Lost and Found

An Adventure by

Tom Williams

Advance Praise for Lost and Found

"An adrenaline filled Rollercoaster ride with a pot of gold as the prize. Tom Williams takes the reader on the ultimate high-tech treasure hunt. Experience a treasure hunt firsthand. This is fiction, but someone in NASA could turn it into reality. A unique story written by a great storyteller. All the wit and emotion of Clive Cussler's best novel. Great read, a page-turner that you won't want to put down."

Ron Polli, Offshore Editor
Extreme Boats Magazine

"While I normally only review books related to the health care business I decided to review this novel because it promised to be intriguing. When I read it I was delighted with the pace, adventure and timeliness of this story. The story centers on energy, starting with oil in Texas to gold in Turkey to a tease for the author's next novel on breakthrough energy discoveries in Poland. Most of the action takes place on or near water, and it makes sense because the author is a master merchant marine officer licensed by the U.S. Coast Guard with special expertise in shipwrecks and salvage. This piece of information should give you another hint about the story line, and if you are willing to accept my opinion, this is a fun adventure with all of the thrills of an Indiana Jones story."

David C. Martin
Publisher & Editor of *Health Care Weekly Review*,
for 24 years the only independent weekly newspaper
in the state of Michigan directed to health care professionals

"Tom Williams really keeps the action moving. Plot twists run deep into the content and the story takes you on some interesting journeys. Just when you think you've got it all figured out, there's a surprise waiting in the next chapter. It's an intriguing read with colorful characters we've encountered in our lives. The compelling story is hard to put down and the ending is well worth the read."

Larry Jewett, Editor
Mustang Enthusiast

"The book *Lost and Found* has more twists and turns than a corkscrew. The story is action packed and full of suspense to keep you turning one page after another. The story leads you through the deceit and treachery of the Corporate Board room to the excitement and turmoil of the Treasure Hunt. This book would make a GOOD movie. I could see the movie in my mind's eye as I read the book. ENJOY!"

Owen Krahn, MBA
Krahn Publishing
Idaho Senior News

"Tom Williams' first novel, *Lost and Found*, has an interesting storyline that threads the reader from high-tech technology and touching on current topics, to mystery and intrigue. If you enjoy pirate stories, mysteries and adventures, you will enjoy Tom's modern-day treasure hunt for survival. Well-written for his first novel. I hope to see more of his work."

Loretta Lynn Leda
Feature writer for the Orlando Sentinel,
The Reporter, and the West Orange Times

"This was a delightful and fun read. The book has lots of subtle humor, the characters well developed, and is a really good adventure story. Highly recommended!"

Ralph L. Webb, Professor Emeritus
Department of Mechanical Engineering
Penn State University

"Florida-based writer Tom Williams' novel, cleverly titled, *Lost and Found*, will be released soon. It cannot be too soon. This extremely unpredictable adventure is guaranteed to keep even the most weary bedtime readers turning pages late at night, telling themselves 'just one more chapter' over and over again."

William Kerns
Entertainment Reviews
Lubbock Avalanche-Journal

"A rip-snorting thriller, rich in vicious international intrigues, corporate treacheries and old-fashioned heroic pulp-fiction gumption— all in a life-like setting that draws as much intense momentum from its technological realism as from the life-or-death urgency of the situation. A cracking good read."

Michael H. Price, Associate Editor
The Business Press Fort Worth

"Lost and Found is a fast and easy read with all of the customary components of an entertaining book...murder, mayhem, madness, mystery and romance. Just the thing to liven up a long boring airline flight or for a lazy day by the pool."

Lynne Christen
Author of *Travel Wisdom*

"With treasure hunting, corporate back-stabbing and a sadomasochist on the heroes' heels, *Lost and Found* has everything you could ask for in a great thriller. It's a business meltdown that makes the story of Enron look tame."

Brian Bandell
South Florida Business Journal

"Lost and Found is a mystery adventure by an author of startling ability. It's common to talk of a novel's "fast pace," but the phrase is hardly enough to describe the fevered action in Tom Williams' story. I'd never have expected such work from a local columnist, but finding it is a delightful surprise. You won't set *Lost and Found* aside easily. That's because Williams, when he talks of seeking undersea treasure, knows his subject. He's skilled, himself, in underwater salvage operations off southern Florida. He knows the hazards. Combine such adventure in a story with corporate malfeasance in the petroleum industry. Then mix it in with local hoodlums off the coast of Turkey—the stew bubbles with threat. Now add a distorted villain of twisted character who honed his vicious skills in the pre-Mandela South Africa. You've assembled a repast that only the dullest reader could put aside. You'll enjoy it thoroughly."

Ed Nelson
Freelance Author, Chicago

"Tom Williams has woven together a masterpiece of adventure, murder and mystery all fueled by greed. This is a must read for anybody who's ever dreamed about diving a wreck and finding a gold doubloon. Williams' characters will pull readers into the adventure and along on a wild ride."

Gabe VanWormer
Producer, Michigan Out-of-Doors TV

"Lost and Found: This contemporary thriller novel has it all: high-tech satellite gimmickry, brainy Brit scientists, corporate chicanery, sunken Spanish galleons, a genuine damsel in distress, arson, an earthquake and nutcase villains of multi international origins. In addition, it's action-packed, fast moving, and totally engrossing. Read it in a hammock and you won't even notice the mosquitoes."

Anne Stinson: Book Critic
The Weekend Star Democrat Easton Maryland

"Lost and Found is an intriguing story. It delivers thrills and surprises. Williams knows how to build suspense as well as creating believable personalities. The heroes are likable though realistically flawed, and Williams manages to make the main villain, Cedric, grow even more unlikable and unstable as the book progresses.

By Lee and J.J. MacFadden
Special to the Herald Courier Tri-Cities

"It has been said that the test of a good book is dreading to read the final chapter. This was the case as I was reading *Lost and Found* during a recent cruise to Bermuda. The excitement was riveting with no letup in sight – my type of reading. Originally, I was planning to read John Adams, a fine book but certainly lacking the adrenaline flow needed to pass the hours of a 7-day cruise. Thank you for making the *Lost and Found* world part of my world. Looking forward to the next manuscript.

Bill Balam
Senior Beacon

ArcheBooks Publishing

Lost and Found

By

TOM WILLIAMS

Copyright © 2008 by Tom Williams

ISBN-10: 1-59507-211-X
ISBN-13: 978-159507-211-5

ArcheBooks Publishing Incorporated

www.archebooks.com

9101 W. Sahara Ave.

Suite 105-112

Las Vegas, NV 89117

Second Edition: 12/2008

Dedication

To Vicki Lynn Williams, my wife and lifelong accomplice, all of my huge Macedonian family, and all of my friends and family at Marriott and Scripps.

Also to my parents Joyce and Seth, who were the best storytellers ever.

Acknowledgements

To Bono, who once on a sailboat near Marco Island, Florida advised me, "Be careful where you set your goals, because you'll probably get them."

To little sister Tami Williams and Richard Blackmore, who took me to all the haunted castles in Germany.

To Ralph Bayer, for reading some of my first work written on a legal pad, and immediately giving me my first computer.

To artist and author Stan Saran, and authors Linda Bilodeau, Michelle Weston, and Prudy Taylor Board for the writer's conference that started the publishing process.

To Bob Gelinas at Archebooks for believing in my work, and to the best and most relentlessly-driven publicist in the world Trish Stevens, a ball of fire from Essex England that is a true shining star.

I also wish to thank Lana and Roger Withers, Tarik Ayasun for all the expertise on Turkey, Monte Lazarus, Jesse at Marco Scuba adventures, Mike Christoff and Rick Barnes for all the expertise on firearms, Ed Shanks, webmaster Tracy Gudgel, cover artist Ricardo Rodriguez, and Captain Jim Martin who placed me on the nautical path to become a Merchant Marine officer.

Lost and Found

Prologue

AUGUST 17, SATURDAY
GOODLAND FLORIDA

Billie slammed the door behind her and stepped out onto the little wooden balcony. She was high above the docks and could see everything clearly. A thunderstorm was building, and climbing up over the Everglades. From inside her second story office, the storm clouds had been hidden as the waterside view looked only over the mangroves and the winding channel leading out to the gulf. Billie, however, was not concerned with the weather, the tropical scenery, or with her appearance. Billie Johnson was looking for her husband.

"Goddamn it, Buddy!" Billie said loudly as she began her descent of the rickety stairs.

Down on the dock, Dotson glanced over his shoulder at Billie's approach. Billie Johnson was a striking young woman dressed in a makeshift combination of sun-faded boating attire. She was a tall figure with a wild tangle of sun-lightened hair on a roving inspection of the South Florida docks.

Dotson, the local dock master, was helping with the lines of a visiting sailboat. A big sloop was nudging her fenders against the well-worn pilings and the current was running fast. A sunburned man at the wheel was hiding under the shade of a Bimini top, while two deck hands, both twenty years his junior and both wearing bikinis were standing on the foredeck. The girls were passing lines to Dotson as Captain Sunburn hollered orders.

"That's perfect, now the old man can handle the rest."

Billie walked over, but her eyes scanned for Buddy. There was a large area to search: eight sailboats tied in the slips, the ketch on the face dock, three crab boats, and the salvage-dive rig. The docks were wide, expansive, and hot. It was August in southwest Florida and the heat was oppressive.

Climbing over the mangroves, the thunderstorm clouds were coming closer and edging up the channel—a silver curtain of rain closing against the open water and the lush green foliage. Lightning spiked in the distance and thunder ominously rumbled.

Without warning, Captain Sunburn turned off the big sloop's diesel auxiliary. He wanted to be finished, off the boat, and away from the storm. The sailboat's motor had been holding the fifty-foot hull against the surge of a very strong flood tide, but now the mooring line began to slip, and the bow began to pull away.

Dotson was seventy and his reactions to the unexpected were slow. His end of the yacht-braided hawser was not yet tied, but only wrapped around a piling. The dock line slipped, snaked away, and dropped into the water.

Both of the girls screamed together, suddenly alarmed that the big sloop was moving and turning sideways away from the dock. Beneath the shaded cockpit cover, Sunburn looked confused. He could only stare as his befuddled command drifted down current toward a large wooden classic with two towering masts.

Below the rigs of Billie's ketch and tied just over the booms were rigged awnings, the glow of varnish rich and soft under the shade. The sun was not yet swallowed by the storm, and poured a final serving of heat upon the classic antique about to be broadsided.

Billie stepped forward, her hand reaching for a life ring—a lifesaver buoy attached to a length of heaving line. She crouched low and threw the life ring like a Frisbee with the line trailing behind. The big sloop was now almost stern to the dock and rushing sideways in the current. In a moment, the metal rub-rail of the modern intruder would clash with the wooden matriarch of the marina. The collision would only affect cosmetics, but cosmetics were time, and time was money. Billie it seemed, always needed money so her reactions were fast.

With an abrupt clatter, the life-ring-Frisbee caught the drifting sailboat by the bow-pulpit railing. After wrapping twice around the sturdy stanchions, the big sloop was captured. Billie however, did not wait for a confirming glance at her target, but had already taken two turns around Dotson's previous dock pile. The line went taut as the big boat stopped and shuddered in the current. After a moment, the girls and Captain Sunburn obediently began to edge back toward the dock. Now with a much longer bowline, the sloop's stern was still moving toward Billie's classic wooden ketch.

Billie looked to Dotson and saw the age on his face, his features molded in concern. He was watching as the tourist boat once again began to shoulder against the dock.

The big sloop was under control, but drifting dangerously close to Billie's family heirloom. As Dotson watched, Billie saw the relief on his features. She also knew that only inches separated the two vessels, a sliver of space between an intruder and the anchor in her life.

Lightning flashed, thunder cracked, and huge raindrops began to pepper the dock.

"Shit!" Captain Sunburn exclaimed; he had had enough. The boat slipping away or the lightning next to the sailboat masts, whatever—he wanted off.

The two girls had already climbed over the lifeline railing and made a beeline across the docks for shelter. Beneath an Old Florida stilt-house, pilings rose over the decking to support the wooden balcony, the rickety stairs, and the living quarters of Johnson Charters, Fisheries, and Salvage. The sunburned man hurriedly followed the girls and watched from under the shelter as Billie and Dotson finished tying the run-away boat. The rain was stronger now and came down in sheets. A scent of wet-hot gravel and dock wood crowded the air.

Billie followed Dotson and joined the new arrivals standing under the house. Water began pouring out of the gutters in a torrent, sounding an accompaniment to the now constant rumbling thunder. The florescent signs above the "Ready Ice" machines began to glow against a suddenly dark and late afternoon.

Billie stepped forward. "Out from Miami?" she asked.

Sunburned man nodded and made a show of glancing at his watch, a gold Rolex that he wanted to show off. "Left at six this morning, out through Hawk's channel and up into Florida Bay, broad-reaching most of the way."

It was Billie's turn to nod, "How long you planning to stay?" Billie was not regarding the older, sunburned man wearing the flowery shirt, but the arm-crossed, pouting figures wearing the bikinis—their body language spoke volumes. The leader was a brunette, and her obvious underling a redhead.

Sunburn looked over to the two girls as they studied the tall blond woman intently. The girls from Miami Beach were making an evaluation.

Billie Johnson was indifferent to her soaking wet appearance. Her shoulder-length blonde hair was matted by the rain, and her long-sleeved white shirt open and rolled up to the elbows. A blue sports bra swelled beneath the now see-through material, and a pair of safari-type, khaki shorts were fastened below the knot of her cross-tied shirttails. Her skin tone was as dark as a lifeguard in September, her cheekbones high, and her nose aquiline. Billie's eyes were the color of living emeralds and the intense green was now gripping. The young women from Miami could not hold her gaze.

The dark haired girl turned away first and was now clinging to the rain-spotted Hawaiian shirt of Captain Sunburn. "Melvin, you said we were going to Naples," her voice was a whine, "to the yacht club," she insisted.

The other girl, the redhead, appeared disappointed and miserable. She was looking around, first to the overhead plank floor supporting the large dock-house they were gathered beneath, then to a workbench littered with tools and boat parts. Finally, she gazed inland to a gravel parking lot and a distant trailer park rinsing in the rain.

Abruptly, Captain Sunburn was reminded of his charges. The redhead pounded the dock with her foot and spoke with a disappointed whimper. "We can't stay here, not on the boat, you promised."

Billie ignored the girls and her focus returned to the man in the Hawaiian shirt. "How long?" she repeated.

"How far is Naples?" The sunburned face screwed tight with the question and looked upward into Billie's features. Captain Melvin Sunburn had to look up. Billie Johnson was much taller.

"Twenty miles to Naples, We charge five dollars a foot, overnight." Billie's words were cut short as thunder crashed after a flash of lightning and a voice called out over the rumble.

"Aw, damn-it-to-hell, Billie, that ain't no way to be friendly! Five dollars a foot? We ain't never charged that much!" Buddy Johnson was moving beside the workbench and the boat parts, his smile cracking as he stepped out of the shadows. He was holding a can of Budweiser with one hand and gripping the remaining six-pack with the other.

"Anybody want a cold beer?" Buddy asked as he raised his cans toward the newcomers. His eyes were red-rimmed, glassy, and trying to focus on the two girls in bikinis. The dark-haired whiner instantly crossed her arms over her chest and the redhead moved closer to the short, portly figure wearing the Hawaiian shirt.

"Come on, girls, how 'bout a beer?" Buddy insisted, waving the cans.

As harmless as the gesture might ordinarily be, there was something dangerous, something not right about Buddy Johnson. At first glance, he looked like a younger version of the Marlboro man, but rough and calloused around the edges. He was dark with a permanent tan in the face and

6

his sandy hair, like his mustache, was too long and sloppy. His blatant attraction toward the girls in bathing suits was obvious, and his lack of concern about offending the shorter, older man was alarming.

"No thank you," said Melvin stiffly.

"What's-a-matter, my beer not good enough?" Buddy's voice dropped suddenly and matched the rumbling thunder in the distance.

Upon Buddy's arrival, Billie had remained silent and watchful. Now she shook her head and disappeared around the corner of a storage locker.

The two Miami girls immediately became concerned with the tall, blond woman's departure. The scant bikinis crowded closer to Melvin prodding him to speak, and the puffy sunburned face began to glance around—looking for help.

"No, that's not—" he began.

"How 'bout you Red? Buddy interrupted. "You want one? Maybe you want something besides a beer?" There was no doubt about the insinuation.

The dark-haired girl now looked sharply over to Melvin as the redhead actually moved behind the sunburned man with the flowery shirt.

"Now, let's watch that language," Melvin sputtered. His words had absolutely no conviction.

Buddy moved in, enjoying himself. "Who do you think you are?" he demanded. "Telling me to watch my language—watch my language in my own goddamned place! You city people make me sick, coming down here with your fancy boat and your fancy women. Look at you in that stupid shirt." He gestured across the waterway. "Don't you get it? You're in the Everglades now! Hell, this is a mangrove jungle. Who do you think is gonna protect you now—some Miami lawyer? Maybe I'll just take that fancy watch, and go for a ride on that fancy boat. And maybe I'll just take these two fancy pants girls with me!"

Melvin stepped back aghast as the girls moved away silently, their darting eyes screaming panic.

"I bet I scare the shit outta you," Buddy advanced, now very close, his sour beer-breath flowing directly into the sunburned face.

With a glance to the two girls, and then over to Dotson, he added. "I bet I scare the shit outta all-o-you! All-o-you!" Buddy motioned around the dock as if to include Dotson, the other boats and even the distant trailer park. His face frowned into a dangerous scowl, and he suddenly fired his beer and the remaining six-pack, down at Melvin's feet. The unopened cans exploded, beer spewed everywhere, and the girls screamed as Melvin's sunburned face turned white.

Suddenly Billie was back, trudging forward from the shadows. "Nobody...scares the shit out of me!" she said. After she spoke, she pulled the lever on a fire hose nozzle and a tremendous blast of water knocked Buddy off his feet. Water was ripping out of the two-inch hose and flying across the underside of the dock-house to pin Buddy Johnson in a corner of the workbench.

Melvin and the two girls were caught in the outer fringes of water but easily kept their footing and immediately started for their boat. The girls were screaming as their captain followed—their voices howling and unintelligible. Sheets of rainfall drenched the bikinis and the Hawaiian shirt, washing them into a blur before they reached the dockside sailboat.

Billie continued her focus and aim, sending the driving spout of water onto a struggling Buddy, keeping him pinned under the workbench. After a moment, she shouted to Dotson. "Help them get away, and don't let them hit the Ketch."

Dotson nodded sadly and moved out into the rain. After the big sloop pulled away, Billie turned off the water. She threw the hose down and the nozzle crashed on the dock. She stood with her hands on her hips and regarded her husband with disgust.

"Goddamn it, Buddy! I just got the credit card bill! Five hundred dollars? Five-hundred dollars at a strip bar?" She shook her head and added. "We can't pay the mortgage and you scare away the only business of the day. Visa says you spent five-hundred dollars at a goddamn, Fort Myers strip bar!"

Billie shook her head again and started back up the stairs.

Chapter 1

"How much longer do we have to listen to this rubbish?" Brian Pauliss whispered.

"Quiet," hissed Peter Clopec

The chairman was droning on and on.

"...with political tensions building around the world, it has become apparent that new methods for oil exploration are now paramount." The chairman, Alex Haggly-Ford, was also British, but his longevity in the oil business and his last twenty years in Texas had given his public school accent a strange twist.

"The justification for the expense of our new satellite is obvious. In the very near future, we will have no choice. The forecast demands for oil production in the twenty-first-century are staggering. Russia will no doubt hoard her vast oil reserves and share her petroleum business only with former eastern bloc countries, and only on a favored nation basis. The rising Muslim population in Africa, coupled with the manipulations of fanatic leaders will create ever growing concerns whenever dealing with this volatile region. And the Middle East..."

Peter felt Brian's elbow nudge, and turned to observe his colleague rolling his eyes upward.

Brian was just like a schoolboy, thought Peter—despite the fact that Brian Pauliss was forty-six, divorced from his second wife, overweight, and smoked *a lot*. Yes, Peter considered, as the chairman continued. Brian is very child-like although not immature, and certainly one of the greatest academic minds that Peter Clopec knew.

Lost and Found

"With this new technology," the chairman continued, "OPC will conquer the forefront of all future petroleum endeavors. All new oil fields and perhaps even natural gas reserves can now be mapped from just above the earth. Even as I speak, our precious *bird* is circling the globe, searching every flat steppe, every rising plain, and even the most rugged and remote mountain ranges."

The chairman paused. Haggly-Ford was amused to use the specialist's term for satellite in front of the board of directors. He glanced over to Brian and Peter with a fabricated smile and continued.

"Our *bird* is indeed precious, as the annual fiscal report will certainly indicate."

A low rumble of laughter rolled through the waiting assembly and fell short just before the first row and the stern-faced board of directors. Befitting his position as chairman, Alex Haggly-Ford was standing behind a lectern and delivering his annual address to the gathered stockholders of Odessa Petroleum Consultants, or OPC. He looked like a television news anchor. He was even wearing makeup. With a quick glance to the rear of the auditorium and the standing room crowd, it was obvious that over two thousand attendees were present at the meeting.

Peter Clopec swallowed hard against a rising bout of heartburn. He knew at any moment, both he and Brian would be called forward and introduced as the new managing directors of OPC's satellite mining division.

"Without further delay...ladies and gentlemen of the board, distinguished guests and honored stock holders, I would like to present Doctors Brian Pauliss and Peter Clopec."

"Christ!" Brian's sidelong whisper to Peter was not even covered as both men rose from their seats and approached the raised dais and the lone standing figure of the perfectly groomed, silver-haired, Haggly-Ford.

A pair of spotlights caught the climbing duo as they gained the center-stage-steps and a thunderous applause broke like a swelling wave and abruptly dribbled off into silence. The glare from the theatrical lighting was dazzling, but in the darkness beyond was the knowledge that a predator waited—a collective beast searching for the presence of fear, or perhaps, evaluating the possibilities of weakness. Two-thousand stockholders were now focused as one, two-thousand critical investors, waiting with the cold and calculating mind of a Wall Street financier.

Silence covered the dais and the lectern with a foreboding presence.

Haggly-Ford looked over to where Peter and Brian were standing. His smile was forced and weak. The chairman was waiting. He was waiting to measure the two men he had just employed. Beads of sweat were beginning to pop through his makeup.

10

Peter Clopec was tall and lean, his hair too long and usually messy. He was gray at the temples before the ends of his troublesome wisps turned to black. He wore a moustache peppered with gray and a permanent stubble of salt and pepper whiskers suggesting more than a five-o'clock shadow.

Brian Pauliss was shorter than Peter, but much heavier. Brian was completely blond with no sign of gray. He combed his hair straight back as a grooming effort, but one could easily imagine long, rebellious strands constantly being replaced behind his ears. Brian, like Peter, also wore wire-rimmed eyeglasses, but he looked like a chubby little boy from an English boarding school.

Both Brian and Peter would always have a youthful appearance. In fact, all that was missing as the two men stood beneath the glaring spotlights were the brass buttons and embroidered crests of boarding school blazers. The Englishmen were of course, not dressed in uniforms, they were wearing suits—Peter in a dark worsted wool from Brooks Brothers and Brian in an British Banker's gray, straight off the rack at Harrods. Brian did not look good in a suit. His red striped tie was obviously constricting and the single middle button of his coat appeared ready to pop.

Haggly-Ford now gestured toward the lectern and mumbled, "Gentlemen." He pulled a handkerchief from an inside pocket and retreated out of the spotlights into the darkness.

"After you, mate," whispered Brian

"Right," Peter's answer was automatic, but he was surprised when Brian turned and followed Haggly-Ford onto the waiting sidelines, away from the focus and scrutiny of the predator.

Peter swallowed against a new rise of heartburn and stepped forward to the podium. He gripped the lectern with both hands and looked at the microphone glinting in the light.

"Good afternoon," Peter instantly felt the sweat break out on his forehead. The local time, he realized was about 10:00 AM. After an endless moment of silence, he began again. "In London, of course, the time is now afternoon." A trickle of laughter drifted out of the darkness. This was not a friendly laughter, but the low growl of a predator sensing weakness.

"But here in Texas, the time is morning, and with each morning, there is an urgency to accomplish one's daily goals—the goals and challenges so eloquently outlined by our chairman." Peter paused and tried to peer into the darkness. He continued smoothly, fortified by the slow Texas drawl he had experienced when meeting most of OPC's board of directors. "The excitement and challenges of prospecting for oil in a new millennium, and the ultimate goal of discreet geological surveys without the troublesome consequences of on-site, in-the-field analysis.

Lost and Found

"As we are all-too-well-aware, the mere presence of a petroleum survey team instantly demands attention from even those most remotely involved. Real estate values and mining rights grow at an exponential rate, political issues become complicated, and greed, one of the most basic human instincts, grows to a level beyond all conceivable proportions."

For a moment, Peter considered that he might have just described the motivation of OPC's chairman and board of directors. Quickly he pressed on. "Satellite mining, hopefully, will eliminate on-site survey teams, restore confidentiality with petroleum futures, and secure the profit margins of Odessa Petroleum Consultants until the next scientific breakthroughs can be accomplished.

"Thank you, ladies and gentlemen, for your kind attention," Peter paused, and glanced over to the darkened sidelines.

"Doctor Pauliss?" Peter's arm was now en-gesture, his palm open as if to bring Brian forward.

After an awkward moment, Brian reappeared in the spotlights, his face shinning with perspiration. He stepped forward quickly, took Peter's place at the lectern and brightly offered, "Good morning!" This remark brought much more than a trickle of laughter. The Texans were now amused.

After a quick glance to confirm Peter's blushing features, Brian continued. "What my esteemed colleague has noted, but thus far failed to expound upon, is the fact that we are both honored and grateful to be part of OPC's new wing of experimental satellite research. Thank you and good day." As he stepped away from the microphone, Brian raised a hand to the spotlights, waved into the darkness, and placed a playful arm around Peter's shoulder.

As he led Peter away from the lectern and the now thunderous applause, Brian Pauliss whispered. "Thank Christ that's over. Let's get a drink!"

Chapter 2

FRIDAY, AUGUST 16
ONE YEAR LATER

"**D**octor Pauliss, the chairman will see you now," the receptionist smiled sweetly after she spoke.

"Thank you, my dear."

She was quite the looker thought Brian as he rose from his seat in the waiting room. The girl smiled again as she opened the door. She was tall and busty with perfect teeth and big hair. Texas women were wonderful. Charlene was her name and—

Brian's thoughts of conquering the feminine Wild West were suddenly derailed upon entering the chairman's office. Haggly-Ford was seated at his desk and Peter Clopec was standing before him. Here was a disobedient student presented before the headmaster, waiting for punishment.

Peter's eyes shifted to an open file resting on the desk. The file: a standard folder for an OPC geological report did not rest long. Haggly-Ford was out of his chair in an instant and the file-folder was flying across the room. Brian flinched as the file papers scattered.

Haggly-Ford roared, "Saltwater!" The chairman now seemed ready to crawl over his desk. He repeated, "Saltwater! I'm not bloody looking for saltwater, am I?" Haggly-Ford was beyond angry. He was livid. The chairman turned away, disgusted.

Peter shot Brian a "don't say anything look," as Haggly-Ford turned and began to pace before his floor-to-ceiling windows. The Midland oil fields lay beyond—endless pump-jacks nodding their horse-like-heads to withdraw the rough Texas crude.

13

Lost and Found

Brian watched as the chairman paced. Haggly-Ford was counting. Brian knew from experience that the chairman silently counted the oil wells. He counted the wellheads to calm his nerves.

"Bloody Hell!" Haggly-Ford's latest comment was announced quietly and apparently intended for the pump-jacks in the oil field. "Another bloody saltwater lake. Another underground, saltwater sea," the chairman continued softly. He was still looking out into the West Texas desert.

The sun was low over the Midland oil fields burnishing the horizon with shimmering heat waves. A fuzzy edge moved at the skyline revealing a dusty wave rolling forward with the silent desert heat. Shadows were beginning to tilt beside the mechanized oil horses and reach toward the OPC corporate headquarters.

Odessa Petroleum Consultants was a sprawling expanse of mirrored windows and snow-white geometric shapes. Twenty acres of executive offices, research facilities, and endless west Texas dust. OPC was a nightmare of ultra modern, too much money, new-age architecture.

Haggly-Ford turned away from his bobbing steel subjects, his desert kingdom and his only reliable source of revenue. A disgusted expression molded his features as he pitched his voice as a mimic of Brian's piping contralto. "'But Alex, me old son, we have recalibrated the ground-penetrating radar and the anomaly carrier-wave signal. No worries, mate! Bob's your uncle and Fanny's your aunt! We'll have it this time! This time we'll find an oil field!'"

With a sudden motion that surprised both Peter and Brian, Haggly-Ford jumped forward and violently swept an arm across his desk. Every carefully placed item went tumbling: an oil well clock, a collection of classic miniature automobiles, and a red telephone.

"Because of you two, because of your incompetence, the board has called for an emergency meeting. Someone in Petroleum Discovery has leaked this latest report. Some moron in mid-level management knows someone on the board. Some *peon* is trying to leverage a promotion. The board will most probably call for a vote—a vote of confidence! I cannot retain my position as chairman against such a vote. Twenty years...twenty years wasted, unless I can make something happen fast."

The chairman glowered. "Well, let me tell you something, Doctor *bloody* Pauliss and Doctor *sodding* Clopec, it's your bones that will be burning on this corporate bonfire, not mine. You have exactly one week to find a substantial oil reserve. One week, or contracts be damned, you're out! Both of you fired! I will even call the state department and revoke your visas. I will *bloody well* have you deported!"

Alex Haggly-Ford looked as if he were ready to explode, and when the misplaced telephone began sounding the off-the-hook busy signal, he turned back to his oil wells and the setting sun. After a moment, he spoke softly, as if to the windows or the dusty desert beyond. His voice was on the edge of panic.

"You have one week... Now get out!"

Peter looked over to Brian's appalled features. Doctor Pauliss was apparently in shock and regarding the cleared desk, the scattered bric-a-brac, and the buzzing telephone resting among the littered sheets of paper.

After turning away from the chairman standing before the windows, Peter nodded to his best friend, and both men quietly exited the room.

Haggly-Ford's receptionist did not look up as the two Englishmen passed; she was too embarrassed. The chairman had been screaming.

Peter only glanced at the blushing receptionist with her face glued to the computer screen. He punched the elevator call button and waited until the lift door opened with a pneumatic rush.

After stepping inside and waiting until the doors closed, Peter turned to Brian, "Happy Birthday Doctor *bloody* Pauliss, August sixteenth and aged forty-seven."

"Too right, aged to forty-seven and sacked all in one day," Brian shook his head. "Well, Doctor *sodding* Clopec, it is a Friday, the beginning of the weekend, and my birthday. Let's get pissed!"

Chapter 3

Odessa in August was like any other city in the West Texas summer, hot to the point of being oven-like. Triple-digit temperatures cooked the landscape and the workforce, and evenly divided the population into two very separate categories. The outsiders were the oil field roughnecks: the men and women who worked for high wages in high temperatures. The insiders were the addicted-to-air-conditioning creatures of the corporate oil business. The outsiders resembled the landscape in which they worked, coarse, cracked, and resentful. The insiders could not have been more different. With very few exceptions, the insiders were fair, delicate, and soft.

Brian was most definitely an insider. When not working, he preferred the franchise bars and fashionable restaurants. In West Texas, "Friday's" was his favorite. Only a small number of the roughneck crowd ever came to "Friday's." Brian of course, was fair-haired, fair skinned, with manicured fingernails bordering on perfection. Brian hated the Texas heat and broke into a sweat whenever caught between air-conditioned cubicles. The only attributes Odessa and Midland could offer Brian were the seemingly endless chain of trendy restaurant-bars and the high-maintenance women that frequented these establishments.

Peter Clopec was also an insider, but Peter was different. Doctor Clopec could easily pass for an outsider. Peter was officially British. He had been schooled in England and attended university in Scotland, although Peter had been born in Africa. Clopec was a Hungarian name and Peter's father

16

came from Budapest. Mining in the Transvaal and East Africa regions had captured the Clopec clan for two generations, and as a result, Peter carried the seasoned, out-of-doors appearance of a geological prospector or an oil field professional. The Texas summer heat was nothing new to a native-born African, and Peter's resulting complexion spoke of endless days by a swimming pool and his dark Hungarian heritage.

"May we please have another round of those delightful concoctions?" Brian's voice was oily with alcohol. He was speaking to a waitress with incredible bust and cleavage.

Brian liked sweet drinks: whisky sours, rum and coke, anything with sugar. Tonight, Peter and Brian were encamped around a small table at the darkest corner of "Friday's" bar. They had been drinking rumrunners, and they were not alone.

"Not here please, a Black Label if I may. No ice." Peter's voice was steady but his eyesight seemed to waver. Clearly, he was transfixed by the cocktail server's low-cut costume.

"I just can't believe you're fired—fired on your birthday!" This was the voice of Pauline Taggart. Pauline was Brian's girlfriend of sorts, and she was attempting to divert Brian and Peter's gaze away from the departing waitress.

"That beats all—all I ever heard of! Haggly-Ford is a goddamned asshole! You two should sue. Yeah, you should sue the shit out of all of them!" This voice was from Becca Raimes, Pauline's friend. She was demanding complete attention from her side of the candlelit table.

Brian chanced a glance at Peter and was not surprised to observe an expression of vague annoyance. Peter was not a snob, but he obviously did not care for the vulgarity of the local Texas woman.

"You still have one week. Don't you think you could *still* find *something?*" Becca's latest remark was addressed to Peter, almost nagging.

Rebecca Raimes was a young woman who had been trying to build a romantic relationship, a West Texas woman with her matrimonial gun sights on a rich oil executive. She found Peter through Pauline, and Peter Clopec was definitely Becca's target of acquisition. Pauline's attraction to Brian had developed almost instantly after Brian and Peter's installation into OPC. Becca was Pauline's friend and had managed to strategically edge her way into a position of opportunity. Becca was physically well armed and mentally determined, as was Pauline.

Both women were young, in their mid-thirties, and attractive. Becca was a dark brunette with chestnut eyes and Pauline blond and hazel. Both were tall, slender, and carried an impressive arsenal of desirable endowments. Musky perfume was always well applied, hinting of the more seductive pheromones that could be uncovered at a moment's notice. Perfect hairstyles complemented the latest in stylish dress, and augmented breast sizes seemed oddly round and out of proportion when displayed in the skimpiest of bikinis.

Brian had capitulated after one week of feminine attack and was currently ensconced into Pauline's intimate bosom. When her finger beckoned, Brian most often responded obediently. The ring finger on her left hand however, much to her frustration, remained unadorned.

Thus far, Peter had not fallen victim to Becca's advances, and her current tone and behavior suggested frustration at a lack of success. She was also quite agitated that her focused onslaught might have been misplaced and her efforts wasted. An oil executive without a job was not a target of opportunity.

The waitress returned, deposited the drinks accordingly, and departed after a brief eye-contact battle with Becca.

"Damn-it-to-hell, why won't the friggin' satellite work?" Becca leaned forward in the candlelight, her face hawkish.

"My dear, must we fall into that again? It's my birthday!" Brian's announcement was met with a quick visual between the two women before Pauline answered.

"Brian honey, maybe we could help," she offered. "Hell, the oil business is nothing new to Becca and me. My daddy was looking for oil in this desert before you two were born… Well, maybe not you, Peter."

Brian winced. He knew that Peter was going through somewhat of a mid-life-crisis; his age of fifty-one, obviously much more acute with Haggly-Ford's earlier ultimatum.

Becca shifted her eyes from one man to the other. "You boys have got to figure this out," she demanded. "If the damn thing won't work—fix it!"

Peter watched as Brian lit another cigarette. Brian was obviously drunk. His face was flushed red, his eyes rheumy, and he was chain-smoking. After another glance at the two waiting women, Peter sipped his scotch and spoke softly.

"The satellite does work," he said. "There is not another or more sophisticated ground penetrating radar anywhere. The oil is the problem. It doesn't have enough of a signature. Oil is too thin. Too thin and buried too deep. But the satellite does work." Peter's eyes were now focused and he held Becca's gaze defiantly.

From the bar, a group of late night Texans began singing *The eyes of Texas Are Upon You.*

"This entire enterprise was destined for failure…even before it started." Peter's voice was stronger now, determined to carry over the drunks at the bar. "The satellite is a fantastic piece of aerospace hardware, but not for finding oil. OPC is up the spout," he said, "Finished."

Becca appeared skeptical as Peter continued. "Three-hundred and forty million wasted, all because Haggly-Ford wanted to be first. And, because he wanted to be first, he hurried. He bullied engineers, forced and threatened subordinates, and lied to the board of directors. No, he is finished, and so is OPC—only a matter of time."

Pauline gasped. Both she and Becca also worked for Odessa Petroleum Consultants. They were administrative assistants—Pauline in Human Resources and Becca in Petroleum Discovery.

Brian was nodding sadly. Peter had spoken the truth and now the facts were out.

More drunks had joined the bar singers. *"The eyes of Texas are..."*

Peter drained his glass and tore his eyes away from Becca's admonishing stare. He motioned for the waitress to bring another scotch.

"Brian? Up the spout? What does that mean?" Pauline asked. "Finished? The company is finished?"

He nodded.

"But OPC is the best place to work in Odessa. Brian, are you sure?" Pauline's voice was pleading and hoping for a denial, but her mind was spinning. She had never been a saver and she knew that Brian was all but broke. He drove a nice new Jaguar, but she knew the car was leased.

Brian lowered his head. He had stubbed out his cigarette and was now rubbing his temples. He did not want to look up.

"Brian... Brian, honey?" Pauline looked around, her tears streaming.

"Eyes of Texas...are...upon you..." Everyone at the bar was singing. *"Louder! One more time..."*

Becca appeared ready to burst. Her hands were now gripping the table tightly. Her face was flushed, and little beads of sweat were shinning on her upper lip. The bad news about OPC was not what she wanted to hear.

The cocktail server returned with Peter's scotch, but before she could deliver the drink, Becca was on her feet and grabbed the glass recklessly. Luckily, Peter's wire-rim glasses protected his eyes, but the double shot of whisky covered his face and hair.

"If the oil is too thin...you fucking moron...find something that's not! Pauline! We're outta here!"

With a violent action that Brian found surprising, Becca pulled Pauline from her seat and began marching her adjutant toward her fellow Texans at the bar. With a dramatic disruption, the unofficial state anthem fell apart as the two women centered themselves among the bar singers.

"You see those two limey assholes." Becca's voice was a whip as she pointed. "They said all Texans are a bunch of inbred shitheads. But I think they're wrong! I think that they're a couple of snobby foreigners, and I think they need a lesson in whoop-ass."

Becca was now entrenched among the singers and holding Pauline tightly, almost like a shield.

A few of the drunks began to grumble. Their song and patriotic focus had been broken. A few of the singers began to scrutinize the two men at the candle-lit corner table.

One of the drunks came up from behind Becca and whispered in her ear. She was focused for a moment before the Texan's tongue came out and licked her on the cheek. After screaming, "Asshole!" she grabbed Pauline and stormed for the door. The entire bar erupted into laughter.

After a moment, Peter motioned for the waitress. She approached carefully and offered a damp bar towel.

"Sweetheart," she said, "I've seen it all before, and believe me..." The busty server jerked a thumb toward the exit. "Those two think that every time they sit down, they're sitting on boxes of gold. I hope it was worth it, but I somehow figure it wasn't."

After Peter thanked her for the towel and ordered another drink, the waitress nodded. "The next time," she said, "I hope you find what you're looking for."

With the suggestion, Doctor Peter Clopec seemed to drift away, his features blank as his mind focused inward, his dark complexion and whisker stubble a silent mask over his lean and chiseled appearance. After a few silent moments, Peter came back. He then looked to Brian and smiled.

"Doctor Pauliss, I think it's time to go to work."

"I think its bloody-well time to get out of here." Brian was covering his lips as he spoke, but offered a quick glance to three roughneck patrons seated at the bar. Three of the former Texas singers were watching the corner table intently.

"Brian, Becca was right! And so was our waitress!" Peter began to laugh and Brian looked worried.

"Right, mate. What are you talking about? Are you pissed? Those blokes are just about to show us some southern hospitality." After speaking, Brian's face drained white as the three big Texans began to hobble off their bar stools, their intent and actions obvious.

"Now hold on boys!" The waitress was back, moving in front of the roughnecks and holding Peter's scotch. She placed the drink in front of Peter, glanced over to the terror-struck Brian, and stood with her hands on her hips. She stood with her chest out and eyed the three Texans suspiciously.

"Well, what'll-it-be," she said. "The drinks are on Doctor Clopec," after a quick glance and wink toward Peter, the waitress continued. "Well?"

"Well shit," the biggest Texan replied. "I didn't know that he was a doctor. I'll have a Jack and Coke, what about you boys?"

The busty woman then turned on her charm and led the troublemakers back to the bar. After a few moments, Brian began to breathe. "That was almost a bollocking!"

"Brian, sort yourself out!" Peter's tone was urgent. "Can't you put it together?" he asked. "Remember your training! What did she say? Think man! You're a scientist! 'If the oil is too thin…then find something that's not!' And then our server, 'Sitting on boxes of gold?'"

Peter shook his head with amazement and began to smile again as he searched Brian's expression. Slowly, through the alcohol and emotional excitement, Brian's academia took over. His features became flushed, his mind accelerating. Suddenly the heavyset, middle-aged little boy became focused. Focused as only a man with two PhD's can become centered.

Dr. Brian Pauliss, hidden in the corner of a dark Texas bar was once again a scientist. After one year of dealing with greed-driven bureaucrats, and dulled by corporate procedures, Dr. Brian Pauliss was back. Gone was the frustration propagated by so many lies, distractions and deadlines. Brian's eyeglasses caught the candlelight as he nodded to Peter. This was the terse signal of a preoccupied mind.

Peter signaled the waitress.

She came over quickly. "Well, well, well," she said. "You boys look like the cat that swallowed the canary."

Peter asked, "How did you know my name?"

The waitress smiled. "I remember every gold or platinum card that comes in here. There aren't many. And by the way, Doctor, your three new friends at the bar are sucking down drinks as fast as they can."

The waitress smiled again, and Peter decided she was quite attractive, much older than Becca, but there was substance here, a distinct fortitude.

Peter handed her the card that she remembered. He touched her hand for a moment as the plastic passed between them, pausing as she regarded him carefully.

"Give our friends a few more drinks," he said, "but cut them off before they become dangerous. Add a hundred dollar tip for yourself, and keep those fellows on their stools until after we leave."

"Is that all, Doctor Clopec?"

"Yes, all for now. Doctor Pauliss and I have a satellite to reprogram. After that," Peter offered, "I think we just might find some new boxes of gold."

Chapter 4

A a red trail of dust followed Brian's Jaguar as Peter drove just over the speed limit. OPC was twenty miles outside of town and well positioned in the middle of nowhere. All roads in the desert were perfectly straight, which allowed Peter a moment to examine the dusty red cloud glowing in the rear view mirror. The lone sedan was the only car on the road—a single pair of headlights racing toward the next horizon as the subtle purr of British engineering basted the drifting desert from the West Texas highway.

Brian was hunched over in the passenger seat and scribbling on a yellow legal pad. The glove box was open and spilling an essential light. A calculator was balanced on one knee and from time to time Brian punched figures into the little keypad.

Peter Clopec smiled. Here was the Brian Pauliss that he knew. A man focused and determined, not the lazy and sloppy individual corrupted by unobtainable corporate goals. For the last year, Peter had watched Brian deteriorate. Haggly-Ford's offer of satellite mining, had at first, seemed irresistible. Here was a position with incredible possibilities and a virtual unlimited budget. This was before Peter and Brian both realized the OPC satellite was too good to be true. The orbital, ground penetrating radar was indeed a breakthrough, but certainly not capable of finding truly deep oil reserves. Brian's added carrier-wave tickler-signal was the only ray of hope for the over-priced, destined-for-failure project. Haggly-Ford had exaggerated the satellite's potential. He had falsified documents and deceived the board of directors.

Peter found and confirmed the discrepancies after only one month. He spoke to Brian and together they privately confronted Haggly-Ford. This was the first occasion that the chairman's anger had surfaced. At first, he had been only annoyed, but his irritation rapidly turned to antagonism as Peter insisted that the OPC satellite was impotent.

Brian had diffused the confrontation with a suggestion. A proper carrier wave, he insisted, could tickle certain underground formations and register anomalies that could point to future oil fields—a potential crutch for the stumbling project. Haggly-Ford had been pacified until recently. He would be satisfied with anything but an announcement of failure to the board.

Peter was distracted from his thoughts and turned away from the probing headlights and the dusty roadway. Brian was tapping his ballpoint against the figures on his legal pad.

"My God!" he said. "It's so simple. Gold is a super conductor and would have one of the most recognizable signatures of any element on the planet. How far down the microwaves will reach, will once again be problematic, but results should be much better with a concentrated mass and shallow deposits. Meddlesome minerals and other potential blockers of the ground penetrating radar will also dissuade the purity and density, but even a small amount of pure gold should register an anomaly reading.

"But carbon, Peter, coal deposits, would certainly cover any veins of gold." Brian was speaking, but his eyes were forward, regarding the rapidly approaching sodium lights of OPC's corporate city. A glowing fence line surrounded the massive installation, suggesting the outline of a military base or an ultra modern prison. Brian swallowed hard against the thought of such confinement. He had always been extremely claustrophobic.

Peter slowed the Jaguar as they approached the entrance and security checkpoint. "Good evening," he said to the guard as he presented his corporate identification.

"Good morning," was the reply as the security officer examined the credentials.

"And your guest, sir?" the guard was looking inside the car.

Peter looked over to Brian. In normal business hours, only one identification was necessary. Peter also noticed the night watchman was armed. A holstered automatic rested high on the security man's hip.

Brian was already responding to the request and reaching for his wallet when the beam of a flashlight invaded the sedan. Caught full in the face with the light, Brian instantly began blinking. After only a glance, Peter realized that Brian still looked drunk—flushed face and red-rimmed eyes.

Brian sputtered as he offered his OPC clearance. "My good man, is this really necessary?"

"Yessir," answered the guard before he took both sets of credentials and entered the glass and stainless steel checkpoint. As the Jaguar idled, Brian nervously lit a cigarette. Peter watched the guard as Brian smoked.

The guard at the gate was not fat and sloppy like the men of daytime security. This man resembled some kind of mercenary. He was tall, very fit, and carried a manner of arrogance and determination. Upon entering his well-lit security station, the sentry instantly picked up a telephone and was now speaking into the handset while making a photocopy of both sets of identification. After a few more moments on the telephone, he returned with the ID cards.

"Park up front, under the lights, next to the main entrance," the guard's voice was curt.

"Can't we park and enter through Petroleum Discovery?" asked Peter.

"Nossir," was the answer.

Bloody Nazi," Brian whispered under his breath, and both men were surprised when the guard leaned forward and said, "Yessir."

Peter parked as directed and Brian muttered, "Bugger all," as another armed guard strode forward from the main entrance. This man was an exact copy of the man at the gate.

"Petroleum Discovery, follow me," the words were out, the guard turned, and Brian and Peter followed.

After a swipe of Peter's all-access card and a rush of pneumatic pressure opened the sealed door to the satellite mining division, Brian and Peter stepped inside and were alone and away from the escorting security.

"Great buggering, bloody hell," Brian announced to the closed door and the sealed-off guard on the other side. He walked with Peter past the cubical map stations, the glass-encased private offices, and the rack-mounted stacks of computer hardware. Finally, they arrived at the split-level den of the satellite control system. At the base of the static-free room, Doctor Brian Pauliss sat at his throne. After a reverent pause, as if the very large plasma-screen monitor was an altar, his fingers began flying over a computer keyboard. After a few moments he stopped.

Both men were now regarding a series of diminishing figures scrolling down on the screen as they waited for the real-time and current position of the satellite to come into view. After a few moments, an image of the earth appeared, turning on its axis. Sunlight was crossing into shadow and daylight into darkness. Bisecting the globe and following the eternal sunset was a series of vertical lines showing the last four orbital paths of the OPC satellite.

Haggly-Ford's "bird" was on a high inclination-polar orbit. With the spacecraft orbiting from south to north, from Antarctic to Arctic regions, a complete worldwide survey could be completed on a routine basis. As the earth continuously turns beneath the satellite path, a new slice of the globe was offered for every 90-minute orbital flight.

Brian reached into his pocket, unfolded his recent notes on the legal pad, and lit a cigarette. Peter as he had done on many occasions when the two men were alone in the dust-free sterile environment turned away from the oversized monitor and approached another smaller computer terminal. He was, as usual, pulling up an encrypted software program to disable the smoke alarms in the environmentally sensitive room.

"There we are, my love," Brian was leaning forward in his seat, his voice almost a purr as he spoke to the satellite control system.

From 210 nautical miles above the earth, Haggly-Ford's bird was traveling 18,000 miles-per-hour and just crossing over Morocco and northward into the Straits of Gibraltar.

As Peter returned to the large monitor display, he stood and watched over Brian's shoulder. After another few moments, and another set of lengthy keyboard commands was entered into the system, the satellite responded and began a fresh download of information. Brian had completed the recalibration of the ground penetrating radar and now a plethora of new figures began marching into columns on the right side of the satellite display. Each individual column of numbers was dedicated to a specific return of wavelength. When the searching beam of microwaves crossed from the Moroccan coast and into the Mediterranean Sea, the wavelength signatures changed dramatically. Water was easy to penetrate, the stony African soil much more complex. Over land, the satellite was forced into dealing with a vast combination of sedimentary layers, the identification of complicated minerals, and a rise and fall of vertical terrain.

"Yes, my darling, take your time and study carefully." Brian's remark to the spacecraft was followed by another series of keyboard commands. "A sharper focus of the radar should yield better results with a solid element, and the tickler beam *should* excite the highly conductible molecules of gold. Shallow deposits that are truly dense would be easily recognized." Brian paused and looked up from the keyboard. "Of course, most gold mining is quite deep, or is it?" he asked.

Peter rubbed the stubble on his chin, a sure sign of collective thought. "As I recall, most gold mining in the Transvaal was very deep, six-thousand, even ten-thousand feet. At almost two miles down, the air in the ventilating shafts had to be refrigerated, simply abominable temperatures. On the other hand, you remember the forty-niners out in California in the California gold rush, Sutter's Mill or something like that. Those old buggers found gold very near the surface, even in creek beds. You remember, panning for gold?"

"Of course, alluvial deposits created and carried by natural erosion. And don't forget, some of those strikes were incredibly rich." Brian paused, checked some numbers on his legal pad, and once again began typing.

Peter continued. "Alluvial deposits in this day and age would be incredibly rare or incredibly remote. Like the diamonds found on the shore in South Africa. Very rare now, but in the 1800's, sizable diamonds could be found walking along the beach."

Brian turned in his seat. "Just like tourists looking for seashells."

Peter nodded and pointed to a column of figures scrolling on the monitoring screen.

"If the microwaves are focused in a tighter beam," he said, "The conductive properties of gold should react with a stronger signature." Peter snapped his fingers. "Too right, Brian, narrow the beam. Smaller search areas with each orbit could quite possibly yield much better results than a wide-range, rummage around approach."

Brian's fingers were now flying over the keyboard.

The wavelength signatures dropped in quantity, but the numerical values rose as the traveling beam of microwaves became more concentrated.

Peter spoke again. "Can we introduce a trigger?"

"Absolutely!" Brian answered, but his fingers on the keypads were unstoppable.

"With the radar beams tighter, and the search pattern smaller, we must have a spiral." Peter was thinking aloud. "Can we do a reverse spiral?"

Brian stopped and turned in his seat. "Of course, when the wavelength signatures, identify a potential deposit, only a small corner or narrow vein would trigger the anomaly display. We need a back-track, a verification."

"Yes, but not the clockwise spiral as in oil anomaly returns, the satellite travels too fast." Peter's comment was acknowledged as Brian nodded and stubbed out his cigarette.

Here was one of the most prominent difficulties with satellite mining. Whenever the ground penetrating radar discovered an underground anomaly, the flight of the orbiting spacecraft was already too far along to register a proper or accurate reading. However, Brian had adapted his carrier wave-tickler beam to probe out ahead of the orbital path and potentially refocus the searching radar beams into a spiral pattern around the triggered area of search. The spiral exploration process was better than the wide range, weak signal returns that were offered from broadband radar, but with a clockwise spiral, the speed of the spacecraft combined with the advancing radar was too much area to cover too fast. Conversely, a reverse spiral would travel backward, counter clockwise, and search in a slower, circular pattern for additional anomalies, a confirmation or denial of an actual deposit.

"There, now you have it, my dear." Brian's voice was a whisper. He had stopped typing and for the first time was leaning back in his chair. He turned and looked up to Peter. "My God, what have we done?"

Peter smiled when he answered. "Haggly-Ford wanted an oil field in one week. Well, we just might have something better. At any rate, we should know by Monday morning."

Brian could not return the smile. He looked dejected. The alcohol in his system was gone, as was the excitement of his efforts. Doctor Brian Pauliss had the beginnings of a hangover. He began to rub his temples and asked, "Could it really work?"

"On shallow deposits certainly" Peter nodded again as he spoke. He was trying to lift Brian's spirits. "It's about time we got out in the field, and away from this desert. Maybe do some panning for gold ourselves."

Brian punched in the shutdown sequence to the satellite interface. He rose from his chair as the big plasma screen faded and returned to normal orbital tracking.

"It's too easy! Why hasn't anyone thought of this before?" Brian's voice was filled with doubt.

"Because, old chum, this is the first satellite of its kind, and all these bloody Texans can think about is oil." Peter frowned after he spoke, and continued in a rush. "What if someone else checks the information download before we do?"

Brian shook his head. "Anyone who checks will only find a copy and paste version of the last five days of input—more underground saltwater seas." Brian now smiled, but his voice was thin. "Only with a password can any gold anomalies be downloaded, and only at a specific time."

"And, what might that password be?" Peter's arm was now around Brian's shoulder as the men were moving toward the pneumatic door.

Brian pulled a rebellious strand of hair back behind his ear. He looked to Peter and whispered, "Forty-niners."

Chapter 5

Cedric Bowles knew everything. It was his job to know. He was the director of security for OPC corporate headquarters. His staff was small, but loyal and very effective. He answered to only one person, Alex Haggly-Ford, and no one else.

After reviewing the security log for early Saturday morning, Cedric pushed his keyboard under his desk, rose from his antique leather chair and entered the washroom of his private office. There was very little lighting as he walked through the spacious workplace. All the window treatments were false. The office for the director of security was in the sub basement, two floors below ground level.

Cedric hated light. He hated the sun and everything about the daylight hours. The security chief preferred to go outside only at night. He was plagued with blinding migraines whenever he was caught in bright sunshine, and therefore always wore the darkest sunglasses available.

Upon entering the lavatory, the security director paused at the washbasin as always. He had entered the room only to gaze at his reflection. A dim nightlight granted the most flattering image possible and showed an overly thin, middle-aged man with a receding hairline. After turning his head to examine his profile, he rubbed his chin and checked for whisker stubble. There was none, Cedric Bowles shaved at least twice a day. After a few moments, he opened the vanity and removed a hand-held mirror. As he turned and began to study his bald spot, he considered the motives for the unexpected, midnight arrival of the two British scientists.

The security chief, of course, knew about the *one-week* deadline and the

28

threat of deportation, he had even called the INS. and checked visa status. The OPC security director was well connected. He had a green card and many contacts at the Immigration and Naturalization Service.

Cedric now replaced the hand mirror and began studying the details of his complexion. He was, of course, pale and his face was dotted with freckles. His hair for *now* would have to do. Strawberry-blond was the color the Americans had clichéd, but his thin strands were still long enough to do a comb-over. This was also an American term, and as Cedric carefully checked the part in his hair, he considered that he hated the two Englishmen almost as much as he hated the Kaffir-loving Americans. At least he wasn't fat. His body, he knew—for a thin frame, was in perfect physical condition. He worked out every day and he was very fit. His hands and arms were very strong.

Maria, he considered, knew of his conditioning and knew of his strength. He made sure of that almost on a daily basis. Cedric smiled at the thought and watched his reflection. The smile turned to a frown as he noticed a glimpse of teeth. The teeth were an imperfection, uneven and jagged he supposed, but quite sharp. Maria knew about the teeth and she knew that he liked to use them.

Outside in the office, the telephone rang. Cedric walked briskly back to his desk and reclined in his chair. He picked up the handset and looked about the darkened room. The glow of ten large computer monitors was flickering the images of OPC's working staff.

"Well, what did you find out?" The voice on the phone was Haggly-Ford—impatient, snobbish, and English.

"They arrived at 12:16 AM Saturday morning, and drove out the gate-post at 1:57. One hour, forty-one minutes." Cedric's South African accent was clipped, curt, and concise—more Afrikaans than English. Still holding the phone, he rolled his chair over to the bank of surveillance equipment and punched three digits into a keypad. Instantly, all ten monitoring screens changed to capture the same image of Alex Haggly-Ford sitting at his desk looking over the oil fields.

"That's it? Under two hours? What did they do?" Haggly-Ford was now leaning back in his chair, pondering the ceiling. He had no idea there was a hidden camera.

Cedric spoke into the phone. "Pauliss smoked and typed on the satellite interface while Clopec disabled the smoke alarms."

"What did he type? And why haven't you confronted Pauliss about smoking and Clopec about disarming fire alarms?"

"If they knew that we knew, we would lose our edge." Cedric now clicked a right mouse button and Haggly-Ford's oversized head with the thick silver hair zoomed closer.

"Well, what did he type? What happened? Did they change the orbit? They better not have changed the orbit!"

"No. No orbital changes were made, however something was done. Something regarding the radar beam, the microwaves."

"Something? Damn it, man, with your budget and staff, I want to know what that something was!"

Cedric now smiled. Haggly-Ford was turning red in the face.

"Yessir, mister chairman, I have already sent a copy of the changes to my man in Cape Town," the security chief lied. "The information is highly technical, but we should have a synopsis in layman's terms within the next few days."

This latest statement seemed to pacify Haggly-Ford. His facial coloring was subsiding, but he had punched in the speakerphone and was now pacing in front of the floor-to-ceiling windows. His next words sounded distant and metallic. "I want immediate notification. Call me the instant know something. No pissing about!"

"Yessir."

"Have you notified the INS? Can their visas be revoked instantly?"

"Yessir," Cedric smiled.

The chairman was nodding, pleased with himself. "Well, keep me advised of any changes, or developments."

"Yessir."

Haggly-Ford walked over to his desk, punched a button ending the call and returned to his windows. As Cedric could see, the sunlight was still too bright to venture outside.

Once again, Cedric reprogrammed the monitoring screens and a dozen different images came into view. He focused on a split screen, third from the top.

Directly outside his office, his administrative assistant was working at her computer. As he thought about the two English fannies, and their discussion about satellite mining for gold, he started to become excited. Gold was certainly much more lucrative than oil, and certainly much easier to acquire. Cedric Bowles had no intention of telling Haggly-Ford about survey satellites prospecting for gold, or about any of the other carefully guarded secrets at OPC.

There was only one problem. The hidden cameras and microphones were not able to pick up the password that Pauliss whispered to Clopec. A man on the security staff *here* was already evaluating a video copy of Brian Pauliss's fingers going over the keyboard. The man was an expert and a staff-member who could be trusted. Most of the input was numerical so any lettered text could certainly be scrutinized. The thought of such efficient security was also exciting. Cedric felt himself becoming aroused. He rolled back to his desk and punched the outer-office intercom.

"Maria? Get in here now!" Cedric licked his lips as he watched the expression register on his secretary's face. She knew about the hidden cameras and quickly pulled herself together, but not before an expression of pure alarm crossed over her features.

This was one of the best parts, Cedric thought: *anticipation.* He could not help himself. He giggled.

•

Reluctantly, Maria Sanchez stood from her desk and approached the polished wooden doors. She would once again go to confession. She would be forgiven. She would block her mind of the evil, give up her body, and somehow explain the terrible bruises that always happened afterward. She had no choice. She simply did as she was told. She must, or her whole family would be deported back to Mexico. She had a husband and three little boys and she would not send them back!

These were the thoughts of the attractive, Hispanic woman, as she entered the security director's office. She was never prepared for what waited. No one could be.

The *Diablo* Bowles was naked and lunged at her the moment she entered and closed the door. His hands were opening her blouse, and after two buttons went flying, his teeth were on her nipples. She cried out as always, but tried to remain quiet as she remembered her anguish seemed to excite the fiend further.

After a disgusting moment, she felt the warm squirt of semen in her hand and realized the instant when *he* became soft. It was over in less than a minute, and as usual, the *Diablo* instantly went to the *bano.*

From the bathroom door, she heard his business-like voice. "That will be all, Mrs. Sanchez."

Maria bowed her head and asked a quick prayer of forgiveness. Afterward, she searched the carpeted floor in near darkness until she found the buttons of her blouse. She crossed the threshold into the outer office, reached into her desk for some wet wipes and after a moment, patiently began to re-sew the buttons. As she worked, she realized that very soon she would need a new box of sewing supplies, some extra buttons, and a new box of wet wipes.

Chapter 6

MONDAY MORNING, AUGUST 19
OPC HEADQUARTERS

Alex Haggly-Ford was pacing. He turned suddenly and faced the door. Cedric Bowles was entering the oak-paneled conference room followed by two of his men from nighttime security. The two corporate guards were carrying cardboard boxes.

Haggly-Ford now leveled his gaze toward Brian Pauliss and Peter Clopec. Both of the scientists had been ushered directly into the formal meeting space upon their arrival. They had been refused entry into Petroleum Discovery and led to the present location by two more of the security staff.

"You bloody well moved it! You came into these offices drunk, after midnight, and you changed the orbital path!" Haggly-Ford was now standing, his hands on his hips. He was having a stare-down across the long polished table, his words dripping with disgust.

Before Peter and Brian could respond, the newly arrived security guards placed their boxes on either side of the seated scientists. Upon a glance, it was obvious the boxes were filled with personal items.

Brian was dumbfounded, his mouth was open as he recognized the private contents of his desk in Petroleum Discovery.

Peter never looked over to the box by his side. He was deeply engaged in an eye-contact battle with Alex Haggly-Ford. When he finally began to speak, his voice was as determined as his stare, level and steady. "The ground penetrating radar was realigned, and recalibrated, but the orbital path was not changed."

"Rubbish! I want you out! Out of here this morning!" Haggly-Ford now motioned to his director of security. "Cedric, make the formal announcement."

"Brian Pauliss... Peter Clopec... You are hereby charged with gross negligence of corporate policy, failure to uphold a contract, damage to company assets, and inappropriate behavior in the workplace. Your employment contracts with OPC have been terminated. You are now dismissed and will be escorted off-property." Director Bowles now nodded to the security officers. The men stepped forward, one on either side of Peter and Brian.

Peter was still eye-locked with Haggly-Ford as he began to rise from his chair, but Brian was slow to start moving. One of the security men now reached forward and gripped him by the shoulders.

"Get your hands off me, you bloody, buggering, cheeky bastard!" Brian's statement of outrage rose in volume as he came out of his seat. He now turned away from the surprised but stern-faced security men and confronted Haggly-Ford.

"I have no intention of accepting these trumped-up accusations!" before Brian continued, he tipped his head toward Cedric Bowles. "Nor, will I lower myself to deal with this refugee from a Boer colony. Clearly, we have been manipulated, falsely accused, and targeted unfairly."

For a brief moment, the security men were derailed by Brian's statement, but Haggly-Ford quickly regained control. "No one has been targeted or treated unfairly. Have you not had over one year? Over one year to produce results, but nothing has been found! There are no new oil fields. Nothing discovered, and finally, you have blatantly disregarded all company policy."

With a decisive movement, the palms of Peter's hands came down on the table. He was leaning forward. He was not moving until he spoke.

"No plausible results can be produced with an impossible goal. The satellite as it *was* programmed, could not have found the geological anomalies required to discover oil! No results were possible! *You knew* that from the beginning!"

Despite Haggly-Ford's eloquent accusations and red-faced demeanor, Peter had captured the room. Everyone was watching him intently, especially Cedric Bowles. Peter continued quickly.

"But significant breakthroughs have been made. You must understand. Our satellite is an infant, a forerunner for geological surveys of the future. The current level of ground penetrating radar is inadequate and not yet capable of finding truly deep anomalies. The technology of deciphering the huge amounts of data is another problem. We need more time for research, time to understand a new language. The satellite is trying to teach us, but we must have the patience to learn." With an indication to Brian, Peter rushed on.

"Doctor Pauliss has doubled the capacity that we can download telemetry. Before the development of his tickler signals, we were entirely in the dark. Now we are on the brink, on the threshold of true discovery.

"Certainly, we came here after drinking. You had given us only one week and therefore, we felt there was no choice. We were inspired, not with alcohol, but with an idea. We came up with a new idea and we acted upon it." Peter was searching the faces around him, looking for a spark of understanding.

"We came here last Saturday and realigned the radar. Realigned the radar and narrowed the search pattern. We *reprogrammed* the telemetry objectives. Don't you understand Alex? We changed the anomaly triggers to search for to a different element."

Haggly-Ford said nothing.

"Aren't you curious? Don't you want to see our new results?" Peter was insistent, his tone beseeching. "Don't you want to know?" he demanded.

"With your permission, Mr. Chairman," Cedric Bowles stepped forward. He was now behind his men and the Afrikaans in his accent was anxious.

Alex Haggly-Ford turned abruptly. His eyes shifted from Peter's gaze and he nodded to his security chief. "Carry on."

"Yessir," the guards responded together.

"Alex! We did not change the orbital path! You have been misinformed," Peter's words dropped to a whisper, but the rage in his voice was a roar. "You have my word!"

"Too bloody right," Brian added. "But not misinformed, lied to—is more bloody likely."

After a bobbing nod from the oversized sunglasses of Cedric Bowles, the security guards picked up the cardboard boxes and thrust them into Peter and Brian's hands.

"Don't you want to know?" Peter repeated, but defeat was now apparent and the guards were pushing toward the door.

"He doesn't want to know or he's not clever enough to understand," Brian spoke over his shoulder.

"It's *gold*, Alex! *Gold*! We reprogrammed the telemetry objectives for a gold signature," Peter was totally exasperated, and his tone was now desperate. "If you don't believe it, go look for yourself."

"I'm afraid that's not possible," Haggly-Ford began. "The satellite is now in a different orbital path, an orbital path that will rapidly decay. You have drunkenly moved the satellite! There is not enough onboard fuel to reestablish a stable orbit, and you may consider your dismissal here as only the beginning of your problems. I am in contact with our lawyers. I have been assured that criminal charges will be filed. Over three-hundred million dollars has been buggered away and you two are responsible."

Alex Haggly-Ford now paused and shook his perfect, silver head. He was frustrated, and obviously distracted by Peter's declaration. He was also bright red in the face and not in his comfort zone of control. He raised a pointed finger for the door. "Cedric, get them out of here."

"Yessir!"

Chapter 7

"Hello?"

"Becca, this is Peter Clopec. I just wanted to call and apologize. I'm afraid I had quite too much to drink and my behavior toward you and Pauline was uncalled-for. Please accept my apologies."

"Well... I don't know. Is it true that you and Brian were led out by security?"

"Yes, that's true. We were dismissed."

"What happened? I thought you still had one week."

"That was my understanding, but obviously this was not the case."

"Pauline and me...we heard you showed up drunk. Showed up drunk and broke the satellite. You know—after we had that fight."

"We did not..." Peter's words were cut short by Brian's hand chopping motion.

Peter and Brian were in Brian's apartment and gathered around the kitchen telephone. Brian was frowning as he listened with a cordless extension while Peter continued on the hard-line handset.

"Yes, as you know, we all had been drinking." Peter hesitated, but Brian motioned him to quickly continue.

"Yes, we were drunk. Again, I apologize." Brian nodded his approval, and urged Peter forward. The telephone call had been rehearsed, but neither of the Englishmen was prepared for the blunt directness of the West Texas woman.

36

Peter continued carefully. "Becca, I was wondering if you could help me. Actually you would be helping Brian, me, *and* Pauline."

"What do you want?" Becca instantly sounded suspicious and Brian rolled his eyes. Peter shook his head and refocused.

"I left something in Petroleum Discovery. Some data."

"Oh, no!" Becca exclaimed. "You guys was fired! Fired and walked out to the parking lot. What do you think? You think I want to get fired too?"

"No," Peter sighed. "We don't want you—"

"Nobody has ever been walked out before," Becca interrupted. "You two were the first." She added, "You broke our *satellite*."

"We did not break the satellite. Someone has lied. We only reprogrammed the satellite, and realigned the radar."

"You *broke* it."

Peter now held the phone at arm's length and stared disbelievingly at the receiver. Desperately, Brian gestured to carry on.

"Becca, I need your help," Peter resumed. "I need your help to be vindicated."

"Don't you talk dirty to me! I'll call the police."

"No, you don't understand. I didn't mean to suggest—"

"I don't even know why I'm still talking to you."

"Becca, I would be willing to pay… Willing to pay for your help. You *do* have access to Petroleum Discovery. Becca, you really could lend a hand. Actually, you could help everyone, including yourself." Peter hated this, realizing his voice sounded pleading.

"Did you talk to Pauline?" the telephone voice demanded abruptly. "Have you told her that you are sorry? Where's Brian? Brian should say that he's sorry, too." Becca was gaining confidence. She sounded, cool, aloof, and condescending. "Have you told Pauline about talking to me— about what you want in Petroleum Discovery?"

"No."

"Good! Don't tell anybody, not Pauline, and not anyone else," Becca's tone hardened. "Now tell me what you need, and how much are you gonna pay?"

Brian looked sharply to Peter, and Peter mouthed the words "How much?"

Brian held up his hand, showing five fingers.

"How does five-hundred sound?"

"Five-thousand sounds better. Now, what do you want?"

Brain appeared shocked at the figure, but Peter pressed on.

"We need proof, Becca, proof that we did not change the orbital path of the OPC satellite.

Haggly-Ford says we moved the satellite, wasted all the stabilizing fuel, and sent a three-hundred million dollar spacecraft on an irretrievable orbit.

"He says we were drunk and therefore criminally responsible. Cedric Bowles wants to press charges. I have spoken to a lawyer and he says that we need proof. We need real proof or we are in serious trouble. Apparently, we are under some kind of investigation."

Peter, even as he spoke, could not believe Haggly-Ford's wild accusations and the downward spiral of recent events. He looked over to Brian. Doctor Pauliss was listening intently with the cordless extension tight against his face.

"How can I get you proof?" Becca's voice was anxious over the phone and Peter pictured her mentally counting the five-thousand dollars.

"In the computer, in Petroleum Discovery."

"How?"

"Do you have a pencil? This might be difficult to understand or to remember."

"All I need to remember is the money, but wait a minute and I'll get a pen."

A scratching sound followed as Becca put down her phone and the sound of a television intruded in the background. After a moment, the television went silent, the phone rattled and Becca was back.

"I'm ready," she said. "Now tell me what you want."

"Do you work tomorrow?"

"All day."

"Good. Now at precisely 4:48 PM, you must be at a computer terminal on the mainframe in Petroleum Discovery. Do you understand?"

"What do you think? That I'm stupid? Of course, I understand. My station is not in satellite mining, but I work on the Petroleum Discovery mainframe all day. 4:30 shouldn't be a problem."

"Becca, I know that you are not stupid, but you must listen carefully. The timing is absolutely critical. At exactly 4:48 PM, you must type, forty-dash-niners-at-search-dash-AU-dash-download. You must have a fresh and empty disk in your CD burner, and when you watch the computer clock on your monitor change from 4:48 to 4:49, you must press enter. The download onto your disk should take less than three minutes.

"Is that it?"

"Yes, but please repeat the instructions. As I have explained, there is a lot at stake. The data is guarded, and the downloading procedure must be followed exactly."

Becca sighed dramatically and surprisingly was able to recite all of the instructions perfectly. Brian nodded solemnly to Peter and re-gripped the phone as Becca started speaking.

"Alright," she ordered, "Now it's my turn to deliver exact instructions. I want that five-thousand in cash, but nothing too small, all in hundreds. I want it in a FedEx envelope—easy to open so I can see the money. Five thousand for the disk. Take it or leave it."

"Very well, as you wish." Peter was nodding as he spoke, but watching Brian scribble on a note pad.

Becca continued, "I'll trade the disk for the money, but I don't want to be seen with you. You and that Brian are bad news. Everybody's talking about how you broke the satellite, how OPC can't stand to lose that much money. A lotta people are *real* mad. I would be careful where I went, careful who saw me." Becca now sounded old before her time and her voice wise and ominous.

Peter swallowed against a bout of rising heartburn, and looked over to Brian's note pad. There was one scrawled word: "Kinko's."

"Meet us at Kinko's."

"No way!"

"Becca, we have to examine the disk, to make sure the information is intact. We cannot spend five-thousand dollars for a worthless disk. This is very important."

"Well, alright...I guess. But let's wait until it's late. How about midnight?" Without a doubt, and judging by the control and excitement in her voice, Becca was enjoying herself immensely. Peter nodded his head.

"Fine, the Kinko's in Odessa not Midland." Peter knew that this was more of a drive from OPC and Becca's apartment, but he felt the need for at least one small victory.

"OK, the Odessa Kinko's at midnight," Becca agreed and added, "Hey, you better wear a disguise, I'm gonna! I don't want to be seen with you, or Brian. And remember, don't tell nobody about this. I could get fired. Don't even tell Pauline!"

"Right, but be careful taking out the disk. Watch out for Cedric Bowles and his Apartheid Nazis."

"Don't worry about me, just bring the money."

After the click, Peter was staring into a dead telephone. He looked over to Brian who was lighting another cigarette. Doctor Pauliss was chain smoking again.

Chapter 8

The chairman waited until everyone was gone, all of the staff from Geology, Fire-Fighting, and especially Petroleum Discovery.

Alex Haggly-Ford was pacing in his office and planning his final move. He knew the timing must be perfect. The OPC stock was still climbing and had been for years. The earlier installation of Clopec and Pauliss was brilliant. Together, the two men had four PhDs, and backed with those credentials, positive speculation on OPC's satellite mining had driven the ailing stock from $9.32 a share, to the current price of $86.40. With the aid of his overseas broker, Alex had ridden the satellite-mining fad all the way to the top. He had secretly acquired seventeen percent of the entire company.

No one knew of his constant buying of the almost worthless OPC stock. No one knew of the months of manipulation, the careful staging, and the constant upbeat performance regarding the hopeful dream and ultimate benefits of satellite mining. After two, carefully nurtured years, OPC stock had climbed and split four times. Alex, by today's reckoning, was a multimillionaire many times over. All of his stock was hidden, secret and controlled, but now ready for market. If handled properly, no trace of his seventeen percent would ever be found. He would sell all his shares at precisely the right moment and no insider trading issues would ever surface.

Timing however, was indeed the issue. The secret percentage must be slipped onto the market just as the board began to rally. With major investors involved, an all-out effort would be launched to stabilize the stock. This was the critical moment when the Securities and Exchange Commission turned off the investigative microscope and went on to other business.

Only the ugly rumors set forth by a missing satellite and gossiping employees could offer an answer. The high hopes of satellite mining dashed by the bumbling of two drunkards and a consulting company paralyzed without the latest tool in aerospace hardware. Everything was now in place, and the schematics and blueprints of the satellite already destroyed. No one would know that the satellite could never find oil, and the only proof remaining was a useless ground-penetrating radar orbiting from Antarctica to the North Pole every ninety minutes with all the damaging evidence tied to an orbital bundle and all those lose ends waiting to come down. With the last bit of physical evidence destroyed, the chairman could skim all of the profits and safely resign from a dying company.

Alex could hardly believe his luck. Despite their academic brilliance, Clopec and Pauliss were fools. The "one-week or your fired" scenario was good enough, but now this was even better. With the satellite missing, there could be no evidence of fraud. No chance anyone could connect the huge offering of stock—all dumped in one week, to the chairman of OPC.

Good rumors could propagate a fortune and bad gossip could destroy an empire. Clopec and Pauliss, drunk at the satellite controls was a brilliant stroke of luck and the perfect excuse for some foreign investor to dump all of his OPC stock. All of the board members had too much invested not to support the company, and as a result, they would be concerned with insider trading charges. Hartock, Barnes, and the rest of the investors would try to offer support, but after the secret seventeen percent was brought to market, confidence would fail, trust would erode, and OPC would plummet. The entire board would be ruined as they tried to support the company. Odessa Petroleum Consultants would certainly crash along with a worthless satellite, but not before the secret seventeen percent could be cashed in and tucked away in Luxembourg.

The scandal of a falling satellite and nasty corporate accident would be the beginning of the end for OPC. Very soon, the stockbrokers would lose confidence and much more than the secret seventeen percent would be for sale. *Very* soon, every *sodding* share would be worth only pennies on the dollar, but not before the chairman could secretly get out. By next week, the company would be in danger, and Alex could picture the day, the emergency meeting, and the announcement to the board—all those bitches and bastards, all major stockholders, and unbeknownst to them, all about to lose everything.

As the chairman walked down the glass and chrome corridor, the harsh tapping of his single set of footfalls was oddly unnerving—the tap-tick-tap-tick, of tangible movement toward a real criminal action.

All of the OPC buildings were virtually empty and as Haggly-Ford swiped his identification into satellite mining, the cool swish of the pneumatic door echoed down the glass-lined passageway. After a confirming glance to ensure that he was indeed alone, Alex filed past the individual workstations, past the former offices of Clopec and Pauliss, and down to the central tier of the satellite control center.

The whir of electronic cooling fans and the glow of the LED read-outs were almost comforting—a gentle stability and a cool symbol of confidence. Alex looked around and smiled.

The entire idea of satellite mining had been absolutely brilliant. Everyone loved the concept of outer space surveys, especially the Texans. These were the men and women from Houston who formed a consulting company and hired an Oxford-educated Englishman as the chairman of their petroleum consultant enterprise.

In the beginning, Alex found himself caught up in the idea: the spacecraft design, the construction, and especially the launch. It had all started after a routine board meeting—a group of Texans out for dinner and discussing the possibilities of finding new oil fields.

Alex could remember the restaurant, the board members, and the evening perfectly. First and foremost was the queen corporate Bitch, Angela Barnes, the lawyer, followed by the fat Roy Hartock and his collection of investment bankers and insurance capital tax-dodgers. Everyone was, as usual, relaxed after a big steak dinner. They were all smoking and drinking Tennessee whiskey. All the investment underlings were bright-eyed, wanting to impress as Hartock or one of his good-ole-boys offered speculations or suggestions. As usual, after a board meeting dinner, the bloody Texans wanted to hear about the future of their company and what clever plans the hired-help Englishman could deliver. This was the night the Queen Bitch watched as the good-ole-boys turned vulgar, primitive and ugly.

Roy Hartock was a fat and sloppy, bad dresser from Houston with the business instincts of a shark. With a quick turn of dialect, and a direct lunge for the only English jugular, Roy had unknowingly provided the key. After leaning his massive bulk back in a chair and blowing out a thin stream of cigarette smoke, he smiled with his shark-like grin. "Hell, to find anything new, we need to look toward the future, to the tools of the future and not the past. Damn it folks, we have to find some new tools! Maybe we need some new blood. Maybe Alex ain't right for our little company."

Just as Angela Barnes began to nod her agreement, Alex had jumped onto the idea of satellite surveys.

He had no idea if the concept was possible, but clearly the Queen Bitch and the "Good-ole-boys" were wondering what the highly paid Englishman was going to bring to the Texas table. With every meeting, and the meetings were becoming more frequent, the corporate mood was deteriorating into desperation. Fighting oil well fires had been a huge profit after the Gulf War, but that had been the last big windfall for OPC. No new prospects were on the horizon, the stock was dropping, and the shareholders wanted much more than a tax-write-off for an already antiquated, new age company.

Earlier in the day, Alex had been looking at thermal imaging charts taken from satellite photographs. He had also been thumbing through the latest edition of *The British Global Geological Report.*

Brian Pauliss had just published an aerospace-survey book in Britain and the idea of outer space oil exploration was born. The Texans instantly loved the idea, especially the bad dressers from Houston.

Alex shook the recollection from his mind and glanced at his Cartier wristwatch. He sat before the large plasma screen monitor displaying the last four orbital paths of the OPC spacecraft. The vertical lines spanning the globe were perfect, no errors in trajectory or altitude. All of the telemetry signals were strong, indicating perfect function and the communications link showed an ideal, five-by-five signal strength. The ground penetrating radar however was scrolling some unusual figures.

After typing Peter Clopec's personal password, "Sasha," Alex watched as a new menu opened on the screen. The new list of options began with "Orbital Mechanics." Following the leading caption was the subtitle, "Ellipse." Below the subtitle were two columns of scrolling figures. Above the first column was the single word, "Apogee." Above the second column, "Perigee."

Alex leaned back in the chair and watched the scrolling numbers. Apogee was the highest point of the ellipse, and Perigee the lowest. Ellipse, Alex knew, was just a trumped up name for orbit. The OPC bird was currently on track and just coming up from South America. Orbiting the earth once every ninety minutes and moving at 18,000 miles-per-hour the satellite would soon be in range of the orbital command transmitter.

The chairman now selected a different menu entitled, "Propulsive Maneuver." Below this option were several choices: "Retrograde Velocity, Prograde Velocity, and Period Velocity."

Alex logged on to Period Velocity and checked his Cartier. Six minutes until the bird was in range. There were now two choices beneath Period Velocity, "Progress" and "Retro." Alex highlighted "Retro." Upon this selection, a column of figures began scrolling the countdown time until the satellite was in range for a course change—5:45, and counting.

So far, everything was perfect. Alex remembered standing over Pauliss' shoulder and asking seemingly innocent questions. Brian had explained,

"For a spacecraft to perform an attitude change, two separate engine burns are required. To increase altitude, the ellipse period velocity must be progressed, the satellite speed increased in the direction of travel. To lower the altitude, the reverse or retro engine must be fired. This is an action slowing the direction of travel. With a decreasing velocity, the spacecraft drops into an elliptical orbit with a perigee equal to the new altitude. After reaching the desired perigee the engine is fired again to reduce altitude and velocity further."

Alex had made a pretense of stressing his point, "But if the satellite were closer to the earth, then certainly the ground penetrating radar would work better. Closer is better, right? Better signals should offer better results." Brian, at this point explained escape velocity and the minimum orbital altitude of 170 miles above the earth.

The countdown was now scrolling through 2:13. After reaching 1:59. Alex was startled when a flashing icon appeared on the screen, "Enter length of burn." After this text, a new window came into view: "Maneuvering fuel." This was the satellite fuel gauge with a computer graphic showing an eighty percent reserve.

Before Alex could become confused, the "length of burn" icon was replaced with a "Burn Execute" button. The chairman dragged the mouse arrow over until the arrow became a hand with a finger on the button. The countdown was now filing through eighteen seconds. Upon reaching zero, a computer bell sounded and Alex pressed the left mouse button. A new icon popped up over the remaining fuel indicator: "Initiating Burn."

Slowly, as the chairman nervously watched, seconds passed into minutes as the fuel reservoir finally began to drop. The period velocity numbers also began to drop, and the altitude figures, which had always remained steady, began creeping downward. Alex held the mouse button until over half of the remaining fuel was exhausted. The OPC bird was now falling. This was the beginning.

Alex now leaned back in the chair. After a reflective moment, he checked the column of figures under "Perigee." I was one hour, fifteen minutes until Perigee, the lowest point in the new earth orbit. He maneuvered the mouse again over a new button labeled "Perigee Burn." Another countdown began as Alex found and highlighted "Length of Burn." He selected 10:00 minutes, and then hit "Enter."

The last burn had used over half of the remaining fuel and had taken only six minutes. Alex now ran his fingers through his hair and rose from the chair. He looked at the big plasma monitor and spoke softly. "Houston, we have a problem."

Alex Haggly-Ford had no idea that Cedric Bowles was watching.

Chapter 9

Becca Raimes felt good. She felt better than when she was in high school, and better than when she won the cheerleading competition. This was exciting and she loved her outfit. The hat with large brim was just right and matched her raincoat perfectly, black on black.

The rain had started around sunset—not really a downpour, but just a steady drizzle. The time was now 11:55 and Becca was alone. She was parked across the street from the Odessa Kinko's, and waiting in Johnny Bacchus' car. Johnny lived in the apartment below, and would do *anything*, loan her a car, money, whatever. Everyone knew her red Firebird, and *her* car might be recognized.

Maybe she would use the five-thousand and help pay off the car. After watching two more strokes of Johnny's windshield wipers Becca thought, hell no! I'm going to Cancun and vacation like a movie star.

"About friggin' time," she announced, as a green Jaguar splashed through parking lot puddles and pulled to a stop in front of Kinko's. The taillights winked out, the doors opened, and the two Englishmen hurried inside. Becca smiled—*perfect*. Kinko's was open 24 hours, but at midnight on a Monday, the green Jag was only one of four cars visible.

Becca hopped out, popped open her umbrella and started across the street. This was *too cool*, her umbrella and purse were also black.

Waiting for the passing of a lone pick-up, Becca caught the expression on the driver's face as he stared at her. Under the streetlights, moving in the rain, she must look like one of those James Bond girls. With a purposeful and saucy stride, she crossed into the parking lot and advanced

45

confidently. Her eyes moving just beneath the hat brim.

"Hello Becca, thank you for coming." Peter was holding the door with Brian waiting nervously inside. A flood of florescent light crowded the store and showed Brian's every wrinkle of concern.

"Show me the money!" Becca had planned her beginning statement, but seemed mildly annoyed that neither Peter nor Brian recognized the famous line from the movies.

Becca closed her umbrella with a flourish and Brian moved forward quickly. "First the disk," he said. "We must examine the disk."

"I said, I want to see the money. Now go over to that jerk at the counter and rent us a computer. I got the disk and *you two* had *better* have the cash." Becca was now pointing with the umbrella and seemingly ready to prod Brian into action.

"The money you asked for is locked in the car." Peter was determined and his voice business-like and matter-of-fact. "When the disk is authenticated, we will give you the money. Now please give Brian the disk."

"Goddamn it." Becca paused, looking around. There were several office-like cubicles stationed along a wall at a right angle to a long glass counter. Two of the computer stations were occupied; five were not. At the other side of the store, two young women were operating a copy machine. They were openly bored and clearly interested in the woman in black and the two rain-spotted men standing beside her. A single attendant was behind the counter, sitting on a stool and reading a newspaper.

"All right, here!" said Becca. Out of her purse, she produced a clear plastic CD container with the silver disk visible inside.

Brian nodded, took the disk, and started for the counter.

"You better have that goddamned money! This was not easy. I did the download just as you said, but right after, two guys showed up. I had just finished, taken out the disk and went to the washroom. When I got back, these two weirdoes were waiting. They were waiting right by my desk— like they were looking for something. I asked them what was going on, but they just said they were electricians checking a circuit. They didn't look like electricians, they looked like cops." Becca's eyes narrowed as she watched Peter's surprised reaction.

"How did you bring out the disk? As I recall, ladies handbags were subject to security search. No electronic data is permitted outside of Petroleum Discovery."

"Use your imagination. I told you I went to the wash room."

"Oh, I see. Very clever," but Peter was blushing.

"I better not be in trouble, that five-thousand…maybe that wasn't enough?" Becca frowned and held Peter's gaze with a practiced pout.

This was going perfectly. Becca knew the Englishmen would have the money and that the disk had been downloaded carefully. She checked *twice*. Everything was perfect but the bright Kinko's lights and those jealous bitches over by the copy machine. They were gawking as if they might remember something. The story about the two electricians was made-up, but not how the disk was smuggled out in the front of her underwear. That was intense, walking past security, feeling the disk—very damned exciting.

Brian was seated in an open cubicle, his fingers hammering away on a keyboard. Suddenly he paused and leaned forward to the monitor. After a moment, he looked up and nodded. He punched the CD tray and retrieved the disk. He was across the room in seconds.

"Everything is in place. It's all there," Brian said excitedly, "all the telemetry—everything. Proof that the orbit was not altered on Saturday morning—and some results. We definitely have anomalies from the new search patterns. I need some proper software to download accurately, but I feel certain the new program found some hard returns."

"All right, good," Becca interrupted. "Now let's have the money! I want to get-the-hell out-of-here," she whispered. "Maybe those women are cops—like the others."

"Police? What others?" Brian's voice was urgent as he looked over to the copy machine women. They were now openly staring.

"Let's go," Becca turned and Peter opened the door.

The rain was coming down harder and bouncing back from the pavement like little silver pebbles. Peter ran to the car and returned with a plastic bag. Inside was a large Fed Ex envelope.

"Just as you asked," he said.

Becca paused, holding the bag and envelope. She turned from Brian's concerned expression and looked to the rain-spattered Peter Clopec. She smiled suddenly and was quite beautiful. "It's all there?"

"Yes, of course, five-thousand dollars in hundreds. Thank you, Becca. You have really helped us."

"Well...I guess," she offered. "Listen..." Becca's face disappeared as her hat tilted downward. "It's not that I don't trust you—you understand—but I had better have a look." Her fingers rifled the envelope, and after a moment, she looked up and her face was flushed.

"Nice doing business with you boys," she said. "But if you need anything else, it's gonna be more expensive. Those electrician guys at OPC, they gave me the creeps."

"Hey," she added just after she opened her umbrella. "You two wait inside for at least five minutes—until I'm out of sight." And then she was gone, her umbrella up in a flash and her rain coat swishing as she walked.

Chapter 10

C edric Bowles was waiting. He had patiently followed, waited, and used his Slim-Jim to enter the old Chevrolet. He was hiding in the back seat and watching as the girl crossed the street and approached the car. He had dismantled the dome light and was now crouched down into a totally concealed position.

Becca unlocked the door, threw in her umbrella, and took off her hat. After slamming the door closed, she took only seconds to turn the switch for the overhead light. She wanted to see the money, but before she could do anything but curse Johnny Backus and his stupid car with the light that didn't work, she felt a ring of fire gather around her neck and a sensation of panic that made her kick wildly.

"There...there...Miss Raimes, don't struggle." Cedric Bowles whispered. "The harder you struggle the greater the chance that you will do yourself harm. You are feeling the pressure of a number three-drapery cord. I could have used wire...but then you would have been cut and possibly scarred for life. My cord is now fastened securely around your neck— believe me, you cannot escape. I may increase the pressure..." Cedric now pulled tighter on the garrote and waited for the anticipated response.

Becca felt her world grow dark, but not before she thrashed violently against the constricting nightmare at her throat, her feet kicking and her fingers trying to grasp the strangling lash.

"Or, I may decrease the pressure..." Cedric was now leaning forward in the back seat and whispering into his victim's ear. He was very close, and now he was pleased that he had worn a special cologne.

48

"I will decrease the pressure, *only* if you stop fighting me!" Cedric relaxed his grip and waited for the only reaction possible. Within seconds, and as planned, Becca Raimes stopped struggling, her hands at her sides, but her chest was heaving badly.

"Before we continue, allow me to explain the rules." Cedric felt himself becoming aroused. He knew that his whispered words were hot on her ear, and he knew that his breath was perfect; he had just taken a mint.

"You cannot speak, Miss Raimes. Therefore, I will do all the talking. There are several questions I must ask, questions regarding the two men you met across the street—Doctor Pauliss and Doctor Clopec." Cedric now chanced a glance in the rearview mirror and was pleased to note the look of terror recognition in the young woman's eyes.

"Our first question will be easy and obvious. What is your relationship with the aforementioned individuals? Are you lovers with perhaps one, or both of the men?" Cedric knew she was not, he knew everything about her, but this was just for fun.

Becca moved her head gently back and forth, a negative response. Her eyes were locked on Cedric in the rearview mirror and her breathing was frantic.

He continued smoothly, "If you are not lovers, then perhaps a business relationship."

Becca carefully nodded a *Yes*.

"A business relationship with OPC?"

Again, Becca nodded.

"You see, my dear, this will not be difficult" Cedric's last words allowed his lips to touch her ear. He checked the mirror. Her eyes were wild.

"Tonight, you received money. Is this correct?" Cedric tightened the cord and was pleased when her breathing became, even more panicked.

Becca tried to nod, but only tapped the floorboard twice. *Yes!*

"Good! You must have completed your assignment." Cedric now paused, his mind racing nicely. "You brought the men information, a CD, a compact disk stolen from OPC."

Again, Becca nodded and tapped twice. *Yes . . . Yes!*

"What was on the CD?" Cedric wondered vaguely if she liked the cinnamon on his breath.

Becca tapped four times and her eyes were darting back and forth in the mirror. She wanted to talk—she wanted the cord off her neck.

"Very well, Miss Raimes, I will release the pressure enough that you can speak. Do not try to scream or to struggle, you may only whisper. Now tell me, what was on the disk?"

Cedric eased the garrote, but retained his grip for instant use. He leaned forward and placed his ear next to her mouth. She was hysterical, her breathing frenzied. He loved this part; he wanted to feel her terror.

"I downloaded the disk from satellite mining. It was proof of some sort. Some sort of proof that they didn't break the satellite." Becca's voice was a hot and panicked pant, directly into Cedric Bowles' ear. For a moment, he thought he was going to ejaculate in his trousers.

"But there was more." Cedric insisted as he twisted the garrote cord onto one handle, his other hand now free. He began touching her breasts, inside her blouse, beneath her bra. He began pinching. He looked in the mirror. She was crying, her tears streaming.

"You must tell me...you must tell me everything that was on the CD." Suddenly he abandoned the breasts and went back to the garrote. He began to pull "Tell me..."

She nodded. Her voice restricted but determined. "It was proof!" she sobbed, "Proof that they didn't wreck the satellite, and something about results of a new search program, some positive results on the disk."

"What is the code to access the program? Tell me the code."

Becca carefully shook her head no. "The program is deleted—gone. They told me to delete the program after I copied the disk."

"The one CD—this is the only copy?"

Becca nodded positively. "I did, just as I was told," she lied. "Take the money, take the money, and let me go." Now it was Cedric's turn to nod positively.

Beyond the rain drumming on the roof, a police siren began to wail a metallic cry, growing in volume and coming closer.

Cedric paused, loving what was next. He was carefully observing the woman's, and his own, reflection in the rear view mirror. "Do you know who I am?" he said.

Becca Raimes shook her head violently, cutting herself with the garrote. "No!" she whispered.

For a moment, Becca was saved. Two police cars raced into view, but they disappeared into a washed-out blur of flashing red and blue.

"Liar," Cedric snapped, closing the garrote. The last image for Becca Raimes was a rain-streaked windshield and the dull glow of the Odessa Kinko's sign.

Afterward, Cedric stripped Becca Raimes of all her clothing and opened his tool bag. He removed a vaginal syringe filled with semen and administered a full dose. He removed several hairs from a plastic bag and placed them throughout her pubic region.

The hairs and semen were acquired with the security director's endless resources and usual efficiency.

Tom Williams

The rain was still coming down nicely when Cedric Bowles had finished. He left the woman in the car and walked down the street to his sports utility vehicle. He was wearing green, tool pushers' coveralls and a baseball cap. His garrote was still inside the old Chevrolet, but his rubber gloves were in his pocket. Gripped in his left hand was his tool bag with all his special items and a new FedEx envelope. The envelope was pleasantly full and as Cedric continued to walk, he began to giggle.

Chapter 11

The funeral, like the weather was drab, depressing and dreadful. For three days, the rain had continued, transforming the flatland desert into a molten sea of tan, brown and amber. Mesquite trees and patches of scrub pine surfaced on either side of the highway and raced ahead to hold back the image of a lost and barren wasteland.

Brian was driving, Pauline Taggart in the passenger seat, and Peter sat alone in the back of the Jaguar. The radio played softly beating time to the rhythmic slap of the windshield wipers. The radio stations were making the best of a seasonal situation. The remainder of a Gulf Hurricane was blowing up from the coast and pouring a hopeless deluge over West Texas.

"It was nice don't you think?" Pauline sniffled—her voice strained from crying.

"Yes." Peter and Brian replied together—their voices automatic, yet strangely unfocused.

"But I just can't believe it," Pauline said. "Becca's mother was so mean to me."

"That was completely uncalled for," commented Brian.

Indeed, thought Peter.

The memorial service had been performed in a small Midland funeral home. A smattering of OPC workers joined the immediate family, and a small cast of neighbors gathered around the local townsfolk. Conversation before and after the service was strained and difficult at best. Peter and Brian had been hardly tolerated and Pauline openly chastised when she approached Becca's mother.

"This is all your fault. You and that wild crowd you run with!" Mrs. Raimes said gesturing toward Peter and Brian. "All you people trying to be so high and mighty. Trying to act better than you are. Don't you know it's your kind that killed her?"

The woman's accusations had drawn all attention. Everyone at the funeral had turned to stare.

"If only she would have listened to me," the ranting continued. "I told her…told her that a simple life was okay. I told her…" The grieving woman then broke down and had to be led away.

This was after the memorial and the pitiful graveside ceremony, where the drizzling rain found the freshly dug grave, the green tent beneath the gray sky, and the huddle of all black umbrellas.

Brian replaced a loose strand of hair, lit a cigarette, and cracked the window of the Jag. He exhaled with a sigh and asked. "Who was that bloke in the brown raincoat—the one who was staring at everybody?"

"He is with the police." Pauline said with a sniff. "I've seen him before. I guess they always send someone official. I think that's nice."

Peter leaned forward from the back seat. "When was the last time you spoke with Becca?" he asked.

"I think it was on Tuesday morning, when I saw her at work." Pauline sobbed. "I just can't believe that she's gone. She was so pretty—so young. Who could have done such a thing? How can this have happened?"

"Yes, truly a terrible tragedy," Peter added. "Do you remember what you talked about—you and Becca?"

"I wanted her to go to the movies—that new one with Harrison Ford." Pauline blew her nose, shook her head, and continued. "If only she had… maybe none of this would have happened.

"You know, Peter," Pauline turned to face the back seat. "Becca thought that you were really handsome. Handsome in a movie star way. She always said that you reminded her of one of those cool European actors, tall, dark, and handsome. She said that you looked like Pierce Bronson with glasses and a tan. I know that Becca was a little rough around the edges, but she really did have a crush on you."

"Did she mention her plans," Peter interrupted softly. "What she was going to do?"

"No, just that she was sick of OPC and wanted to get-the-hell-out-of-here." Pauline laughed a little laugh and dabbed at her tears.

"That's all, nothing more?" Peter was trying to sound nonchalant but he could hear the edge in his voice.

"Now you sound like that man in the raincoat, the one from the police."

"You spoke to him?" Peter and Brian asked together—both alarmed that they had done so.

"Well, yes, I was her best friend. The policeman—he called me at home and asked if he could come over." Pauline was now looking at back and forth, between the front seat and the back. "Why not?" she insisted, "He just wanted to ask some questions. She *was* murdered. Don't you think I should try to help?

"He told me to be very careful. He said that because I was her best friend, that I probably know the murderer. He said that normally, people aren't killed by strangers." Pauline now looked down at her crumpled tissue. "I don't like to think about it—you know, a killer and a rapist. Maybe someone who knows me. What if I'm next?"

Brian lit a fresh cigarette, the last one sucked down and abandoned out the window. "Try not to worry Pauline," he said. "Peter tell her—this is a time you must count on your loved ones, through good times and bad."

"Of course," Peter's response was automatic.

"The policeman," Pauline sniffled. "He did ask about—you know—if Becca had a boyfriend. I told him about the fight we had, the fight with Becca and us on Saturday night. I told him your names and how we all were friends. I told him that Peter—well, that Peter was Becca's special friend. I also told him about how you got drunk, went to work, and broke the OPC satellite. The policeman...he wrote it all down."

"Christ!" Peter's expression was a hiss from the back seat.

Chapter 12

" **A** re you certain? Certain they have proof?" Alex Haggly-Ford was standing and facing the rain-streaked windows and the oil fields beyond.

"Yessir," Cedric Bowles replied, sitting at the guest side of the chairman's desk wearing sunglasses even though the day was gray and bleak.

Thunder rumbled in the distance as Haggly-Ford cleared his throat. "How was this done? How did they gain access?" He began to pace.

"Obviously, someone on the inside."

"Cedric, sometimes you can be quite boring."

"Yessir,"

"There has always been trouble in Petroleum Discovery—always a leak." Haggly-Ford shook his great silver head. "Someone on the board was getting information—early reports regarding poor satellite results."

"Only someone with access to the satellite mainframe could produce such proof, or give such precise information to a board member." Cedric reached for his briefcase and withdrew three personnel files "I have a list of three possible suspects." After placing the files on Haggly-Ford's side of the desk, the security director leaned back in his chair and began to recite.

"Silvers is 56, a closet homosexual, and therefore subject to blackmail. He is the software engineer for all of Petroleum Discovery. Denise Stone is the extreme feminist liberal who frequently files harassment complaints in human resources. She manages all the computer servers and also has access to the satellite mainframe. Finally, and this file has been terminated—was Rebecca Raimes." Cedric Bowles began to examine his fingernails, his head

55

tilted and his sunglasses were very dark in the late afternoon.

"Was it the girl...? The Raimes girl?" Haggly-Ford turned suddenly and stepped forward, his voice dropping to a conspiratorial whisper, "My God! Do you think that they killed her? Killed her for the proof?"

"Possibly," Cedric paused, then added delicately, "They *were* falsely accused. They *are* desperate. Perhaps she tried blackmail—holding the satellite information for ransom." The dark sunglasses now centered on the chairman and the skeletal head with the red-sandy hair nodded. "The scenario is certainly logical."

"Yes, quite," Haggly-Ford offered. "The newspaper did say there could be other motives—other than rape. The police are apparently quite suspicious as the strangulation appears to have been professional."

Cedric was once again scrutinizing his manicure. He frowned suddenly and his Afrikaans accent became academic. "They have a disk, a disk with an accurate telemetry schedule. A schedule of hours, minutes and days. They have proof that they *were* dismissed under false pretense. Proof that someone *else* altered the orbital path. They were discharged from this property before the satellite was moved." Cedric now removed his sunglasses and began to rub his eyes. He continued sadly. "Pauliss and Clopec have proof of conspiracy."

"Well, I want that possibility eliminated. I want that disk! Within days, that satellite will be finished—downed somewhere in the ocean. There must be no proof!" Haggly-Ford was now red in the face, his fists clenched at his sides."

"Yessir, I understand perfectly."

"Cedric, I know that we understand each other, the hopelessness of this company. There was no choice. I was forced into these actions, forced by that God-cursed board—by that bloody bitch Angela Barnes and that sodding hillbilly Roy Hartock. All these years wasted with those country and western fools. Don't worry. You take care of our little problem and I'll take care of you." Haggly-Ford now paused and his eyes narrowed. "I want them followed," he added. "Put one of your best men on it."

"Yessir."

"Your account in Cape Town—you can expect $50,000 as soon as I have that disk—and make sure that's the only one, no copies." The chairman was pacing again, his mind in overdrive.

"I understand, thank you, sir. No copies, no proof." Cedric now stood and replaced his sunglasses. He turned for the door.

"Oh, and Cedric?"

"Yessir?"

"You had better sell your OPC stock and stock options...immediately."

Chapter 13

Peter slammed the door of his red Cherokee Jeep and began walking under a grove of pines headed for Brian's apartment. The parking lot was carpeted with pine needles, still wet from the rain, the scent of evergreens earthy and soothing. The morning was clear and cooler as if the last four days of precipitation had washed away all the troubles of Texas.

Peter, however, did not appear to be trouble free. He was carrying a plastic grocery bag and his movements were impatient. Before he gained the condominium sidewalk, Brian was coming out through an opened door. He had been waiting. The entrance of the two-story building was still in shadow with the red brick and green shrubbery soft in the early light.

"Good sweet Christ. Thank God you're here." Brian said quickly. "You will never believe what I found! It's amazing!"

"Something good, I hope." Peter tried to sound bright, but he looked very tired. "I could use some good news right about now, and some coffee."

"What's wrong, mate? You look mismanaged." Brian clapped a hand on his friend's shoulder.

Peter tried a smile but was truly exhausted. He had been too worried to sleep. His thoughts were in turmoil: Becca's murder, the irrational Haggly-Ford, the falling satellite, and Pauline's statement to the Odessa-Midland police.

Brian on the other hand was the picture of health. *Sex*, thought Peter. After the funeral, Pauline had needed comfort—Brian as well.

"First, some coffee," suggested Peter. "Then tell me. What have you found, and why is it so amazing?"

"It's all on the disk! Everything!" Brian's smile was youthful and contagious, but Peter did not respond. Brian now became insistent. "Come in, let me show you. I still can't believe it."

Peter nodded dejectedly and both men started along the juniper-lined path.

"What's in the bag?" Brian asked, his mood buoyant.

"Trouble," Peter offered darkly.

"What do you mean? What kind of trouble?"

"This was left on my doorstep." Peter held the bag almost at arm's length and explained thoughtfully. "The doorbell rang, and after a moment, I went to the door. No delivery staff and no one from the post, just this." Peter nodded at the bag.

"Well, what is it?" Brian was now looking at the grocery bag carefully, as if something poisonous or dangerous might leak out.

"Come on." Peter tilted his head toward the door and Brian nodded and followed.

Brian's apartment was extravagant and expensive, and among the finest condominiums in Odessa. Winding walkways led through perfectly manicured grounds, water splashed happily in bubbling fountains, and the whole complex was sheltered with shade trees. The apartment was large with three bedrooms, a cooking-show-style kitchen, split-level-den, and two marble baths. Brian rented the flat monthly and the fee was exorbitant.

Peter went for the kitchen. He pulled up a stool at a large oak bar and opened the grocery bag as Brian poured coffee. Inside the bag was a black videocassette and a brown paper envelope. With exhaustion mirrored on his features, Peter wearily pushed the envelope over to Brian's side of the bar.

With a furrowed brow, Brian sat down with his coffee, opened the envelope, and began to scan the single page note. After a moment, he gasped, "Mother of God!"

"Yes."

The message was written on OPC corporate stationery. The text was short and to the point. Brian placed the paper flat on the bar and both men sipped coffee as they re-examined the wording.

> As you must now realize—for whatever reason, the OPC
> satellite is doomed as well as the solvency of the company. A
> young woman has been murdered, a piece of aerospace
> hardware destroyed, and a year of exclusive, geological
> surveys wasted.

Rebecca Raimes came to me and told me of your request for the downloading of files. As the satellite was already beyond repair, I allowed her to proceed. Afterward, and as the download disk was encrypted, she was to report back to me with the details found on this stolen piece of OPC private property. The girl was murdered before she could return and make such a report. I took the opportunity to acquire all of the surveillance camera footages within one-half-mile of Ms. Raimes body on the night she was killed. When considering the aforementioned circumstances and the contents of the videocassette, the complications of an upcoming murder investigation would seem inevitable.

Therefore, at this time, I offer a chance for exoneration. Whatever positive results you found with your gold prospecting attempts—if any—will be the only chance for a destitute and failing company. As I have been informed, there is a 30-day time-period before one can be charged for withholding evidence. (The type of evidence found on the enclosed videocassette.)

I now offer this 30-day period as a chance to clear your names with a murder investigation, save OPC from financial ruin, and reverse the legal action that will be taken for tampering with the O.P.C. satellite. You have thirty days to go out into the field, locate your lost and drunken pipe dream, and return here with enough physical proof of future mining potential to save OPC.

The ultimatum was dated and finished with an oversized signature—Alex Haggly-Ford, August 20th, The day after Rebecca Raimes was murdered.

"Have you played the tape?" Brian asked carefully, his face tight with concern.

Peter nodded. "It's a copy of the security camera at Kinko's. It shows Becca and us quite clearly. There is no sound, but that makes it very incriminating. We look absolutely guilty of something."

Brian grabbed the videocassette and within moments, the fuzzy image of Becca, Peter, and Brian, appearing to argue, flickered across Brian's large-screen television. A wall clock in the store was showing just after midnight. Just before Becca Raimes was murdered.

"But we're innocent. We had absolutely nothing to do with whomever killed Becca," Brian insisted.

Peter was looking at the note, turning it over. Suddenly he frowned.

"We should have suspected that Becca would go to Haggly-Ford or to someone on the board. I don't want to speak ill of the dead, but I don't believe this was Becca's first attempt at charging for corporate services rendered. No wonder she wasn't concerned about slipping past security with an encrypted disk. She had Haggly-Ford's blessing. I now believe Becca was the mysterious connection to Petroleum Discovery and the board of directors. The rape must have been a cover-up. Either Becca or Haggly-Ford must have spoken to the killer or someone on the board generating a motive. Maybe the object of her death was to stop her from delivering the disk and destroy the proof of our innocence."

"My God!" Brian gasped. "If we get wrapped up in a murder investigation, OPC has a perfect scapegoat. Maybe the killer was just moments too late for completing his mission—retrieve the disk and frame us for murder. And, rape and murder combined."

"That's it," Peter said with conviction. "This can be the only explanation. I am absolutely certain." He looked up curiously. "But we *do* have a valid disk—the telemetry date that confirms the satellite's position. Proof of our innocence. And…" he asked carefully, "what else was on the disk? What have you found?"

A fraction of Brian's earlier smile returned. "No worries about the telemetry, we have absolute proof the satellite orbit was not changed during our last night at OPC, but as for the rest, you won't believe it," Brian shook his head and pulled back a rebellious strand of hair. He motioned toward his office.

One of the oversized bedrooms was now filled with a collection of desks, crowded bookshelves, and the little green lights of glowing computer equipment.

Peter followed and watched as Brian sat and touched the nearest keyboard. After only a second, a screen saver disappeared and the monitor showed a satellite map of the earth as viewed from 210 statute miles aloft.

As designed, the OPC satellite traveled south to north mapping the globe vertically with the space between orbital tracks at about seventy miles. As intended, the spacecraft would continue the mapping process until each rotation of the earth provided a new opportunity and another path of unexplored territory. With one earth orbit completed every ninety minutes, an entire global survey was routinely completed.

The current sector under observation was the near-coastal waters just off the coast of Brazil.

"Here!" Brian said excitedly. He touched the screen with a finger. "This is the first anomaly that came up."

A small cluster of bright red pixels was dotted on the display, a tiny jumble of red flecks, speckled on the South Atlantic Ocean. "And look at this one." Brian was clearly eager as he maneuvered through the disk that had been downloaded by Becca Raimes.

After a moment of scrolling and many miles of ocean and coastlines, another group of bright red pixels appeared. This time there were three separate clusters of little glowing dots—three haphazard circles of red flecks on a blue water background.

Brian now turned away from the computer and gave Peter his complete attention. "All of the anomalies I found have been over water, all of them!" Brian shook his head, ran his fingers through his hair, and reached for a cigarette. After his lighter flared, he spoke as he exhaled. "I have scanned the entire disk. There are ninety-seven hard returns."

"What can it mean? A mistake?" Peter now moved closer to the screen. He took off his glasses, rubbed his eyes and looked again—but nothing had changed. The three tightly grouped clusters of red were glowing and holding steady just off the north coast of Cuba.

"But gold underwater?" Peter looked bewildered. "There could be no gold deposits on a Caribbean island. The geological properties are all wrong, completely wrong! There is no gold mining in the Caribbean."

Brian smiled, but said nothing. He now rolled his chair away from the satellite imagery glowing on the largest monitor and approached another computer standing-by with a screen saver. After a quick click of the mouse, an Internet webpage sprang into view. The title, *Lost Spanish Treasure and Antiquated Shipwrecks*.

"My God!" It was now Peter's turn to gasp.

"Yes." Brain echoed, "Ninety-seven hard returns, all over water, and all over the world! But here!" he exclaimed. "In this hemisphere alone, we have found all the lost treasure of the Spanish Main—every legendary treasure and every lost ship, all the secrets from the past, and all the maritime mysteries undisturbed for centuries. Every shipwreck that hasn't been salvaged and every bit of gold that remains lost and scattered on the seafloor."

Peter just stared at the image on the screen.

Brian asked, "Can we even begin to understand what this means? The forgotten riches of generations after generations—everything revealed by a satellite. Peter, you were right, shallow deposits without an overlay of meddlesome minerals, shallow deposits of gold covered only by water, and water the easiest medium to penetrate. And, gold as a superconductor will always offer the most available signature of any element on the planet. Just consider." Brian paused breathless, but his voice was in a run-on. "Where there is gold there are most probably silver and precious gemstones. This is absolutely unbelievable! And, don't forget the historical artifacts, an unprecedented find in priceless historical treasure!"

Peter shook his head speechless, his mind in overdrive. "Christ-all-bloody-mighty!" he finally muttered. "Are you sure? Can we be certain? There *is* no mistake?"

With another click of the mouse, Brian opened an antiquated mariner's chart complete with ancient calligraphy and bold Spanish crosses. Available at a glance were the antique trading routes traveled by the old treasure fleets. Broad arrows darted around the Spanish Main and indicated specific dates and points of departure. The harbor of Havana Cuba was clearly the starting location for many of the treasure ships outward bound for Spain. Many of the arrows started from Havana but swept eastward, north, or even west into the Gulf of Mexico.

Brian maneuvered the mouse arrow onto a purple up-link labeled, "Fleet wreck of 1733." With a double click, the following heading came into view, "From the recovered log of Capitan-General Juan Diego Garcia, Admiral of the fleet."

Below the modern Internet heading and the English translation, was a photocopy of the original manuscript archive.

Rapidly, Brian scrolled over the English transcript and began to scan the original Spanish text. As Brian was born in Buenos Aires and spent the first twelve years of his life in Argentina, his Spanish was flawless.

After Brian began to read and simultaneously translate, Peter pulled over a rolling office chair and both men crowded next to the computer screen. The makeshift office was cool and dark, the shades pulled always, and the glow of the two computer screens the only light in the room.

Whenever possible, Brian rolled his "r's" and twisted his tongue eloquently around the Castilian names and the Old Spanish landmarks. As he moved over the words his voice sounded oblique and almost reverent, the meaning of the ancient pen strokes obviously captivating.

> *On this 26th day of Augustus, in the year of our Lord 1733, we find ourselves in the service of the Holy Madonna Maria, the Mother of God, and his Royal Majesty, King Phillip of Spain. After the death of our beloved Consulate of the fleet, Capitan-General De Marcos de Vega, I find myself burdened with a weary heart, but honored with the authority to lead our ships home. His appointed Excellency, Don Mendoza Ortega, the governor of Havana, has ordered our ships post-haste to Cadiz.*
>
> *We are four galleons and eighteen merchant ships of various tonnage and size, laden with the responsibility and prosperity of the last five years of holy conquest. Together and collectively, we*

are over one thousand souls in service to his Most Catholic Majesty's high Spanish crown.

Our ships, I fear, are over burdened with weight and afflicted with the perils so common in these hot and tropic waters. Havana's bay, from which we so recently departed, was so crystal, and so clear that the many faults of our aged and earth-born vessels was too easily noticed. From the wicked sea-worms below that must surely feast on our very timbers, to the devil-rot, which hides in all places and makes the mighty oak weak, our prayers must be joined with the fabric of our vessels as the Holy Madonna carries us over her blessed creation.

I pray that our efforts please and do not blaspheme, and that our mission to enrich the kingdom of Spain, leads only along the path that the Holy Madonna will allow us to follow.

His Majesty's obedient servant
Capitan-General Juan Diego Garcia

Brian edged forward, clicked on the mouse button, and scrolled the text forward. The following penmanship was strained and jerky, with the elegance and flourish of the earlier entry replaced with an urgent need only to communicate.

The Internet text continued: From the flagship, Lourdes de Conception, and the hand of Capitan-General Diego Garcia, Admiral of the Fleet.

Find us now, on the fifth day of our voyage, during the Holy month of the first day of September, in the year of our Most Holy Lord 1733.

A tempest has befallen our fleet and scattered us over the green and white mountains, which have been so recently created. Of the twenty-two ships that set sails together, only three of our galleons and one of our merchant ships remain in sight.

The wind has backed and veered, but has now gained in augmentation to drive our failing vessels over the cresting waves at a frightening pace. Every soul aboard joins in the most earnest of prayers hoping for the divine intervention gained by our noble Christ on that most famous of storms upon the Sea of Galilee. Without such help, I fear that we are lost.

With my own eyes, I have seen three of our lesser vessels succumb to the churning waves and fall below the surface to embrace the Madonna. Even now, our own ship speaks loudly in protest to the suffering she must endure. Her timbers, below decks grown a continuous bedlam, as the howling winds aloft scream to declare a terrible blasphemy. The tempest in the rigging can only be described as the cry of the unfaithful, with every breath of the storm offering a new episode in the tale of our destruction. As with the heretic fables of the whirling dervish, every soul aboard is naked with fright, as our own vessel has been stripped of her sails. She now points her broken spars to heaven and offers only the tatters of her former clothing to be snapped in the rising wind. Green water is climbing in the hold and makes a mockery of the knowledge that we are heavy with a King's treasure. Our mission, as we endure, purveys a sense of guilt and punishment, and launches a fear that no earthly price can buy a heavenly salvation.

Our other vessels, which remain in sight, are equally stricken, without sails, and only able to ride before the wind. As far as the remainder of the fleet, I cannot imagine any ship able to withstand such punishment and survive. I now submit this account into a ship's bottle sealed with a candle and dispatched onto the waves. With the Holy Madonna's blessing, this record of our strife will be preserved and revealed. I had hoped to once again to see Cadiz, but now I can only wait to embrace the Holy Mother. I pray for our fleet, and for our lost one thousand souls.

Juan Diego Garcia
September 1, 1733

Brian finished reading and sat back in his chair. "I believe they turned back," he said. "Diego didn't mention it in the log, but I believe that they turned back, at least some of them."

Peter shook his head, his mind in overload.

"Look," Brian said. He was pointing with a pencil eraser and tapping the monitor. "These three groups of red are three separate anomalies that would equal three separate shipwrecks—the three galleons that remained together in 1733." Brian now paused to light a fresh cigarette. He rolled his chair away from the computer, leaned back and exhaled. "They turned back, but it was too late," he said simply. "The hurricane was already upon them."

"It does seem logical. When the weather becomes rough you return to port." Peter removed his glasses and rubbed the bridge of his nose. He replaced his eyewear and added doubtfully, "But Brian, ninety-seven anomalies? It just seems impossible. How can we determine that your little glowing dots are actually sunken shipwrecks or deposits of gold?"

Brian puffed on his cigarette and smiled again. "Oh, Peter, I know you so well. Peter the doubtful—always looking for proof. Well then, sit back and prepare yourself. I saved the *coup-de-grace* for last. I think *this* should offer much more than a coincidence."

Once again, Brain moved to the Internet computer and typed in a web-site for the *Miami Herald*. He accessed newspaper archives for 1975. After a few moments of scrolling, a grainy headline appeared complete with pho-tographs. Encircled by his French crewmembers, the leading man of the article was easily recognized. Here was the famous undersea explorer with the large Gallic nose and tear shaped eyeglasses.

The headline read, Jacques Cousteau offers to help Castro with Lost Treasure Ships. The editorial explained the Frenchman's theory that three galleons from the treasure fleet of 1733 were lost in the north side of Ma-tanzas bay in Cuban waters. Located in 701 meters of water, the wrecks would certainly be a challenge to salvage, but not unattainable.

Quickly, Brian scrolled to another later article, zoomed in on the fine newsprint and sat back smiling as Peter leaned forward to read. Castro thanks Cousteau, but declines Frenchman's offer to help. This article was also accompanied with a photograph showing a frustrated Cousteau, ani-mated with a typical Gallic shrug.

Patiently, Brian waited for Peter to finish reading and rolled his chair over to the main computer showing the satellite map.

There were no labeled landmarks on satellite imagery, only the familiar coastlines with the unmistakable shapes of Cuba and the Florida Keys. With a double click of his mouse, Brian added software and Castro's island nation was suddenly overlaid with topographic legend and boundary lines. A detailed chart showing cities, towns, and roadways, complete with har-bors and ports of call.

Glowing brightly in the deep-water bay on the north side of Cuba were the three red dotted clusters from the OPC satellite. The name given to the scalloped out cove was Matanzas bay.

"Unbelievable!" Peter pushed his chair away from the screen. "This is simply unbelievable," he added.

"I know, but with Cousteau's research, and now with our three clusters of anomaly, there can be little doubt.

"Diego Garcia turned back," Brian continued smoothly, "And three out of four Galleons sank in Matanzas Bay."

Before Peter could deny the obvious, Brian was scrolling the satellite imagery up from Cuba and northward onto the east coast of Florida.

"Watch carefully," he said as he zoomed in on the Atlantic beaches.

From time to time, a single glowing dot would appear. Red in color but not as big and bright as the anomalies found in Matanzas. All the dots were spaced well apart but in very shallow water. Almost all of the red pixels were near the entrances to old Spanish harbors: Boca Raton, Sebastian, and St. Augustine, but a few were near Ft Lauderdale and Palm Beach. As Brian maneuvered the mouse and therefore the OPC disk, the computer purred and made the little clicking sounds of a machine burning a compact disk.

"I'm making copies. Extras for both of us," Brian commented, adding, "Do you want to see the fourth Galleon? The one that went missing when Diego Garcia turned back for Cuba?"

Before Peter could respond, Brian was navigating the disk, down across Florida and out into the Gulf of Mexico, down past Tampa, Fort Myers, and Naples, to a cluster of red dots glowing just offshore of the extreme southwestern peninsula. The coastline below Naples, south to the Florida Keys was charted as the Ten Thousand Islands. The name labeled just above the red dotted anomaly was Cape Romano Shoals.

"This must be the missing Galleon." Brian was tapping his eraser. "The water in this area is extremely shallow. Too many sandbars for a large vessel to cross over safely. When the wind is strong, shallow waters become extremely rough. Even at miles offshore, the water is less than 30 feet deep. Think of it, Peter, a King's treasure *waiting* in thirty feet of water."

Brian now stubbed out his cigarette and reached to retrieve the newly copied compact disks. After carefully placing the original and the two copies into plastic cases, he began the shutdown procedures for both computers.

Clearly, Peter was overwhelmed, his mind weighing the possibilities of such an incredible find. The scientist in him was struggling for control, but the spark of a newfound adventure was growing and beginning to burn away the anxiety and exhaustion of the ultimatum from Haggly-Ford.

"What are you doing? I thought you never turned off the computers." Peter's voice was no longer weary or depressed. He now sounded jovial and almost mocking.

Brian, for years, had always insisted that it was far better to leave computer equipment running, he was adamant that start-up and shutdown were the hardest functions for the hard-drive to perform.

After a quick glance and a smile at Peter's remark, Brian reached over to the Internet computer's printer tray and pulled out a single sheet of paper. "Here," he said. "This is our itinerary. We have a plane to catch in El Paso and only four hours to get there."

"Then we're going?" Peter grinned. "We're going to look for Diego's lost Galleon?"

"Absolutely! How long will it take you to pack?"

"Never mind packing," Peter shook his head. "I think we should just buy what we need on the way. For some reason, I don't think money is going to be a problem. Time is our only challenge."

Brian stood after he completed the computer shutdown and Peter followed him back into the kitchen. Both men were drawn to the ultimatum resting on the bar.

The note was dated August 20th.

"Becca was buried yesterday, the 23rd" Peter was thinking aloud. "Today is the 24th and tomorrow the 25th. After tomorrow, we only have 24 days until the Haggly-Ford deadline."

"But you realize," Brian looked up from the note. "We already have proof that we didn't move the satellite. The telemetry schedule on the disk confirms our innocence."

"Yes, thank God, but there's more going on than a falling satellite. Haggly-Ford is as slippery as a snake. He *does* have that video placing us next to Becca's murder, and if Becca was killed, who knows what could happen next. I think it's better if we play along—find some proof if we can, that we really did find gold."

"So, we're off and into the field," Brian held up the itinerary. "Panning for gold?"

"Definitely," Peter nodded. "When we find proof that the satellite really did work, we're off the hook with the OPC board, Haggly-Ford, and any problems with Becca's murder. With the Kinko's video out of the equation, the police won't be distracted and directed to us. Then they can find the real culprit and I'll wager anything that the genuine trail goes back to Haggly-Ford."

"Then that's it," Brian smiled. "We go for the gold!"

Chapter 14

Alex Haggly-Ford was standing in the oak-paneled conference room and facing the board of directors. There were twelve members on the OPC executive panel, eight men and four women. The board members were seated, but clearly impatient and irritable. Everyone had been called to an emergency meeting.

"As you all know, our stock is under attack." Haggly-Ford paused for effect. "I would suggest that no one in this room feed the flames of hysteria and offer negative comments."

Angela Barnes was the attractive woman near the head of the table. Sadly, she shook her head.

Before she could speak, the gruff voice of Roy Hartock interrupted. "Goddamn it, Alex! Is the satellite lost, falling, or crashed? This whole company depends on that fancy piece of hardware." Hartock was the founder of OPC, and the big oilman from Houston who was tied into twenty other companies and sat on twice as many boards.

Most of the other board members were snobbish figureheads, having no personal or vested interest in the company. These were the investment banking and insurance people who represented the largest blocks of OPC stock.

Alex raised his hands protectively and began smoothly. "NASA holds a routine press conference every month, a briefing regarding the flight status of redundant orbital hardware. During this very informal and sparsely attended meeting, an updated list of falling space junk is released to the press." Alex now settled into the role of an English professor. He had rehearsed this part.

"As you must know, there are currently about three-thousand satellites in orbit around the Earth. Older spacecraft have exhausted maneuvering fuel, suffered communications failure, or wobbled into an unrecoverable and irregular orbit. Most spacecraft are small, like ours, and weigh under a thousand pounds. Older and much larger satellites, like the former Soviet military equipment, can weigh up to three or four tons. These, when they fall, have the potential to be dangerous. Smaller satellites, upon reentering the atmosphere become heated to the point of total disintegration. Others could fall like meteorites, crashing onto the Earth."

Haggly-Ford now glanced about the room. Some of the board members were wandering, two were actually doodling on their note pads. One of the women was inspecting her nails and another younger man had flicked open his cell phone and was checking text messages.

Angela Barnes however, was watching intently. So was Roy Hartock. As always, Roy was dressed in a bad suit and the rolls of his flesh were constricted by a badly chosen tie. He seemed to have gained even more weight, and he now clutched a white handkerchief and dabbed at the sweat beads that were popping on his forehead.

The air-conditioning in the conference room had been lowered to the lowest setting as Alex hoped the frigid temperature would precipitate a quick closure to the meeting. Hartock's sweating was mildly disappointing, but Angela Barnes appeared to be thriving in the cooler environment and this was alarming.

Angela was a trim, very attractive woman in her early fifties. She wore her hair in a strict blonde pageboy and appeared to be a cross between Martha Stewart and Peter Pan. Angela Barnes was well educated, well traveled, and a very good dresser. And she was, as the Texans so often coined the phrase, "Sharp as a tack." Today, Angela was wearing a cobalt business suit, and even sitting, her posture was perfect.

As the intensity of her blue eyes and the sharp color of her dress blended with the frigid boardroom, Angela seemed to reach out with icy fingers and grip Haggly-Ford—squeezing him for the truth.

Alex swallowed uncomfortably and tore his gaze away from the scrutiny of the corporate Queen Bitch. "Our OPC satellite, I'm afraid, will be on the next list of falling space junk. Destined to reenter the atmosphere and fall somewhere into the Indian Ocean."

"This is criminal. Absolutely criminal!" Roy Hartock exploded. He was turning red in the face and his chubby fist pounded the polished table. "I want Pauliss and Clopec charged with criminal negligence. Angela, you're the goddamned lawyer. You're the legal counsel for this board. Let's file some charges."

Angela Barnes now turned away from Haggly-Ford. She was focused on the heavy-set Hartock seated across the table, but when she spoke, a chill in her voice claimed all attention and galvanized the room.

"Criminal charges are not possible without proof," she said. "However, all the proof I need is on that up-coming NASA press release. The moment our doomed satellite becomes public knowledge, we are no longer bound by the SEC and insider trading issues. At that moment, I will resign from this board and offer all of my OPC stock at whatever price I can get."

Bloody hell!

Haggly-Ford had not expected this. Alex had expected initial support and an all-out effort to save the company. The Queen Bitch was beyond ultra-savvy and ready to ruin everything. This was *not* part of the plan! If Angela sold her stock, and her stock was considerable, the entire board would dump as an obligation to their investors.

Sodding Bitch!

The entire room was now centered on Roy Hartock. He was lighting a cigarette against all the no-smoking regulations. "Alex! Find me a goddamned ashtray!" Roy exhaled expansively and nodded across the table. "Angela, I'm gonna lose millions on this one. But I know enough to steer clear of those bastards at the SEC. Maybe we could work a deal, divide geology and fire fighting into two, new and separate companies. Reissue a new stock, put out the fire, and call off the witch hunt."

The other board members were looking around hopefully, all very attentive. Doodle-pads were abandoned, cell phone closed, and manicured fingernails were fidgeting under the table. Heads would roll if this company failed.

Angela shook her head no, and for a moment, the remaining board members hung on to the possibility that the negative action was in response to Roy Hartock's smoking.

"Not enough time, and not enough real value." Angela continued thoughtfully with no apparent malice toward Hartock's cigarette. "Alex, please *do* find Roy an ashtray, I can't imagine damaging this fine furniture."

Now it was Haggly-Ford's turn to go red in the face. He bent quickly to a highly polished sideboard, opened a door, and removed an empty tumbler. After placing the short glass in front of Hartock, he stepped back a pace and stood with his hands on his hips.

Bloody Ice Bitch, thought Alex—almost in an inward panic, if everyone dumped the stock on the same day of the press release, the trading price would instantly go to pennies on the dollar. His seventeen percent would be almost instantly worthless. Never did Alex consider that Hartock would not support the company. He would be down a fortune. And the Barnes bitch—certainly she would lose over ten million. But how was this possible? The Texans were only hillbillies. Hartock, Alex knew, did not even have a university degree.

Angela Barnes reclaimed the room as she leaned back in her chair. She tapped her pencil thoughtfully on her note pad and examined as if for the first time, the great, silver head of Alex Haggly-Ford.

Everyone was watching intently.

"Alex has served us too well," she said. "He offered a new idea, followed up with a brilliant publicity campaign, but failed to offer one shred of proof that the spacecraft would work. I think that satellite failure is the real problem and not a falling satellite. I now believe our trio of elegant Englishmen have sold us a pig-in-a-poke." With the last of her words, Angela enhanced her southern accent and felt the room tighten with her focus.

In a new voice that reflected her Radcliff education, the lawyer in Angela Barnes continued. "Our chairman has guided our corporate cart on the path to ruination. We have stupidly placed all of our eggs in one basket and we have cooked the golden goose. Mister Haggly-Ford was the pied piper of greed and we have followed him obediently into fiscal destruction."

The attorney now paused, staring, but as Alex tried to remain stoic, his mind was reeling. He had never expected this. He was all-but being accused of fraud, and heaped together with Clopec and Pauliss. His collar felt very tight and he felt flustered that he must be as red in the face as Roy Hartock.

Alex stammered, "But, my dear, the board voted on satellite—"

"Don't you, 'my dear' me, you smooth son-of-a-bitch. Your shenanigans will cost me at least fifteen million." Angela now appeared hawkish, determined, and clearly a woman scorned. In the following silence, the tension in the room became electric.

Alex shook his head and grasped at a final straw. "Pauliss and Clopec, on the night they moved the satellite, they also reprogrammed the ground penetrating radar." He smiled weakly.

"They reprogrammed the satellite to search for gold. Apparently before the satellite went off-line there were some positive results."

The entire room now exploded into a multitude of conversations.

"Alex, this had better not be bullshit." Roy Hartock spoke over the bantering noise. "You have proof? You have data?"

Quickly, Haggly-Ford nodded—his mind in a desperate turmoil. He explained about the surveillance footage in satellite mining, and exagge-rated about Peter Clopec's last-day description of the newly acquired gold-searching-orbital-radar. He also, now fueled by the obvious excitement, allowed that at least thirty days would be required before the telemetry da-ta could be deciphered into hard and specific geological sites. His command of the English language had never been smoother. He also added that he was saving the gold prospecting news for last, as he hoped to call a press conference and announce the positive gold mining results before gos-siping rumors could erode stock confidence further.

Angela Barnes, throughout the non-stop rhetoric watched intently, her icy gaze leveling.

Afterward, as the conference room filled with bonhomie and a very animated Roy Hartock smoked, nodded positively, and drilled Alex exci-tedly with speculative questions, Angela continued her unmovable vigilance.

When there was a notable pause in the multiple conversations, Angela stood from her chair and walked around the room. After passing the enthu-siastic bankers and excited insurance crowd, she paused by the door. Without trying, Angela Barnes commanded all attention and spoke loud enough to override the last of the English chairman's dwindling dialogue. "Alex Haggly-Ford," she said, "How long before the NASA press confe-rence?"

"Well...that was my point in calling the meeting today." Alex faced the door and opened his palms in explanation. "The orbital flight status information was just released. The monthly NASA meeting was yesterday. Our satellite will not be mentioned until the next press conference, thirty days from now. About the same time required to decipher the Pauliss and Clopec gold mining data. We have thirty days to save our company."

Angela Barnes nodded and offered a chilling corporate smile. "Alex Haggly-Ford," she said. "I shall be watching you...*very* carefully."

Chapter 15

After a quick stop at Peter's Odessa Bank to visit the safety deposit boxes and drop off the original OPC satellite disk, Peter and Brian arrived at the El Paso International Airport. They parked Brian's Jaguar in long-term parking and crossed into the welcome air-conditioning of the multilevel terminal at 12:05 PM. The high, vaulted ceiling produced a canopy of echo as a multitude of travelers bustled through checkpoints, mounted escalator platforms, or dropped luggage in front of various airline desks.

Both men were suddenly aware they were the only potential passengers without substantial luggage and that the police and airport authorities regarded this type of traveler as either fugitives or possible terrorists. Brian shouldered a lightweight, leather carry-on containing his laptop computer, global cell phone, and a small hand-held GPS. Peter however, carried nothing but his passport, wallet, and a copy of the OPC disk in a pocket of his short khaki trousers.

After a few moments of deliberation, an airport gift shop was located whereupon both Peter and Brian emerged with roll-behind luggage stuffed with an assortment of loud and flowery vacation attire and the clothing they had been wearing upon entering the airport. Peter was now animated in a pink oversized shirt covered with white hibiscus flowers and Brian in a comfortable sea-foam jogging suit. Peter went off to reserve a rental car in Miami while Brian queued up in front of the Delta Airlines counter.

As promised with Brian's itinerary, the Delta connection to Atlanta arrived on schedule and allowed both men to cruise through the Atlanta concourses and board Delta's final flight of the day to Miami. With Brian's usual stubbornness for luxury, he had booked both flights in first class. Without delay, the A-310 airbus roared through take-off and reclaimed the Georgia skies at 2:35 PM.

"May I offer you gentlemen something from the bar?" asked the flight attendant. She was a strikingly beautiful black woman in her late twenties.

"Of course, my dear," Brian purred as he stretched out comfortably in the big leather chair. "A Cuba Libre please—a rum and coke."

"And for you, sir?" The woman was now regarding Peter's bright pink shirt with the white flowers.

"A Black Label, if I may, no ice," Peter replied.

The flight attendant smiled and nodded pleasantly, her uniform, scarf, and short hairstyle immaculate. When she returned and served the drinks, she smiled again and asked, "On vacation?"

At the same instant, Brian answered, "Yes," as Peter said, "No."

Brian recovered immediately. "Well, that certainly reflects a point of view doesn't it?" Brian sipped his drink, glanced over to Peter and continued smoothly. "My colleague tends to look on the darker side of things. However, I believe that even the most routine travel can offer wonderful possibilities and endless adventure. All a state of mind don't you think?" Brian now turned in his seat and looked around the near-empty first class cabin. There were only two other passengers forward, both older men wearing business suits and both reading newspapers.

"Won't you sit down, my dear, I'm afraid my drink will be in need of constant attention." Brian was now indicating the empty seat across the airliner aisle-way.

There was no surprise when the young woman laughed and sat down. Peter sighed, tasted his whisky, and looked out the aircraft window. Brian was, as always, a disarming and insatiable flirt, and as a result, women usually found him charming and sensitive. Doctor Pauliss carried his old world flair like an aristocrat, but always with the behavior and enthusiasm of a young and inquisitive gentleman.

As Peter listened to the harmless banter between his best friend and the flight attendant, he sipped his drink and looked out over a sea of clouds the aircraft was so effortlessly passing over. With Brian's charm blending with the droning jet engines, Peter closed his eyes and let his mind wander.

Brian, of course, was his *best* friend and only life-long true friend. Peter had met Brian when they were both children in an English boarding school. Peter had been older by three years when Brian had just arrived from Argentina. Even then, Brian had appeared young for his age and as an overweight, spoiled little boy, he was immediately targeted for ridicule.

Peter remembered finding Brian, locked into a toilet stall and crying. Anyone that was a foreigner or an ex-patriot and not born on English soil was always an easy target, and Peter remembered all-too-well his own experiences after arriving from Nairobi.

Peter's family was Hungarian, from Budapest, but his father and grandfather had both been mining engineers destined to work in Africa. The wild bush of the Transvaal was all the early childhood Peter could remember and he would never forget being the only white boy among the native Africans and his youthful dream of becoming a Zulu warrior. With the aid of his *Bibi*—his native African nanny—he had learned to speak Swahili and trek along the veldt with his childhood friends. This was one of the happiest times Peter could ever remember. That, of course, had all changed, when at the age of twelve he had been packed off to England and boarding school. He remembered his own tears and the painful goodbyes to his *Bibi*, even more painful than the farewell to his own mother and father.

The first months away from Africa were a lonely and agonizing existence, especially with the insistence that all foreign nationals spoke only English, a language that was to Peter as unfamiliar as Chinese.

Brian, at least, spoke English as his mother and father were from Scotland. He had been born, however, in Buenos Aires. His Scots father was a successful railway engineer with expertise on mountainous terrain, and, as a result, the Pauliss family lived most of their lives in South America. The Andes between Chile and Argentina were the new highlands for the transplanted Scotsman, and the entire Pauliss entourage often traveled to the most remote, rugged, and difficult challenges of railway construction.

Brian was also raised by a nanny who taught him Spanish and German. The Pauliss family was almost identical to the Clopec's as both parents were highly social and lived large lives around wealth, prosperity, and well placed political connections. Proper children were raised by servants until they could be educated in England. This, generations had proved, was the recipe for world-class success.

Peter opened his eyes, sipped his whiskey, and settled himself deeper into the broad-backed, comfortable leather. Brian was still pouring on the charm, and the flight attendant appeared to be mesmerized.

Brian had always had a gift with charisma and with the ladies. After Brian's childhood rescue from the toilet stall, he and Peter had become fast friends. After boarding school, Peter and Brian both attended university, Peter in Edinburgh, and Brian at Cambridge.

It was later, during a second session of graduate school in Scotland that the two old boarding school friends became reacquainted. Brian had finished Cambridge with honors, completed his thesis, and qualified for a doctorate in geology. Peter, meanwhile, had done the same at Edinburgh, although his doctorate was in chemical engineering. When Brian arrived in Edinburgh for his second doctorate in aerospace physics, he found Peter working on his second PhD in mechanical engineering. Their reunion at Edinburgh had reestablished a lifelong friendship, a friendship that was always to be closely guarded, with many worldwide holidays together.

The senior Clopec and Pauliss families were drawn together by the relationship and were brought together by major events such as weddings and funerals. Peter had stood up as Brian's best man for two weddings and Brian for Peter on one.

As always, when he recalled the weddings, Peter's mind focused and flashed painfully back to Monica, their beautiful wedding in Budapest, and the traditional ceremony at the riverside church on the Danube. The birth of his daughter Sasha, always followed the delicate wedding memory, but was dashed by the horrible afterthought of the phone call, and the news that both mother and daughter had been killed by a terrorist bomb in London.

Peter bit his lip against the painful memory, swallowed some whisky against the inevitable heartburn, and looked up as the flight attendant was playfully placing a pillow under Brian's head. The jet engines droned onward as the voice of the airline captain made his routine announcement.

"Ladies and gentlemen we are now headed southward over Florida. Tampa Bay to the right of the aircraft and I anticipate an on-schedule landing at 5:40 Eastern Standard Time, about one hour from now. The weather in Miami is a balmy ninety-two degrees with a light wind out of the southwest. I would like to thank you..."

Peter looked over to Brian. The flight attendant had returned from visiting her other two passengers, but Brian was now asleep. The attractive woman reached into the overhead for two of the lightweight blankets. She gently wrapped her favorite passenger with the first coverlet, and offered the other to Peter. Peter took the blanket and closed his eyes.

The beautiful girl with the silky coffee skin—she looked a lot like his *Bibi*.

Chapter 16

"Gone? Where have they gone?" Haggly-Ford sputtered. He was rifling through his desk looking for some stationary.

"They have apparently left the state," Cedric Bowles replied smoothly.

"And the disk, do you have my disk?" the Chairman looked up.

"Nossir,"

"Bloody hell, Cedric! I told you to have them followed. I want that disk." Haggly-Ford abandoned his desk search and began to pace before the darkening windows. OPC was closed for the day and the chairman's receptionist was gone as was most of the daytime staff.

Through the bronze-tinted windows, the sun was a golden burnishing ball, fallen and captured by the desert horizon. This was Cedric Bowles favorite time of the day—nightfall.

"Our personnel are totally inadequate for this kind of work," Cedric spoke to the pacing figure. "Our man followed Pauliss and Clopec to the airport in El Paso, and into the terminal. Afterward he was not allowed beyond the passenger's security checkpoint. There were twelve flights leaving within a two-hour period, and I do have those destinations. However, I believe that their final destination was Miami."

"How can you be so sure?"

"Our man was following closely and was behind Clopec at the Hertz rental car desk."

"Damn it, Cedric. Do I have to draw blood to get the story? Explain!"

Lost and Found

As the sun slipped beneath the West Texas sand, Cedric Bowles sighed and removed his sunglasses. "Clopec made a car reservation for the Miami airport." The security director added, "This, of course, could have been a ploy, if Clopec recognized our man."

"Don't be ridiculous. You're over-thinking."

"Yessir," was the clipped Afrikaans response.

"Cedric, listen to me. Clopec, Pauliss, and that damned disk represent the future of this company. I want them followed and I want it done right. I want you to go out and find them. Follow them, do whatever it takes, and make daily reports back to me!" Haggly-Ford paused and lowered his voice. "I don't care about expense and I don't care about legalities."

"We could hire a private investigator——."

"I don't *bloody* well want a Private Dick. I want *you*! With your background in the South African transition period, as you and I both know, there could be no better choice. This could get dicey, messy, and complicated. If they really did find anything with that *sodding* piece of overpriced space junk, I damn-well better be the first to find out.

"Now get on the phone, get on a plane, and for God's sake find them before they disappear."

"Yessir," Cedric now rose from his chair and joined Haggly-Ford at the floor-to-ceiling windows.

Soft little lights were beginning to wink on in the distant desert. At least two overtime crews were working on pump-jacks in the Midland oil fields.

"Mister Chairman," Cedric spoke softly. "In Cape Town, during the transition period, I had total autonomy and therefore I was able to achieve results. A successful campaign to be sure, but certain compromises had to be made, certain situations and actions that must forever remain discreet. To achieve positive results here, I will require the same type of autonomy and complete discretion. My former employers understood such requirements. Do you?"

Haggly-Ford now turned to face his security chief. The chairman's office was quite dark with the OPC sodium glow and the distant lights from the oil fields the only illumination in the executive workplace.

"Oh, for Christ's sake, Cedric, whatever are you talking about? Just find them, follow them, and call me every day with an updated report. Five *sodding* minutes on the phone will do! After all, I'm not *bloody-well* asking you to go out and kill someone am I?"

"Nossir."

"Well then, let's carry on and get the hell out of here."

"Yessir."

78

Abruptly, Haggly-Ford turned, crossed the office and held open the big double door. After Cedric Bowles passed the receptionist's desk and disappeared into the corridor for the elevator, Alex Haggly-Ford shuddered and shook himself like a dog.

Chapter 17

Cedric Bowles drove the extra hour to the San Antonio airport and boarded a non-stop flight to Miami. The American Airlines flight was packed with tourists traveling in coach, and Cedric had been relieved to find the first class cabin pleasantly empty. No one was sitting next to the OPC security chief or in the two seats across the aisle way. This allowed several windows to be closed against the terrible glare of daytime air travel.

After takeoff, Cedric ordered a mineral water, popped a breath mint, and opened the latest copy of the *Odessa Daily Sentinel*. The West Texas newspaper carried the details of a local murder investigation on page 4.

Before her murder, Rebecca Raimes had been sexually assaulted. Forensic pathologists were now tracing certain evidence to track and bring to justice the fugitives responsible.

That was it, Cedric thought as he folded the newspaper and leaned back in his seat. The one decisive word out of the whole article was "fugitives," a plural term meaning more than one. The vaginal syringe had been over-filled with two different semen donors. The police were now looking for two men. There were other clues that had been left behind, but this type of information would not be found in a newspaper. The district attorney, as Cedric knew, always liked to gather everything necessary before making any arrests. This was the best approach to guarantee a conviction. Yes, everything was going perfectly, and with an anonymous phone call, Pauliss and Clopec could be fugitives in no time—incapacitated and out of the picture and just part of a contingency plan that was beginning to form.

The security chief closed his eyes behind his extra dark, daytime sunglasses and considered his options. He was well prepared. He carried three separate sets of identification—all with U.S. passports and one very good badge and ID from the United States FBI. The badge was from a federal agent from the Food and Drug Administration, and the FBI ID copied from the television series "The X-Files."

Most Americans watched television and every American believed what they saw on TV. The ID was complete with photograph, frank-crimped by a public notary tool, and was enclosed in a very expensive leather case. Just the flash of a federal badge would be enough for everyone, even minor law enforcement officials.

All of the credentials, with the exception of his Texas driver's license and OPC identification, were sewn into the bottom of his carry-on luggage—just in case. There were also the usual items tucked away in the checked baggage in the hold of the airliner—innocent items if inspected by a baggage handler or an airport police officer, but very effective tools in a surveillance operation. Cedric smiled again and then stopped himself as he focused on his plans for the Miami airport.

The direct American Airlines fight would arrive twenty-eight minutes before Delta's connection from Atlanta, allowing just enough time to hire a car from Enterprise and watch for Clopec and Pauliss at the Hertz desk. The security chief would follow, take the disk or not take the disk, or force one or both to reveal the location of the disk, or simply continue the surveillance and see what happened.

What was much more exciting than Haggly-Ford's disk was the thought that these Kaffir-loving Englanders just might find what they were looking for. After thinking about the two Englishmen looking for new sources of gold mining, the silver-haired chairman reclaimed Cedric's attention. Haggly-Ford was so predictable. Everything about the man was pompous, self-centered, and greed driven. Any behavior that Haggly-Ford might display was easily calculated—as was the other two Englanders.

The OPC security man that followed Pauliss and Clopec to the El Paso airport had immediately called with the rental car report about Miami. He had also relayed the fact that Pauliss was lined up at the Delta airlines counter, a counter that showed the next two flights departing for Atlanta and Miami. Two plus two equals four, *ergo* Clopec at the rental car desk and Pauliss at Delta, the two men were undoubtedly going to Miami. It was a simple deduction to establish airlines and flight times, and even the connecting flights from Atlanta.

Pauliss at the Delta counter was, of course, not reported to Haggly-Ford, and this omission of verifying information would allow slack time in any reports back to the chairman. It was all so easy, and this was going to be fun. Anything away from Odessa, Texas and the boring routine of OPC would be like a vacation.

Cedric smiled briefly and quickly covered his teeth. Someone might notice his only flaw. He cracked his eyes and checked seats in front of him. No worries there. Both of the flight attendants were obvious bitches and preoccupied with the other passengers forward in the cabin.

Good. No one would remember the man seated alone with the newspaper, and this was a mission that called for discretion. As always, for a successful operation: stay out of sight, don't be noticed, and use discretion, discretion, discretion. In this case, follow the two Englishmen until something happened, make daily reports, and listen to Haggly-Ford scream over the telephone. After this latest thought of the chairman red-faced on the telephone, the security chief almost giggled.

Cedric now took a mental grip, closed his eyes tighter and let his mind drift to the last days in Cape Town, to the last few days of Apartheid and his position with the South African Security Force. With an effort, Cedric kept his smile controlled as he remembered his field promotion to Major.

He had earned that rank by eliminating three separate cells of Mandela-loving Kaffirs. He had followed their moves by using simple logic, found them one by one in their filthy tenements, and dispatched entire families with a quick midnight attack and endless bursts of machine gunfire. No other officers had been so efficient, but afterward, when the Security Force was betrayed, Cedric made his way unnoticed into the veldt and over the border into Rhodesia. Identity papers were forged, and eventually through Austria the former Major of the South African Security Force found a home in West Texas.

In three years, there had been five others like Rebecca Raimes, but none in Odessa or Midland. None so close to home—discretion, discretion, discretion.

Cedric awoke as the American Airlines Flight 154 touched down in Miami. The local time, the captain announced, was 4:58 PM. The flight was early. Cedric could no longer control himself. As he unbuckled his seatbelt, he began to giggle.

Chapter 18

"Where are we going?" Peter asked. "Are you sure this is the right road?"

"Of course this is the right road," Brian answered. He was looking up from his South Florida map. "Just a little further and we should cross over a bridge and see the posted signs for Goodland. That's the fishing village. The village with the salvage company," Brian added.

Peter refocused on the sun-battered pavement crowded by a jungle. He was driving a new Chrysler LeBaron from Hertz, and the rental car's color was gold.

Upon speaking to the attractive Cuban girl at the Hertz desk in Miami, and after signing the papers to hire the car, both Peter and Brian had stopped in their tracks after turning away from the counter. The girl had spoken as an afterthought. "Your car is the gold convertible—bright gold—you can't miss it!"

After becoming confused in the Miami rush-hour traffic, Brian finally directed Peter out of the city and onto the old Tamiami Trail. Shortly after leaving the Miami suburbs, the late afternoon sun tilted over the Everglades and led the way past endless wetlands, palmetto filled hammocks, and rising sable palms.

As the gold rental car turned away from the inland thoroughfare and rushed closer to the gulf coast, the two-lane highway became lined with rising mangroves and narrow waterways. Peter spoke again over the droning road noise. "What do you know about this place, about this salvage company?"

Brian opened his leather carry-on and referred to their itinerary. "Only that Johnson's Charters are listed as a salvage operation and positioned perfectly to explore the Cape Romano Shoals. Our wreck site is only eight miles from the fishing village harbor."

Peter nodded thoughtfully as the convertible rounded a bend and began to climb a large causeway bridge. The setting sun was visible as the car topped the rise, but was hidden again upon descent by a canopy of orange clouds and endless green foliage.

"Here, just as I said," Brian pointed to a sign. "Goodland, turn to the left."

Peter followed the instructions and the car turned off the main highway onto a badly paved, twisting path. The narrow road was hardly more than a track with each shoulder crumbling into black water pools and the reaching fingers of mangrove roots. Falling into tropical darkness, the final colors of sunset faded as the open car cruised.

"I repeat, are you sure this is the right road?" Peter asked again as he switched on the headlights.

"It is desolate," Brian remarked after he folded the map. "But this is the Ten Thousand Islands. This is an area protected from any further development."

After a few more winding turns, the Chrysler emerged from the mangrove track and faced a fork in the road. Brian pointed to neat, but hand-painted signpost, "Johnson Yacht Charters, Fisheries and Salvage." Beneath the lettering was an arrow that indicated the left fork.

As Peter drove along the designated route, a ramshackle trailer park appeared on the right as a small restaurant and stacked crab traps passed on the left. A spangle of stars defeated the last light of the day as the gold convertible crunched into a loose gravel parking lot. Behind an expansive boardwalk, the rising masts of a sailboat fleet climbed into the tropical dusk.

Brian was out of the car and headed toward the Salvage and Fisheries sign before Peter could unfasten his seatbelt and turn off the engine. Peter followed after raising the cabriolet and locking the car. He met Brian waiting on the seawall.

Rising above the boardwalk and dock system was a stilt-house office supported by pilings. Beneath the roof shadows, a weather-beaten signboard offered, "Johnson Charters, Fisheries, and Salvage." The windows of the house were dark with no sign of life.

A balmy breeze was pouring into the little crescent-shaped harbor carrying the rich scent of salt, creosote, and backwater musk. The scooped out boating-basin was seemingly dug out of the mangroves with a winding channel disappearing into darkness on either side of the semicircle of docks. All-weather courtesy lamps were situated along the dock piles, with just enough light spilling along the green planking to carry from one lighting station to the next.

Abruptly, the sound of metal banging on metal was heard, followed by a stream of curses. "Goddamn it," was the last of the expletives voiced from the stern of a moored workboat.

A halo of light was rising from the troubled quarterdeck, and as Brian and Peter approached, they could see two figures sitting with their legs dangling into an engine compartment. Tools were scattered around a dismantled engine, and a pair of wire-caged trouble lights were glowing from the open bilge.

"Excuse me, please," Brian asked as he stood at the edge of the dock. "Could you please tell me where I might possibly find someone from Johnson Salvage?"

Peter moved up quietly, also looking down into the boat.

A young woman, dressed in grease-stained, worker's coveralls looked up, her blond hair in a ponytail and trailing from the back of an Atlanta Braves baseball cap. "I'm Billie Johnson," she said. "What can I do for you?"

Brian turned to Peter, but Peter was just staring—mesmerized.

Although Billie Johnson's hands were dirty and her face had a grime-streak, she was absolutely stunning. The green of her eyes captured the dim lighting and held Peter and Brian speechless.

"Well, boys, I don't have all night. Is there something that you want?" Billie was now standing in the boat, her hands on her hips as she looked up to the two figures waiting on the dock.

"We are interested in hiring a salvage boat for the Cape Romano Shoals," Brian answered finally.

"And some divers," Peter added.

"What for?" asked Billie.

"A shipwreck," Peter answered.

"Yes, a very old shipwreck filled with artifacts," Brian offered.

Billie nodded, still holding the two men with her gaze. "Cape Romano is a big shoal, and a large area to search. Tons of sand, and the sand is always moving. A salvage job like that could get expensive."

It was Brian's turn to nod. "Yes, but we have exact coordinates from a GPS—giving us a very small area to search."

Billie Johnson now turned to the older man sitting on the deck of the workboat, "Looks like we got a pair of treasure hunters, eh Dotson?" The older man who was dressed in greasy coveralls merely nodded. He then reached for a wrench and resumed his work on the engine.

Billie climbed out of the boat, stepped onto the dock, and regarded Peter and Brian thoughtfully. She was much taller than Brian and even a fraction taller than Peter.

"With a small area to search, a thousand a day shouldn't be too pricey. That would include Dotson and me, the salvage rig, and the vacuum line to shift away the sand.

"You provide the location and Dotson and me will work all day, every day, for as long as it takes—or until you run out of money."

Billie now smiled in the near darkness and added. "Don't think that you two are the first out here to look for treasure," she jerked a thumb toward the older mechanic in the boat.

"Dotson and me, we already had our share of treasure hunters, and we know just how much to charge. Everyone knows that these shoals are rich with shipwrecks, but so far, zilch. Nothing has been found."

"When can we start?" Peter asked patiently.

"Tomorrow morning, if you have the money," Billie replied

"Do you take American Express?" asked Brian.

Billie shook her head, "No. Just Visa or Master Card."

Peter reached for his wallet and withdrew his platinum Visa. He offered the card, and Billie took it. Quickly she scanned the expiration date and nodded. "All right, I trust you. You keep the card and at the end of every day, we tack on another thousand. Does that sound fair?"

As she passed back the plastic, Peter and Brian responded together. "Yes."

Billie smiled. "I'll give you one thing, you sure sound confident. By the way, where are you boys from?"

"Argentina," Brian offered.

"Africa," added Peter.

"Well, you sure sound English to me, but as long as the credit card holds, you can be from anywhere you want."

Brian looked perturbed. He was obviously becoming frustrated with the local woman's flippant behavior. After looking around the docks and seeing only two other workboats and the shadowed masts of the sailboat fleet, he asked. "You mentioned a salvage rig, may we please see the equipment—the boat that we will be using?"

"Fair enough," Billie replied as she pulled a rag from a pocket in her coveralls and began wiping her hands. "Follow me," she motioned with her head, "on the other side of the dock house."

With a glance to the older man in the boat, she added. "Come on Dotson, let's show 'em the rig." The older man grunted and climbed out of the boat. He followed Peter and Brian as Billie Johnson led the way.

Around the far side of the stilt house-office, a flat rusty barge was rigged to a very old, dented tugboat. Darkness covered the rig with slanting shadows, and the only inspection possible was from the muted lights on the dock pylons. The tugboat was a double-decker around fifty feet in length, and the barge was larger, at around sixty. The two vessels were strapped together with heavy wire cables, and the wood-slatted decks were littered with oil drums, pump engines, and coils of rope. A crane with a boom was rigged to a pair of vertical spars that ran through channels in the barge to anchor into the harbor. A tinge of diesel oil blended with the salt air as tidal water churned between the barge, the tugboat, and the dock.

"She might not look like much—a little more rust than paint, but everything works." Billie was looking at the rig but was also checking the reaction of her two latest customers.

"Is it safe?" Brian asked, but his question was interrupted by Billie's laughter. With the explosion of her laugh, so unexpected, and so warm, her cool indifference melted away.

"Of course she's safe, depending on how far we go." Billie grinned and now patted Brian on the back. "Don't worry, Argentina, I'll keep my eye on you. You'll be safe enough." Billie turned to Peter, "How about you, Africa? Are you worried about the state of our little rig?"

Peter shrugged and rubbed the stubble on his chin. "The safety and success of every vessel depends on the skill of her captain."

"You got that right. Now listen." Billie made a smoothing motion with her hands. "The weather forecast is good for tomorrow and if you guys are really serious, I want to cast off no later than seven—seven sharp.

"I'll give you a full day's work for a full day's pay, and I'll even get Dotson to grill and make sandwiches. But be here on time. If the weather holds and the wind stays down, we can be out on the shoal before the rich folks are finishing breakfast." Billie smiled again with her hands on her hips.

"Is there a hotel nearby? A place we can stay," Brian asked.

"Well, Argentina, there's a Marriott over on Marco Beach, and the Piña Colada Inn here in Goodland."

Brian actually rubbed his hands together. "A Marriott, that sounds great," he said, but frowned as Peter interrupted, "Anything closer?"

"If you promise not to track sand aboard, you can stay on the Ketch." Billie was now pointing to a large sailboat with two towering masts. A warm glow of lighting poured from classic portholes, and spilled onto teak decks. The wooden boat was easily the most handsome in the marina and obviously the most cherished. "Valkyrie" was inscribed in gothic, gold leaf across a wineglass transom.

"We wouldn't want to be a burden—" Peter was about to continue, but Billie cut him off.

"No burdens here, Africa, I'm being selfish. I don't want you to change your mind about a thousand-dollar charter. Besides, I charge fifty dollars a head to sleep on the *Valkyrie*, but that includes breakfast in the morning." Billie now paused as she watched for Brian's reaction.

"Don't worry, Argentina, she's fully air-conditioned, with a state rooms fore and aft, and guaranteed the most comfortable night's sleep you'll ever have. Shower's rigged with fresh water and there's beer in the fridge."

"Sounds like a deal," Peter offered, but Brian looked doubtful.

"Come on, Argentina, let me show you my boat." Billie started across the docks and Peter and Brian followed.

"I'm Doctor Brian Pauliss," Brian offered as they walked toward the sailboat.

"And, I'm Doctor Peter Clopec," added Peter.

Billie laughed again—the sound rich and full. "I like Africa and Argentina better."

Dotson remained in the shadows of the stilt house until Billie and the two Englishmen climbed aboard the ketch. He remarked to no one, "Well, I'll be damned."

Chapter 19

Cedric Bowles was checked into room 5 of the Piña Colada Inn. He was disgusted with the accommodation and very disappointed that the Englishmen had decided to stay on the boat. The Marriott would have been better—a large, comfortable hotel and easy to stay out of sight. In this tiny kaffir-hole, the window-mounted air-conditioner rattled loudly, hardly worked, and complicated badly the first report to Alex Haggly-Ford. The only consolation was that Haggly-Ford *did* have to scream over the telephone.

"Cedric, do you have the disk?"

"Nossir, not yet," Cedric replied softly.

"What? What did you say?"

Before answering, Cedric paused for a moment, waved the telephone toward the air-conditioner and giggled. He resumed with his clipped Afrikaans manner of speaking.

"There has been no opportunity to recover anything, or gain much information."

"Why not? Where are you? Where are Pauliss and Clopec?"

"At present, we are situated in a coastal village in South Florida. Clopec and Pauliss are sleeping on a sailboat and I am calling from a small room in a motel."

"Bloody hell! What are they doing there? I thought Miami would have led to South America. This is bad news. They are supposed to be looking for potential gold mining sites."

"Yessir."

"Cedric, no more pissing about, I want that disk, and I want it tomorrow. Angela Barnes has been calling twice a day and I must have something as a muzzle to keep her quiet."

"Yessir."

"And, Cedric, I don't care what it takes. Retrieve that CD or find out what's going on. I need information and I need it quick. Make something happen! I'm running out of time."

"I understand, Mister chairman."

"Oh, and, Cedric?"

"Yessir?"

"Don't do anything that can be linked to OPC."

"Nossir." Cedric now replaced the telephone, popped a breath mint, and began to examine his unpacked baggage laid out on the threadbare bedspread.

The first and foremost of the surveillance tools was special cell phone and GPS unit that was linked to a transmitter attached to the inside bumper of the gold rental car. The cell-phone frequency transponder would send out a homing beacon easily picked up as long as the car remained in an area with cell phone service. As long as the transponder battery carried a charge, the gold rental car could be tracked anywhere. This was possible by a Global Positioning System interfaced with the cell phone receiver. The transponder had been friction-taped inside the bumper when Pauliss and Clopec were speaking to the old man and the woman on the docks. This had been easy, and now the security chief knew he could relax. The rental car could be followed easily for at least a week.

After checking that the transponder was showing an immobile and steady signal, Cedric began his rub down. He was naked as he opened the plastic bottle of rubbing alcohol and began his evening ritual. A motel washcloth was used, and as Cedric considered his options, he chemically cleansed every portion of his body.

As soon as conditions would permit, Haggly-Ford's disk would be retrieved and $50,000 US dollars would be deposited in the Cape Town Bank of Good Hope.

But, how to get the disk? Maybe the disk wasn't that important. The disk was certainly encrypted and could not be deciphered immediately. Perhaps Haggly-Ford suggestion was the best approach. Find out what's going on by making something happen. Accelerate the situation.

The morning would certainly bring some answers and with answers came opportunities.

The answer would most probably be found—somewhere in the Englander's behavior. A key as to what would be found on the disk.

The security director now lifted a foot to the edge of bed and began threading the alcohol soaked cloth between his toes.

Cedric, of course, realized that to follow the rules of discretion, an empty substitute disk must replace the vital CD that was to be sent to Haggly-Ford. The Englanders might take a week before they discovered the CD had been stolen and replaced—or they could find out almost immediately.

Also, the security chief was troubled by the fact that he was unarmed. Only an amateur would try to smuggle a weapon on an airliner, but Cedric was relieved to note that on his bedspread arsenal there was a length of No. 3 drapery cord. He also knew that soon, this operation could quickly deteriorate and that the only answer for uncontrolled and accelerating events was firearms. Unfortunately, the ultimate weapon was not readily available in the United States. A real, wooden stocked, Russian manufactured, Kalashnikov AK-47, the most dependable, and wonderful, fully automatic weapon in the world.

Now shifting his stance to clean the other foot, Cedric thought of the most effective and available weapon in America. A 12-gauge pump shotgun with the stock and barrel sawed off. The shotgun, shells, and a hacksaw, could be purchased at any sporting goods store, and hopefully, there would be plenty of time for gathering the necessary equipment.

After a rapid knock on the motel room door, the alcohol cloth froze in place as Cedric was cleaning his testicles. The knock sounded again and Cedric ran to the bathroom and emerged with a towel around his waist.

He now took a quick inventory—on the bed was the complicated GPS and cell phone receiver along with his recently opened carry-on bag with the sliced open bottom. His straight razor was lying open next to the three sets of identification as well as the fake FBI ID and the federal food and drug badge. Also was the conspicuous coil of white drapery cord next to an open map of Florida and an open telephone book.

"Damn!" Cedric hissed as he grabbed the section of drapery cord and moved toward the door. Just after the security director unfastened the chain-latch, a key was turning in the outside lock and a feminine voice called out cheerfully. "Hello! I know that you're in there! I'm coming in— I'm the manager."

As the safety chain fell away, the door opened wide, and Cedric Bowles stood with a white motel towel clutched around his middle.

"There you are! I just wanted to drop by and make sure that you have *every little thing* that *you* might want." The voice was slurred and the woman's breath was thick with alcohol.

Instantly, Cedric recognized the over-sized bleached-blond from the shabby check-in-desk where he had paid for the room earlier. For her evening attire, the heavy-set woman wore a pink-flowered sarong and a black bikini top barely containing her overflowing breasts. She held a pitcher of cream-colored liquid in one hand and two short motel glasses in the other.

"It's just me, the Piña Colada welcome wagon." The woman wiggled a little dance, winked, and made a pouring motion with the pitcher and the two glasses. Her make-up was heavy, her red lipstick smeared, and she was drenched in perfume.

"I'm Molly, and you are…Cedric Bowles," she said. "I remembered your name from the registration." She now pointed dramatically at Cedric holding the towel, and with a lurch, the woman was across the room and plopped down on the bed. "Oh now nice! I just love these soft old mattresses. Don't you honey?"

Cedric was speechless. He was still clutching the towel and standing in the doorway, but he had turned with the woman's entrance and was now openly shocked and staring. He was also holding tightly, the length of No. 3 drapery cord.

Molly seemed indifferent to her staring motel patron and was now pouring two portions of Piña Colada mix into the short stubby glasses.

"Here ya go, honey. This will put hair on your chest," Molly the manager offered. "It looks like you could use some," she added with a snicker.

Inside, Cedric's mind was screaming as he visually scanned the room. The woman was on the end of the bed with the three sets of ID and the forged FBI credentials behind her. The ripped carry-on bag was open next to the straight razor—the fake bottom exposed, and the cell-phone-GPS receiver was resting by the pillows. Molly the manager was sitting on the unfolded map of Florida, and the local phone book was open to the yellow pages and the firearm section. A digital alarm clock on the nightstand was showing 11:05 PM and blinking.

"Come on honey, ain't you glad to have a little company—I am. After all, it's August and you and me are the only ones in this whole damn place—just us." With this admission, Molly offered Cedric one of the drinks, and stuck out her chest with a jiggling motion.

The drapery cord was hidden within the two hands that gripped the towel, but the knowledge of that cord was burning. At the same time, another part of the security director's brain was shouting, discretion …discretion…discretion…not now, later.

Discretion won this round and Cedric Bowles dropped the towel and the No. 3 drapery cord at the same time. He had an erection. Calmly he walked toward the motel manager and stood in front of her.

"Here, honey," she said as she sat down the drinks. "Let me help you with that."

Chapter 20

Billie surfaced at the diver's ladder beside the barge and looked up at Dotson in the wheelhouse of the tugboat. He nodded, but gestured upward to a blue sky dotted with puffy clouds. A small red and white airplane was circling high overhead.

"Hey, Argentina, give me a hand here!" Billie commanded as she unhooked her swim fins and threw the dripping flippers up onto the barge deck. She popped the snaps of her buoyancy compensator that held her scuba tank and octopus regulator.

"Ready," Brian said as he reached over and took the weight of the cumbersome scuba equipment. "Anything new?" he asked as Billie climbed out of the water.

"Looks like a big hole in the sand, but much bigger than yesterday and giant compared to the day before." Billie shook her head and her hair fell down her back in a tangle. She now looked back to the diving ladder as Peter surfaced through erupting bubbles.

"What do you think, Pete? How does it look to you?" Billie asked as she and Brian helped with Peter's fins and diving gear.

"Getting deeper," he gasped as he climbed on deck. "Like a huge bowl dug out of the sand—or a sea-floor swimming pool. I can't imagine having to go much further," he added excitedly.

Billie grinned at the boyish response and once again, Peter and Brian were both frozen in place by her staggering beauty. Standing tall on the deck with her feet slightly apart, she was dripping wet, and clad only in a deep-blue two-piece. She was the girl-next-door, with the ultimate swim-suit figure.

After an awkward and silent moment, Billie once again resumed her confident stance with her hands on her hips. "OK, you two," she ordered, "sort yourselves out and stow this dive gear!"

Shading her eyes and looking up to the wheelhouse, Billie shouted, "Dotson! Start her up!"

After the older man cracked a grin in response, he pulled the throttle cable on an 871 Detroit Diesel and engaged 800-horsepower into a deck mounted dredge pump. The bobbing rain-cap ripped wide-open and black smoke poured out of the diesel smokestack. At the same moment at thirty-two feet underwater, a steel standpipe began vacuuming seafloor sand off the Cape Romano shoals.

The water around the tugboat and barge was an emerald green until three hundred feet away a flexible hosepipe surged into a doughnut-shaped float lined with metal mesh. As the diesel roared and pumped a slush of sand and water through the pipe and into the mesh grating, the beautiful water churned with the muddy discharge a hundred yards away.

"We'll let her run an hour this time," Billie spoke over the engine noise, glancing at her dive-watch. "No more than an hour," she added. "We might be getting close." After her statement, she clapped a hand on Brian's bare shoulder, grabbed a towel, and started across the deck to climb up to the wheelhouse.

"Aaaah!" Brian exclaimed after Billie's touch, he was sunburned, but hoping to catch up with Peter's darker tan.

Billie spoke over her shoulder. "You had better get a shirt on, Argentina. This sun can be a killer."

Brian could only stare as Billie climbed the ladder to the top of the tugboat. He grabbed his shirt hanging on some oxyacetylene cutting gear and went to help Peter with the scuba tanks.

"I know that I must have said it a hundred times, but Christ what a looker!" Brian exclaimed as he approached Peter by the diving ladder.

"Yes indeed! What a beauty and what a character," Peter agreed as he watched Billie's lithe figure duck into the shade of the pilothouse.

"And, what an adventure!" commented Brian as the two men pulled the diving gear off the wooden deck and placed the Scuba equipment into a galvanized tub filled with fresh water.

"Best experience of my life—even if we find nothing," Peter grinned.

It was true, thought Brian. After casting off the lines in Goodland and motoring out to the shoals, neither Peter nor Brian expected an overnight stay on the rig. Nevertheless, that had been three days ago and tonight would be the fourth night.

The first morning had been uneventful with the exception of finding the exact satellite coordinates and anchoring the rig over the wreck site. The entertainment began as Billie stripped out of her cut-off khakis and her white work shirt, down to the first of her two-piece bathing suits. The first one Peter and Brian would never forget, was bright red. She had stood with her arms crossed over her breasts and looked down at the two men she had named Africa and Argentina.

"Who wants to help me with the diving? It's not safe to dive alone, and Dotson has to stay topside to keep an eye on the rig."

Peter and Brian instantly responded together. "I will!"

"OK, but first, let's make sure you guys can be divers," Billie had said. With her every-ready grin that both men found intoxicating, she rigged up two sets of scuba gear and sat Peter and Brian on a bench near the back of the barge.

There they had sat, with fins and mask in place and diving gear on their backs breathing compressed air out of regulators. Completely high and dry and sitting on the boat, Brian recalled that he was almost beginning to feel foolish as he looked over to Peter, until Billie went to the side of the barge and scooped up a pitcher of seawater. She walked over to Peter, tilted the top of his mask away from his forehead and filled it with salt water. She insisted that Peter keep his eyes open, watching her through the burning and briny liquid, as he continued to breathe normally out of the regulator in his mouth. As Brian watched, Peter had absolutely no problems and stared at Billie through the water and continued his steady breathing. When it was Brian's turn however, he could not breathe the Scuba air with the mask full of water. He had choked, gagged, and ripped off the facemask gasping.

Billie had once again crossed her arms over those lovely breasts. "No diving for you, Argentina. You're gonna be my number-one topside man!" She turned to Peter. "Pete! You and me, we're gonna be diving buddies," she commanded. "Just do everything I do, and stick close by my side."

At that moment, Peter's face broke into a grin as if he had just been awarded another doctorate. That was the first day, with Billie and Peter diving down to explore the sandy bottom.

Even from the deck, the perfectly clear emerald water revealed no shipwreck, just underwater sand-drifts rippled across the seafloor. Billie had explained with her usual perky demeanor, "Every wreck on the shoal gets covered by sand. Even the recent ones. But you never know. Better to dive and make sure, before we start ripping up the bottom."

Standing beside Dotson and watching the divers and their rising bubbles, Brian could not help but feel a touch of jealously. On the very first day, Peter had become Pete, but Brian, even on the fourth day was still Argentina.

The nights on the rig were even better than the days. At the end of the first day, just before an incredibly beautiful sunset, Billie had climbed down from the pilothouse and shouted for Dotson to shut down the big diesel pump. As the engine wound down and clattered into silence, Billie approached Peter and Brian smiling. She was holding six-pack of iced beer.

"It's Miller time!" she said brightly.

This was a moment of sheer distraction, Brian recalled. Billie had been wearing her red two-piece all day but now she was only wearing the bottoms. Her top was now the long-sleeved, white shirt rolled up at the elbows and cross-tied at the shirttails. The bottom of the shirt was closely tied, but there were no buttons, and a natural movement was obvious from underneath.

Peter and Brian pretended not to notice, but after Billie raised her arm to clink beer bottles, Peter had to clear his throat and speak to redirect Brian's attention. "When do we start back? After sunset?" he asked.

Billie took her eyes away from the towering clouds and the golden light spreading on the horizon. "I thought you boys wanted to find a shipwreck," she said. "We don't go back till we find something or we give up. That's the salvage business," she added.

"We stay out here? On the boat?" Brian's comment was totally unguarded, and he began to look around as if for a rescue.

"That's right, Argentina, right here in mother nature's arms," Billie grinned. "You're up for it, aren't you Pete?" she asked.

Peter nodded. "We couldn't have better weather—the water is so calm. Moreover, just look—"Peter gestured with his beer, as the sun appeared to melt on the horizon. The rig at that moment was bathed in an incredible unearthly light and the entire south Florida sky reflected orange, crimson, and purple in the mirror-like sea.

"Damn-straight, Pete, not too many light-shows like this one." Billie called to her partner up in the pilothouse, "Hey, Dotson, let's fire up that grill."

Dinner on the first night was tenderloin filets wrapped in bacon, the second night, grilled chicken and hot Italian sausage. The third night, grilled pork chops and roasted potatoes. For tonight, Billie had taken her spear gun and shot a black-tip shark that had been attracted by the dredging. As Dotson had cleaned the little four-footer, Billie announced, "Shark steaks for dinner!"

Abruptly, Brian's recollections of the last few days were interrupted as

Billie began shouting for Dotson to throttle back the diesel dredge. "Whoa—shut her down," she insisted. "Did you hear that?"

As the big impeller ground to a halt and the Detroit Diesel idled, Billie demanded all attention as she jerked a thumb toward the distant float, the discharge pipe, and the metal strainer.

"I'll-be-damned, Dotson," she shouted. "But I heard something running through that pipe, something besides sand and water!"

Peter and Brian were instantly galvanized by Billie's excitement, and stared breathlessly upward to the salty old man in the pilothouse. "Yep, I heard her, too," Dotson replied. "Sounded like wood...metal, or maybe both."

"Goddamn it, boys, let's go look! Argentina, crank up that outboard." Billie's cry of enthusiasm was beyond contagious as she nodded toward the zodiac inflatable that was floating and tied to the barge.

This was Brian's topside job—driving the little inflatable boat back and forth to the spoil area and checking for anything other than sand and water coming out of the dredge pipe. Brian was in the boat and had pulled the outboard to life before Billie and Peter could scramble onboard.

"All right, Argentina, give her some gas," Billie said as she cast off the only line.

Without comment, Brian gunned the throttle and the Zodiac flew along the sunken hosepipe until the flexible tube rose off the sandy bottom and emptied into the floating strainer.

After tying the zodiac to the strainer float, everyone climbed up on the doughnut shaped surface and looked as the pipe-end dripped water into the strainer. The metal mesh of little one-inch squares, ten feet in diameter, was completely clean with no foreign objects.

"Nothing!" Peter muttered.

"Now hold on, Pete, what I heard is probably still in the pipe," Billie explained. "Hey, Dotson!" she yelled as she waved her arms. "Run her up a little bit—just enough to get some flow. Nice and slow."

With sluggish rumble and a noticeable vibration in the dredge pipe, water and dark sand began to sputter from the end of the pipe.

"It's much darker than before," Brian said quickly, "much darker."

Billie said nothing, but her eyes were wide as she nodded.

Suddenly, the pipe began to convulse—almost jumping away from the tethers that held it to the float. A gush of dark water exploded and bits of black wood began popping from the end of the pipe and accumulating in the strainer. These foreign particles were the only non-sand objects that any of them had ever seen in the metal mesh. Gleaming wet in the sunshine, the shattered fragments were obviously wooden with worn grain-lines apparent on every scrap and splinter. A stench of sulfurous rot also began to belch out of the pipe between gushes of dark water and more of the thick wooden bits.

"Damn!" Billie whispered

Peter and Brian instantly said, "Yes!"

Before further comment was possible, the pipe convulsed once more and a length of badly eroded chain fell into the strainer. The pattern and links of the old forged metal was instantly recognized, but even as the chain appeared, it was covered with more fragments of the sodden black wood. The strainer was rapidly becoming covered with the broken wooden splinters, more sections of broken chain, and occasionally a broken piece of shell or pottery. After a brief tacit in falling particles, and another gush of sulfur-tainted black water, a tiny tarnished spoon fell from the pipe-end along with a small glass bottle half filled with an amber liquid.

At the same instant, Billie, Brian, and Peter all raised an arm skyward and yelled toward the rig. "Stop!"

Almost at once, the pipe stopped all vibration as Brian whispered, "Holy mother of God! We really found it! We found Diego's lost Galleon!"

After his statement, Doctor Pauliss was suddenly off the edge of the strainer-float and climbing carefully over the sodden wood bits toward the little glass bottle and the badly tarnished spoon. Pausing only once to stop and lift one of the broken lengths of chain, Brian smiled at Billie and Peter as he tested corroded metal for strength. He frowned briefly as he looked at his hands that were now stained black with the wrought iron residue. Quickly after wiping palms on his bathing trunks, Brian slowly moved forward and picked up the tiny spoon and the worn glass container.

"Medicine and a dosing spoon," he explained with a quiet reverence.

Billie leaned forward and retrieved a shard of the recovered wood. "Boys, I have to tell you the truth, I never thought this would happen," she said. "It's just like something out of the movies. I can't believe it." Billie focused on Brian as he climbed back to the edge of the float. "Do you know what that spoon and bottle are worth? Thousands to collectors. I've read about this kind of salvage," she insisted.

"Now, of course, there can be no doubt," Peter said. "The satellite imagery is verified. Brian, do you concur that the spoon and the flask are from the correct period?" Peter asked, as he took the relics from the Galleon and examined the ground-glass stopper of the medicine bottle. He shook the amber liquid and held the little bottle up to the sunlight to see the yellowish fluid more clearly.

Brian nodded. "It certainly appears to be eighteenth century. The spoon, I feel certain, must be pure silver. However," he added, "neither of us has any expertise with archeology."

"What do you mean?" asked Billie looking up. Peter had handed her the little spoon and she was turning the medicine ladle over in her hands.

"I thought you guys were Doctors. You know—scientists," she added.

"Scientists, yes, archeologists no," Brian explained.

"Then how did you know about this place? How did you know exactly where to look?" Billie asked, as she passed the spoon to Brian and took the medicine bottle from Peter. She followed Peter's example, shook the amber fluid, and held the bottle aloft into the sunlight.

"Billie, it's a long and complicated story," Brian confessed. "A whirlwind of events with some very exciting, and very sad episodes," Brian nodded to his partner before he continued.

"But I think Peter will agree...you've earned the right to hear it all. Without your thoughtful patience and expertise, Diego's wreck may have never been discovered."

Billie shook her head. "No, that's not fair. Any salvage rig could have done the job." She added quickly, "I didn't mean to pry. After all, it's none of my business. With all the excitement I just got curious," Billie shrugged. "Besides, me and Dotson...we're just the hired help." After speaking, Billie handed the little bottle to Peter and looked dejectedly back to the rig.

Brian now moved over to where Billie was sitting on the float. He lifted his arm and placed a hand on her shoulder. "Billie," he said. "We knew where to look, but not how to explore, or how long to search. With any other crew, we would have given up and gone back the first day. After all, four days in these primitive conditions is a new slant to our lifestyle. Without your perseverance, and your charming manner this..." Brian held up the little spoon, "this would have never been found."

"Billie, Brian's right," Peter nodded and looked into her eyes. "You made all this possible, and you also bring a great deal of joy into the process. Everything here, all of this, has been the greatest and most wonderful experience—all because of Billie Johnson—right, Argentina?" Peter now grinned and winked at Brian as he used Billie's term of endearment.

Billie shrugged, looked up and nodded. "Fair enough," she said with the beginnings of a new smile, "But I have to tell you, it's been fun for me, too," she added, "real fun."

"All right, good," Brian said. "Now that we know we're all on the same page. What do we do next?" he asked, "Start up the dredge?"

Billie shook her head playfully, "Hell no, Argentina. Pete and me are going for a scuba dive. We have to go see what it looks like down there."

Chapter 21

After the third day, Cedric realized he hated Florida even more than Texas. The sun was hotter and brighter, and the humidity almost unbearable. The entire fishing village smelled as if it were rotting. Cedric also realized that he was becoming dangerously bored and frustrated. The two Englanders had vanished, although their rental car had remained stationary for almost three days.

A thunderstorm had broken the tedium of late afternoon, bringing a mass of cloud cover to block the ever-persistent sunshine. The windy weather had cooled the stinking village and allowed the security director to venture out and walk down the docks to where the gold rental car still waited. Perhaps, Cedric considered, if he could speak to the old man or the young blond woman, he might find a clue as to the whereabouts of the two English fannies.

The rain was still coming down in a welcome drizzle as the security chief walked along the waterfront under a green and white umbrella that advertised "Enterprise-Rental-Cars."

After finding no activity around the docks, the "Johnson Charters, Fisheries, and Salvage" sign appeared to be the only source of potential information. Cedric popped a breath mint and began to climb the well-worn stairs of the old silt house.

After a repeated knock on the door brought no response, the security director turned away and started down the steps. He was stopped halfway by a squeak of hinges and voice thick with the aftermath of slumber.

"What da ya want? Are you from the bank?" the belligerent voice belonged to a sleep-tousled man with sandy hair and a thick mustache. The shaggy figure was badly in need of a shave and his eyes were red-rimmed and glassy. Before Cedric could respond, the man narrowed his eyes and opened the door to stand on the balcony.

"What-in-the-hell are you looking at? Ain't you ever seen a working man before?"

Cedric smiled without showing his teeth, tilted back his umbrella, and adjusted his sunglasses. Without missing a beat and using his best American accent the security chief flattened his voice-tone and climbed back up the stairs, opening the fine leather case with the big gold badge, smoothly announcing, "I'm Special Agent James Marshall. I'm with the FBI."

With a plethora of emotions showing on the disheveled man's face, Cedric now held the federal badge and the ID at arm's length in front of the red-rimmed eyes.

"Are you Mister Johnson?" Cedric guessed.

"Well, ya... But you know that—right?"

The security director now nodded seriously. "Yes, Mister Johnson, I need your help in locating two men. Two fugitives," Cedric added.

With a more than obvious relief, Buddy Johnson nodded positively, but remained speechless.

Cedric now had to look down—to keep from smiling. "The two men were driving the gold rental car that is now parked in your driveway. The car has been abandoned for the last four days. Would you have any information regarding the whereabouts of these two individuals? They are foreigners, with English accents." Cedric added flatly. "One of the men is short and heavy-set, with glasses and long blond hair, the other is taller with a thinner frame. He also wears glasses, but has darker features with salt and pepper hair."

Buddy's forehead knotted as his eyes squinted. He was looking out to the far end of the gravel parking lot where the gold Chrysler was apparently abandoned. "Well..." he said, scratching his chin, "I don't know? I mean... I ain't seen them. What you want em' for? Drugs?"

"There are several charges. However, I am not at liberty to disclose that information at this time. There is a reward offered for information leading to their capture. They are also wanted by Interpol," the security chief embellished.

"Now, hang-on-there—what did you say your name was? Hell, come on in," Buddy Johnson now apparently realized that it was drizzling rain and that he was getting wet. He started inside the door and motioned for the FBI man to follow.

Cedric closed the umbrella at the threshold and stepped inside. There was a neat desk with a silent computer and bookshelves lined with paper-back volumes. Beyond a partition, an apartment waited—well kept and, thankfully, almost dark with pulled bamboo blinds.

Buddy now scratched his head and walked over to the desk. He picked up a single sheet of paper and scanned a note. Abruptly he wadded up the paper and threw the message into an empty trash bin.

"Well…" he stalled. "How much of a reward are we talking about?"

"There are also penalties for withholding information," Cedric now leveled his dark glasses at the shabby figure standing by the desk.

"Now, wait-a-minute. I don't know nothing about the car, or the men that you're looking for. I just got back from a little trip over to Ft. Lauderdale. Me and a couple a boys from the crab house went over on a little picnic." Buddy snickered, adding, "Got myself one hell of a hangover. You woke me up and I ain't thinking right. Not just yet, at least."

"What was on the note, Mister Johnson?"

Buddy's eyes instantly went to the trash bin and Cedric knew at once that everything he needed was on that piece of paper. Buddy Johnson looked up, saw the thin man watching intently, and knew that he was caught.

"Aw…you can't blame a feller for trying to work the system. It's just that I need the money—the reward. You know how it is," Buddy reached into the trash basket and unfurled the note. He grinned with his lopsided smile and handed the paper to Cedric Bowles.

The message read:

> Gone out to the shoals with a good charter.
> Two English guys looking for an old shipwreck.
> Pie in the sky treasure hunters and I won't be back
> until they're out of money.
> That's their gold car in the lot, and <u>don't</u> bother it.
> You had better get those crab traps ready, October will
> be here before you know it.
>
> Billie

"Looks like that little note from my wife is going to get me a reward," said Buddy.

"That depends on what happens next," the security director replied.

"I ain't never talked to an FBI man before—just the deputies out from the sheriff's office." Buddy paused and scratched the stubble on his chin.

"You know, I wasn't never convicted with them arson charges—only the bad checks. I did my time, and now I only got six more months of probation. Hell, I don't even drink and drive!"

Cedric nodded approvingly. "That's good to know," he said.

Chapter 22

Huddled around the fixed dining table in the tugboat salon, Billie, Peter, and Dotson watched as Brian tapped on his recently completed chart of a Spanish-Warship Galleon.

A noisy air conditioner was grinding away, but dipped suddenly with the lighting in the cabin as the rumble of the below decks generator faltered and regained momentum. When the air-conditioner ground on and the lighting resumed normal brightness, Brian turned away from the windows and the darkness beyond the rig and returned to his hand-drawn diagram.

"Our first two attempts have pierced the galleon somewhere. However, I believe that we have encountered the back of the ship. Where the—" Brian cleared his throat, "—heaviest cargo might be found. I believe that vessels of this type were about one-hundred feet in length and even three or four decks in the stern. This is all so difficult," he added.

"Heaviest cargo," Billie laughed, and made a show of clearing her throat to match Brian's attempt at subterfuge. "Why don't you just say treasure, Argentina? You know—as in treasure chests, gold doubloons and pieces of eight," she added.

Brian was clearly flustered with the latest events, and appeared impervious to Billie's goading tease. He refocused on the chart and ran his finger down the deck tiers of his penciled Spanish ship. "I cannot believe that our medicine bottle and dosing spoon would be found in the forward part of the galleon and with the discovery of the broken chalice there can be little doubt as to our finding the aft part of the ship."

104

Peter nodded his agreement. "When loading a ship of this size, with particular heavy objects, most of the weight would indeed be placed in the stern and in the lowest hold, or even in the ballast. The crew was kept in the forward berths and certainly no crewmember would have access to a silver chalice. The silver goblet proves the second drilling site is correct. We must be into the stern of the ship." Peter now gestured to the tarnished and broken wine cup resting on the table.

Billie shook her head, "But how many years and how many storms have passed over this shoal? Nobody knows for sure, and our wreck could have been broken and scattered everywhere." Billie looked over to Dotson.

"She's right," he said. "A hurricane sank this old boat, and a few more have probably torn out her belly long before she ground into the sand. And remember, anything heavy would always work down to the bottom. We might need a bigger dredge, and much more time—and time right now, is something we ain't got." Dotson didn't speak often, but when he did, his voice was filled with conviction and experience.

Billie tilted her head toward her age-old companion and shrugged her shoulders with resolve. She cracked a grin, walked over to a sliding cabinet and produced a bottle of rum.

"Pete! Argentina! Let me buy you a drink. I wish we had more time, but what we already found should cover the cost of salvage. Hell, this stuff is valuable," Billie offered as she indicated the silver chalice, the dosing spoon, and the medicine vial. "We'll pull the anchors and head back in the morning, but tonight we'll have a little celebration and chase the blues away."

After finding the initial wood bits, chain, spoon and medicine bottle, Billie and Peter's diving investigation revealed nothing but the dredge pipe driven into the center of a deep sand crater. No amount of hand excavation, or water jetted around the standpipe offered any clues or additional artifacts. Discovering only frustration, the dredge pipe had been lifted and moved to a far side of the underwater basin.

Slow pumping had continued until a silver wine cup had been found in the spoil strainer. This discovery had once again boosted excitement and morale, but at the same time offered more frustration. It was obvious that the silver chalice had been whole until traveling through the dredge pipe. Fresh silver showed at a break in the cup and left little doubt as to the primitive method of excavation. The fifth day had passed without more discoveries other than additional wood bits and more of the black and sulfurous water.

Dotson became even less talkative and more intent on listening to the marine weather information. Hurricane Debra was coming, and she was moving fast. Debra was a category three hurricane with winds over 130 miles-per-hour and traveling westward through the Old Bahamas channel. The National Oceanic forecast had issued a hurricane watch for all of South Florida, and the watch was to take effect in the next forty-eight hours.

Billie made the announcement as the dredge pump idled down at sunset. "Boys, we gave it one hell of a try, but now it's time to go home. The wind will start by late tomorrow, and Dotson and me have to get back and tie up the marina. Besides, if we stay out here too long, we could end up like the Spaniards below us."

Brian had looked to Peter, then back to Billie. "But we can come back—after the storm."

Billie nodded, "Sure we can, if you boys found her once, you can find her again—right?"

"What do you mean? Find her again. I have the exact coordinates," Brian insisted.

"Argentina, this old shoal shifts like a desert in a sand storm, and that's just yearly movement, not including a major hurricane. Hell, this could be the biggest blow for South Florida in fifty years. After Debra, I might not even recognize Coon Key or the entrance into Goodland."

Into the evening, Billie's words echoed repeatedly as Brian tried to battle the upcoming storm with logic, educated reason, and scientific approach. Nevertheless, the euphoria and excitement of the initial discoveries was fading and disappointment was turning into depression. As focused and academic as Brian became, Peter knew that the troubles in Texas, and the ultimatum from Haggly-Ford was looming closer as the 30-day timetable and the good weather diminished.

During the third round of dark rum over ice, Brian was clearly worried and chain smoking and Peter had fallen into a moody silence. When Dotson went below to shut down the failing generator, Billie lit kerosene lanterns. The hint of a breeze sighed into the cabin as Dotson returned and Billie ordered the salon doors opened as the air conditioner was no longer working.

"Argentina, I get the feeling you and Pete are in some kind of trouble. And bad trouble by the look of it." Billie poured another rum for Brian and looked to Peter for some kind of response.

Peter shook his head sadly. "Earlier, Brian promised to tell you our story. A story filled with many episodes. Some tragic, some pathetic, and one incredible stumbled-onto discovery. Perhaps the greatest breakthrough in marine archeology ever."

Billie topped off her own glass and added to Peter's. Dotson covered his drink with his hand and shook his head no, but like Billie, he had also pulled his chair closer to the table—ready to listen.

The rig was now very quiet with the water over the shoal still and calm. The air moving through the cabin was heavy with humidity, salt tinged, and slow.

Peter glanced at Brian before he began. "Our predicament is linked to a thirty day calendar, and a fixed agenda outlined by the chairman of a greed driven company." Rattling his drink, Peter continued. "After tomorrow, we only have eighteen days left."

Brian looked up after lighting a fresh cigarette. "Yes, eighteen days to produce much more than this." Brian's glowing cigarette circled around the Spanish artifacts resting on the table.

Billie appeared flustered. She leaned back in her chair and crossed her arms. "So what's going to happen if you don't find more than our little antique collection? You get fired?" she asked.

"We have already been fired. Now we face criminal charges for tampering with a corporate satellite and ruining a company," Brian confessed. "That's how we found this old Spanish wreck. We altered the program of a geological survey satellite—a ground penetrating radar housed in an orbiting spacecraft. A very expensive piece of aerospace hardware that is now out of control and destined to crash."

Brian's eyes now shifted to Peter, and Peter nodded his consent.

"We found ninety-seven hard returns before the satellite went offline," Brian explained. "Our Galleon is only one of ninety-seven salvage sites that registered a strong signature for gold."

"And, a young woman has been murdered—" Peter broke in, "a beautiful young woman who worked at our former company and a person that I was connected with socially."

"That we were both...connected with *socially*," Brian added softly, and then downed his rum to the ice cubes. "May I please have another," he asked, but Billie could only stare open-mouthed across the table.

"Murder," she mouthed.

Peter made a little encompassing gesture. "As you can see, we are in quite the—."

"Shhhh—quiet!" Billie insisted, raising her hand for silence and cocking her head to listen. They all heard it—the sound of a motorboat approaching fast. As the whine of twin outboards grew louder, everyone rose from the salon and gathered outside the wheelhouse.

An open fishing boat was moving fast over the water and making a beeline for the salvage rig. A crescent moon was high overhead adding a cloudy glow of moonlight to the phosphorescent wake produced by the oncoming vessel. The speeding boat showed no running lights, but a single shadowed figure was visible beneath the shade cover of a center-console.

Peter's gaze refocused when he observed Billie's posture stiffen and her hands tighten around the tugboat railing. Just before the intruder thundered alongside and the racing outboards dropped to an idle, a bright spotlight exploded from the center-console and raked along the tugboat wheelhouse. With Peter and Brian shielding their eyes against the sudden glare, it was obvious that Billie and Dotson were riveted by a hidden tension.

"Well, I guess I caught you this time!" a slurred voice called out. "I know all about your two new boyfriends—I know that you have been screwing them. I know all about it!"

The shadow figure in the boat stumbled and the spotlight wavered until it recaptured Billie and Dotson with Peter and Brian standing on either side.

"Just look at you—you don't even try to hide it. Out here and screwing two guys at once! At least now you're interrupted—forced to put your pants on. Don't you know there's a hurricane coming or were you too busy to notice? Billie, you goddamned slut."

"Now see here—!" Brian began loudly, but Dotson grabbed his arm and whispered, "No!"

"Hey! You fat little faggot—you want a piece of me? How about both of you? You limey bastards!" As the drunken voice dribbled off abruptly, the spotlight winked out, the outboards revved-up, and the open boat lurched into the barge with a crash. After a stagger from the fishing boat to the barge deck, a swaying Buddy Johnson stepped forward with obvious intent. He swayed briefly and tied a mooring line to a cleat on the barge.

"Do I have to come up there? It will be worse if I have to come up there!" he added as he visually searched the upper deck of the tugboat. "Billie—you whore! Do I have to come and get you, too?"

With the latest threat, Peter turned and noticed Billie was gone. Only the silent Dotson remained between Brian and himself.

"Goddamn it, Buddy. Get the hell off this rig, or so help me, I'll light you up."

Peter leaned forward on the upper deck railing, as did Brian and Dotson. Billie was now visible below decks and standing on the wooden deck of the barge. She was also holding with outstretched arms, what appeared to be a short, but oversized pistol.

"She's got a flare gun," Dotson offered quietly.

"Oh my God," Brian muttered.

"Billie—please be careful and don't do anything to regret later." Peter's voice was steady and loud enough to be heard by all. He sounded very calm and matter-of-fact.

"That's right, Billie. You better listen to your new boyfriend," Buddy sneered to Billie, redirecting his voice to the upper deck. "Billie, Billie, Billie—did she ever tell you her real name? She married me to get Johnson and her high school cheerleaders made up Billie. Her real name is Irmgard—Irmgard Finkelmeyer. I bet she didn't tell you that, I'll bet she didn't tell you that she's a goddamned kraut. Just like her daddy and her Nazi grandpa. Look at her now with that star-shell pistol—just like a Nazi, but she's a Nazi that's a *slut*!" Buddy seemed fortified with his latest statement and took a menacing step forward.

Everyone heard the click as Billie cocked the flare gun. "I've got three witnesses that heard you threaten me and my charter. Now get off this rig, and get off now! Get off, or get burnt real bad. Buddy, I mean it."

Buddy nodded, but then offered a sly grin. "I'll go," he said. "But next time you won't hear me coming." After Buddy turned and groped across the open deck, he paused beside the fishing boat. "I got rights, too," he said. "And I can do things without witnesses—and you know that—don't you, Irmgard?" After Buddy fumbled away the mooring line and climbed into his boat, Billie visibly shuddered.

"Hey, you limey bastards!" Buddy yelled. "There's a cop looking for you! He knows you're out here!" After his latest slur, Buddy slammed the throttle stops home and the battered fishing boat tore out over the water.

Chapter 23

Cedric was tired of waiting. He desperately needed something to happen—something exciting. After phoning a taxi company from Marco Beach and sending a bottle of Jack Daniels to the door of Johnson Charter's, Fisheries, and Salvage, the OPC security director waited in his car until the shaggy figure of the cowboy fisherman staggered down the old wooden stairs. The timing had been perfect. The afterglow of sunset was just beginning to fade.

Cedric had approached and planted a seed. "Mister Johnson, I believe you should know that the two Englishmen spent the night with your wife before leaving on the off-shore charter. As a federal officer, I have no jurisdiction in Florida state waters, but as we both have interests in locating the fugitives, I felt that you should know about the two foreigners and the affair with your wife. Mister Johnson," Cedric continued smoothly. "I need those men to come back—I need to follow them further. The FBI knows how to pay a reward and knows how to wipe away probation."

After the noisy fishing boat raced away from the dock, Cedric waited until full nightfall and then found the electrical breaker box located beneath the house. He also found a few useful tools littered on the workbench. With the electricity turned off, the docks were completely dark with no sign of movement. The security director returned to the trunk of his Enterprise rental and removed two five-gallon gas cans. The cans were full of high-octane fuel, and there were six filled cans.

Cedric giggled as he splashed gasoline around the oil and fuel drums stored under the house. The big containers were labeled, "Flammable—No

110

Smoking." With the smell of the fuel almost overpowering, Cedric moved along the docks and added a splash here and there along the cracked and dried planking until he reached the first of the workboats.

He carefully climbed aboard, and with the aid of a penlight, found the fuel tank opening. After three raps with a hammer and a wood chisel, the fiberglass-covered wood parted and filled the air with the rich scent of diesel fuel. A few more splashes of high-octane were mixed with the fuel oil and Cedric moved on to the next boat.

With each boat, the preparations became easier and the gasoline cans lighter. On the final and largest of the rough-looking crab boats, a raised engine hatch and the searching penlight found a glass-bowl fuel filter. A quick tap of the hammer smashed the glass container and this event produced a seemingly endless flow of the pungent diesel fuel. For a moment, Cedric froze as he heard the click of a switch and the soft whir of an electric motor. After scanning the docks and the distant lights of the trailer park, the sound of water flowing overboard reclaimed all attention. Two fingers placed into a stream just below the gunnels confirmed the old crabbing vessel was not pumping water, but the overflow of diesel fuel flooding into the bilge. Cedric smiled when he thought of war movies he had seen with fuel oil burning on the water. After a pause to judge the potency and the magnitude of the total fuel seepage, the security director moved on to the large wooden sailboat.

Standing beneath the canvas awnings and above the fuel-soaked wooden decking, Cedric dropped his last empty gas can overboard into the oily water. Even though the security director had run out of gas, the old sailboat should go up like a funeral pyre. After another glance confirmed no apparent movement among the lights of the trailer park, Cedric climbed down to the docks and began the final part of his plan.

All along the docks, accent lighting was fixed alongside electrical receptacles for visiting boats. As the electricity was now turned off, the security director moved between the shadows from dock pile to dock pile. As he passed each darkened lamp, the workbench hammer made a quick but effective tap-tap and reduced the outer, weatherproof lens and the inner light bulb to glass splinters. Earlier, each lamppost had been given an ample dosing of the high-octane gasoline.

Upon returning the hammer and wood chisel to the workbench beneath the house, Cedric opened the gas tank of a rugged old pick-up truck and forced the receptacle-end of an extension cord deep into the fuel source. He found a roll of friction tape and once again approached the electrical breaker-box. With a quick pause to look over his shoulder, he now taped his glowing penlight just above the largest switch on the panel—the electrical lever labeled, "Main"

Returning to his rental car, Cedric smiled when he saw the dull glow of the penlight shining beneath the house. He checked his watch. The drunken Buddy Johnson had been gone one hour and fifty-five minutes. The timing was probably good, but the security director had no idea how long the conflict on the salvage vessel would last. The distance offshore had been calculated after flying over in the chartered airplane, but there were too many variables to rely on the unpredictability of a drunken fisherman.

Cedric now unfolded his cell phone and punched in the number for the Piña Colada Inn.

"Hello—Piña Colada Inn. Molly speaking," the familiar voice slurred.

"Molly, this is your tenant from room five—your *new* friend Cedric."

"Oh! There you are—I went to your room. I was looking for you. I was wondering if you were feeling lonely."

"Well yes, but I have been detained and I need your help."

"What kind of help? Where are you?"

"Right now, I'm driving back from Miami, but unfortunately I'm behind schedule. That's why I'm calling. I made a promise to Buddy Johnson—I promised to turn on his lights." Cedric cupped his hand over the phone and giggled. He cleared his throat and continued smoothly. "Apparently there have been some problems with his electric system and I promised to switch on his electrical panel just after nightfall."

"Buddy Johnson? How do you know him?" Suddenly, Molly sounded sober. "That's one bad son-of-a-bitch," she said. "Listen, honey, stay away from that one—he's dangerous. He's as mean as a snake."

"Well, yes. Now you understand my predicament. I am very late and I know that he is out on the water. I have some business dealings with him and his wife, and I wouldn't want him to return to a dark house or a darkened marina. He made a point of telling me his concern over criminals in the trailer park."

Cedric pulled the phone away from his ear as Molly laughed rudely. "That's a new one," she said. "No one in their right mind would ever cross Buddy Johnson. He's just too damn mean."

"I'm glad you see my concern. He promised to leave a small torch—I mean a flashlight taped to the electrical panel. Apparently, only one lever needs to be switched on. The main lever,"

"Well I don't know…" she began.

Cedric bit his lip as the woman's voice hesitated.

"You want me to go there now?" she asked uncertainly.

"Yes please. Just the one favor. I have a big surprise waiting if you do as I ask. A big surprise."

Chapter 24

Buddy knew that something was wrong as soon as he rounded the final turn in the channel. It was too damned dark. He pulled the throttles back on both engines and waited for the boat to drop off plane. As the bow settled and water rushed nosily around the stern, he roughly considered that Billie might not have paid the electric bill. This thought was reinforced as he saw the lights from the trailer park glowing behind the marina. With a fresh rage swelling as he idled toward the docks, Buddy began to contemplate the correct amount of revenge he would take out on his wife.

This time she had gone too far. She had threatened him with a god-damned flare gun and now she had forgotten to pay the power company. Buddy's anger grew as he motored closer. Something had to be done.

Billie didn't understand him anymore. It was not like it used to be—not like when he was the high school quarterback and she was the cheer-leader. That had been fun, but that was many years ago. Now the only fun for Buddy was drinking with the crab-house boys and chasing the strippers in Fort Myers and Lauderdale. The Lauderdale girls were the best—much better than the west coast, but they were bitches and more expensive. At least the Fort Myers girls would go out after hours—

As the boat moved along the seawall, Buddy sniffed the air. It smelled like oil—like gas and oil mixed. A strong smell like something was leak-ing. After pounding the steering wheel and punching the center console, Buddy cursed under his breath and fumbled for the hand-held searchlight. Something was leaking for sure, and by the smell of it, something bad.

Lost and Found

"Jesus Christ," Buddy muttered after he thumbed on the searchlight. The water was covered with the unmistakable rainbow shine of fuel oil on the water—and it was everywhere. All around the dock piles—all around the boats. There were even oil marks on the waterline boot-stripes. This was one hell of a fuel spill and the bastards from the EPA would have a field day with this one. The older the marina, the more often they showed up, and they were just here last week. Now they would be back with a god-awful fine.

Wait a minute! Buddy's mind screamed as he switched off the spotlight. This must be on purpose. This was someone trying to get even, someone who was pissed.

Buddy nudged up the throttles and steered for the center console's slip at the docks. Maybe it was one of the crab-house boys, pissed-off about the money he owed them. No, they wouldn't have enough balls to do this. Maybe it was Burt Loomis and his crabbers from Everglades City, still upset about those cut-away and missing traps.

After he shouldered between the pilings and shut down the engines, he heard it—someone walking on the docks.

"Hey! Who the hell is that? What the *hell* have you done to my marina?" Buddy yelled and at the same instant pointed his searchlight over toward the workbenches under the stilt- house.

Before she could speak, Molly the motel manager covered her eyes against the glare of the unexpected light. "It's just me Buddy, Molly from the Piña Colada," she said as she moved toward the glowing penlight and the electrical box.

"I'm just here to turn on the lights. Do you smell all that gas? I think something is leaking. It smells real strong under the house. We had better see what's going on. Just a second and I'll turn on the switch."

Buddy was so pissed he wanted to get on the dock fast. His Jack Daniels buzz was all but gone, and now he had that burnt-out wiry feeling. He needed another drink, and he wanted to show that slut from the Piña Colada who was boss, but just as he stepped onto the stern of the center-console and began to reach for the nearest piling, all of the dock lights began to fizzle with electrical sparks. This image only lasted a second. After that, a giant hand or a giant sun-splashed wind completely swept him backward into the water.

Buddy went deep and he seemed to stay down a long time, but when he finally clawed his way to the surface, everything was on fire—even the water. Luckily, he surfaced almost in the channel and was well away from where the entire marina was burning and where oily patches blazed on the water's surface.

Tom Williams

Flames were rising all over the docks, spilling into the boats and climbing the masts of Billie's sailboat. Just as Buddy was weighing the chances of a fire department rescue, a tremendous explosion rocked the stilt house and sent a mushroom fireball out over the water. The house sagged as some support pilings were blown away and now the tilting structure was totally engulfed with flames. Orange flames with red tongues were climbing onto the roof and flickering firelight was showing brightly through the windows—the windows of Billie's office and her bedroom. His bedroom on the corner was still dark.

At the same instant Buddy realized he was treading water, he remembered Piña Colada Molly. As he recalled Molly standing under the house, he saw a slow motion, moving figure, staggering between billowing columns of oil-fired flames. The figure, although unrecognizable, was clearly human and could only be Molly.

She moved slowly—like Frankenstein, one foot heavily in front of the other and her arms outstretched like the monster. She looked like a roasted marshmallow, but a marshmallow that had been in the fire too long. She was still burning in some places, but she was mostly just blackened. Finally, she reached the edge of the dock and went head-over-heels into the harbor. Buddy knew it was impossible, with the snap-snarl and crackling of the flames, but he thought he heard her sizzle as she touched the water.

Suddenly Buddy Johnson felt like a very little boy, all the past years melting away and all the trouble. He didn't want to be a bad-ass anymore, just as much as he didn't want to be frightened. His memory, he realized, would never be free of that startling image of a woman burned to death, but still walking—a true Frankenstein. Without knowing why, he broke the rhythm of treading water, and began to swim toward the marina—not toward Molly or the stilt-house, but to the mangrove border and the edge of the docks.

"Mister Johnson, over here!" Cedric was waving from the only finger pier that was not on fire. He was fairly certain that he was safe from further explosion after the detonation of the oil and fuel drums under the house.

"Over here!" he repeated. The security director was of course wearing his sunglasses, but also shielding himself from the flames with his back to the fire.

To Buddy Johnson the FBI man looked like the devil outlined by flames—a pale, skinny devil wearing sunglasses.

After helping the cowboy fisherman climb out of the water, Cedric kneeled beside the sodden local. In the blazing firelight, it was comically obvious that Buddy Johnson had not totally escaped the initial explosion. His face and forearms appeared to be badly sunburned, and his mustache

115

and eyebrows were gone and singed into tiny black curls on his skin.

Without warning, one of the crab boats next to the stilt-house rose out of the water on the flames of a fuel detonation. The force behind the explosion lifted most of the thirty-foot vessel and sprayed burning fuel and fiberglass over the entire semi-circle of docks. Now the fire line perimeter was enlarged as flaming debris fell in the gravel parking lot facing the trailer park. Before Cedric turned away from the newly expanding firelight, he could see a group of locals gathering around a central stand of mailboxes and the doublewide entrance for trailer traffic.

"Mister Johnson, are you injured?" Cedric began. "I think we should move away from the pier, the fire seems to be getting worse." After his comment, the security director ducked as a secondary explosion rocked a small fishing boat and sent an outboard gas tank rising into the night.

The climbing missile looked like a controlled rocket in a nighttime launch, unstoppable until a trajectory change demanded a self-destruct over the wooden sailboat. Before the sound of the sky-bound explosion registered, a cascade of flames descended over the far side of the burning classic and delivered a falling ring a fire to a group of sailing boats that were previously untouched. Now, they too, began to contribute as sail covers and canvas tops ignited and added firelight to the green foliage beyond the farthest pier.

"Mister Johnson! Please!" Cedric was now truly insistent. The fire was getting worse and spreading fast. In the distance, the ardent howl of a siren rose above the popping of the flames but was muffled by the hidden crash of something large and structural. The Johnson Charters, Fisheries, and Salvage sign followed with another crash, and after the stilt-house resettled, burning embers began falling into the water.

"Yeah, I'm coming," Buddy finally answered. He stood and began to follow the skinny man from the FBI. "Did you see her? Did you see her go into the water?" Buddy coughed as he spoke. The two men had crossed into a wall of smoke, downwind from the fire, and emerged in the gravel parking area facing the marina.

The smoke was not only caustic, but also poisonous. Burning fiberglass combined with chemicals used to treat the dock wood was turning the flames into a menagerie of firework colors and producing an unnatural amount of thick boiling smoke.

Two fire trucks arrived with fading sirens, and a jumble of red flashing lights began searching through the drifting pall. Immediately, a team of firemen dressed in respirators and bulky safety gear uncoiled hoses, and as Buddy Johnson and Cedric Bowles moved forward, streams of silver water began to spay into the night.

From the center of the parking lot and facing the mounting disaster, the firemen's actions appeared to be too little too late. When the reaching arcs of water touched the multi-colored flames, a deep and darker smoke began to rush out vehemently as if the flames were alive, malevolent, and vengeful toward the attacking firefighters.

"Did you see her?" Buddy Johnson repeated. He was now gripping Cedric Bowles tightly by the arm.

Cedric coughed and shook his head no. He pulled away and indicated a county sheriff's cruiser that had just skidded into the parking lot.

"Away from the smoke," Cedric coughed again.

Abruptly, a flashlight beam stabbed through the smoldering haze and captured the two reeling figures moving away from the fire trucks.

"Buddy Johnson, is that you?" The deputy was a big man, not overweight, just big. His accent was pure southern everglades.

"It's me," Buddy croaked. He was a staggering mess, still wet from the harbor. His hair was singed and flash-fried and his face was blackened with soot.

"Where's Billie?" the deputy asked. "And how about the old man, Dotson?"

Buddy shook his head and his words stumbled out on a string. "Out on a charter. Out on the salvage rig. Out on Cape Romano."

Cedric almost giggled. This was so predictable. The sight of the burning woman had obviously unhinged the cowboy fisherman. Now he was overwhelmed and a puppet to be manipulated.

Of course the native Floridian would be intimidated by his past, and the local sheriff would certainly know about the previous arson charges. Small communities in America knew everything about each other, especially the law enforcement and criminal types.

"All right, Buddy, you had better tell me what you know." The deputy's remark was relaxed, yet foreboding. Clearly, he was beginning his well-practiced and personal approach to interrogation until a second police cruiser appeared with all lights flashing.

After the tires crunched to a stop, an older deputy climbed out of the car and slammed the door against the drifting smoke. The senior man was just that—senior. He was also a big man and obviously well beyond his prime. His hair was white in the multicolored flashers, but his face was red with anger.

"Richard Johnson, you are under arrest. The charge is arson," the older deputy spat. His handcuffs were out, and just before he reached for an unbalanced and cringing Buddy, Cedric Bowles stepped forward. He flattened his voice and did his best West Texas accent.

"Sheriff," he said. "You are right about the arson charge—an investigation will reveal that fact, but I can vouch for Mister Johnson, he wasn't the man responsible." The security director now produced his credentials. The FDA badge was omitted but the smooth leather case with the X-files—FBI credentials was opened with a flourish.

"I'm special agent James Marshall with the FBI and I'm here on an undercover assignment. I saw the woman responsible, but unfortunately was unable to react in time. Apparently there was an accident and the woman was killed when the fire started prematurely."

Both of the deputies were now examining the offered credentials. Flashlight beams crisscrossed over the photo identification and the face of the OPC security director, still wearing sunglasses.

"It was Molly, wasn't it?" Buddy Johnson asked. He seemed amazed. "Piña Colada Molly?" he repeated.

"I don't know the woman's name," Cedric lied. "But I saw her under the house with a fuel can. She must have triggered the explosion by mistake, unless it was a suicide."

The security director now turned to the fire-blackened Buddy Johnson. "Do you have any idea why this woman would have done this?"

Before Buddy could speak, the senior deputy sheriff raised his hand for silence. "This is my jurisdiction," he said. "This is under county authority—not state, and damned sure not Federal. I'll ask the questions here."

"Of course," Cedric replied. He added, "Perhaps I could be of service and drive Mister Johnson to the hospital, he obviously needs attention. Afterward, we could drive into the county seat and make a formal report."

Before the older deputy could answer, the fire chief approached, ripped off his respirator and interrupted.

"We need help," he said. "Those fumes are dangerous. We should evacuate the trailer park, and we should do it now!" The chief continued with his explanation about the danger from polystyrene-fiberglass vapor and when the fireman had finished, the FBI man and Buddy Johnson were gone.

Chapter 25

"Wake up!" Peter was shaking Brian.

"What's going on?" Brian sat up. He, like Peter had been sleeping in the tugboat salon. "Are we moving?" Brian asked.

"Yes."

"Why? I thought the shoals were too dangerous at night—too many sandbars."

"Come on," Peter insisted.

"But why? Tell me why."

"Can you smell it?" Peter asked.

After he sniffed the air, Brian offered, "A campfire?"

"Billie thinks it's more, and Dotson seems worried."

When Peter and Brian entered the pilothouse, they found Billie behind the tugboat wheel with the rig moving slowly forward. Down on the wooden barge deck, Dotson was a shadow between the red and green running lights. His image further diffused by the distant glow spreading on the horizon.

"Billie, what's wrong?" Brian asked.

"It's a fire," she answered softly. Her eyes were trained on the orange blur rising over the water, but suddenly she looked down to the compass glowing in the binnacle. After a brief calculation, Billie bit her lip. "It's Goodland," she said. "Marco is too far to the west."

Without a pause, Billie reached to the overhead and pulled down the microphone for the VHF marine radio. "Johnson charters, this is Johnson salvage, over," she transmitted. "Johnson charters, please answer."

After a moment of waiting in silence, Billie replaced the microphone and began with a sigh. "Well, as you might have guessed, that was my husband earlier. That was Buddy."

After Buddy Johnson's tear-away departure from the salvage rig, Billie had withdrawn into herself. She was obviously embarrassed, deeply troubled, and once again immersed into her dysfunctional lifestyle. She had refused to comment on the strange altercation, and Dotson had become equally stoic and incommunicado.

"He wasn't always like that," she continued. "But somewhere between twenty and thirty, he changed. In the beginning, after high school, I thought he was just frustrated." Billie paused, and checked the compass heading, then started again with a faster pace, as if she decided to unburden her emotional load.

"Then, as he got older he couldn't find himself," she explained. "He couldn't find a niche. He got seasick offshore, he has no patience for tourists, and he has always resented the marina. The bad things started after he stopped playing ball."

The tugboat diesel churned slowly, sounding a cadence to Billie's narrative. On the front of the barge, Dotson raised an arm and pointed to the right. Billie responded and turned the big wheel until the signaling arm dropped, then continued.

"All he ever wanted was just to play sports. He was very good at everything. Football, basketball, even softball, but he wanted more. After high school, he even had a tryout for the Miami Dolphins. One week after he was turned down, the coach, the one that told him no, his car was fire-bombed.

"There were never any questions, not from the police, but Buddy had definitely changed. He seemed to have gotten mean. After that there was always trouble and never enough money."

In the dim lighting, Peter and Brian watched as Billie shook her head. Her voice did not change, but they could not fail to notice her tears. Brian moved closer on her one side, and Peter on the other.

"There were fights, and some of them were very bad. He always found fault with everyone, especially the smaller guys—the ones who had no chance against him.

"Once, there was a softball umpire. He called Buddy out and Buddy put him in the hospital. The umpire, he was going to press charges and put Buddy in jail, but that was before his house burned down. No one was hurt, but the man moved away. He moved away and then Buddy was happy for a while.

120

"About a year later, there was another fire—this time in Everglades City. It was a crabber's trailer, a man who was our direct competition. There were constant arguments over fishing grounds, and Buddy openly made threats. He made threats in public and bragged about the softball umpire and the football coach in Miami. After the trailer fire, Buddy was arrested and went to trial, but he was never convicted. This was all my fault."

Billie paused as Dotson lifted his arm in another signal. She turned in the direction indicated, briefly wiped her eyes, and continued in the same soft voice.

"All my fault, because after my dad died, I was the one in charge. My dad left me the marina and the *Valkyrie*—the sailboat you slept on. I mortgaged the boat and the marina and hired the best lawyer I could find. I got Buddy off. He should have gone to jail, but the lawyer found a loophole."

"That's what lawyers do." Peter offered.

"But I promised, for better or worse," Billie pounded the wheel with frustration. "I always hoped things would get better," she said. "But we were married too young. We grew apart. Buddy started to drink and I began to read."

"When you're married," Brian said, "you're always obliged to help, for whatever the reason. Better or worse, richer, poorer. I should know," he added. "I was married twice."

Billie seemed not to hear. Her eyes were on the orange glow. Even to Peter and Brian the glow seemed to be getting brighter. Standing on the front of the barge, Dotson was now more of a blackened silhouette than a shadow, a dark figure before a troubled and premature sunrise.

A depth alarm sounded over the rhythmic churning of the diesel and after a quick scan of the shallow water indicator Billie toggled a switch and silenced the irritating buzzer.

"How long have you been doing this—driving tugboats and doing salvage?" Peter asked. His voice was soothing and well-placed and Brian instantly recognized the disarming tactic.

Billie was obviously under a lot of stress. Piloting the hundred-foot rig over a treacherous shoal in darkness, toward an uncertain disaster, was mounting into a tangible anxiety.

"My dad," Billie said. "He came to Florida and bought the marina. He came from Germany, but he was not a Nazi. He was too young for that. My mother was Austrian, but she was killed when I was very young—she died in a traffic accident. My father was driving and he never forgave himself. Dotson worked for my dad and together they raised me. I guess that's why I'm not so lady-like.

Lost and Found

"I grew up sailing, fishing, and exploring the Everglades. We never ate anything that wasn't pulled out of the gulf. When I was too young to pull a crab trap, I drove the boats. Daddy got sick when I was a senior in high school and died just after I graduated. He taught me everything—diving, welding, the weather, everything. I couldn't have had a better childhood."

Billie fell silent, either lost in her thoughts or absorbed with the task of piloting the rig.

"*Und Deutsch? Können Sie sprechen Deutsch*"? Brian asked in German — *And German? Can you speak German?*

"Of course, but I'm not a Nazi." Billie responded instantly in the same language and Brian was impressed with her High German accent and the rekindling of her perky spirit.

Forward, on the barge deck, Dotson signaled again, but this time he pointed upward. Billie responded by reaching for a handle in the pilothouse roof. After she pressed a switch, a searchlight beam stabbed into the darkness and found a distant wooden tower rising over the water. A reflective green square was captured in the light and after a quick calculation with the compass, the spotlight winked out.

"That's the first marker into Coon Key. We're out of the shallows now and into the channel. It's lucky for us we're riding the high tide," Billie explained. "Without the extra water we would have never made it."

"I still don't understand," Brian said. "Why did we have to come back at night? Is the hurricane coming sooner or are you concerned that the fire might be near the marina?"

Billie shook her head and turned to face Brian. In the glow from the binnacle, she appeared flustered as she pulled her hair into a rough ponytail.

After her baseball cap was firmly in place and her hair streaming out the back, she glanced to Peter but jerked a thumb over toward Brian.

"Pete," she said. "For a smart guy he sure misses a lot. Argentina," Billie continued. "Haven't you been paying attention? This shoal is like the back of my hand. I've been through here thousands of times. Coon Key is the beginning of my driveway. That fire in the sky—that *is* my marina."

Chapter 26

Dotson threw a line and captured a piling on the only finger dock that was not burned down to the water. Billie eased the tug into neutral and the outgoing tide gently moved the hundred-foot rig over against the seawall.

Although the fire was out, the fire engines and firefighters remained to spray the smoking rubble into final submission. It was clear by the actions of the smoke-blackened, stumbling figures that the firefighters had had a long night.

After Peter and Brian followed Billie down from the pilothouse, they watched as a heavyset deputy-sheriff approached. The law enforcement officer appeared disgusted as he made his way along the fire-blackened seawall—a seawall that once was covered by an expansive dock system but was now only a desolate border between partially sunken boats and the ruins of the dock house and marina.

"Not much of a morning…is it Billie?" The deputy offered after he walked to the end of the finger pier.

Billie's answer was a negative shake of her head.

"Do you know where we can *find* him?" The deputy had removed his cap and was asking his question, hat in hand.

Again, Billie shook her head.

"He was here earlier—when I first got here," the deputy gestured back to his cruiser. "He was supposed to go into the courthouse. He was with an FBI man, a federal agent who told us that a *woman* had been killed." The deputy kneaded the cap in his hands and made a face. "Hell, Billie, until now I was afraid that woman might have been you.

"We pulled her body out, but there was no way to make an identification—not without dental records." The county official now scratched his head. "Damn! I knew I should have taken him right then. After all, this is arson and murder, but I just got too busy and I trusted that federal badge. Billie, I sure am sorry. You damn sure don't deserve this."

"No, she don't," Dotson said as he stepped up to the edge of the barge. He was now standing with his hands on his hips and facing the deputy. "And she damn sure doesn't need to have her nose rubbed in it—by you, or the likes of them." Dotson pointed to a Fort Myers television van pulling into the parking lot next to the fire trucks.

A drifting pall of smoke was rising over the fire-blacked rubble and apparently offending a young woman reporter as she stepped out of the van. Quickly, she held a handkerchief over her nose against the pungent odor of burned fiberglass. She shook her head and climbed back into the air-conditioning, her perfect hairstyle and sharp features visible in the passenger seat. Two of the camera crew began laughing as they set up their equipment.

"Well, I guess the stink of Buddy's mess will give us a few minutes," Dotson offered. He turned back to the deputy. "Do you need Billie—I mean for anything legal?"

Again, the deputy scratched his head, "Nope, not unless she wants to file a complaint against her husband. The insurance people might want to talk to her. I don't think they'll pay—what with Buddy's past."

"I don't care about that," Dotson shook his head. "What I want to know is, can she go? Is she free to go right now?" he insisted.

"Well...I suppose, but I'm not sure. The sheriff, he might want a statement, or Billie might have to sign something." The deputy looked over his shoulder. The dish antenna on the television van was rising.

"I'll do that," Dotson nodded. "Billie and me have signed power of attorney over to each other. Just in case of something like this," he added.

Now it was the deputy's turn to nod. "I guess that would have it covered. As long as *you* stick around—I mean we gotta have somebody to answer questions."

"Good," Dotson said. "Now maybe you could keep those busybody reporters out of our hair while I have a few words with Billie."

When the deputy turned to look, he could see the female reporter talking and the camera crew panning over the burned-out docks and marina. They were visibly scanning the rubble until they stopped and focused on two blackened masts rising from the charred decks of a sunken sailboat.

The masts were tilted as the sunken wreck now rested on the shallow bottom. All that was visible were the blackened decks and the standing rigging.

"The old *Valkyrie* will keep 'em busy for a while, but then those buzzards will find their way over to us." Even as Dotson finished speaking, two local firemen had wandered over to the camera crew and one of the firefighters was pointing down to the water and the salvage rig tied to the finger dock.

"Billie, I'll be proud to buy you a few minutes," the deputy said. "You have a ride?" he asked after a quick glance to the fallen stilt-house and the burned out shell of a Ford pick-up.

When Billie didn't answer, Dotson demanded. "Well? Does she have a ride?" The older man had turned to the silent Peter and Brian who were standing behind Billie on either side.

"Of course!" was the dual response.

"That's our car—the gold one," Brian remarked to the deputy, pointing past the destruction to the left of the fire trucks. Standing alone and dusted with ashes was the only car in the gravel parking lot.

"Good enough," the deputy turned and replaced his cap before moving down the ravaged seawall.

"But I can't—" Billie began.

"You can. You will. And it's about time that you did." Dotson's hands were back on his hips and his gaze was leveling. Clearly, he was not going to accept any argument from either Billie or the two Englishmen at her side.

"Billie, I'm telling you right now," he began. "You have tried to make this work long enough, and now there is nothing left to work with." Dotson paused. "Don't look over there," he demanded.

Billie's eyes had wandered to the charred remains of her father's sailboat—to her anchor, her family, her childhood and her life. A single tear welled and ran down her cheek.

"Listen to me," Dotson moved forward and placed his hands on Billie's shoulders. He saw the tear and wiped it away with a rough and calloused finger.

"Now listen," he said again. "I helped raise you, and me and your daddy did the best we could. I always figured that after he died you needed something that was missing, and that's why you married Buddy. I guess neither of us ever imagined that Buddy Johnson would turn out as bad as he did. But now..." Dotson shook his head. "Now it's time to go on—to start over." Dotson hesitated after his voice cracked with emotion. "Billie, these last few days with old Pete and Argentina... Well, I haven't seen you happier since your daddy was alive."

Dotson now paused to gather eye contact with Peter and Brian. "Now you two. Last night, you said that you had more than ninety more wreck sites—all over the world. Is that true?"

"Yes, sir, it is." Peter answered solemnly.

"Absolutely," Brian echoed.

"Well, I figure that you boys know what you're up to—even if you are in a little bit of trouble. At least you know what you're doing on the high-tech end of things." Dotson shook his head. "One thing is for damn sure. Nobody else has ever found anything on that old shoal, and many have tried. So what I figure," the calloused old man continued. "Is that you're good for Billie and she would be good for you. Hell!" he exclaimed. "You two wouldn't know a good salvage operation if it fell on you. And most likely the wrong kind of outfit would either rob you blind, or worse, if you really find what you're looking for."

Dotson now paused to examine all three faces that were looking to him. He glanced over his shoulder to the deputy, the firefighters and the television crew. The young woman reporter was now rechecking her make-up and holding a microphone. In a few moments, the early morning disaster would be perfect. The camera operator was holding a light meter. They were all searching the scene. They were looking for an angle to enhance their story.

"Alright, listen up," Dotson's voice became stern. "I want you boys to take good care of my Billie—real good care. You treat her right and share what you find." The salty old man turned to Peter. "Where is the next salvage site—the one with the best chance of finding something?"

Peter turned to Brian and said, "Cuba is out of the question. The wrecks are too deep and the political situation impossible."

"Not Cuba," Brian shook his head. "Turkey," he said, "A remote location in Turkey with an unbelievably strong signature and a wreck site well positioned in shallow water. It's very near the coast on the Black Sea."

"Billie, is this possible?" Peter asked. "Would you really want to go with us?" Doctor Peter Clopec was searching the deep green gaze of the young woman before him.

"Yes," she said simply. "I want to go."

"But your things," Brian motioned to the smoldering remains of the stilt-house. "You need a passport, and identification."

"My boat bag on the rig," she explained. "I always carry my driver's license, dive card, Captain's license and passport. It's a Coast Guard thing—you have to have everything in case you're boarded."

"Then it's settled," Dotson was now looking from Peter to Brian and back again. "Get her away from here and away from this mess."

A sudden gust of wind cleared the smoke and Billie could see the female reporter staring across the burned debris. A low cloud began to scud over the mangroves, and as the wind gusted, a burst of rain spattered across the scene. The television woman was now confused. She suddenly seemed torn between the striking young woman on the tugboat, the early morning fire, and the beginnings of Hurricane Debra.

Chapter 27

"What do you mean you don't have the disk?" Haggly-Ford's words sounded distant and metallic over the cell phone and Cedric was forced to concentrate. Rain was drumming on the rental car roof with such a force it was difficult to hear.

"The disk has apparently been destroyed," the security director reported. "A fire," he added. "The sailboat that Clopec and Pauliss were sleeping on was destroyed by fire. Along with an entire marina and their personal travel gear," Cedric embellished.

"Are you sure? How can you be certain?" the chairman demanded through cellular static. "And Pauliss and Clopec? Are they dead?"

"Nossir, they were out on a salvage charter, a salvage charter to uncover a treasure ship."

"What?" Haggly-Ford's voice seemed to reach into the phone.

"Yessir, a treasure ship. It seems the satellite data is linked to an old sunken ship."

Cedric Bowles smiled during the following silence and looked out through the rain to check on the cowboy fisherman. The local crabber was inside a convenience store buying beer and cigarettes. He was comical with his singed hair and shiny face covered in burn ointment. He was fumbling with money and still trying to hold the Enterprise rental car umbrella.

Haggly-Ford was back. "This treasure ship—did they find it? Did they find gold?" he asked urgently.

"They must've found something. It would be illogical for them to return to Odessa with a salvage expert. They must be moving on to another site—another shipwreck."

"Of course, what a brilliant concept," Haggly-Ford thought aloud. "Highly concentrated deposits of gold covered only by water. The satellite worked. But how many of these underwater salvage sites are possible?"

"Impossible to determine at this time," the security director replied smoothly. "As I said, I believe that the disk was destroyed by fire."

"This fire," the chairman's words now sounded suspicious. "Was it arson?"

"Yessir."

"Was it Pauliss and Clopec? Did they actually start a fire to cover their research—their findings?"

"I imagine that *could* be possible," Cedric continued. "You remember the girl from Petroleum Discovery, Rebecca Raimes. She was quite possibly liquidated. The potential of what has been found could be extremely valuable—even priceless."

"Where are they now? What are they doing?"

"At present they are in route to Miami." Cedric referred to his cell phone-tracking device. The gold convertible was showing a steady blip on the GPS screen.

"And you are following them now?

"Yessir."

"Tell me about this salvage expert."

"A woman, but apparently well qualified in marine operations."

"Cedric, listen carefully," Haggly-Ford continued. "You must not allow them out of your sight. You must not fail. The disk, if it *was* destroyed, must not be the only one. They must have other data—other sites waiting to be explored. This could be the biggest find in years—the biggest find *ever*! You keep after them and bring me results. You do this, and I promise …you will be a very wealthy man. Consider your first installment of $50,000 secure in Cape Town.

"Call me every day with updates."

"Yessir."

Cedric closed his cell phone as Buddy Johnson approached. The feeder bands from Hurricane Debra were sweeping across South Florida and the tropical rain, driven before the wind, was a sliver slant washing into gray.

After he closed the dripping umbrella and slammed the car door, Buddy opened his cigarettes and threw the cellophane on the floor.

"Don't do that." Cedric's remark was casual and preoccupied. He was backing the car away from the parking lot. He checked for traffic and accelerated onto the old Tamiami Trail.

"Don't do what?" Buddy now had a cigarette in his mouth and had punched in the rental car lighter.

Lost and Found

"You may drink beer, but no smoking, and kindly do not litter the interior of my car."

"The hell with you, I will do whatever I—"

Buddy Johnson never finished his sentence. Even with the torrential rain and gusting wind, Cedric nailed the steering wheel hard left and quickly pulled the emergency brake. The result was a controlled Bootleg turn that the security director had learned in the South African Security Force. Even with the wet road, the radical maneuver unfolded perfectly.

The back of the car suddenly slipped forward and the front of the Enterprise rental was now traveling in an apparent reverse. Cedric pumped the foot brake and turned the wheel hard to the right. Instantly the car skidded to a stop on the tropical shoulder. A transport truck appeared through the rain and blew a non-stop signal of warning before thundering off in a gray cloud of mist.

Before Buddy Johnson could react, the security director had grabbed the cowboy fisherman by the throat and was holding the red-hot cigarette lighter just beneath the local man's left eye.

"Whenever I speak...do not consider my remarks...as only a suggestion. You will follow my *every* direction...as if your *life* depended on...*the ...tone...of...my...voice.*"

Buddy did not struggle or even make a sound. He had no chance. This skinny FBI man was gripping his windpipe with one hand and holding the red-hot lighter just an inch away from his eye with the other. The heat was incredible that close, and Buddy knew that if he moved, the skinny man with the sunglasses would blind him.

"I need your help. That is why we are traveling to Miami and you are not in jail. Without me, you will be charged with arson and homicide. Do you understand and agree?" Cedric's ultimatum was in a quick whisper with his mouth and teeth very close to the local man's ear.

The security director had used the automobile ploy many times. He knew that with every second the lighter coil lost heat, the threat of blindness became less intimidating. After the cowboy fisherman gently nodded yes, Cedric abruptly released the startled man and calmly pulled back onto the road.

As the windshield wipers beat back the rain, Cedric replaced the cigarette lighter, and popped a breath mint. He looked over to the shabby figure who was sullenly rubbing his throat. The security chief suppressed a giggle. The cowboy fisherman was clearly terrified.

After a few moments, Buddy Johnson cracked open a beer. He needed one.

Chapter 28

Cedric knew that he was good, but he also realized that he was lucky. Pauliss and Clopec had disappeared into the masses of the Miami airport and it was not until he saw the local Florida woman that he knew he was not too late. The woman was standing alone at a Delta airlines counter and the security director had just enough time to join a line at another counter and pretend to read the newspaper.

Pauliss and Clopec joined the female salvage consultant and presented their identification and passports. After all three had cleared security for the international concourse, Cedric returned and purchased a ticket to London at the same Delta counter. It was not until he saw Clopec looking at his watch and speaking to an attendant at a boarding gate that the security director knew that he had the wrong destination. The woman, along with Pauliss and Clopec were traveling to Frankfurt, Germany with an ongoing connection to Istanbul.

With the brim of his Panama hat pulled down low Cedric adjusted his sunglasses, rolled up his newspaper, and backtracked out to the main terminal. He pretended to be disgusted with his cell phone and explained to the counter attendant that he must switch his London ticket for the flight to Istanbul. A new ticket was issued without question, and after regaining the international concourse, Pauliss and Clopec were easily found speaking to the young woman at the nearest airport bar.

The security director found a perfect section of crowded seating amidst a gaggle of passengers waiting for an upcoming flight to Paris. The view to the bar was ideal with the two Englanders and the local woman visible behind artificial plants and glare-proof glass. The boarding gate for Germany and Istanbul was three seating sections away, and the crowd for the Paris flight was noisy with impatience. Almost all of the seats were taken, and as Cedric sat and unrolled his newspaper, he watched the rain pouring over a taxiing aircraft and thought about how the cowboy fisherman had died.

Everything was timing and the timing had been perfect. Cedric had simply waited until Buddy Johnson drank the entire six-pack of beer. After the first three cans, the scorched simpleton began to ask questions.

"Why are we going to Miami? I thought you were taking me into Naples, to the county seat. You told the deputy that we were going to the hospital. I think we had better turn around. What if those cops think I had something to do with that fire, with what happened to Molly?"

Cedric had pretended indifference, but secretly suppressed a giggle. During the drive, he had only offered an occasional glance whenever his rambling passenger's comments seemed to mount into significance. Finally, after the crabber's last beer, when a road sign confirmed forty-five miles to Miami, the cowboy fisherman insisted that he had to urinate. The security director had immediately looked at his watch, but ignored the request. After an additional ten minutes, the oncoming hurricane showed a break in her feeder bands and offered a clearing section of sky with only a light gusting drizzle. A side road appeared conveniently on the right shoulder and Cedric turned off and stopped after rounding a slight bend. He placed the rental car in park and gestured forward along a ditch-lined gravel track.

As planned, the local man immediately opened the door, lit a cigarette, and cupped his tobacco against the occasional raindrops. He looked back only once as Cedric climbed out of the car and unfastened his zipper.

When the smoking man's stream finally reached into the ditch, the security director placed his knee firmly into the cowboy fisherman's spine and pulled very hard with a new section of No. 3 drapery cord. As usual, the entire struggle lasted under two minutes.

Afterward, when a strangled Buddy Johnson was released, he tumbled lifelessly and fell into the muddy water. Without looking back, Cedric threw the makeshift garrote into the ditch and climbed into the car. Within minutes, he was back on the Tamiami Trail, and all of the problems with the cowboy fisherman were over.

With the hurricane coming, the rain would continue for at least forty-eight hours. Even with critical thinking, the body of the local man would not be found for several days, if at all. The alligators, which were everywhere, would enjoy an uninterrupted meal and the law enforcement officials would have a fugitive for their investigation. Johnson was a local who had a reputation for arson, and a man who had escaped from a federal officer—a federal officer who was missing. Buddy Johnson was now wanted man and wanted for much more than questioning. He was the principal suspect in a crime of arson involving murder.

As the security director collected his thoughts, he pulled the newspaper closer. He had to; the image of the flash-fried drunk with his penis out was hilarious. One of the alligators would certainly enjoy an appetizer.

Cedric giggled until he could not catch his breath. He bit his own lip and finally tasted blood. He knew he had to control himself, discretion...discretion...discretion.

Chapter 29

For the flight to Europe, Peter and Brian insisted upon comfortable clothing. While Billie waited at the ticket counter, the two men shopped. They returned with soft jogging suits, similar to the variety Brian had worn from Texas. Peter was in navy blue, Brian in his original sea-foam, and they had procured a dark burgundy for Billie.

After boarding the airliner, the Captain made his announcement. Within the next hour, no further flights would be leaving Miami until the danger from Hurricane Debra was past. He also explained there would be considerable turbulence climbing out of the tropical weather, but a smooth ride up the eastern seaboard and across the North Atlantic was expected.

Billie sat in an aisle seat, Peter next to the window, and Brian on the opposite aisle of the center section. The first-class cabin was pleasantly empty with only a smattering of big business Turks, and a complaining German who loudly voiced his opinion that Lufthansa was far superior to the substandard service of Delta. The after-most, and coach section of the aircraft was noisy and completely full.

Before takeoff, Brian sipped champagne and ordered a double dark rum for Billie, another for himself, and a double black label—no ice, for Peter. During the bumpy climb up through Debra's feeder bands, Billie sipped her drink as she and Peter looked out through the split-level layers of clouds. After the airliner smoothed out and turned away from the sunset, Brian was fast asleep.

As Brian began to softly snore, Peter looked over to Billie and asked, "A penny for your thoughts?"

"I just can't believe it—all that's happened," Billie said quietly. "Buddy was bad and getting worse, but burning down the whole marina? And murder? Who could the burned woman have been? It just doesn't seem possible. I know Buddy better than anyone. He's a baby deep down, and only tough on the outside. Maybe the whole thing was some kind of accident, some kind of freakish bad luck."

Peter signaled the flight attendant and ordered another drink for Billie and himself. He frowned as he considered her words. "Perhaps you're right. From the beginning, very soon after we reprogrammed the satellite, a streak of very bad luck has begun to unfold. A beautiful young woman has been killed, a billion dollar company placed in jeopardy, and Brian and myself forced into a position of basic blackmail." Peter paused as Billie took the newly arrived drinks.

"And now," he continued. "Bad luck has followed. Out on the shoal, we did not find the gold we so desperately seek, and upon our return, we find the marina destroyed and your husband missing. Another woman has been killed, and all we found were some artifacts. At the end of the day," Peter summarized. "All we really found was an exciting distraction."

Billie nodded. "After you told me about the murdered girl in Texas, and about the trouble with the satellite, I never even once considered that you might have done something wrong. You and Brian," she tilted her head and smiled. "You two just don't seem like the dangerous type. All I could think about was what bad luck, and the more I think about it, it's like you guys are cursed. Cursed because of what you found. And now," she added. "It's spilled over to me."

After a quick glance over to Brian, Billie reached down to the control buttons on her armrest and switched off the overhead light. With the reading lamp dark, she leaned toward Peter and continued softly.

"We told you before about other treasure hunters that came to Cape Romano. They never found anything, but they sure spent a lot of money trying." Billie shook her head as if she was hesitant to continue. "But there is one story that's different," she whispered. "A story I will never forget."

Peter sipped his drink. "I like stories," he smiled. "Especially ones that can never be forgotten."

Billie's grin flashed, but then she became serious. She placed her hand on Peter's arm and leaned closer. "For years this research specialist—Mel Fisher, searched these southern gulf waters looking for lost Spanish Gold. He explored forever. He dragged a metal detector off the back of a tugboat looking for old iron cannons. This is how most treasure hunters work. He found cannons from the right era, but none from the missing treasure fleet he had read about in Spain. When he was desperate and almost broke, he finally found the *Atocha de Conception* off the Marquesas. That old ship was in thirty feet of water and only about 60 miles from our wreck site on Cape Romano. To date, that was the richest shipwreck ever found."

Billie paused to search Peter's gaze. "The first night after they found the treasure—there was an accident. Mel went into Key West to announce his success, and that night, in perfectly calm water, the tug that was anchored over the wreck rolled over and sank. Mel's only son, who was an excellent swimmer and diver, was drowned."

"Even today," Billie added, "down in Key West, they sell pieces of eight and other coins recovered from that Old Spanish ship. It's a tourist thing. They make the coins into jewelry."

Billie shifted in her seat. "I know this guy," she explained, "a Captain in Sanibel. His wife bought him a gold coin that was made into a necklace. He wore it for three months and had terrible luck. Then one day, on an offshore charter, he threw the coin back into the water." He said it was simple. He threw the coin back and the bad luck was over. I don't know," Billie shrugged. "Maybe some things are better left alone. Maybe it's like that old fairy tale—the one about King Midas. All he wanted was gold, but it eventually killed him."

"Try not to worry too much," said Peter. "And please don't frighten me with sea stories and old superstition. I've got enough on my mind—look." Peter gestured to the softly snoring Brian. "We should be more like Argentina and try to relax. We need our rest. After all," he added, "we are traveling halfway around the world and looking for something that could potentially equal your friend's treasure ship. You know," Peter insisted," this Turkish wreck site is the strongest anomaly recorded from the satellite—the strongest out of all ninety-seven."

Billie nodded, but then frowned. "After Mel found the treasure, the state of Florida and the Federal government wanted to keep everything. They wanted to confiscate the entire shipwreck. After about a week, the state of Florida ordered every recovered article impounded. What will happen in Turkey if we actually find something? This could get very tricky."

"You're right," Peter answered. "But consider that the real value of our satellite discovery is the fact that it's real. Proof is all we need to make the ninety-seven hard returns priceless. Any government would be willing to pay a percentage to learn about lost treasure. Don't worry Billie. All we need is a little proof, a few gold coins, and a few ingots, actual evidence that the satellite really did find gold."

Billie smiled. "Then we're not really looking for the whole mother lode? We're not going to become big time smugglers?"

"No," Peter grinned. "Not big time. All we need is a little proof."

Chapter 30

Cedric was amazed. Following the Englishmen had been simple. They were so typically overconfident. They had not noticed the OPC security director even as he had passed through the first-class cabin. They had been totally absorbed with their preflight champagne and the young Johnson woman who sat between them.

Even after landing in Turkey and passing through customs, the two Englanders seemed to be in a non-stop competition for the blond woman's attention. The three travelers had collected their meager luggage and immediately filed out to the waiting chaos that was the Istanbul taxi lines. Just as the situation began to appear difficult—as it would have been if Clopec and Pauliss jumped into a cab, a Four Seasons transfer van rolled through madness of the horn blaring taxis.

There were other hotel limos, but Pauliss instantly signaled the Four Seasons driver and after a quick vocal exchange, the three new passengers were quickly installed through a side door of the van. The driver waited to help an elderly couple who also boarded, and then edged into the tangled snarl of the Istanbul traffic.

When the van was away, Cedric approached a knot of men standing around a taxi kiosk. He addressed the nearest driver and spoke with authority. "Hotel Four Seasons."

"But, effendi, you have missed the transport bus," the man said in English. "One moment and I will signal their driver." Instantly, the Turkish Taxi man unclipped his radio and began speaking into the device.

After transmitting a barrage of Turkish, the man's handlebar mustache lifted as he smiled at the crackling radio. "The Four Seasons bus will now return. The driver from the Four Seasons is my cousin. He will make the turn-around and return for you at once."

Cedric's head darted back and forth. His bulbous sunglasses looking like the eyes of an insect. "No," he insisted. "I don't want to ride in the van. I want a taxi."

"But, effendi, you asked for the Four Seasons Hotel. I would take you, but as you can see it is not my turn," the man explained. He gestured to the bricked in swarm of taxis stationed along the airport curb.

"Never mind, I want a taxi and I want it now. Do I look like a common fool who would ride in such a public vehicle? No," the security director explained, "I am a man of privilege and require a private car. Make the arrangements immediately."

"Of course, effendi, your request is on the top of my head." The Turk then returned to his radio and launched a new vocal onslaught.

After the man finished, Cedric spoke. "Does everyone here speak English as well as you?"

"No, effendi. But I am an educated man."

"What is your name?"

"Mustafa Kemal, effendi," the Turk removed his flattened, short-billed cap and bowed with a flourish. "Clearly you are a man with special needs. You will perhaps require a translator and a guide. I could provide such a service, for a fee." Once again, the handlebar mustache rose as Mustafa Kemal smiled. His eyes were dark brown, like his hair, and his teeth beneath the mustache, very white. Even from a distance, Cedric could smell cologne.

Abruptly, over the jammed lines of idling cars, another taxi driver shouted in Turkish. The man was signaling in Cedric's direction.

"You car is ready, effendi," Mustafa explained. "Will you require my services as translator and guide?"

"Are you discreet and truly available? My business is private and might require immediate travel. You might be engaged for several days."

The man replaced his cap. "My fee for such an important job would be five-hundred US dollars every day."

"Ridiculous!" Cedric replied, walking toward the pre-arranged taxi.

"But, honored effendi, for a man of your obvious importance, perhaps a smaller price could be negotiated. Perhaps 300 US per day?" Mustafa was following.

"Too much," the security director now increased his pace.

Standing beside a battered Mercedes sedan, another driver waited. He was an older man with dark clothes and a cigarette in his mouth.

"I wish you good luck, effendi, with your travels in Turkey," Mustafa offered. "May the prophet smile upon you and bring you success."

"200 US," Cedric barked over his shoulder."

The driver of the battered Mercedes was holding open the door. The inside of the car was obviously reupholstered leather and immaculate.

"I can see, effendi, that you are a shrewd businessman." After Mustafa spoke, he addressed the older driver in Turkish as all three climbed into the cab. A brief exchange followed as the car jerked into gear and moved out into traffic.

"For 200 US per day," Cedric said carefully. "I will certainly require more than the services of a guide and translator. I will require specific information from specific sources."

Mustafa turned from the front seat to address his new employer in the back of the sedan. "There was someone on the Four Seasons bus?" he said as a statement. "Someone that you wish to follow, but someone that doesn't know you are here, a person who would recognize your face?"

"What did you say your name was?" Cedric asked as he looked out at the Istanbul traffic and adjusted his sunglasses.

"Mustafa Kemal, effendi," the passenger in the front seat replied.

"Mustafa," the security director said. "I believe that I just made a good investment."

Chapter 31

"Do you speak English?" Brian asked.

"Of course," replied the driver.

"Do you have rooms available at your hotel?" Brian inquired, his voice pitched to override the noisy traffic.

"Of course, effendi. Several choices are available, very nice. We have the best hotel in Istanbul." The driver seemed incredulous that anyone would ask such a question.

"Peter, what do you think? After all, we need to rest and a place to start." Brian's remark was addressed to Peter, but he was watching Billie. She seemed fascinated.

Peter nodded, but he was also regarding Billie's spellbound expression. The choked lines of traffic clearly demanded attention, as did the masses of workers and travelers flowing in and out of the Ataturk International Airport. But Billie herself was also a part of the distraction. Standing an average head taller than most of the Turks, her striking features and tangle of blond hair was demanding an unnatural amount of interest. More than a few of the Turkish women had stopped mid-stride and were openly gawking as they made hurried conversation.

The van driver was no exception. He smiled toothily, popped open the door with a flourish, offering his hand to help Billie into the van. Peter and Brian followed, and after an elderly British couple boarded, the little transfer bus was moving away from the airport and onward into the city.

Istanbul was old, new, crowded and exotic. Even with the August sun high overhead, the temperature of the city was much cooler than Florida and the humidity virtually dry. There was a scent in the air and it seemed to be everywhere. It was like old dust, allspice and liquorish, fading at times, but then rushing back stronger than ever.

"It's the aroma of age," Brian teased, "and the ghost of Constantinople."

The open van stopped, started, and snarled through tight bottlenecks until traffic moved faster onto wide boulevards. The local time was 1:00 PM—seven hours faster than Miami.

"Billie, are you tired?" Peter asked as he looked as his watch.

"No way. How could I be? I'm too excited. Look at this place. Oh my God, what is that?" Billie was pointing as the van rounded a wide curve in the thoroughfare. A huge domed building appeared as the transfer bus continued. Six thin spires rose far above the monolith and framed the sprawling structure with an air of majesty.

"It's the Blue Mosque," Brian offered, "One of the most famous landmarks in Istanbul."

"It's the most amazing thing I have ever seen." Billie's voice reflected her awe. "Is it a church, a church for Muslims?" she asked.

Peter nodded. "Yes, it is quite impressive."

"I had no idea. It's so beautiful. Everything is so different."

"Billie," Brian said quietly. "Dotson was right—you needed this."

For a brief moment, a cloud crossed Billie's features, but then she smiled. "Argentina...you always know the right thing to say."

"Alright good. Here's the plan. We must not rest," Brian insisted. "We have to stay up until its Turkish bedtime, then in the morning, we wake up and we're acclimated. This is the best method to beat the time difference and jet lag. Tomorrow," he added. "We hire a car and travel to the Black Sea coast."

Peter looked at Billie and they both rolled their eyes. Brian had slept through the entire flight.

After check-in at the hotel, Peter and Brian took Billie shopping. They toured the Grand Bazaar and the spice market, and when they returned to the Four Seasons, a bell cart was needed to carry their parcels.

Billie had no clothing apart from her new jogging suit and the boating clothes and swimsuits she had on the rig. She was very private when she shopped for her clothes, and sent Peter and Brian out on their own as she made her selections.

After sunset, the men waited in the "Seasons" five star restaurant until Billie made her appearance. When she emerged and walked into the fine-dining foyer, all conversations stopped and every head turned to watch her entrance. The Turkish Maître d' blossomed like a peacock, rushed to her side, and walked with his elbow extended as if the extraordinary young lady was an angel on his arm.

"My God, she is absolutely stunning," Brian exclaimed as he stood.

"Beyond stunning," Peter corrected as he also rose from the table.

Both of the Englishmen were wearing new suits. Brian in gray and Peter in a dark charcoal, but neither of the elegantly dressed males were prepared for what had just arrived at their table.

Dressed head to toe in flowing white gauze, Billie wore gold hoop earrings and several slim bangles. She looked all the part of an angel, an exotic middle-eastern goddess in flimsy, semi-see-through material that teased the eye for a clearer view of what lay beneath. Her high sandals were nothing more than thin strands of gold wrapped around her ankles and produced the overwhelming effect that she was walking on air.

"Hi," she said. "Do you like it? Do I look all right?"

"Madam," the Maître d' explained with a click of his heels. "You are the essence of perfection. It is truly an honor to serve you."

"*Tesekkur ederim*," Billie's effort at saying thank you in Turkish, clearly flattered the headwaiter beyond words. He responded with a signal that compelled two underlings to rush forward and deliver menus.

After Billie sat, Peter and Brian fell into their seats.

"Quit staring," Billie whispered. "You're making me self-conscious."

"Right," Peter and Brian obediently responded together.

Billie chuckled at the rejoinder but then became serious. "This is the first time I've ever been this dressed up. But being here in this foreign place…it just seemed right—like a show of respect for the past."

Brian glanced to Peter and mouthed, "Wow."

After cocktails Peter asked, "Billie, may we order for you."

"Sure," she said, "but nothing weird."

Peter smiled. "No frog fish from the river?" he whispered. "No camel's lungs stuffed with goat meat."

"Yuck!" Billie made a face.

Brian cleared his throat as the headwaiter approached. "Chateaubriand for three please, Caesar salads, and please service our cocktails!"

After the waiter had made a fuss over unfolding Billie's napkin and placing the serviette in her lap, he made a hasty retreat for the kitchen. Clearly, Billie was unaccustomed to having strange man's hands smoothing fabric around her upper thighs.

As the waiter fled before Billie's leveling stare, Peter suppressed a smile as Brian muttered, "Cheeky bastard!"

During the salads and dinner, the headwaiter allowed his underlings to serve while he was content to hover in the background. After dinner, Brian ordered cherries jubilee tableside and the Maître d' smiled with Peter and

Brian as Billie clapped her hands in delight. The display of the flaming dessert in the near darkened restaurant offered a respite in Billie's features that even a stranger could see. For a moment, in the firelight, she was a child again with her recent and tragic past temporarily forgotten.

Afterward, when the restaurant was deserted, only one of the underling waiters remained in attendance. A few oil lamps marked the boundaries of the room, and after the table was cleared, Brian ordered a cognac and reached beside his chair to retrieve his laptop computer.

When the monitor was lifted and the machine came to life, Brian tapped on the screen.

"This is it," he said, pointing to a map. "Here along the northern Turkish coast is a sheltered bay protected by a narrow strip of land. On the western side of this isthmus is the open Black Sea, but on the southeastern side there is a sheltered bay and a great natural harbor. For centuries, this natural and protected anchorage has been a major seaport on the southern Black Sea coast."

"Peter looked around the darkened restaurant and pulled his chair over next to Brian. Before Billie could rise, the lone waiter rushed to the tableside and helped adjust her chair so she could also see the screen.

Billie repeated the Turkish words for thank you and the man was gone.

"This natural harbor," Brian said softly. "Is the location of our strongest satellite anomaly. A small town named Sinop straddles the isthmus. Here—" Brian pointed to the narrow strip of land on the screen. "The harbor side of Sinop will be the base of our operations."

"How deep is the water in this harbor?" Billie asked.

"It varies," Brian said, "but according to nautical charts, our specific GPS location lies in about 33 meters—around 100 feet."

Billie nodded, but an expression of concern crossed her features. "That's a little deep for recreational scuba. Bottom time at 100 feet is around 15 minutes. That's not much."

"But this isn't recreational diving," Brian frowned. "When we were out on Cape Romano, you and Peter stayed down for almost an hour. I remember because I was beginning to worry."

Billie's concern vanished as she smiled in the laptop's glow. "Argentina," she said. "Out on the shoals Pete and me were diving in only twenty-eight feet of water. That's only one atmosphere. At 100 feet, you're in a whole new ball game. The longer you're down, in deeper water, the more you become saturated with nitrogen. If you stay down too long and come to the surface too quickly, you get the bends. That's when your blood boils with nitrogen bubbles. A mistake with a deep dive can be very dangerous, or even fatal."

"Billie," Peter said. "If this is not safe, or you're not comfortable, then we forget it."

Billie held up her hand. "No, it's not that. It's just a simple diving rule. When you dive deep, you pay attention. You follow the rules."

After a moment of holding Billie's gaze, Peter returned to the map on the screen. "What do you think we will be looking for?" Peter's question was directed to Brian.

"Here's the good part," Brian said excitedly. "This town of Sinop is ancient. I did a little research even before we left Texas." After a sip of his cognac, Brian brought up a fresh page on the computer.

"The Hittites," he read, "came to northern Turkey in 2000 BC. They were eventually conquered by the peoples of the Aegean Sea, but this happened much later at around 1200 BC. The point being, all of these people used our harbor, but the most interesting time for us is what happened afterward." Brian sat down his drink, tucked a loose strand of hair behind his ear, and lit a cigarette.

"Among and after the migrating tribes from the Aegean, was another race of people called the Phrygians. These were a very advanced and prosperous group, and controlled most of ancient Turkey until the death of their King. This happened at around 700 BC."

"Argentina," Billie interrupted, "I appreciate the history lesson, but somehow I get the feeling that you're holding something back."

Peter nodded his agreement. "And, Doctor Pauliss, what does all this suggest for three treasure hunters from the 21st century?"

Brian could not contain his smile, "This Phrygian King who died. He built a huge tomb similar to the Egyptians—not a pyramid, but still a large burial chamber hidden under a great mound. It was filled with hundreds of funeral gifts and thousands of coins."

"And this funeral chamber is underwater?" Billie asked.

"An earthquake submerged the tomb?" Peter chimed in.

"No, and that's the beauty of the story. Our King was buried many miles from the harbor of Sinop. His tomb was found by archeologists in the Phrygian capital of Gordian. After finding his skeleton, all the scientists found was bronze, bronze everywhere, hundreds of statuary, thousands of bronze coins and lozenge-shaped bars. Everything made of bronze, but not one piece of gold."

"I don't get it," Billie said. "Then what are we looking for?"

"The lost treasure of King Midas," Brian exclaimed. "He was the Phrygian King."

Brian continued quickly and did not notice the glance that Billie gave Peter.

"King Midas," he explained, "as we all remember, was obsessed by gold. He was fanatic about his wealth and very secretive about its location. At the end of his reign, he was under attack by a well-organized but barbaric tribe known as the Kimmers. Before he was eventually trapped and committed suicide, he was rumored to have moved his entire treasure, by sea, to a secret location. Can anyone guess," Brian asked with a rueful smile, "which is the closest Phrygian seaport to the king's capital city?"

"Mother of God!" Peter's voice was raw.

"This place! Sinop, that's it!" Billie exclaimed.

Brian leaned back in his chair and lit a fresh cigarette, the look on his face triumphant. "It's one possibility," he said as he exhaled. "But I must admit, it certainly does seem to be the most logical explanation."

"Then the tomb that was found was a decoy, and the bronze coins a trick?" Billie asked.

"That would reinforce the theory," Brian nodded. "After all, everyone knows about the greed of King Midas. He must have been absolutely paranoid with his kingdom under attack."

"And this missing treasure ship?" Peter asked. "It could have also fallen under attack and sank in the harbor? And Midas killed himself when he found out?"

"I never thought of that, but yes, it would certainly fit the personality type. But my God," Brian offered, what a terrible fate, and what horrible luck."

"Argentina," Billie said. "You're beginning to catch on."

Chapter 32

From Istanbul, the coastal road to Sinop was roughly 350 miles. The route was filled with breathtaking scenery, and as Billie sat next to the Turkish driver who spoke only Turkish and German, the hours passed quickly as she and Brian translated for Peter.

"He said that long ago, the local people from Sinop loved to eat the Hungarians from the Austrian Hungarian Empire," Brian said to Peter.

"That's not what he said," Billie giggled, and translated for the driver who also laughed.

Peter who was stationed beside Brian in the back of a Fiat sedan nodded at the joke, but winced as the hired car bounced over another pothole. "Ask him if he is required to hit every dip and crater on the road."

"Now, Pete, let me tell you. I don't believe anyone could do any better. This pavement is a nightmare." Billie was holding the overhead safety handle as the Fiat bumped along.

"At least ask him to slow down," Peter winced again as the car bounded over another section of bad macadam.

"No, Peter, please," Brian insisted. "I would very much like to see the harbor before sunset."

"Me too," Billie said. "Look at this countryside, Pete, and don't think about the ride. Isn't this the most beautiful coastline you've ever seen?"

Peter smiled his private smile for Billie. "Alright," he said. "Just tell him to not to drive over the edge and tumble us into the sea."

Billie returned her attention to the driver and spoke in the German she learned from her father.

"She's good," Brian said to Peter, "very good. Her accent is perfect. She speaks like a native from Hamburg. It's amazing."

"You're smitten," Peter whispered, knowing his comment was covered by the road noise of the open sedan.

"*You* are!" Brian rebuffed as quietly. "You are absolutely taken with her."

"Don't be ridiculous! At my age, I could almost be her father."

"And I couldn't?" Brian was openly staring. "Oh my God! You've gone over! You're completely mad."

"I repeat! Don't be ridiculous."

"OK, what are you two whispering about?" Billie had turned in her seat.

"Nothing," they replied together.

As the hired car traveled eastward, the Black Sea became blue and the low mountains showed a sandy forefoot as they stepped into the sea. The route rose and fell, curved and twisted, and disappeared into rich green forest until the ancient track stumbled back onto the coast and into the bright sunshine. Ruins passed from time to time, some overgrown with incredible wild flowers, and others that had been turned into local dwellings. With every mile traveled away from Istanbul, an era from the past seemed to be unfolding. Horse drawn wagons appeared on the roadside loaded with pears, apricots, or hazel nuts, and on one occasion, the car was forced to stop and wait for a crossing herd of sheep.

"Yuck! Those things smell horrible," Billie exclaimed as the dirty wool bundles passed in front of the car.

"I'll never eat lamb again," Brian agreed, and lit a cigarette, as did the Turkish driver.

Throughout the day, Billie had been in constant conversation with the driver at her side. The older man's name was Alper, and from the moment she climbed into the front seat and discovered that he spoke German, another facet of her engaging personality was revealed.

The Fiat stopped only once for gasoline, the toilet, and bottled water. As the day advanced with the mileage traveled, the warm Turkish sun slanted and cast lengthening shadows.

"How much longer?" Billie asked the driver in German.

"Insha'Allah," Alper replied in Turkish, and for a moment, Billie was confused. He switched back to the language that she understood and explained a Muslim way of life. "Insha'Allah, means, 'As God wants.' Only God can determine the time of our arrival, or *if* we arrive at all."

Billie smiled. "That's very wise," she said, then launched a barrage of questions regarding the subject of Islam.

"Are you offended, that as a woman, I do not cover my hair—that I do not dress as a Muslim? What do the women of Turkey think, when they see a woman who is not covered? Why do they stop and stare whenever I walk by? What are they really talking about whenever they huddle together and whisper?"

"Oh brother," Brian said from the back seat.

"What?" Peter asked, "What did she say?"

"Quiet!" Brian insisted as Alper began to answer.

"Since you ask, missy, I will tell you. A good Turk will never lie." Alper paused and seemed to collect his thoughts. Every time the older man addressed Billie, he used the popular English slang for miss. "The women of Turkey, they think, missy, that you are a foreigner and a harlot. They also will believe that your hair is colored, like all harlots, but why do you bother as this fact will easily be revealed when you are naked."

As Billie's face flushed to red, the driver focused on the road ahead and explained further. "I, of course, understand that as a foreigner, your ways are different, and I am personally not offended that you do not choose to dress as a Muslim. But, missy, is it not obvious that you are traveling with two men who want you—two men who want your sex?"

"What did he say?" Peter broke the following silence as the car topped a rise.

"Christ!" Brian muttered.

The twinkling lights of a coastal town were just beginning to defeat the day as the hired car began to descend and wind onto an isthmus. When the Fiat turned north and faced the Black Sea, the last of the setting sun was a burning copper bar melting on the western horizon. On the eastern side of the ribbon of land, a smooth bay waited in shadow, the water very dark with the exception of the lighted waterfront. Beyond the town and the narrows of the isthmus, the land widened again and climbed into a small diamond-shaped mountain. After the mountain, the shadows of the bay joined the last light from the sea.

Alper spoke again after he switched on the headlights. "Do not worry, missy. I do not think of you as a harlot—only the women of Turkey." He continued quickly, "Look, missy, God has smiled upon us. We are here. This is Sinop."

Chapter 33

A ngela Barnes was in her law office in downtown Odessa. She had been going over a list of OPC stockholders when her assistant called and reported that there was a young woman who wanted an appointment. The woman was waiting in the outer office and insisting that her business was urgent and related to OPC. With her curiosity rising, Angela cleared her desk and ushered in a nervous young lady in her mid-thirties.

"Please have a seat," Angela said. "How may I help you?"

After the two women sat on opposite sides of a large and well-polished antique, the younger woman opened her handbag and produced a black videocassette.

"This should explain a lot," she said. "I know that you have interests with OPC—I know that you are a major stockholder and sit on the board of directors."

The younger woman paused after the black tape was placed on the desk. "I don't really feel comfortable speaking to Mister Haggly-Ford," she said, "he kind of scares me."

After a moment, Angela smiled. "I don't feel comfortable speaking to him either—in fact I don't like the man."

Pauline Taggart did not smile, but she nodded toward the videocassette. "Can we watch this? And can it be private, like an attorney and client privilege?"

Angela frowned. "But you are not my client. I don't even know your name. Do you work at OPC?"

Pauline nodded, but dropped her eyes. She retrieved the cassette and replaced it in her handbag. As she started to rise, she spoke softly. "I'm sorry I've wasted your time. I don't have enough money to become a client."

"Do you have five dollars?" Angela smiled. "That would be enough to establish a legal relationship."

"Really? I mean this office. It looks so expensive."

Angela punched her intercom. "Rita," she said into the device. "May I have a new client retainer form?"

When the administrative assistant was gone and the paperwork and personal check for five dollars complete, both documents were nervously pushed across the desk. "My name is Pauline Taggart, and yes, I work for OPC."

Without looking at the check or the retainer, Angela leaned forward at her desk. "Okay," she said, "What's on your mind Miss Taggart?"

Once again, the purse was opened and the black cassette reappeared. "It's all here," Pauline explained. "It's a short tape. It will only take a few minutes."

Within seconds, an elegant cabinet was opened, a television turned on, and the black tape was inserted into a VCR. As both women watched the fussy surveillance footage, Pauline explained.

"This tape was delivered to my apartment. It came in the mail with no return address—no note, nothing." The younger woman shook her head and continued in a rush.

"The girl with the hat in the black raincoat was my best friend—Becca Raimes. She was murdered, and she also worked at OPC. But I think you know that." Pauline once again dropped her eyes and did not see the alarmed expression of the elegant lawyer.

"The two men are friends of mine," Pauline continued. "They worked at OPC, before they were fired. The blond man, the one that's kind of heavy, he's my...special friend. We were lovers," she admitted with a blush. "But now, he's gone. He hasn't called, and now I'm worried. I don't know what to think." An expression of helplessness crossed the younger woman's features before she could continue. "The other man was Becca's special friend and he's gone, too."

"My boyfriend there," Pauline pointed. "His name is Brian Pauliss. Becca's friend is the taller man. His name is Peter Clopec. But I think that you already know that, too."

Angela nodded, but remained as quiet as the silent film.

"I believe this was taken the night Becca was killed," Pauline confessed. "The first night it began to rain. You can see that Becca is holding an umbrella and she is wearing a raincoat. And Brian and Peter—they kind of look like they had been sprinkled on. And it's dark. And the clock says midnight." Pauline began to sob. "Becca was murdered just after midnight. I'm afraid that Brian and Peter might be involved and that's why they have disappeared."

Without speaking, Angela opened a drawer on her desk and offered a box of tissue.

"Thanks," Pauline sniffed.

"Why haven't you told the police?" Angela Barnes probed. "Why bring this to me?"

"Because Becca told me about her special reports," answered Pauline. "She told me about the special reports from Petroleum Discovery and also about the money, the money that you gave her."

"I see," Angela replied carefully.

"Becca said it was like a part-time job and it made her feel cool—like she was some kind of spy, like in the James Bond movies."

"Pauline, I want you to listen very carefully. The relationship between Rebecca and this law office was a private affair. A business relationship in which she performed the role of a private investigator. You must understand," Angela Barnes continued with her best legal voice. "I have reason to believe that a major fraud has been committed at OPC, a premeditated crime to manipulate a public stock. That's not only a felony in the state of Texas, but also a Federal crime."

"And did she find out?" Pauline asked softly. "Did Becca find anything—anything that might have gotten her killed?"

Angela shook her head. "Definitely not. Her reports were menial, and only a preview of official geological reports that were released later. I only wanted advanced geological data that could be examined against actual monthly surveys. OPC wasn't finding any oil with the new satellite and I only wished to verify the truth."

"In case someone lied," Pauline asked, "Someone like the chairman—Mister Haggly-Ford."

"You are a very bright young lady," Angela nodded. "Who do you think sent you this video?

"I know this sounds crazy," Pauline leaned forward. "But I believe the tape is from the OPC security director. I don't know if you know him, or know who he is, but he's a really creepy guy. His name is Cedric Bowles and he's some kind of foreigner. He tries to hide it, but he has a weird accent. I even heard when he was overseas, he was in some secret police."

Pauline now gestured to the television that was showing the final footage of the black and white surveillance. "After all," she added and tilted her head. "It is a security tape, and who else but an expert in security would know how to find something like *this?*"

Angela arched an eyebrow. "Is this only your woman's intuition or is there something else?"

"This man, the security director, Cedric Bowles," Pauline said. "He's gone, too. I've asked around and he hasn't been to work for days. I believe he sent me this tape to make Brian and Peter look guilty. I think he wanted me to take it to the police."

"Now that," Angela mused, "is a very interesting theory."

After a moment of silence, Pauline raised her eyes and met the practiced legal stare. "I believe with all my heart," she insisted, "that Brian and Doctor Clopec are completely innocent—I just know it!"

After a sob, Pauline placed her hand over her heart. "Deep down inside ...with all my feelings...I just know they had nothing to do with what happened to Becca. Brian is a big little boy, and he's the sweetest man I ever met."

"Unfortunately," Angela shook her head. "Feelings have little to do with reality."

"But everything that's happened," Pauline rushed on, "It seems so controlled and premeditated—like it was all planned. Brian and Peter are smart—heck they're brilliant—but they're not the type to premeditate something as evil as murder."

As the last of her words seemed to have an effect and break through the thick attorney's shield, Pauline became determined. "I believe Becca's rape and murder, *and* the falling satellite was all part of some big crazy plan," she confessed. "And that Brian and Peter are supposed to get blamed, but they got away before they were made to look guilty."

After Angela picked up a remote and switched off the television, Pauline continued. "I also believe they're out there somewhere trying to prove their innocence—at least about the falling satellite. I just *know* that that creepy man Cedric Bowles is after them, and I believe Mister Haggly Ford is directly responsible."

After a pause, the younger woman added. "I also believe that you are the only person who can help."

After a long moment of holding each other's eyes, Angela Barnes said, "Miss Taggart, you just might be onto something."

Chapter 34

After finding a small but beautiful hotel on the harbor side, Billie and her entourage checked in for the night. Brian booked a separate room for everyone, including accommodations for Alper, the driver from Istanbul.

During an evening meal on the waterfront terrace, Alper explained in German. "Tomorrow I return to the city, but when you need me, I come back. Please, missy," he added with a pleading expression. "I do not think of you as a harlot—only *some* of the women of Turkey."

Billie remained silent for a moment and then burst out laughing. "It's all right," she said. "Thank you for being honest."

The following morning, Brian led an expedition through the harborside town. There were three dive shops in Sinop, but only one that had a boat available for a private charter. Another problem was the fact that Peter had no diving certificate. The owner of the shop had finally relented after examining Billie's Dive Master credentials.

"He is my student," Billie insisted. "We have done open-water dives before, and I take full responsibility. After all," she added, "I've instructed as many as four divers at once. This will be simple, one on one, one student and one instructor."

The dive shop owner was a stubborn Dutchman, but his equipment was the best and the dive boat immaculate. The boat driver, however, was a young Turk who spoke only broken English. The youth was only a teenager, but he seemed capable enough as he climbed over the transom and began to stow the dive gear.

"No worries, missy," the youngster grinned. "I know all of the harbor, and all of Sinop. And all about boats."

With the noontime sun beginning to reach toward the west, the dock lines were cast off, and the inboard diesel chugged away from the waterfront. After the juvenile captain had steered out into the bay and away from other boats, Billie stripped down to her bright blue two-piece. The youngster dropped his jaw at the sight, but pulled himself together and tugged down the plastic brim of his tourist style Captain's cap.

Brian smiled at the boy's reaction, but then stepped up beside the steering station and produced a GPS. "We go here," he said, as he showed the screen of his global positioning map. "To this place."

With his eyes torn between watching Billie pull on her wetsuit and Brian's liquid crystal display, the boy shook his head.

"No! No!" he said, "This not a good dive. This is the place where..." The young man was now apparently confused and did not know the English words to continue. "This bad place," he finally offered.

"Why?" Brian asked.

"This place bad, when storm come, very bad," he replied.

"There is no storm today," Brian gestured to a beautifully clear sky.

"Never mind, this place bad!"

"What's the matter? What's wrong?" Peter asked over the diesel engine. He was also struggling into a wet suit.

Brian appeared flustered. "I don't know," he said. "It must be some kind of bloody superstition."

"Tell me," Billie asked. She was now dressed in red neoprene and standing next to the boy at the wheel. "Tell me why this is a bad place?" she insisted.

"Fingers of fire come from the sky. Always in this place—when storm come."

"Lightning, do you mean lightning?" Billie asked. She made a zigzag motion with her finger and said, "Boom!"

"Yes, missy, very much yes, always lightning." After trying the new word, he asked. "You wish to dive on the airplane—the old airplane?" The boy removed his cap and looked up to meet Billie's gaze. "The airplane is deep, and not for fun," he said. "I know many good places. There is much good diving in the harbor of Sinop, many places which are better, more shallow and easy to reach. I know more than you. I am a professional diver."

"An airplane?" Brian nudged in and returned to the point.

"Yes, effendi, a big airplane and very old."

Peter had now joined the others at the wheel. "Well, that certainly blows the King Midas theory," he said.

Brian looked perplexed. "It is the strongest anomaly," he insisted. "I'm certain this is the correct location."

Billie smiled. "An airplane sounds better to me than a spooky old ship filled with bad luck. Please, Captain Benjamin," she used the boy's name. "Can you take us there? This is the only reason we came to Sinop."

After a moment of hesitation, the teenager nodded. "OK, missy," he said reluctantly. "But only today, and not when the storm clouds come."

During the following half hour, the diesel boat cruised as Brian smoked and checked his GPS. Benjamin stoically ignored the modern technology and only regarded the receding landmarks and rhumb line on his compass. When Brian said excitedly, "Yes, yes this is it," the Turkish boy nodded and the noisy engine rattled to a stop.

With the warm sun slanting toward the fuzzy image of Sinop, Brian watched as Peter and Billie checked their dive gear. The bay was wide and tranquil as a lake, the water color a deep dark blue. Benjamin, after they stopped, had thrown over an anchor, but the line went straight down and offered no suggestion of holding.

"Is the flash on the camera working and the film loaded?" Brian was pointing to the rented underwater Nikon.

"Yes, Argentina," Billie replied. "I have film in the camera. I have checked the flash, and I have dive bags to bring up the treasure." After Billie's latest comment, both Peter and Brian looked sharply to the teenager with the Captain's cap.

The youngster was still watching the anchor line and seemed not to have noticed or understood the English word "treasure."

Billie caught her mistake and bit her lip. "Sorry," she mouthed.

After she opened the air valves on both scuba tanks, Billie reclaimed the scene and spoke with authority. "OK, Pete," she said. "This will be different from the diving in Florida. The water is deep and we don't know anything about currents or what we might find on the sea floor. As I said before, our bottom time will be limited."

Billie now paused to indicate her wristwatch-style dive computer.

"For our first survey," she explained, "I want to take it easy and see how things go. Maybe just a quick trip down, a quick look around, and then a slow assent to the surface. If you have any trouble equalizing your ears, or you don't feel comfortable, give me a thumbs up and we'll come right back topside. But, if everything goes well, and we're careful with our air supply, we can stay down for the whole bottom time and get a good idea of what were facing and what to do next."

Peter nodded, but he did not look confident. He, like Billie, was fully covered in a bright, red wetsuit. The color of red was necessary for good visibility in a deep dive. All of the dive gear was first rate and in good condition. Billie had checked thoroughly.

After Billie gave her all-round winning smile, she pulled on her dive mask, nodded to Peter, and both of the red neoprene suits disappeared over the side.

Brian instantly looked at his wristwatch and then over to the teenage captain. "About twenty minutes," he said. "Then they will be coming up."

The young man was staring down at the water until the divers bubbles vanished. He looked up to Brian and spoke solemnly.

"Insha'Allah, he said, "As God wants."

Chapter 35

After setting the bezel on her dive watch and watching carefully to make sure Peter's buoyancy compensator was empty, Billie waited until her diving partner made eye contact and gave the circled thumb and forefinger symbol for OK before they began their descent.

The water was brisk, in the lower seventies and immediately Billie felt the cold, even with the wet suit, especially on her face and hands. She instantly recalled her father's ever repeated warning: *The most dangerous thing about the water is the temperature. Even with ninety-degree water, you can still freeze to death. The cooler the water, the faster you die. Hypothermia is always the greatest danger.*

Once again, Billie looked into the eyes of her diving partner. The eyes behind the faceplate always told the truth. A good dive master at a glance could always evaluate beginners. Fear and apprehension furrowed the brow, wide-eyed wonderment represented awe and curiosity, but the most dangerous expression was a pair of unfocused eyes looking upward and clawing for the surface. This was the old killer—panic.

Billie checked her depth gauge. At fifty-five feet, Pete's expression was somewhere between curiosity and apprehension. His breathing was a little fast—he was showing too many bubbles, but that was understandable. Everyone new to scuba sucked a lot of air.

After receiving another positive OK from Pete, Billie looked down and tried to see the bottom. She also tried to judge the current. As far as she could tell there was none. The anchor line trailing from the boat was well inside her range of visibility—a non-straining, white vertical streak going straight down. That was a plus, she considered. Underwater currents could be a nightmare in scuba, sweeping students away from instructors, and experienced divers away from their recovery boats.

The water in Sinop was even clearer than in Key West and maybe even better than Mexico. The light however, was fading, the water getting darker, and the bottom was...moving?

Billie looked over to Pete and saw him pointing straight down. The entire seafloor beneath them was moving. A dark mass, like a gray underwater river was flowing and getting closer as the two divers continued to descend.

Then they were absorbed. Billie reached over just before she was swallowed and pulled her partner close. She was gripping the webbing on Pete's BC as she watched the expression in his eyes. There was no fear, only wonder followed by bewilderment.

The two red suits of neoprene were suddenly surrounded by a thick new environment of undulating gray. The moving mass was so dense that no visibility was possible outside of the two faceplates staring at each other.

They're mullet, Billie thought with amazement—thousands and thousands of the tightly schooling fish she remembered from the South Florida waters. But never had she imagined such an incredible population of the harmless vegetarian creatures. And then, with the same abrupt manner in which they were engulfed, they were below the living river with the rocky seafloor rising up to meet them. With the multitude of fish still traveling overhead, the diffused light from above was only a weak green flicker.

After receiving yet another diver's OK from Pete, Billie checked her watch, dive computer, and her depth gauge. She was eight minutes into the dive at ninety-two feet.

Ahead and to the left, Billie observed the anchor line trailing into the rocks below. On the right side of the near vertical rope, the rocks subsided and a sandy seafloor reached to the limit of visibility. Purple sea fans rose like alien flowers, motionless and still with the lack of current. In the distance, a dark shape loomed on the sandy bottom.

Billie pointed to the darkened mass and continued the descent. When her depth gauge registered 101 feet, the crashed wreck of a large aircraft was easily recognizable. The airplane was huge, with an incredible wingspan. It had four engines, two on either side rested with bent propellers plowed into the sand.

Suddenly, from above, the weak light became stronger as the migrating school of mullet passed overhead. When the full sunshine filtered down to the bottom, it revealed the airplane's fuselage broken into three pieces. The flight deck was still attached to the wing section, but behind the wings several cracked openings showed in the tubular airframe. The tail section still pointed a great vertical stabilizer skyward, but a torn and broken rudder tilted to embrace a huge mound of rising stones. Beyond the lifeless eyes and nose of the aircraft, more of the sea fans grew but failed to reach behind the wings as a tumbled rocky hillock rose to support two upright columns of barnacles and minerals. The story of the rapidly descending plane was clear. The airliner had made a full stop after reaching the two towering columns and the rising outcrop of stone.

Billie watched as Pete's flippers touched the sand. A plume of sediment rose around his feet, and once again, she checked her depth and dive watch, 118 feet at twelve minutes.

Quickly, she motioned him over and reached for his dangling pressure gauge. Pete was showing 2,400 lbs of remaining air. They had both started with 3,400. A check of her own air supply revealed 2,900 lbs. Billie nodded and tilted her head toward the broken airplane.

As the two divers approached, it became obvious that the airliner was quite old. A thick layer of sediment rested like gray snow covering the horizontal surfaces and the once shiny metal was now pockmarked with pebble-like formations of marine growth.

Before Billie could react, her newest student was swimming awkwardly toward the largest crack in the torn-open fuselage. The tear in the metal was large enough for both divers to enter at once, but before Pete could gain the threshold, Billie tapped her dive knife against her scuba tank. The abrupt sound pierced the monotony of underwater breathing and caught Pete unaware as he turned in a cascade of his own rising bubbles.

After his eyes focused and his brow furrowed in question, Billie shook her head.

"No," she signaled, producing an underwater flashlight and switching on a probing beam of warmth.

Pete nodded his understanding, reached for his own light, and added another glowing probe to reach inside the aircraft.

Before he could make an entrance and follow his light beam, Billie recaptured her student's attention as she reached down to the seafloor and selected several fist-sized rocks. Without delay, she swam to the top of aircraft and the highest point of the torn and waiting crevice. She motioned Pete away from the entrance and dropped the stones inside.

With an incredible rush, an explosion of silt billowed out of the broken fuselage and was followed by a fish so large, both divers, forgot to breathe. Billie nodded as she exhaled and pointed to the retreating giant. Billie knew the oversized fish was a Goliath grouper, and that any wreck site with a sizable opening was a perfect home for such a monster. She also knew that the large fish were relatively harmless, unless trapped by divers in a confined space.

Peter shook his head with disbelief, and gave the thumbs up divers signal to return to the surface.

After a quick glance at the dive computer, Billie signaled, "No." She then swam down to the torn open fuselage and looked inside.

After gaining entrance, a thick layer of silt was visible lining the floor of the old plane. Billie quickly indicated the rising clouds of disturbed sediment. Peter nodded his understanding to be careful as both divers continued cautiously into the decreasing visibility.

It was obvious that the main hold of the airplane was empty, and it was also apparent that the old aircraft had been used for some kind of heavy cargo. There were no passenger windows, and the interior of the airframe was lined with heavy netting—heavier now as silt and barnacles clogged the once open ropes.

As the divers exhaled and their bubbles continued forward, the green flicker of sunshine began to fail. The inside of the airliner was a gray cave with the only illumination from the searching beams of the underwater flashlights. After passing the overhead supports for the wing section, forward progress was denied by hanging cables, bits of damaged fuselage, and more of the cargo netting.

Billie turned to examine Pete's expression through the window of his faceplate. He appeared calm enough, though his head tilted to indicate the blocked passage to the flight deck. After a quick shrug, Billie unsheathed her dive knife and began cutting through the heavy net.

Within minutes, Peter had pulled away the trailing bits of cable and wreckage as Billie opened a passageway to reveal the two closed doors of an aircraft bulkhead. With both divers awkwardly pushing on the lightweight panels, a crack appeared as the first metal gate was forced open. A descending fog of sediment blurred visibility as the second of the flight deck doors was pulled ajar.

After quiet moment to allow the silt to settle, the two streaming flashlight beams were centered on the backs of the pilot and co-pilot's flight chairs. As Peter moved forward, he expelled a gush of bubbles.

Sitting at their stations, in the seats where they died, were two human skeletons. Their white bones were a sharp contrast to the gray metal and sediment around them. Both figures were staring forward with eyeless sockets at the sandy powder that covered the undamaged windscreen.

At this depth inside the airplane, the marine growth was minimal, and the labyrinth of flight instruments and control levers were only coated in the underwater dust of time.

Peter was startled back to the present as the underwater strobe of Billie's Nikon camera flashed. She took several shots in quick succession and then motioned her partner back into action. Sitting on the floor of the flight deck, between pilot's seats, were several pieces of silt-covered luggage.

On Peter's first attempt to retrieve the largest satchel, he was rewarded with only a broken handle. This action prompted Billie to unroll a mesh dive bag and together, amongst a torrent of rising bubbles, the dead pilot's belongings were encased in the lightweight netting.

Billie refocused her attention on the dive computer. Bottom time remaining at the current depth of 120 feet was four minutes. When she looked up, she gave the thumbs up, the "Let's surface" message.

Upon returning through the empty cargo hold, Billie's underwater Nikon, flashed repeatedly as Peter struggled with the silt-smoking mesh bag. With a quick pause at the torn entrance to the plane, Billie peeked out and looked for any sign of the Goliath Grouper.

The only sight was the purple sea fans, the mound of rocks, and the welcome vision of watery sunlight filtering down from the surface.

After clipping a short tether onto Peter's diving gear, and then from her own webbing to the heavy contents of the netted bags, Billie pushed the inflation button on her buoyancy compensator. As the two divers began to rise over the drowned plane and the two rising columns of stone, the underwater strobe flashed again and again until the Nikon was out of film.

The river of mullet had migrated elsewhere as Billie coached Peter into a safety stop between 20 and 25 feet. They waited at the decompression stage until Peter had 200 pounds of air remaining. When they finally surfaced, Brian, Benjamin, and the open dive boat were only about fifty yards away.

Brian saw them surface and stood up in the boat, Benjamin beside him.

Billie looked to Peter and pulled the regulator out of her mouth. "Oh my God!" she said. "Those poor pilots—their skeletons."

Now it was Peter's turn. "What about that fish! That huge fish, hiding in the plane!" he gasped.

"It was a giant grouper," she said as she raised her mask.

"How did you know? How did you know it would be there?"

"Pete, it's my job to know."

Peter shook his head dejectedly as the diesel boat rumbled into life. "But the plane was empty," he protested. "Empty, except for the pilot's bags. What if this is some crazy mistake, and all of our time wasted?"

Billie reached over and pulled Peter close. She pressed the inflator button on his BC and again on her own inflatable device. After the hiss of compressed air was silent and the two divers bobbed easily on the surface, the South Florida woman chopped the water with her hand and splashed the Englishman in the face.

"Pete!" she exclaimed. "I know this is important, but as far as wasted time, I just can't see it. That was the most exciting scuba dive of my life!" Her voice was building, "This whole thing—this adventure—Turkey! You and Brian—everything!" Billie shook her head. "I was asleep in my other life, and now I'm alive. My God, I never knew I could be so alive!"

She dropped her eyes and her tone softened to just above a whisper. "Thank you, Peter," she said.

Chapter 36

With the sunset fading and the dusty streets of Sinop falling into darkness, Benjamin Farouk made his way down a narrow alley. After rounding a final corner, he turned back to check the rough plastered walls and the cobblestone passage. No one was there, no one was following. The only sight was the empty trash containers and the backdoor shadows of the harbor side shops. With his palms sweating, and his lightweight shirt sticking to his back, the young harbor captain pressed the doorbell buzzer of the old garage.

Almost at once, the grimy door opened and a thin, dark eyed man with a pale complexion appeared. The man removed a cigarette from his mouth and stood staring. His hands, like his t-shirt were marked with the grease stains of an auto mechanic.

"I have come to see the headman," Benjamin said without preamble.

"And what would such a little fish, have to offer the wolf of Sinop?" The doorman now replaced the cigarette between his lips. His fingers were filthy. As he smoked, his stare became more intense.

"I have news," Benjamin blurted. "Important news regarding foreign strangers." The boy's speech was a rush of the local dialect.

"The wolf is a busy man. You should be warned. He has no time—"

From behind the door, distant laughter erupted and a deep voice boomed. "What keeps you, Emil? Have you forgotten your manners?"

At once, the auto mechanic pulled open the door and motioned the boy inside. After following the doorman down a hallway lined with hanging auto parts, Benjamin entered a cavern-like garage with the rich scent of oil, sawdust, and gasoline. Several cars were stationed beside darkened workbenches in various states of repair. At a far corner, a glass-paneled office spilled electric light from a bank of overhead fluorescents. A single door to the office was open and as Benjamin approached, he tried to calm his breathing as he felt his heart race faster.

As he stepped through the threshold, Benjamin heard the office door close behind him. Before he had time to consider the sound, his eyes focused on a very large man sitting in a modern office chair. The man was huge, dressed in dark slacks, with a white shirt and a loosened red tie. He was clean-shaven except for a small neatly trimmed mustache. His silver hair was slicked back close on his skull. The man was sweating, but cooling himself with a small electric fan stationed on his desk. Sitting around the well-lit office were three other men all like the mechanic who had answered the door—thin, dirty and dangerous. Everyone was smoking.

"Greetings, little brother," the big voice boomed again. "How are you? Will you have a cigarette?" As the big man's ritual Turkish flowed over the room, Benjamin pulled himself together.

"No, thank you, lord."

"May I offer you something? Some baklava perhaps, or something to drink? Emil, serve our guest. Serve him at once!" With the latest command, a sharpened edge appeared in the big man's words.

Instantly, the auto mechanic who answered the door reached over to another desk and retrieved a picked-over platter of the sticky-sweet Turkish pastries. Several black flies were swarming over the abandoned desserts, and as the lowest man in the pecking order offered the baklava, the entire room turned stoic and watchful.

Carefully, Benjamin selected a small-sugarcoated pastry nearest a dirty thumbnail. "With your permission, lord?" the teenager asked.

"Of course, little brother, enjoy."

Promptly, Benjamin popped the candy into his mouth.

"Some tea, Emil, certainly our guest will have some tea."

Before the mechanic could set down the tray, Benjamin offered, "No thank you, *Aga*. I have troubled you enough."

The big man nodded, continuing the tradition. "It has been a long time since we saw each other last. Please remember me to your family."

"Yes, thank you, lord." It was hard for Benjamin to speak with the sticky pastry was caught in his throat.

"You will forgive me," the booming voice explained, "but you must understand. With a town full of growing boys, it is hard for a busy man to remember. Who is your father? How do you know me?"

"Please excuse me, lord, but I have no family here with me. I was born in Ankara." After his initial admission, Benjamin approached, half kneeled and kissed the Wolf's extended hand. He continued formally. "Forgive me, *Aga*, but we have never met before. I only know that you are the *Agam* and the headman of Sinop. I also know of your beautiful fantailed launch—the most exalted craft on the waterfront. I know about your beautiful boat because I am a Captain in the harbor. I work for the—" Benjamin's words fell short as the men in office began to laugh.

"A Captain?" one of the mechanics snorted.

"What man would hire a boy to drive a ship?" another asked laughing as he stubbed out his cigarette.

Benjamin stiffened. "I work for the Dutchman—Van Hymning. He owns the dive—"

Another bout of laughter crowed the room.

"That explains it," Emil, the low man offered with a chortle. "Only a cheap Dutchman would hire a boy."

"Quiet!" the big voice demanded as a massive hand slapped on the desk.

Instantly the office fell silent and the only sound was the buzzing of the flies and the hum of the fluorescent lights.

"But it would take more than a boy to approach the headman of Sinop. Tell me, my young Captain," the wolf continued. "Why have you come? What do you know?"

Suddenly Benjamin was chilled by the tone of the big man's voice. And, just as suddenly, he knew why the headman was known as the wolf. Not only was his hair gray, but his eyes were also the pale color of the predator. And now, for the first time, the man was smiling and his yellow teeth were jagged.

The moment seemed frozen, or perhaps Benjamin realized he was mesmerized by the wolf. He wondered why he was here. Clearly, these were the most dangerous men he could ever imagine. Even with the seemingly harmless banter and the innocence of a second rate garage, the whispered rumors of the wolf and the power of his black hand suddenly rang true. Here was the overlord of the waterfront and the real power in Sinop—the *Agam*.

Now as he stood before the headman and focused to hold back his fear, the young harbor captain concentrated on the one English word and the way it had been guardedly spoken. He considered the poverty he had known all his life, his existence in Ankara as an orphan and a homeless street urchin, his childhood and ever-present love for the sea, and his only mental escape—the fantasy, and then later, the reality of underwater exploration.

165

With the image of such divine beauty and blissful harmony, the teachings of the fundamentalist Muslim came into view—the new teachings that were becoming ever more popular with the up-and-coming Mullahs, the young cleric leaders who focused on politics as well as religion. Opportunities to thwart the English and Americans did not happen often. It was clear they were the enemy and only here as the ancient marauders came in the crusades. They were here to steal the wealth of Turkey. They were here to pillage Islam.

Benjamin stepped forward. "There are strangers in Sinop," he said bravely. "They are not like the normal tourists. I have taken them on the Dutchman's boat. They are looking for something under the water. I think they know a secret about our harbor… Something that has been hidden, but something that I'm certain will be valuable, something that belongs to Turkey."

"I'm listening," the wolf explained, but his eyes never wavered.

"The foreigners," Benjamin confessed. "They have an electronic map—a GPS and they wish to dive and search in a very bad place. Other divers have drowned there."

"Please continue," the yellow teeth smiled.

"They brought something up from the bottom, something in a net. And these foreigners," Benjamin added softly. "The two men are the horrible British. They are so arrogant they must think that I have wax in my ears. Standing in front of me, they mentioned King Midas, and the American woman, the harlot with the yellow hair, she spoke the word, 'treasure.'"

"Please tell me more, my little captain, but now I must insist that you start from the beginning." The wolf leaned back in his chair and lit a fresh cigarette. "Tell me everything," he said as he exhaled. "Tell me all about the horrible British."

Chapter 37

Brian pulled back a strand of hair and lit a cigarette. He was looking through the recently developed photographs from Peter and Billie's dive. "I don't understand," he said. "The satellite coordinates are perfect. There can be no mistake!"

Peter swirled his scotch and took a sip. "It is a big plane, but it certainly is empty," he sighed and crossed the room. "I doubt if there's any gold in that old pilot's box. It just doesn't seem heavy enough." Peter shook his head and studied the underwater photographs.

He continued with a somber voice. "Brian, I know you feel confident, but maybe this is a mistake—a big mistake, a software glitch or some kind of failure in the telemetry program." Peter looked past the open French doors to the terrace beyond.

Billie had her own room, but she was now standing on the open-air balcony of Brian and Peter's suite. Even with her new clothes, she appeared comfortable and causal. She had reverted to her trademark attire: a pair of jeans and a long sleeved shirt. The shirt was extra-large, rolled up to the elbows, and cross-tied at the waist.

The second story balcony overlooked the waterfront and the darkened harbor. After the first night in the single rooms, Brian insisted upon the most extravagant accommodations available.

"I can't concentrate in cramped quarters," he had complained. "We need the space for planning and privacy, and luxury is always the key for inspiration." After the expensive upgrade, all of the staff in the little hotel were beyond obsequious and treated the English-speaking foreigners as if they were visiting royalty.

Lost and Found

Billie reclaimed all attention as she walked into the suite. "It's not a mistake," she insisted. "It's just part of a puzzle. And I say," she added, as she placed her hands on her hips, "That the latest clue is ready to be opened."

After returning to the waterfront Inn, Brian and Peter helped as Billie placed the contents of the mesh diving bags into a bathtub of fresh water. After a few moments, disappointment had flooded the Turkish tiled bath.

The pilot's belongings consisted of four satchel bags, two of which were filled with the remains of sodden books or hardbound paper files. The paper inside the volumes was beyond readable and only a mush of gray and white mud.

The third case contained more destroyed paper, two bottles of what looked like wine or spirits, and a small leather folder that had once held identification or pilot's credentials. The brown dye from the leather had totally corrupted any readable information.

The forth container held a metal box fused with rust, bubbling corrosion, and marine growth. "The bottles and the box had better soak a while," Billie offered. "The fresh water will loosen the salt."

"Let's try the bottles first," Brian now suggested.

Billie nodded as all three gathered around a large glass-top table. She produced a new pocketknife and lifted the first wine-shaped flask. Carefully she tilted the bottle and watched the liquid inside. After scraping away the corrosion, she easily twisted the metal top.

"It smells like cherries," she grinned.

After sharing her discovery, the second bottle was just as easily opened and exposed more of the cherry liquor.

Brian poured the spirits into a glass and examined the clarity. It was perfectly clear.

"Don't taste it," Peter warned. "The metal from the top might have dissolved and caused some type of contamination."

Brian sat the glass down and focused on the drying metal box. The container was a perfect square, about the size of a large dictionary. "Billie," he said. "May I borrow your knife?"

Within minutes, a pile of crusted marine growth littered the table. Brian sat in his chair and pulled on a large corroded latch. After a moment of struggle, the lid popped open and the rich scent of oil filtered into the room.

"Oh my God," Brian whispered. "It's dry!—It's dry inside!"

A khaki cloth covered the contents, but after the oily rag was removed, Brian lifted an automatic pistol with a long snout. The pistol, like the inside of the box was completely dry, but shinning with oil.

"It's a Luger, A German Luger," Peter exclaimed as he reached to take the weapon.

"And ammunition," Brian voiced as he began removing box after cardboard box of what was obviously new cartridges. At the bottom of the metal container were two loaded clips, each with bright new bullets showing at the top of the magazines.

"Then the plane was German? From World War Two?" Billie asked excitedly.

"Of course," Brian added. "The age would be about right, and the liquor—cherry liquor. All the Germans in Argentina were mad about cherry schnapps."

Billie nodded. "They call it *Kirsch Wasser*," she explained.

Peter pressed a button on the side of pistol and a magazine easily slipped out. The gun had been loaded. He worked the cocking mechanism and pointed the barrel to the floor. The dull click of the firing pin sounded as the trigger was pulled.

"Wow," Billie commented. "I guess it still works."

"Perfectly," Peter offered.

"But how can an empty old plane and two dead Germans trigger a survey anomaly searching for gold?" Brian paused and once again lifted the glass of cherry liquor. He sniffed the clear contents and stared into the glass. "How can this be part of our puzzle?"

Peter slipped the magazine back into the gun and released it again. He seemed fascinated, his mind elsewhere.

"Maybe," Brian offered, "the gold slipped out of the plane—during the crash. It could be under the wings or under the fuselage."

Billie shook her head. "No, Argentina. The bottom of the plane is intact, and so are the wings."

Brian frowned at the comment as he continued to examine the schnapps glass. "The satellite survey is accurate," he said firmly. "I am absolutely certain."

Peter raised an eyebrow to Billie and placed the Luger on the table. He picked up the stack of underwater photographs. One by one, he spread out the glossy prints and stood staring.

After a few moments, Billie was beside him. "What if the plane is not part of the puzzle?" she asked. "What if the plane is only a distraction?"

"What do you mean?" Brian looked up. "There can be no mistake. The satellite survey is linked to a precise GPS location. An exact position with only a few meters of discrepancy, the German aircraft site is the only possibility."

Billie now reached forward and began gathering the photos taken inside the plane, the multiple shots showing the empty hold of the airliner, the crashed tail section, and finally the cockpit with the two white skeletons sitting in their chairs.

"But if the airplane is empty," she insisted. "Why should we continue to look there?" She pushed her gathered photos aside and realigned the remaining glossies. The photographs which remained were the ones taken after leaving the interior of the aircraft. The pictures showed the outside of the sunken airliner and the surrounding seafloor.

As Brian stood to watch, and as Peter looked over Billie's shoulder, her finger pointed to the sandy bottom. "Listen," she said. "I'm a diver—right? I never really traveled that much, but I always read the diving magazines. It's fun to read about exotic and faraway diving."

After a pause, Billie pointed to the Luger. "That gun!" she said excitedly. "It reminds me of something. I just remembered a story about a place called Truk Lagoon. Truk is an atoll in the Pacific. A big battle was fought there in the war against the Japanese. Many ships were sunk and now it's a diver's paradise."

"So...?" Peter and Brian asked together.

Billie grinned. "The Japanese lost a lot of ships, but what no one knew until years later, was that there was another ship—a ship from the first world war—a German ship trapped under a new one from the Japanese."

"Christ-all-bloody-mighty," Peter muttered.

"Oh my God," Brian exclaimed. "That's it! It's under the plane!"

"Maybe, maybe not," Billie continued carefully. "Look here," she now pointed to the two photographs that showed the best view of the entire airplane.

The first of the glossies captured the fuselage and wings, but also showed an endless sandy bottom interrupted only by the purple sea fans. The other photo showed an almost identical view of the sunken aircraft, but filled the far side of the frame with the rising hillock of marine growth and the two columns of crustaceans that were so prominent upon Billie and Peter's descent.

Behind the left wing and the torn open fuselage, the oblong mound of crusty rock seemed to crowd the old airliner as the two rising columns tilted away. The barnacle-crusted hillock looked like other stone formations nearby, but as Billie tapped her finger on the two rising stone columns, she began to smile. "How old was the King Midas ship?"

"Around 700 BC," Brian reported, but his face was puzzled.

Billie now looked to Peter. "Do you see it Pete?" she asked. "Do you think it's about the right size?"

"Yes, but my God, how could we have missed it." He was staring at the side-by-side photographs.

"Missed what?" Brian now insisted.

"Argentina," Billie explained, "you sometimes don't see what you're really looking for. What do you think a 2,700 year-old shipwreck would look like?"

After a pause, she pointed to the hillock and the rising fingers of stone. "Here, Argentina, this is it. This is your ship. The hull is crusted over and the rising columns are the masts of King Midas's ship."

Suddenly, there was a shouting voice calling out in Turkish and a scraping sound coming from the open balcony. The shouting voice was obviously one of an alarm and clearly disturbed.

Brian and Billie were first to the balcony and were surprised to see a figure drop from their second story railing and collapse onto the street below. Then the man was up and running, but clearly favoring a damaged ankle. The Turkish voice called out again and Billie and Brian turned to see another man in pajamas shouting after the retreating runner. The man in pajamas was yelling from a nearby balcony. Obviously, a neighboring guest had surprised a man hiding in the shadows.

"Wow," Billie said. "What do you think that was all about? He was here! Right here on our balcony!"

"Yes," Brian agreed, and asked, "Do you think he was a thief?"

"No," Peter said quietly. "He was listening."

Chapter 38

"No, this is not possible," the Dutchman spoke in heavily accented English. "No diving today," he explained.

"But why?" Brian insisted.

Peter, Brian, and Billie, were standing across the counter from Van Hymning, the owner of the local dive shop. The Dutchman was a tall man in his late sixties with a florid face and a full head of white hair.

"Perhaps the day after tomorrow something will be available," Van Hymning offered vaguely.

"Captain Benjamin assured us that he and your boat were certainly for hire. We came in good faith and we expect a boat, dive gear, and a guide." Brian now leaned forward and leveled a stern gaze at the dive shop owner. "We want our boat today."

"Benjamin Farouk cannot speak for the dive shop," the Dutchman shook his head. "He is only an employee. He has no knowledge of previous reservations."

"Apparently your knowledge of future reservations is also in question," Peter countered dryly. "Will your next boat be available the day after tomorrow or not?"

Van Hymning flushed at the remark and made a pretense of looking through a hardbound ledger. Abruptly he closed the book. "I must confer with my local clients before I can commit to any future dive charters."

"Oh my God!" Brian could hardly control his rage. "This is ridiculous," he added, pointing to the open dive boat tied to the waterfront dock. "Where is your charter? Where is Benjamin? We would be willing pay double the regular price."

Again, the Dutchman shook his head. "I am afraid this is not possible."

"But, sir," Billie stepped forward. "It is such a beautiful day. Maybe you would have something other than diving. The small sailboats—would one of those be available?"

Billie was looking out through the dive shop windows to the sun-splashed waterfront. A light breeze was flowing in through the open door as the masts of three different sailing rigs bobbed on the dockside wavelets.

"I am an experienced sailor—I have a Captain's license," Billie smiled sweetly.

Van Hymning seemed to hesitate, but surrendered after Billie reached across the counter and took his hand.

"Please," she said.

"Very well, but no diving gear, and I must insist that you stay well in sight. If you cannot see the dive shop, then you are too far out. If you cannot see the dive shop, then I cannot see you. I must insist that all my sailing boats remain in sight. After all," he added. "What if you become disabled and need assistance?"

After making somewhat of a pretense and shopping for a picnic lunch, Billie cast off the lines of a seven-meter sailboat. She waved to Van Hymning as Brian and Peter pushed away from the dock.

With a quick pull on the main halyard, the mainsail was set, Billie sat by the tiller, and the boat heeled as it caught the breeze.

"Bloody bastard," Brian remarked as he glanced over his shoulder at Van Hymning.

"Not now, Argentina," Billie instructed. "Pete, pull up the jib and we'll be outta here."

Peter obeyed and the little seven-meter was soon under full sail. The on-shore wind was just beginning to whitecap, and as the sleek little boat footed across the harbor, Brian reached into a canvas bag. He removed his hand-held GPS and retrieved a new pair of high-powered binoculars.

"Careful," Billie advised as the boat heeled over with the wind and increased speed.

Brian scrambled to a less precarious position, handed the GPS to Peter, and lifted the safety strap of the binoculars over his head.

"Billie," he asked after he was settled, "How did you know?"

"It's just another part of our puzzle," she answered as she reached to trim the headsail.

After agreeing to hire the sailboat, Billie insisted upon a picnic lunch. She led the way as all three hurried through Sinop to the two other diving shops. As Billie had guessed, in every dive shop the story was the same.

Each of the diving boats and charters had been mysteriously booked, but every boat was deserted and tied to the dock.

Peter and Billie bought bottled water and takeout lunch while Brian shopped for binoculars. Within the hour, they had returned to Van Hymning's sailboats.

"Local clients," Brian mocked the Dutchman's accent as he cracked open a bottle of water.

"Well, if we have any luck," Peter commented. "We might get a glimpse of the locals that were listening at our window. It's just all too convenient."

"Yes," Brian exclaimed darkly, "too convenient to be anything but trouble."

"This is totally my fault," Billie said regretfully. "I opened my big mouth and Benjamin heard me. He must have been the one listening at the window. I'll bet he wasn't around today because he has a sprained ankle—a sprained ankle from jumping off our balcony."

"Billie, please don't blame yourself," Peter shook his head. "Face it. We are a suspicious lot," he gestured. "Two decrepit, expatriate Englishmen and a beautiful American girl. We're bound to be up to something besides an innocent holiday."

"Me? Beautiful?" Billie mouthed and pointed to herself. She eased the mainsail and pulled back on the tiller. The boat responded and fell off the wind, reaching for the bight of headland and the nebulous edge of the Black Sea.

"I don't know, Pete," she said after her course correction was complete. "I don't think that you and Argentina are so decrepit. You two make a pretty good looking pair."

"Thank you, Billie," Brian grinned, but Peter was blushing.

After a few repeated tacks, the boat skimmed across the water and was on an approach to the sunken airplane. Brian peered through the binoculars until his eyes hurt. He then referred to his GPS. "You were right, Billie, someone is there. Stationed just over our wreck site."

"I can see that, Argentina—even without your fancy eyewear," Billie was squinting.

Peter took the binoculars and looked for himself. "It's a large sailing vessel at anchor and quite old," he said. "But we are too far away to see any activity on deck, or in the water."

"Here, Pete, you steer," Billie commanded. "Just keep her on the same heading." After Peter took the tiller, Billie lifted the binoculars.

"She does look old, and around ninety to a hundred feet. That was a hell of a schooner in her day. I'll bet she is at least fifty or sixty years old, maybe older." Billie fell silent as she continued her inspection. "Ah, now that's interesting," she said. "They have her main boom rigged over the water—like they are using it as a crane. For lifting," she added.

"It's hard to believe," Brian sounded dumbfounded. "They acted so fast and on such a tiny bit of information.

"Yes, but that's the difference between winning and losing." Peter's voice was dejected.

"Wars have been won or lost on less intelligence," he added. "A spy in the right place and all bets are off."

"Last night I was so excited," Brian remarked. "I could hardly sleep. I thought that this time we would really find an example—an example of lost gold. I cannot believe that someone has beaten us and plundered our satellite research."

Peter interjected. "I'll wager they have been over the wreck since first light. I wonder," he paused to look up at the sails and then over to the black schooner lying in the distance. "How long it will take to excavate an ancient ship and salvage what is really there? If it actually is King Midas's treasure, can you imagine such a quantity of wealth?"

"No matter," Brian sounded defeated. "When an entire town can be controlled and made to turn a blind eye, what chance do we have? We are only three tourists."

"Brian, you're right," Peter nodded. "The power to control Sinop and the waterfront must be substantial. They are obviously well organized, and obviously, with what is at stake, dangerous."

"We do have ninety-five more anomalies," Brian offered. "I have already marked the next best site. It's a lake in Mongolia. A place called Uvs Lake. It's cold but very shallow—"

"I cannot believe what I am hearing!" Billie interrupted. She had pulled down the binoculars and was staring. "You guys are actually thinking about walking away from this?"

Billie made a show of pounding her head with the palm of her hand. "I can't believe it," she continued. "Tell me that I'm wrong. Tell me right now. Please tell me...that...we...are...not...walking away! Tell me!" she insisted.

"But, Billie," Peter began. "What are we going to do? Call the authorities and complain that someone has beaten us to a treasure trove of Turkish antiquities, a treasure trove that we did not ask permission to excavate. Perhaps we should explain that we are illegal archeologists, and upon success, potential smugglers."

"Peter's right," Brian chimed in. "We have no chance against whoever that is." He tilted his head toward the black hull of the distant sailboat.

Billie shook her head. "No," she said. "We are not giving up." After a moment with her jaw firmly set, she began. "Listen, I didn't want to tell you before, but I don't think Pete and me could have hacked our way through that marine growth without major help. We would need a lot of equipment, more divers, and at least a week to recover anything. Now, we have that problem eliminated."

The two men looked at each other.

"Don't you see," she said. "We already have the bad guys doing the hard part for us. All we do is wait until they're finished, watch that old boat, and take a little sample of what is rightfully ours. Just like you said, Pete—we don't need the whole treasure, just enough to cover expenses and prove that your satellite works."

"But how?" Peter and Brian asked together.

"Don't worry, boys," Billie grinned. "I've got a plan."

Suddenly, the intimate huddle was broken and all concentration flew away from the little sailboat creaming over the waves. In the distance, toward the wreck site, a low rumble of thunder rolled over the water.

Quickly, Billie refocused the binoculars. After a moment, she passed the eyewear to Peter.

"Pete, check it out," she said. "But, before those hydraulic waves subside, you'd better let Argentina have a look.

Brian nodded after the binoculars dropped to his chest. "My God," he exclaimed. "They're using underwater explosives!"

"Argentina, you're catching on fast." After her comment, Billie took the tiller and tacked the boat. Once the boat turned, the weight shifted, and everyone switched sides, she eased the headsail. The little seven-meter was now broad-reaching toward the isthmus and the waterfront of Sinop. With the wind white-capping the water nicely, the hazy effect of salt spray softened the town and blurred the distant image.

At a glance, Peter guessed that they were sailing five or six miles offshore and that the black-hulled schooner was anchored over the wreck site at about ten. He looked over to Brian who was trying to light a cigarette in the breeze, and at Billie who winked at him as soon as she caught his eye.

Peter smiled instantly, but his brow furrowed as he spoke over the wind. "I think that with the underwater explosives, our week of excavation just turned into one day. Tomorrow in fact."

Billie nodded, "Pete, you're right. This new life style is just getting faster and faster."

Chapter 39

The Wolf of Sinop was standing on the wooden deck of the old schooner. He was joined by his two closest confederates, Sali Tuz, the mechanic, and Yarin Dun, the knife. All three were exhausted. The last forty-eight hours had been an exercise in excitement that none of the men ever dreamed possible.

"Alright listen," the Wolf began. "We don't want any more mistakes. We already have too many loose ends and the gossip onshore must be building into a climax."

Yarin nodded as he passed out cigarettes. He looked across the harbor to the waterfront lights of Sinop. A chill in the evening air was spreading across the anchorage as the three figures began smoking on the darkened quarterdeck. The long black hull of the little ship was nearly invisible as she now rode deep in the water. Her masts showed no anchor light although she was moored very near the waterfront and the coastal village.

"I know how to handle loose ends," Yarin explained quietly. He tilted his head toward the well-lit docks and the harbor-side hotel.

"Loose ends are easy, but not even the prophet can stop gossip," Sali the mechanic offered.

"The foreigners are to be ignored," the Wolf's voice broke in. "They are only trouble if they turn up missing. An investigation from Ankara is the last thing we need. We will open the garage tomorrow and stamp out any rumors as we continue our normal routine."

"This is crazy," Yarin spat on the deck and looked up with a grimace. "How long do you believe this old hulk can stay afloat?"

"You're right, little brother," Sali agreed. "Everyone knows an old boat is held together only by habit. The wood is so old she rides the water as if she is already sinking. Are we to lose everything because we fail to act, because we waited too long?"

"Enough!" The wolf's voice was menacing. "Have you both forgotten your place? Have the last two days challenged your minds? Perhaps the knowledge of what we carry pulls away the fabric of loyalty."

After a pause, the headman ground out his cigarette and let his fluid Turkish flow over his men. "Who would believe that an old, abandoned boat could hold a king's ransom? I will tell you," the Wolf confirmed. "No one! Do you not believe that I have thought this thing through? This vessel has been afloat for over sixty years and she will certainly swim for a few more days. Would you consider that I am a fool—a fool that has taken in the dregs of Sinop? You were nothing when I found you! Nothing!"

In the following silence, the Wolf suppressed a smile as he evaluated his subordinates. He felt certain they would remain loyal for at least a few more days, but with the building and burning knowledge of what had been found, the basics of human nature were completely unpredictable.

The men from the waterfront were simple and uneducated, but he had trained them well. They were only muscle without a brain—energy without direction. It had taken five years of careful planning to conquer Sinop, five safe years in a backwater town, away from the limelight, and away from Interpol.

The Wolf's given name was Tarik Oclay and he was a wanted man. An international fugitive wanted by Interpol and the Italian and French authorities.

"Excuse me, lord," Emil had climbed on deck and was now another underling waiting before the Wolf. "I think the boys," he continued nervously, "I think the boys are getting worse."

Without comment Tarik Oclay motioned his men forward. The Wolf began his descent down the companionway. Below decks, the schooner smelled of pine tar, mold, and years of neglect. The old hull creaked as a pressure lantern hissed and forced threatening shadows into hidden corners.

After gaining the main salon, Oclay dropped to one knee and looked in on Benjamin Farouk. The young harbor Captain was sweating even though the Turkish night was cold. He was huddled under a moldy blanket and obviously in great pain.

Without hesitation Oclay pulled away the cover and signaled Emil to fetch the lantern closer. As the harsh lighting invaded the berth, the boy's eyes fluttered open.

"Help me, lord," the clenched jaws begged. "It's the sickness, the de-

178

compression sickness. We did as you asked. We removed every piece—every piece of the—" A spasm gripped the young man and forced him into the fetal position. As the convulsion raged, Oclay studied the hands, which were drawn into claws, and the bulbous joints of the wrists and elbows that were swollen like misshapen potatoes. The ankles and the knees were equally afflicted. After a moment, the inner struggle subsided.

"Please, lord," the desperate voice gasped. "We must get to the hospital. How are the others? I tried to explain—we stayed down too long—too long and too deep. How are the others?" he repeated.

"They are well," Oclay lied. "It is only you that contracted the sickness from the deep."

With defiant exasperation, Benjamin shook his head. "No," he said. "That is not possible. We were all down together. We were all down too long—you insisted we recover everything. We did as you asked." The face in the lantern light twisted. "The hospital..." he pleaded.

"No, my son, not now, there would be too many questions. You must endure the night, and then tomorrow, perhaps—"

"No! I cannot." Benjamin was beginning to ride a new crest of pain. He cried in panic. "Please, for the love of Allah! Have mercy!"

Oclay looked over his shoulder. "Yarin, spare him further pain."

Before the Wolf moved away, Yarin Dun was ready, the blade of his stiletto shining in the lantern light. With the practiced skill of a professional, the boy was instantly dispatched and wrapped in the sodden blanket.

"The others? Are they as bad?" The wolf looked to the shadows of two other bunks.

"The young one is gone," Emil broke in. "The other in a coma."

"Finish your work, Yarin, and then join us in the hold."

With the hissing lantern guiding the way, the Wolf led his remaining men out of the salon and into the depths of the schooner. The ribs of the little ship cast shadows along the planking but could not hide the running-rust streaks bleeding down her sides. Above and across the original sole of the bilge, new timbers had hastily been installed to reinforce the old and weak flooring.

Advancing now to the mid-ship of the hold, the Wolf of Sinop smiled as he stopped to inspect his cargo. A strange transformation had changed the lantern light from a cold wash of white to the warm glow of gold. Lined and stacked along the entire centerline of the schooner were hundreds upon hundreds of lozenge shaped bars.

The radiant bullion captured the light, melted the shadows, and transformed the interior of the old trading vessel into a palace of golden delight.

Mesmerized by the shimmer, the five men stood in silence as the wooden hull rocked on the water and creaked under the newfound weight.

Yarin appeared in the glow and nodded, his task complete.

"Three of us will remain onboard at all times," the Wolf began. "Then, when the time is right, in three or four days, we will sail the ship down the coast and rendezvous near Toplu. Sinop is out of the question—too dangerous and too many people. There have already been inquiries and there could be complications. The American woman I am told is a hell-cat and the British men are not stupid." Oclay glanced around, studying his men, looking for defiance.

"Once we are safely docked," he continued, "I have made arrangements and we will be met by three special men—the drivers of three trucks who will arrive and transport our retirement into Istanbul."

Before the underlings could digest this new and unexpected information, the Wolf nodded to the oldest of his men who was the master mechanic. "How is the engine, Sali? Can she make a voyage of sixty kilometers?

"Not without work. The diesel is Chinese and original—as old as the ship."

"So," Oclay frowned, "you have three days. I assure you the effort will be worthwhile."

"But the parts, Tarik. I told you the engine is Chinese."

"And I told *you*! You have three days."

In the following silence, the Wolf considered his position. His body was tired, but his mind seemed to be fueled with an energy that was somehow magical. As he stood watching Sali, he knew that his mechanic could restore the old engine and he could also sense that the naturally gifted engineer would relish the work so near the old king's treasure. All of the men had a new light in their eyes, even the stupid Emil. The gold had a life force, and it was all-consuming and all-powerful.

After commandeering the old vessel and watching Sali crank the antique diesel into life, the expedition for the Wolf and his men had almost been like an outing or a holiday. The young Farouk had been well prepared, and brought two other youngsters out from the harbor. The two harbor boys flitted importantly around the deck checking their frogman gear as the eager young captain steered the old trading tramp to the correct location. After the boys went down and confirmed what Emil had heard on the balcony, the French plastic explosives were lowered into the water.

When the undersea explosion finally detonated, the old ship rocked as giant bubbles rose to the surface. This again had seemed like a boy's adventure out on the water, playing with fireworks, until the three boys went back over the side and came up almost immediately. When they surfaced, the life force of the gold was already upon them.

The Wolf now understood how the life force worked. When the Farouk boy rose to the surface, his eyes were wild as he ripped off his facemask. He then raised an arm and a hand, and a single gold lozenge rose out of the water and caught the light. The other two boys had surfaced afterward and their single gold bars joined to form the three points of a triangle glinting in the sun. The boys could only surface with one lozenge at a time, as the gold bars were simply too heavy. This was the moment when everyone on the little ship caught the fever—the moment when the life force of the gold slipped inside each man.

Everyone was transformed and changed. It was as if they were drunk, but not on something as primitive as alcohol, but something more pure and almost divine. Every man was beyond excited, joking, and filled with compliments and good humor. With every full net hauled aboard, the men cheered as if they were all winners at some unbelievable soccer match. The excitement levels did not stop with fatigue, but only intensified into a brooding and private calculation. Every man was focused and alert, but inwardly lost as each contemplated future fantasies previously unconsidered.

Even the low-brained and clumsy Emil had suddenly become nimble and full of useful ideas. He had immediately suggested a heavy net be lowered to the bottom so more of the life force could be recovered and brought to the surface.

All the men were fortified and pulled for all they were worth as net after net of the precious gold bullion was landed on deck. Every suggestion, from every man was considered as the life force increased and the dripping lozenges of gold collected heavily.

After the boys came to the surface, their air tanks and their bodies exhausted, the Wolf began his questions. "How much more remained, and how much longer?"

Grimly, the Wolf listened as the already exhausted Farouk made his explanations. The explosives had opened the marine growth, minerals, and barnacles, the boy explained, and now a cave-like entrance was exposed to enter the ancient wreck. Inside and beneath the seafloor covering, the old wooden hull had been incredibly intact.

The multitude of gold bars was lined for and aft, but shifted and tilted as the old king's ship lay on her side. Recovery had been a simple and straightforward effort, but time-consuming as the three young divers were forced to reenter again and again into the ancient and cavern-like hold. Miraculously, most of the lozenge–shaped bullion was unaffected by the great time underwater, and only the surface layers of the primitively cast ingots were slightly pockmarked by underwater contaminates. The gold bars from the center of the treasure appeared like polished jewelry with the decorative scribing of ancient hieroglyphs.

After the first of their air tanks were empty, all three divers insisted that a surface interval must be observed and that an immediate rest was needed, as they had already broken the safety rules of deep water diving.

Tarik had chided the youths with his "hail-fellow-well-met" exuberance, and playfully insisted as fresh scuba tanks were handed down that this was a once in a lifetime experience. The three boys would be rushed to the hospital after their work and every effort would be made to protect the heroes of the hour. But after the fourth and final exchange of air cylinders, there was little doubt on the troubled and beleaguered faces, and as the final net was pulled to the surface the three boys abandoned their dive gear and shouted that the job was complete.

The decompression sickness began one hour later, but even as the three boys began to obviously suffer, the welcome knowledge that fewer hands in the pot could only mean more gold to share.

The Wolf was brought back to the present, as were all the spellbound others, when Emil spoke over the hissing lantern. "I think we should all stay on the ship—all the time," he suggested. His voice was even and strong like the rapidly growing life force that had slipped inside him.

"Emil, you are partially right." The Wolf began carefully. "But it will be my choice as to who will stay aboard and guard our fortune well. If something should happen over the next three days, and anyone should fail," the wolf lowered his gaze, "then pray that you never see my face again."

After a silent moment in the golden light, and his latest statement answered only by the hissing lantern, the Turkish voice continued with a business like tone. "There will be no more suggestions regarding opinions or leadership, or with any other direction that I might offer."

Tarik Oclay took a moment to examine each man before him. They were all stronger now, he considered, and more dangerous. All filled with the magic and the life force that was rapidly turning to greed.

"Yarin, go with Emil," the wolf commanded. "Wrap the boys in their blankets until we return with bags of plastic—the bags of plastic used for trash. Then they can be sealed and we will not be troubled by the smell of their spoil."

"But Tarik—" Sali began his protest. "Why wait? We can weight the bodies with chain and put them over the side. And by the way? Who are these special men with trucks, and why not dock at Toplu? What is this place you speak of...*near* Toplu? Where are we going?"

"No!" the voice of the wolf boomed. "*I told you,* no more opinions and suggestions. And now, I will add to *that*, no more questions. Because you are all now rich, would you believe that you have become more intelligent? Would you believe that we are now a committee? No!" Oclay insisted. "The last thing we need is bodies in the harbor, breaking loose, and washing onshore."

After a thoughtful pause the Wolf continued darkly. "I have had this experience before. In Italy. Near Capri, there were two bodies. Weighted with stones and tied with chains, but after a time...they still came up. Now understand, and listen carefully." The Wolf shifted his gaze as he was brought back to the present. "I have made careful and well-thought-out arrangements," he continued evenly. "The rendezvous location and the men that will come to help are none of your concern. Anyone who does not wish to follow my guidance will join the boys in their blankets."

Chapter 40

Cedric unfastened his safety belt and popped a breath mint. The small airplane had been a pleasant surprise and the nighttime air travel pleasing. The Black Sea coast was cool and dry and very much like the weather in Cape Town. The night was perfectly clear, the salty wind rising, and the tiny airport of Sinop deserted. Stretching his legs, the security director stepped off the boarding ladder and onto the rough tarmac.

Mustafa closed his cell phone and looked up quickly. "The taxi is late, effendi. Would you care to wait in the airplane? Or perhaps the men in the fueling station have prepared fresh tea."

"No," Cedric replied. "I would like to know, with complete certainty, where my Englishmen are staying."

"Of course, effendi. But unless they have moved, the English are still at the Harbor Side Inn with the tall blond woman. I made a call before we left Istanbul. My latest information is only a few hours old."

"I see," Cedric suppressed a smile. Mustafa was very efficient, even more so than the best of OPC's nighttime security—even better than some in the South African Security Force.

With the aid of Mustafa, the surveillance of Pauliss and Clopec to the Black Sea coast had been simple. The Turkish guide was clearly well connected. He had immediately established a link to the hired car that had taken the two Englishmen and the American woman to Sinop. After three phone calls, Mustafa was speaking to an innkeeper at the harbor-side hotel. The presence of the three foreign tourists was easily confirmed.

184

"Effendi?" Mustafa's voice interrupted. "Do you wish the aircraft and the pilot to remain after tomorrow—to remain here in Sinop?"

"Yes, make all the arrangements necessary. I want the plane available until further notice. Make sure the pilot can be ready for takeoff within the hour. Any hour," the security director added, "twenty-four-seven."

Mustafa stepped up to the aircraft cockpit and unloaded a Turkish barrage. Before he finished speaking, the pilot began delivering a reply. With animated gestures toward the aircraft radio, the Turkish aviator spoke forcefully.

"What was that all about? What did he say?" Cedric demanded.

"Some weather is coming, effendi," Mustafa offered, "A low pressure system moving down from the north. The locals have a name for this weather condition. The 'Poyraz' is a fast moving line of high wind and thunderstorms. These summer storms, they come from Russia. Our pilot says sometimes they can be quite severe."

After stepping down from the airplane and closing his door, the pilot now joined Cedric and Mustafa on the tarmac. "I know a little English," he explained. "To operate an aircraft, across international borders, one must have some basic English. I will tell you something," the aviator continued. "We could have high winds by morning. Wind and storms. We have no good weather to fly. No chance." The pilot now folded his arms. "Tonight, I will tie down the airplane, very tight."

Before further comment was possible, Mustafa's cell phone rang. After briefly acknowledging the caller, the Turkish guide listened and hung up.

"Effendi," he began. "The Englishmen and the woman, they have left the hotel. My sources report some activity in the harbor. Apparently they have taken a small sailing boat."

"You?" Cedric was addressing the pilot, "What is your name?"

"Ahmed, effendi." The hired aviator was a slight man in his late twenties. He was prematurely bald and in the darkness, his Ray-ban sunglasses rested high on his forehead. The young man was curious and attentive, his eyes intelligent.

"If the aircraft is grounded I will require your service elsewhere," the security director explained. "As a pilot, you must know something about boats—about the water."

"Well, yes, effendi. I have some experience with boat."

"Good, I will make new arrangements with your pay scale. You will be well rewarded."

"What?"

"Never mind! Mustafa get on the phone and find out what has happened to the car, and make arrangements for the harbor. We need a taxi and we need to hire a boat. Do it now!" he ordered.

Before the security director could finish, a pair of headlights probed across the airfield, and as the car turned and began driving down the runway, a yellow taxi sign became illuminated.

After the car stopped and all three men were installed, the Black Sea Taxi man began rattling away in the local dialect. Mustafa and Ahmed immediately joined in and a three-way conversation erupted as the car left the tarmac, bouncing along the single-lane road leading from the airstrip. When at last, there was a lapse in the dialog, and the pilot and Mustafa fell into an obviously troubled silence, the security director spoke.

"Alright," the Afrikaans accent insisted. "Tell me. What's going on?"

"There is more trouble than the weather, effendi," Mustafa offered. He was distracted as Ahmed interrupted. After a heated and gushing exchange, the private pilot returned to his facing-forward position in the front seat, his mind made up and his attitude determined.

After a moment to reflect, Mustafa lowered his voice. "Effendi," he began. "These small coastal towns, they are not like the big and modern cities. Not like Istanbul and Ankara. Here along the Black Sea there are many old traditions. In these regions, there is always a man, an *Agam*, a headman who is apart from the police and the official authorities. This is an individual who is always a man of business, but a man who secretly runs the town. He controls crime with a very strong fist, and as a result, there usually is none. No criminals, no theft, no fights or arguments. The local police, you must understand, with a man like this, they can relax and have a very nice life." Mustafa paused and glanced at the silent figures in the front of the taxi. It was obvious the driver and the pilot in the front seat were concentrating and trying to understand the English words spoken in the back.

"And your point is...?" the security director now sounded impatient.

"Effendi, this head man of Sinop, he is a very dangerous and powerful man. Our driver has explained that the entire harbor has been shut down. This headman who controls everything, he is known as The Wolf. He has complete control. There is no chance to hire a boat."

"Don't be ridiculous," the Afrikaans accent graded. "If my Englishmen have hired a sailing boat, then I must have something better—something faster."

"But, effendi, the English and the woman, they did not hire the boat, they took it. They were due back after sunset. The owner of this little boat has already made a complaint. He has spoken to the management at the hotel. Effendi, you must understand. Nothing has been said, but our driver has spoken of an old sailing ship anchored in the harbor. There are many rumors. No one has seen anything, and yet everyone is watching. Something important is about to happen. Also, every person knows about the American woman and two English who follow her as if she is a dog in heat."

Mustafa paused and added quickly, "Should I instruct the driver to take us to the hotel—the hotel where the British and the American woman are staying?"

"No, have him drop us at the harbor—to the docks or the pier."

After the driver was paid and dismissed, Cedric led the way along the harbor-side quay. Mustafa and the pilot moodily followed. The street beside the wharf was deserted, the wind rising, and the lights of the waterfront the only illumination.

As the three men moved among the shadows, a fleet of boats bobbed uneasily under a lowering sky. Above the harbor lights, and the old Mediterranean buildings, the streaming fringes of fast moving clouds were rushing away from the land and out toward the darkened anchorage. In the distance, a multitude of boats was silhouetted against the darkness with only a few showing anchor lights. The largest vessel in the crescent-shaped bay was a black-hulled sailing ship with rising masts reaching toward the clouds. The old-style coastal trader was at once conspicuous, anchored alone and away from the other boats.

The security director stopped beside the most handsome cruiser tied along the wharf, a fan-tailed launch of about thirty feet. The sleek craft was obviously cherished, well maintained, and expensive.

After looking up and down the waterfront, and satisfied that they were alone, Cedric began."Until now, it has not been necessary to identify my position, but as the politics of this region have now been made clear, steps must be taken to ensure success." The security director paused as he took a moment to regard each man carefully. He reached for his wallet, opened the folded leather, and produced the forged FBI/X-files credentials.

"I am a Federal Agent of the United States Government," Cedric lied. "And I am here in Turkey to apprehend fugitives—individuals who have committed crimes against the United States." The security director waited for the appropriate reaction as he looked into the faces of the two men who were watching. After receiving a suitable and astonished response from Mustafa, Cedric waited until the Turkish guide translated for the pilot.

"But, effendi, what can we do?" Mustafa stammered. "We have no training as police!"

Cedric shook his head. "I have all the training necessary, but I must have help. I am now in a position to offer a substantial reward for important services rendered."

"What? What do you say?" Ahmed the pilot broke in. Quickly Mustafa explained.

As he listened to the flowing Turkish words, Cedric Bowles jumped down into the fan-tailed launch.

"What are you doing, effendi?" Mustafa's voice was an urgent whisper as he looked up and down the waterfront. "That is a private boat," he insisted, "private property!"

Without an upward glance, the security director disappeared under the canvas top that swept back from the windscreen and covered the steering station. After only a few minutes, with Mustafa and the pilot waiting nervously on the wharf, the sound of a well-tuned engine broke the silence and rumbled against the quay. When the marine motor idled down nicely, Cedric appeared on the fantail and motioned the two men into the boat.

"Mustafa, get the pilot down here! I can get any engine started, but I prefer not to drive. Don't worry, I have complete authority to conscript this vessel. Now get aboard and let's get started."

Before the launch was well away from the quay, Cedric had found a flashlight and was searching through the forced open storage lockers. He was pleased to find the harbor craft well equipped. There were no firearms, but many useful items that inspired a roughly thought-out plan.

As the handsome little vessel motored through the swells, the security director sat on the fantail and examined the two Turks who stood in animated conversation beside the steering wheel. He raised a pair of binoculars and peered through the darkness until he found the old trading vessel. Very quietly, he began to giggle.

Chapter 41

Billie handed the binoculars over to Brian and again gripped the tiller of Van Hymning's sailboat. "Alright, here we go," she explained. "Those two on the quarterdeck must be the only ones onboard. This should be simple," she added. "After you guys get on deck, I'll climb up from the stern and create a diversion."

"What kind of diversion?" Brian asked quickly, his voice a whisper.

"Don't worry about that, Argentina, just be ready."

"Billie, are you sure?" Peter was also speaking softly. "I have no doubt these men will be dangerous. We could all be placing ourselves beyond our limits."

"I'm telling you, Pete, this thing will be over before it even starts. We have the element of surprise and believe me, that's everything."

Full darkness had covered the anchorage an hour after sunset, and as Billie tacked the little boat through the harbor and around the other boats, Brian smoked and fidgeted while Peter checked the gear.

Earlier in the day, Van Hymning was approached and agreed to rent the seven-meter for a sunset and evening cruise. Billie had then shopped for a small rubber raft that was normally sold to beach tourists. It was now inflated and tied to the foredeck of the sailboat.

"OK, Argentina, get ready." Billie steered the seven-meter directly in front of the old schooner and the rising bow now blocked out any view but the front of the ship. With the tiller pushed over, the sails back-winded and Van Hymning's day-sailor drifted to a stop.

189

Lost and Found

Nervously, Brian pulled the slipknot that held the raft in place. After a brief struggle, the raft bobbed in the water and Peter and Brian scrambled onboard. A canvas bag followed along with two small paddles.

"Alright, just like we planned, climb up the chain plates quietly, hide behind the cabin-house and give me about ten minutes." Billie was looking down at the two shadows crowded in the raft.

"Ten minutes from now or ten minutes after we get on deck?" Brian was checking his watch.

"Argentina, just play it by ear. These guys aren't the military and they're certainly not expecting to be boarded. And remember, be careful with the bag and don't use that flare gun unless you really have to. That old boat could catch fire like a box of matches."

Brian nodded in the darkness and Peter whispered, "Billie, please be careful."

"Don't worry boys, you'll see me on deck," Billie promised. She ducked under the mainsail and with a tug on tiller, she was gone with the breeze.

"This is crazy," Brian hissed. "How did she talk us into this?"

"Too late to think like that," Peter offered. "Let's paddle for Christ's sake."

With Peter's instruction, the little toy paddles bit the water and the tiny inflatable moved ponderously toward the darkened schooner rising from the water. Before they could reach the worn planks of the hull, they could smell the pine tar of an old wooden vessel. Small wavelets splashed white along the waterline, and as Peter looked up, the blackened masts and rising rigging seemed to reach all the way to the stars. He looked over to Brian and felt another bout of rising heartburn.

Brian looked ill. Even in the darkness, Peter could tell that he was sweating profusely. His skin tone was shining and very white against the black turtleneck and trousers that he wore, and his hair was wet and plastered to his forehead. With a quick glance toward the waterfront, Peter tried to focus on Billie's darkened figure beneath the ghosting sails, but she was already gone, also dressed in a black turtleneck and trousers.

Just after the little raft bumped into the curving wall of timbers, Peter checked the German Luger that was tucked into his waistband. The pistol was loaded and he had both of the extra magazines tucked into his pockets. In the canvas bag was Brian's flare gun—also purchased earlier in the day, as well as additional star shells and assorted items from a local hardware store. With every paddle stroke along the worn and blackened hull, Brian was looking upward as if the silent dipping of the oars might attract attention and cause Turkish turmoil to rain down on their heads.

After a few more tentative strokes, Peter reached out and grabbed one of the heavy wire cables leading aloft to the foremast. The terminus of the shroud that supported the mast was connected to the hull with heavy bolts fastened into the planking. Three such chain plates stood proud from the hull and each rose into the darkness to become part of the old schooner's rigging.

With a loop of line, Peter quickly tied the little raft to the center guy-wire. He then shifted his weight and pulled himself onto the side of the hull. An easy foothold was found on the chain plates between the rigging and the rusty fittings fixed into the planking. As he stood carefully gripping the first of the rising wires, Peter looked up to the bulky railing that led to the main deck. With one hand on the rigging and another on the bulwark, he placed his other foot on a section of rub rail. With a natural movement, he pushed, pulled, and quickly found himself standing on deck. After a quick glance, fore and aft along the weather-beaten topsides, he looked over the side and motioned Brian upward.

Within seconds, Brian had passed the canvas bag over the railing and after a precarious minute of scrambling, he was another silhouette on the long narrow deck. The foremast rose from alongside their position and led aft to the mainmast that towered even higher. From behind the masts and beside the steering station of the schooner, a dim light glowed and cast lengthy shadows.

As Peter placed a vertical finger across his lips, he nodded to the glow and the Turkish voices that murmured from the afterdeck.

Brian nodded and reached into the canvas bag to retrieve his flare gun. After quietly cocking the signaling pistol, he looked at his watch and tilted his head toward the glowing light and the distant voices. "Let's go," he mouthed, "over ten minutes." He then darted around the foremast and disappeared behind the cabin-house on the other side of the deck.

With every step leading aft, Peter's heart pounded faster and his heartburn rose higher. He now held the German automatic in his right hand as he made a crouched and cautious advance. He was very worried about Brian on the opposite side of the deck.

Billie insisted that a two-pronged approach was necessary, but Peter knew he would never forget Brian's expression as he ducked and disappeared along the other side of the bulwark. Academic professionals, like Brian, were simply not cut out for this type of cloak and dagger operation.

This is madness—what were they doing? Peter's mind screamed. He paused to look across the cabin house for some sign of Brian.

He could picture his friend with flare gun in hand, creeping toward the voices he couldn't understand, and the soft glow of light from the stern. Peter considered the fact that the ammunition for the Luger was sixty years old and had been stored for six decades underwater. Even if the gun worked perfectly, Peter's mind raced, what was he going to do? Murder two Turkish strangers? Kill for a sample of what *might be* lost gold?

Before his imagination could speculate further, Peter was crouched beside the aft-end of the main cabin and watching the mysterious apparatus that had taken control over Sinop—the men with power over every dive shop owner and the hidden force responsible for the spy on the hotel balcony, the calculating figures which had brutally used explosives to plunder a 2700-year-old shipwreck, and a well-organized group that without thought managed to destroy a priceless archeological find.

Aft across the quarterdeck and sitting at a camping table, were two ordinary Turks who appeared to be playing cards. A lantern on the table illuminated the little scene, but forced the men to hold their cards almost flat on the table. With every card drawn from the deck or as another was discarded, a remark, a curse, or an outbreak of laughter followed.

Just as Peter was trying to determine what was being said or what type of game was being played, Billie jumped over a section of bulwark and landed on deck. She still wore her black trousers, but her turtleneck was gone. She was topless and even in the dim lantern light her breasts were exquisite. For a moment, Peter was paralyzed by the sight, as were the two Turkish guards. Billie stepped forward with her chest out and her hands on her hips.

"All right, by God," she said loudly. "Have a good look at a true American harlot. Get your eyes full, so my Africa and Argentina can get the drop on you!"

When Peter finally looked back to the Turks, they were standing in front of their knocked over chairs and gaping at Billie. With a quick glance across the decking to the other side of the cabin-house, Peter saw that Brian, although captivated, was ready with his flare gun extended. Without thinking, Peter crossed the open decking and stood with the German Luger leveled. He was facing the backs of the two Turkish men when Brian moved up beside him.

"Turn around slow—" before Peter could finish, both of the Turks turned in surprise their faces registering shock. With a reaction so fast that it seemed impossible, the first of the guards pulled a knife and was now waving the long blade as a challenge in front of the German Luger.

"Pete, watch out!" Billie cautioned.

Suddenly, the skinny Turk with the knife lunged and Peter stepped back. With a double snap-bang, the Luger popped two very loud rounds that shot splinters up from the decking. The bullets from the German pistol had fired into the deck on either side of the man with the knife, but before the skinny man could drop his blade, and the knife tumbled down, Brian was under attack from the other guard. This man had simply reached forward and was now struggling with Brian for control of the flare gun. Before any weight could be lent to the altercation, the struggle was over. The flare gun belched a star shell of flame soaring above the rigging and onward toward Sinop.

Peter fired the Luger again, this time aloft, and after the loud report, both of the Turkish guards raised their arms and their expressions registered a miserable defeat.

"Good job, Pete. Argentina." Billie spoke as she stepped forward. She had just pulled on her black turtleneck and was standing in the lantern light smiling.

Quickly, she circled behind the Turks, and approached Brian. After giving him a big bear hug, she knelt to the canvas bag and removed several large, zip-strip wire ties. She winked at Peter after she approached the Turkish men and kicked away the fallen stiletto.

Within minutes, both of the guards were sitting on the deck, back-to-back, and bound tightly with the new-age plastic binders. With another flash of her grin, Billie reached into the canvas bag and unrolled two long sections of duct tape. The skinny Turk, who had been so dangerous with the knife, started to fight the tape across his mouth but soon relented after Billie pulled at an exposed section of chest hair.

The other man offered no resistance to the gag, but soon after Billie was finished, two sets of dark malevolent eyes stared outward above several layers of heavy silver tape.

"My God, Billie, you were fantastic," Brian began. "You were right," he said. "We captured the schooner. I can't believe it was all so easy."

"And Peter," Brian gestured, "You with that pistol. It was as if you were trained by MI-6. You were bloody brilliant!"

"That's right, Argentina, Pete was great, but so were you. I've never seen such bravery. That guy," Billie pointed to the heaver-set of the two staring Turks. "He tried to take away your flare pistol."

"It was so *exciting*." Brian had crossed the deck and was now standing next to Billie. He raised an eyebrow. "Especially your diversion and entrance, my God, but that was clever. You were so—"

"Yes indeed," Peter stepped forward, the Luger securely replaced in his waistband. "Billie, you *are* perfection beyond description."

For a second, Peter was confused. The look of shock that accompanied Billie and Brian's expression was unnerving. They were both frozen and staring, but seemingly gazing through him with great alarm. For an instant, before he could react, he understood why. There was a third Turk, one that had been below decks.

When the blow came, it was not really a surprise, only when the deck of the schooner rose and slapped him in the face did Peter realize that he was hurt.

After Peter's collapse, Billie's words reflected her disgust. "You god-damned sneaky bastard," she muttered.

Like Brian, Billie was staring at the waterfront Turk who had climbed out of companion way and struck Peter with an oversized wrench. The dar-kened man from below decks was older, of medium build and height, and still gripped his chosen weapon tightly.

With Peter immobile, and face down on the decking, Brian started his reactionary move to help. This action prompted Peter's assailant to gesture with his wrench, shake his head violently, and shout something that was easily interpreted as "no." Before Brian could stop, Billie began inching her way toward the other side of the deck, her intention at flanking the Tur-kish man obvious.

Even without the feeble lantern light, it was easy to establish that the third man on the schooner was a mechanic. His shirt and trousers were fil-thy with grime, and with his emergence on the quarterdeck, the scent of diesel oil crowded the salty air.

Once again, the grease-blackened Turk shook his wrist with the wrench and shouted for Billie to stop. Before she could react, the afterdeck of the schooner was flooded with powerful searchlights.

Chapter 42

After years of practiced surveillance, the security director knew when it was time to react. The sound of gunshots was defiantly an indication to move, but the orange streak of a signal flare was even more compelling. Without hesitation, Cedric ordered Mustafa and the fantailed launch into action. The distance between the old sailing vessel and the recently acquired boat was covered in a matter of minutes.

"Blind them with the searchlights and tell them we are the police—the secret police" the security director added. He reached into a storage locker and produced a portable electric bullhorn. After a few seconds, the device was turned on and thrust into Mustafa's hands.

"But, Effendi—" Mustafa began to protest.

"Do it, tell them now!"

As the harbor launch settled into its own waves, Cedric braced himself against the rolling of the boat and passed a second spotlight to the Ahmed the private pilot. "Here!" the security director commanded.

Within seconds, the powerful twin light beams defeated the single lantern shining on the schooner. The entire afterdeck was flooded with the harsh lights as Mustafa's voice rang out with a loud metallic resonance. Even before the Turkish warning finished, Cedric roughly signaled the pilot to advance and pull alongside. With his shadowed expression revealing only shock, the misplaced aviator complied and the harbor launch bumped into the wooden hull with a sickening thud.

"Here, take this," Cedric handed over his light. "Stand high enough to keep them blinded," he ordered. "And tell them that they are under arrest.

Tell them not to move."

Before Mustafa or Ahmed could respond, their recent employer was scrambling over the launch and climbing up the battered sides of the old coastal trader.

When the security director landed on the deck, he crouched into the standard military position as if he carried a pistol. He smiled when he realized this maneuver was unnecessary.

Upon a glance, it was obvious that the situation was under control. There was only one man who had the potential to be an obstacle, but he was standing with his hands on his head with the international stance that was the symbol for surrender. Two other men were sitting back-to-back on the deck, gagged with tape and obviously tied and restricted. Near a cabin house entrance, three other figures were huddled on the deck—one prone and laid out, with the other two kneeling alongside.

"Mustafa, get up here," Cedric ordered loudly.

"On the top of my head, Effendi," was the answer from below.

Just after the blinding spotlights winked out, and the surrendered man with his hands on his head became suspicious, Mustafa and the pilot were also onboard. At once, they tied the grease-stained hands behind the man's back and soon the obvious mechanic joined the two other captives sitting on the deck.

"Oh my God!" Brian exclaimed as his eyes readjusted. "You're Cedric Bowles."

The security director could not help himself, he giggled. "What a profound discovery, Doctor Pauliss."

Cedric crossed the deck and retrieved Brian's abandoned flare gun. Quickly, he snapped open the barrel and ejected the spent cartridge. He bent to explore Brian's canvas carryall and shouldered the bag after reloading a new signal flare. After a quick appraisal of the wooden-spoke ship's wheel and glance around the lantern-lit stern-quarters, the South African approached and looked down at Billie. She was now sitting on the deck and holding Peter's head in her lap.

"How is he?" the security director asked dryly.

"Unconscious," Billie replied without an upward look.

"Alright, tell me everything," Cedric insisted. "Why are you here and what have you found?" The security director was halfheartedly pointing the flare gun.

"What do you mean what have we found?" Brian was rising from the deck. "What the *hell* are you doing here, and how did you *find* us?"

"Doctor Pauliss, please try not to be boring. Quite obviously, I have followed your exploits since leaving Texas. You were easily tracked to that miserable village in Florida and onward to here. I am in direct contact with the chairman of OPC and represent the interests of the satellite mining division. The stolen interests, I might add. Now tell me, what have you found and why are you onboard this vessel?"

"My God," Brian sputtered. "You *followed* us—like a spy?"

"Argentina!" Billie interrupted. "Get me some water. If Pete has a concussion, he needs to wake up. Do it now," she demanded.

Without thinking, Brian crossed the deck to the Turk's camping table retrieving one of the guards' glasses and tea pitcher. He returned to Billie's side and gently began to pour the dark liquid over Peter's forehead. Within seconds, Peter gasped, he shook his head, and his eyes opened.

"That's my boy," Billie said softly. "Can you see me? Can you focus?"

After a silent moment of regarding Billie's features, Peter raised his head and looked around. "Billie," he said. "When I first saw your face, I thought you were an angel. But now," he muttered, "I see the devil, and he looks like Cedric Bowles. I must be in hell."

The security director crossed his arms. "Well, almost, Doctor Clopec. But before you can contemplate your after-life further, perhaps you can fill in the missing gaps and tell me what international crimes you have committed, where are the firearms I heard earlier, and *why* you are here?"

"International crimes? Whatever are you talking about?" Peter tried to rise but Billie held him back. She adjusted herself, smoothed her turtleneck and helped Peter to sit up.

After rubbing the back of his head and checking his fingers for blood, Peter glanced at the two men standing on the quarterdeck. "Who are they?" he asked.

"Never mind," the South African accent was determined, "I'll find out why you are here, and what's going on." Before his words were finished, Cedric Bowles crossed the deck and took the lantern from the camping table. He then disappeared with the light down the companionway.

When the cabin entrance went dark, Brian shook his head. "My God!" he exclaimed, "I can't believe that bloody bastard is here in Turkey!"

"Well, he is," Peter offered. "I guess we should have expected this."

"Wait a minute," Billie interrupted. "Who is this guy?—some kind of cop? Could he be the FBI? The same FBI man the deputy was talking about in Goodland? The one who supposedly took Buddy to the county seat, but never showed up, the one who was at the marina when the fire trucks came?"

Peter shook his head, still groggy. "No," he said. "He's not the FBI, just a security man from OPC—our petroleum company in Texas."

"But a buggering bastard all the same, and a cold blooded one at that,"

Brian added.

"A bastard that knows what you two are looking for?" Billie's eyes were searching. "A bastard that might do anything to find what we have found...a person so desperate that he would do anything to cover his tracks?" After a pause, the probing gaze settled on Peter.

"Don't forget, there was a woman killed at the marina fire—a woman that the deputy thought was me." Suddenly Billie bit her lip. "Buddy is a bastard too," she said, "but never for a minute did I believe that he could really kill someone—especially a woman. And, the more I think about Goodland and the fire, I know that Buddy would never burn down the marina. He knew that after his arson charges my fire insurance was canceled. Without the marina, Buddy would have been homeless. Homeless and an arson suspect."

Across the deck, the two Turks that arrived with Cedric Bowles were watching intently. They obviously understood some English and their ears were focused.

"I got a bad feeling about this guy," Billie lowered her voice and tilted her head toward the companionway. "I have the feeling that *he* may be the source of all of our bad luck. I am also getting my woman's intuition signals that Buddy might have finally met his match."

Even in the near darkness, Brian and Peter could not fail to notice the single tear that was hastily wiped away.

"Oh my God!" Brian exclaimed. "If he followed us here—all the way to Turkey, and to Florida, he could certainly have followed us to Kinko's on the night that Becca was killed."

"Brian, you're right, it could all be that simple." Peter's face suddenly registered shock, and his voice began rushing. "Remember the ultimatum letter and the video. Only a security man would think of a surveillance tape, and only Becca's murderer would want to frame us for her death. The buggering bastard could have easily followed her to Kinko's and killed her when she came out. He quite possibly raped and killed her, but discovered he was too late. That's why he followed us all along, because on the night that he killed Becca, he didn't find the disk or he couldn't crack the encryption. He was forced to follow to see what we found."

"And speaking of bastards," Brian's tone reflected his disgust. "What if Haggly-Ford is behind all of this—manipulating everything to save his skin and the company, controlling everything from Texas, everything including murder, mayhem and the lot." Brian jerked a thumb to the darkened cabin house. "That bloody South African is only an Apartheid hatchet man. He could never have financed this on his own. Haggly-Ford must be the culprit, the head of the snake, and ultimately responsible."

As Billie and Brian helped Peter to stand, Cedric Bowles emerged from the companionway. He looked shaken, flushed, and was holding the lantern loosely as if he might drop the light. His eyes were darting around the deck and finally he giggled.

"It's true," he whispered, "all of it," his words dribbled on, "more than I could have ever imagined." The OPC man now seemed beside himself and on the verge of losing control. He giggled again.

"Effendi?" Mustafa interrupted as he stepped forward from the shadows. "A boat is approaching," he warned. "It looks like we have visitors, and by the looks of these scoundrels, I cannot believe we can expect a friendly meeting." The hired Turk was regarding the three tied and sullen figures staring upward from the decking.

The security director now tore his eyes from the passage to below decks, and peered out over the water. After a moment, he replaced the lantern on the table and turned to the two Englishmen and the American woman standing at the railing.

"Its decision time," he said, "and from now on, I make the decisions. "From now on," he repeated, "I am in charge."

With a glance at the flare gun in his hand, an obvious change shifted in the South African's demeanor. "Now tell me," the Afrikaans accent demanded. "Where are the firearms I heard earlier? I heard a handgun, some kind of pistol. Where is it now?"

"It was his." Billie said without delay. She tilted her head toward the nearest of the three Turks tied and sitting on the deck. "The greasy one, he threw it overboard," she embellished, "When you blinded us with the lights," she added.

The security director winced. Across the anchorage, a small boat was racing over the rising waves. In the distance lightning streaked across a cloud-line and thunder rumbled ominously.

Ahmed the pilot stepped forward and pointed to the clouds. "The weather report was right," he said. "The Poyraz is coming. I told you," his voice grated, "these storms from Russia—they can be very dangerous."

From across the water, toward the harbor lights and the waterfront, the wind was rising dramatically as a heavy bank of low rolling clouds was tumbling over the isthmus. A flurry of whitecaps was racing over the darkened water as the old decks began to lift with the waves and move underfoot.

Chapter 43

"**M**r. Chairman, Angela Barnes is here to see you," Haggly-Ford's receptionist spoke into the intercom on her desk.

"I'll just slip in," Angela offered with wink. She was already in mid-stride headed for the big double doors. Today she was wearing a black pants suit and the pressed seams were sharp enough to cut.

"But, Ms. Barnes," the receptionist objected. The busty girl was half out of her chair with her heavily made up features registering a scowl.

"Don't worry, honey," Angela whispered before she opened the door. "He won't be your boss much longer."

When the door closed, Haggly-Ford was rising from his desk. "Angela, what a pleasant surprise," he said. "I was just thinking—"

"A surprise yes, but pleasant is hardly the word that comes to mind." After she interrupted, Angela crossed the room, squeezed by Haggly-Ford, and sat down in his chair on his side of the desk. After a quick scan of his computer monitor, the elegant lawyer began.

"Alex...where is Peter Clopec?" she asked the question nonchalant.

"Well...I'm not quite sure. Why ever would you want to know?" Haggly-Ford was now on the guest side of his desk and looking down. He felt his face flush with the question, and his heartbeat quicken.

"What about Brian Pauliss? Where is he?"

The collar of the chairman's Valentino shirt suddenly tightened. "As you know they have been dismissed—terminated from the company," he hesitated. "They moved the satellite. They were drunk—"

"*So* I have been told," Angela's voice was cutting and dry as ice. "Alex," she continued, "I don't have time to chase you around the merry-go-round. Kindly answer my questions and do not cover the facts with your fancy English pudding. I repeat, where are Pauliss and Clopec?"

Haggly-Ford could not hold the icy-blue gaze. He turned away from his desk and began pacing. His hands gathered behind his back as he toured the floor-to-ceiling windows. His eyes shifting to the nodding pump jacks and the bright desert day.

"Clopec, I believe is Hungarian—perhaps he is in—"

"No, Alex. Don't even go there," Angela shook her head. "For your own best interests I strongly suggest that you drop all pretenses. I want the truth and I want it now."

From across the room Haggly-Ford turned and raised his hands. "Angela," he began in protest. "I really don't think—"

"What about Cedric Bowles? Where is he?"

Haggly-Ford shook his great silver head, determined to remain silent, but his face was a flushing red mask.

"Alright, fine," the practiced lawyer's resolve seemed to melt a little. "How about a trade, quid-pro-quo? I'll give you something vital and interesting, for every honest answer *you* give me."

"Well, I don't—"

"Good, I'll go first," Angela leaned back in the big executive chair. "I know that the satellite never really worked. And I also know that if your fancy spaceship was a fake, then *you* are an accessory to fraud."

"That's not true," the chairman protested, "It worked in the end, and they definitely found results."

"Who did? Pauliss and Clopec?" Angela leaned forward.

"Yes," Haggly-Ford admitted. "If you must know, my security director has followed them. Cedric Bowles followed them to Florida and then onward to Turkey. Positive results from the satellite surveys have now been authenticated."

"Well, at least that's something—although it doesn't really matter to me." The gambler in Angela Barnes now showed her poker face. "I am here to formally tender my resignation as a member of the board."

"But why?" the chairman stammered. "With your investments, I thought you would certainly—"

"No...no...no... That's not how it works, "Angela shook her head, "quid-pro-quo—I give you something, and then *you* enlighten my side of the picture. The more we share, the better we feel."

"Very well," the great silver head wobbled. "Pauliss and Clopec are in Istanbul—they have been there over a week—at the Hotel Four Seasons. Now," he asked. "Why would you give up a seat on the board?"

"Oh, that? That's over now. I resigned from the board first thing this morning—just before selling my stock."

Haggly-Ford's color now began to drain. Slowly, he took the necessary steps to rest his hands on the desk. "But that's not possible," he shook his head. "The insider trading issues—the SEC."

"Doesn't matter anymore," Angela cracked a smile. "You remember that NASA press release on falling space junk—'the redundant hardware' as you called it. I have an old friend down in Houston. We went to school together at Radcliff. She works at the Johnson Space Center in public relations."

"What?"

"Yes, Barbara Stone, she really was quite obliging. She agreed that the once a month press conference was simply inadequate for this day and age. She started the first of the new weekly reports this morning—early this morning."

"That cannot be possible," Haggly-Ford felt the office tilt as his temples began to throb. A high-pitched note began in his ears as the queen bitch continued.

"After the OPC satellite was publicly listed as lost," she explained cheerfully, "I sent my resignation to the board—in certified mail, and then called my stockbroker. I really did get a good price, but that was hours ago, before the sell-off really started." The Texas lawyer raised an eyebrow. "I think OPC is now trading at about ten dollars a share, but that was earlier," she added, "before I came over."

Haggly-Ford was staring, his face registering disbelief.

"I can see that you're a little preoccupied, so how about if I go ahead and give you one more—a freebee for our quid-pro-quo?"

Angela now leveled her gaze. "After the press conference," she continued, "I called Roy and all the investors from the board. I believe they also sold most or all of their OPC shares. I have a clear conscience on everything, but there is one...*little*...troubling aspect."

With Haggly-Ford hanging on the last of her words, Angela frowned, shook her head and offered a pout.

"Alex, did you know there is a least fifteen percent of OPC stock that is unaccounted for? Fifteen percent." she repeated, "At least fifteen percent that nobody can figure out. I'll just bet it's from an overseas broker, a broker that hasn't heard the news about the sell off."

"You Bloody Bitch!" the curse was pure contempt.

"Why Alex, I'm shocked," the Texas lawyer enhanced her southern accent. "Such language to a lady, and from an English gentleman."

"You bloody...buggering...sodding...*bitch*!" Haggly-Ford gasped. He

202

pulled at his tie and ripped open his collar. There was no air in the room and his lungs were on fire. Clearly, the OPC chairman was having trouble breathing. He lunged for the telephone. Paperwork went flying. The oil well clock tumbled to the carpeting, and the elegant red telephone disappeared behind the desk.

"I'm ruined," he croaked. "You've ruined me! Get *out* of here! You whore from the devil! Get *out*!" the chairman was stumbling.

"Alex, you must really learn to control your temper—you don't look well." Angela was standing from the desk. Are you having chest pains?" she asked. "Do you want me to help you with the telephone? Maybe I should call someone? Someone like an overseas stock broker, the SEC, or maybe even 911?"

Just after his left side became fully numb, and his vision darkened, Alex Haggly-Ford felt the pump jack in his chest explode. In the growing darkness, over the endless sound of the off-the-hook telephone, he heard the queen bitch for the very last time.

"Alex," she said sweetly. "Never screw with a Texas woman and her money."

Chapter 44

After an abrupt flash of lightning, and the following rumble of thunder, all focus shifted away from the schooner's quarterdeck to the little fishing boat bouncing over the waves. It was now very apparent that a thunderstorm was building and the approaching outboard was beleaguered by the rising wind and seas.

Another flicker of lightning streaked across the clouds as raindrops began to pepper the deck. With the added illumination, it was obvious that several anxious figures were huddled around the little center console and very intent upon converging with the anchored sailing ship. It was also clear that the wind was increasing as the old schooner turned her head to face the building storm.

"Pete, Argentina, let's get out of here." Billie spoke over the rain spatters and the freshening wind. She crossed the deck and looked over the bulwark. The fantailed launch was moving in the swell and grinding against the wooden hull.

"Hey, you two," Billie was regarding the two men that arrived with Cedric Bowles. "It's time to go—do you speak English—do you understand? We need your boat," she insisted. She looked across the afterdeck and focused on Van Hymning's sailboat. The little seven-meter was now well astern, its mainsail luffing wildly as it had obviously broken loose and was drifting downwind.

"No! We are not going anywhere—no one is," the Afrikaans accent explained. Cedric Bowles shook his head. "You!" he pointed to Billie. "You're the expert. Get this vessel underway—away from that boat." He pointed

Brian's flare gun at the approaching center-console.

"You're crazy," Billie replied with her hands on her hips. "Those guys are going to be armed and they're going to be dangerous."

Cedric cocked the flare pistol and pointed at Billie's face. "I won't tell you again," he threatened.

Billie took a step forward and stared down the barrel. "You shoot me and you'll never get this hull underway."

"Now see here, you bloody apartheid Nazi," Peter interrupted. He was approaching with Brian in tow, but suddenly lost momentum after checking a missing portion of his waistband.

"Very well," Cedric shrugged. He shifted the flare gun and pointed the makeshift weapon at Peter. "Perhaps I should make an example of one of your boyfriends," he said. "Then you would know that I'm serious." The security director now tilted his head and gestured to the carryall bag draped over his shoulder. "I have more than enough cartridges to ruin both of these English fannies and anyone else that chooses to interfere." He paused for but a moment. "I am becoming impatient," the South African accent warned. "We are running out of time."

"My God, man, have you lost your mind?" Brian's voice exploded, as did another strike of lightning and an almost instant crash of thunder. The offshore wind was mounting and the waves in the harbor ghostly white in the near darkness. "There is no time for this—don't be foolish," Brian shouted and gestured over the whitecaps to the approaching boat. "Don't you realize what is at stake?"

But as everyone turned to look, it became apparent that the little fishing boat was having trouble. The center console was clearly visible—laboring at about one hundred meters away, but dipping into the rising waves badly. As a fresh spatter of rain swept across the decking and another stoke of lightning cracked across the sky, it was suddenly clear that the men in the converging boat were several minutes away.

"No, Doctor Pauliss," Cedric raised his voice over the wind. "It is you who does not understand! You haven't been below—it's obvious! None of you could understand unless you've been below." With his latest statement, the security director whirled around and focused on Mustafa and the reluctant pilot. "Get over here," he motioned roughly.

Obediently, against the wind and the increasing rain, the two Turks gathered.

"Mustafa, ask him if he can get this thing under sail."

After a quick exchange, the aviator-boatman shook his head. "No, effendi," Mustafa replied. "But perhaps with the motor—"

"No," Cedric interrupted. "The engine is dismantled—completely out of order—no chance for the motor! I have been below, I have seen every-thing," he now insisted. "I have made a complete inspection." The security director was now thoroughly soaked, as was everyone. His entire being, however, seemed elsewhere, his head turning and his eyes darting about, blinking against the rain.

"What did you see below—what have you *found*—what is so impor-tant?" Peter's voice was pitched above the wind.

After a glance over his shoulder, and a confirmation that the little cen-ter console was still battling the waves, Cedric Bowles began to giggle. "It's all there, in the hold," he insisted. "Beyond everything I could have hoped for."

Suddenly the roving eyes centered and the pale features focused. The OPC security director was back. "Young woman," he said, "either you get this ship sailing immediately, or Doctor Pauliss dies now!" Cedric took the necessary steps to place the barrel of the flare gun against Brian's left eye.

With an automatic reaction, Brian started to back away, but with a sa-vage reaction that surprised everyone, the trained security officer grabbed and twisted, and held his victim fast. It was clear that the pistol was al-ready cocked, and with the determined expression on the South African's face, Billie shrugged and reached into her pocket. She produced her pock-etknife, opened the biggest blade, and handed the knife to Peter.

"Get forward, Pete," she said, "and find the anchor line. Pray that it's not chain or wire, but don't start cutting until I tell you."

Reluctantly, Peter took the blade and disappeared as he moved into the foredeck shadows, his dark clothing masking his movements.

"Alright, I've heard your demands, now *you* listen to me!" Billie's voice was determined. "It takes a crew to sail a boat this big, and if we are going to get this old lady moving, I'm going to need everyone's help. But first, let go of Doctor Pauliss and un-cock that flare pistol."

"Very well," Cedric replied. He lowered the signaling gun and gestured to Mustafa and the private pilot. "Do it—whatever she says."

"Argentina," Billie tilted her head toward the steering station. "Stand by the wheel and get ready."

"Ready for what?" Brian's expression was equal parts puzzlement and panic.

"Just get ready. You're going to drive."

"But I never—"

"I know, but I need you here—OK?" Billie held Brian with her gaze. "No matter what happens, stay by that wheel. Don't worry," she added. "I'll tell you how to steer once we get started."

After a disgusted glance at Cedric Bowles, Brian nodded.

206

"Now the rest of you, come with me!" Billie ordered.

With the wind alive in the rigging and the deck beginning to roll, Billie grabbed the lantern from the camping table and led the way to the forepeak of the schooner.

Peter was there, leaning over the edge, his hair and clothing wet from the rain. "I found it," he shouted over the storm. "Its rope, but it's big— maybe too big for your knife."

After only a glance," Billie nodded. "That's OK," she answered. "That blade is plenty sharp, and the anchor rhode is hemp. Hell, that old line is probably as rotten as the sails." Billie shook her head and pointed to the tied and bundled canvas on the old schooner's booms. She shrugged, looked up and down the decking, and then aloft into the foul night. "This is getting pretty crazy, Pete. I hope you can forgive me for talking you into this."

Peter shook his head. "No Billie, its Brian and me who should apologize. We had no right to involve you in such danger."

Cedric Bowles crossed the deck, abandoning Mustafa and the pilot, his eyes darting from the approaching boat until he stopped and focused on Billie. "I realize this is a wonderful night for romance," he said sardonically, "but I must insist that we get moving." He tilted his head, and pointed to the upcoming intruders. "That lot will not give up until they take this boat. And they will not take prisoners who can turn into witnesses."

"How do you know that?" Peter demanded, wiping the rain from his eyes.

"Never mind, Pete," Billie interrupted. "Get back to that anchor line, but don't start cutting until I tell you. Then be careful. That old line could part easily and snap back like a whip, especially with all this strain from the wind."

After Billie's warning, another bolt of lightning flashed nearby and the rising waves were illuminated before the following crash of thunder. Coming closer, the outboard boat with the center-console was larger, and the rain-soaked men onboard were staring malevolently. Without a doubt, the distance between the two vessels was closing.

"Alright now—the rest of you, over here—quickly," Billie's voice was pitched over the wind, and when she moved to the base of the foremast, Cedric Bowles and his hired companions gathered.

"These are halyards," she explained loudly as she gripped a rising rope. "We pull here to raise a sail—once I figure out which one." Clearly, she was flustered as she wiped her eyes and looked aloft.

There was a spider's web of running rigging leading up the mast and down again to different parts of the deck. Some of the lines were tied and coiled to the bulwark while others were attached to cleats around the foremast. Rainwater trickled down the ropes, dripped from the heights, and waterlogged heavy bundles of furled sailcloth. The storm was tugging wildly through the spars and slackened lines, and made a jumble of the loose and foreign rigging.

"You," Billie jerked her thumb at Mustafa. She climbed to the forward cabin house and began pulling at a bundle of sailcloth. "You see these ties," she shouted, "these little ropes that hold the sails together?"

"Yes, missy," the rattled Turk answered after watching the binding lines being cast aside.

"Take all of these off that front sail—do it now!"

"Yes, of course." After he spoke, Mustafa was a blur in the rain as he moved to emulate the young woman at the second larger sail.

"Now, *you*—you son-of-a-bitch," Billie shouted as she focused on Cedric Bowles. "Start pulling on those halyards until you find the one that starts lifting his sail—not mine but his. We need to raise a headsail to fall off the wind." Billie now pointed to Mustafa who was bent to his task.

The security director offered the grimace of a smile, tucked his flare gun into the carryall, and motioned the panic-stricken pilot to help. After both men tried several lines, the headboard of Mustafa's jib began flapping in the rain-sodden gusts.

"Alright—good," Billie yelled as she watched the sail rising. "That's it. Now pull, damn you! Mustache—you help them."

"Yes, Missy," Mustafa offered. He joined the straining figures pulling beside the foremast.

With every fraction of sail area exposed, it was obvious that the wind's strength was considerable. Even with the heavy trading vessel canvas, the tall and narrow sail was thrashing wildly as if determined to rip its self to tatters.

"Pete!" Billie yelled over the flailing noise. "Cut the cable! Cut it now!" To her crew at the foremast, she shouted, "Get it up! All the way to the top! OK good! Tie the halyard! Tie it off! Now my sail—the second one. Hurry up and pull!"

Slowly, the much heavier foresail began to rise, but it was clearly wet with rainwater and difficult to handle. All three men were pulling and using a winch as instructed, but as the sail climbed the gusting wind tore at the canvas and once again fought the effort. Multiple curses in the Afrikaans spurred the two Turks onward, but their own complaints rang out strangely over the flailing sails and the rush of the wind.

When a new episode of almost non-stop lightning began to flash, Billie stole a moment to search for the intruder's boat. She was beyond alarmed when she saw the center-console, closer than ever, rise with the waves and

Tom Williams

two of the waterfront Turks leveling automatic weapons.

Before any reaction was possible, a torrent of tracer rounds ripped through the sailcloth above and tore into the lower foremast and the bulwark railing. Even with the wind and the rain, the bullets were fingers of deadly fire and left glowing and smoldering holes in the wildly flogging sails. Without any need for a warning, the crew at the foremast was flat on the decking and covering their heads.

Billie was on the safe side of the forward cabin house deck, and calling to Peter when the machine gunfire stopped. She took a quick peek under the now raised foresail boom, and pitched her voice forward. "Pete, are you all right!"

"Yes, for Christ's sake, but it's a bloody miracle!" Peter yelled. "Those bloody bastards!"

"Well, you better get back to that anchor line before they reload." Billie was crawling past the foremast crowd, two of which were in heavy Turkish conversation.

"Christ—" Peter's latest remark was cut off by another hailstorm of gunfire. But as Billie moved up beside him, he was sawing on the anchor rhode, his hands above his head wildly hacking with the knife.

"How much further?" Billie shouted.

"Almost there!"

"No more time!" Billie's response was almost sad.

She jumped to her feet, grabbed the end of the clattering jib boom, and rigged the sheet line to pull the headsail to one side. "Pete! Watch out!" she warned. "Get away from that anchor line."

Instantly, after Billie's effort, the tall sail filled with wind, and the schooner groaned as the masts and rigging took the strain.

Abruptly, the old trading vessel came to life. She tossed her head away from the gunfire as the remainder of the anchor line parted with what sounded like a cannon shot. Then she was away—pivoting and turning, and pitching her bow down with the wind. As she continued to turn, the luffing foresail caught, filled, and offered a much bigger section of canvas to the storm. With the bulk of the sail area now loaded aft of the foremast, the old lady shouldered her burden as she had been designed, lifted her bows, and heeled over with the wind.

When her lee bulwark reached to embrace the water and began to rise again, this was the signal that the little ship was turning directly downwind and approaching the most dangerous maneuver a sailing vessel can carry out in high wind—the dreaded out-of-control jibe. The abrupt and perilous action that can shift the entire load of pressurized canvas from one side of the rig to the other. The amazing stress levels on a modern and racing-style boat are sometimes tolerated, but mostly avoided. But on an aged and neglected wooden vessel, the result could be disastrous. Both the towering masts and the two foreword sails could easily come down, crashing into the water, and pounding the hull into pieces. This was precisely the instant that Billie remembered Brian at the wheel. Without thinking, she began running down the tilting deck, past the foresail, past the mainmast, until she was at the after end of the cabin house.

"Argentina!" she screamed over the wind. "Take hold of the wheel—stop it from turning."

Upon Billie's approach, it became suddenly clear that Brian needed help. A flash of lightning etched the quarterdeck in shadows, and showed a determined figure bracing against the tilting deck and trying to hold the spokes of the wheel that were still turning.

"Mother of God!" Brian exclaimed as Billie joined him at the helm. "Thank God you're here. I can't stop it," he yelled.

Billie lent her weight to the effort, and as both of the struggling figures strained, the wheel was finally grasped and the spokes stopped turning. Slowly, the steering was reversed, and the towering masts and the rolling deck became stabilized. After the treacherous moment, the schooner once again heeled over as intended and the leeward bulwark tilted toward the water.

"Thank Christ," Brian's voice was a rasp.

"Yes!" echoed Billie.

The sailing schooner dipped her bow into a heavy sea, leaning more heavily with the beam-reaching wind. Even with the horizontal rain, the darkness, and the storm shrieking in the rigging, it was obvious that a heavy weight had shifted deep inside the hull. Now the ship was struck with a new affliction. She was heeling more than normal for the wind and seas, and it was clear that a new and unknown peril was active below decks. An incredible weight had been displaced within the old wooden vessel and now the leeward bulwark was dipping dangerously into the sea.

"Oh my God, what now?" Brian voiced, alarmed at the sudden and abnormal heeling of the little ship.

"I don't know, Argentina," Billie responded. "But I have a feeling it has something to do with King Midas's cargo."

Chapter 45

"**M**ake for the other boat—quickly," the Wolf shouted over the storm. He was holding the center-console for all he was worth. The Poyraz was rising, the wind and stinging rain coming at a slant, and the building waves alarming.

After raking the old trading vessel with the four full magazines from the Russian weapons, it was as if the little ship had had enough, broken her tether like a horse driven mad, and charged off before the wind. With the lightning almost non-stop, the breakaway was an unbelievable sight that Tarik Oclay knew he would never forget. He had seen the young woman stand to force the sail, amid the gunfire, and then she was gone only to reappear by the helm as the schooner showed her stern to the little outboard pounded by the waves. This was when the fantailed launch broke away and began drifting alone as if abandoned by an over-wrought and fleeing parent.

"Get to my boat!" the Wolf repeated his command, wiped his face, and stared after the black-hulled ship retreating into the rain and heeling before the wind.

Abruptly, the harsh clatter of gunfire broke the spell of the disappearing gold as Emil emptied his AK-47 into the night. All of the ammunition was tracer rounds, and even as every man watched, the glowing streaks of fire were wild and falling short as the platform of the rolling fishing boat was too low and unstable to permit accurate firing. The distance between the automatic weapon and the disappearing fortune was obviously becoming greater and more hopeless with every pounding wave and rushing heartbeat.

"Enough! Emil, enough!" the Wolf released one handhold from the console to grip his subordinate by the shoulder. "Enough I said!" Then to the boat driver, an elderly local fisherman who had been conscripted at gunpoint, "If you wish to ever see your family again, get me to *my* boat! And then to my ship!"

"Yes, lord," the fisherman replied after checking the angle of the battering waves. He was the only man on the tiny boat dressed in rain gear. The others still wore the ever-stained auto mechanic coveralls, now salted from the waves and storm-soaked from the downpour.

After a few moments of carefully gauging the safest course and trying desperately not to be caught and capsize between the torn apart seas, the skill of the native fisherman eluded the breaking waves and the ghosting white crests and now the Wolf's broken-loose launch was only meters away from where the little center-console was pitching heavily. With an abrupt crash, the fishing boat slid into the side of the fantail as every hand onboard tried to muzzle the two grinding hulls together. The rising sea won, and the vessels were forced apart. With another dull thud, the two boats were once again chafing alongside.

"By the mother of the prophet, I have crushed my hand," Emil shouted against the raging waves, the storm, and the other men in the boat. The Wolf ignored the curse as he had already led the way after the old fisherman had temporarily tied the two grinding hulls together. When Emil and all of the weapons were safely aboard the much larger boat, the Wolf pulled out his revolver. "Leave your boat, old man. I need you to drive."

"No lord, this boat is all I have. Please, *Aga*," the gnarled hands gestured and the hooded raincoat shook.

The Wolf pointed his pistol inside the smaller boat and fired. Over and over, the heavy caliber weapon barked, the reports still very loud against the wind, waves, and cries of anguish from the older man. After the gun was empty, it was obvious the little outboard vessel was holed. Several jets of streaming water were evident even in the near darkness.

With Emil complaining loudly about the crushed condition of his hand, the gnarled old fisherman shrugged and climbed across the two pitching decks.

He looked up into the face of the Wolf. "What now, lord?"

"Pray that you can get me aboard that ship. Pray for your life, your family, and all your generations. Because if you fail—" Tarik Oclay motioned to Emil who was sitting in agony, moaning, and cradling his battered hand. "If you fail, his suffering is nothing to what your family will endure."

"Yes, *Aga*." After he uttered the only appropriate response, the old fisherman bowed his head and focused. Quickly, he offered a silent prayer, but was distracted from Mecca as the engine of the harbor launch rumbled into life. With the aid of a flashlight, the Wolf crossed the wires necessary to start the engine. The ignition panel was smashed, all of the storage lockers were forced open, and all along deck, various items had been discarded as if in a wild and frantic search. As the old fisherman stood behind the fine polished wheel, under the protective canvas and behind the windscreen, his gnarled old hands gripped the steering and pushed the control lever into gear. As the finest launch in Sinop began to plow forward through the storm-tossed sea, the old man shuddered.

With all the evidence of such arrogance and theft, and such blatant signs of vandalism, one frightening factor was certain: there was more than one Wolf afloat tonight.

Chapter 46

With the old schooner struck by a new but obviously dangerous burden, Cedric Bowles appeared on the high-side windward railing followed by his two hired Turks and finally by Peter holding the lantern. All four were gripping the weather deck railing to brace themselves from falling into the steering station or beyond the tilting decks and into the churning water.

"What's wrong?" the security director screamed. "Can't you steer? Don't you know what you're doing? Straighten the deck or we will capsize! Do it now!" his screeching voice was a demand.

Billie shook her head, partially to clear the rain from her eyes but also in frustration. She knew in her heart that the evil little man was right, and that she could not afford to release her grip on the wheel. After another glance down to the tilting deck and the foaming water creaming over the bulwark, the seconds passed with the waves, and after a moment, a generation of experience produced a decision.

"Get *down* here, *you bastard*!" Billie yelled, and her eyes were riveted on Cedric Bowles. "And bring your men!" she added. "We can't hold her much longer. We need some relief!"

Driven by the logic that no two persons alone could hold the slanting decks from a roll over, Cedric and his hired Turks were soon at the wheel and taking the spokes from Billie and Brian.

"Thank Christ," Brian sputtered after he was relieved. He wiped the rain from his face and climbed the angled deck to join Peter at the high side of the bulwark.

After Billie was beside Peter at the rail, he looked into her eyes and asked with his voice above the wind. "Can they manage? Do they know enough to steer?"

"They can handle it," she said. "It looks worse than it really is."

"Mother of God, I hope you're right," Brian offered.

"I hope so too, Argentina, but listen," Billie paused to look at both men. "We have to get below and we have to see what's gone wrong. If I'm right, we're going to need all the help we can get and were going to need it fast, but if I'm wrong and if the keel is broken, or if the hull is shipping water..." Billie left the rest unsaid, but she was staring down at the three waterfront Turks who were still tied, but tossed into a tumble on the downward side of the decking. The three men were obviously in a panic as the surging water rushed around their legs and threatened to wash them overboard.

"But if I'm wrong," she repeated, "We could be trapped if she rolls over. We could easily be killed."

"And if we stay on deck and take our chances?" Peter asked. "Or find some life preservers and go over the side?"

Before Billie could answer, another flash of lightning lit up the storm and showed a wind-tossed sea consumed with breaking waves. In the distance, the fantailed launch was visible laboring over the swelling whitecaps.

"Even if they weren't out there," Billie tilted her head. "Or even if they missed us in the dark, the water is too cold. We would freeze to death before morning."

"Christ! Not too many bloody options," Brian muttered.

"That's right, Argentina, so let's move!"

After receiving a baleful glare from Cedric Bowles at the wheel, Peter held the lantern and led the way below decks.

The stairs of the companionway were awkward at such a tilted angle, but after gaining the main salon, it was very good to be out of the wind and rain, even if the cabin was slanted at an almost impossible degree. The hull of the little ship listed heavily to starboard, and all unlashed items were strewn haphazardly and lying about as if a spoiled child had had a temper tantrum. A clutter of dive bags and wetsuits rested in a lopsided berth, and several scuba tanks rolled and clanked with each pitch of the waves. In another forward berth, three bundles of black plastic were heavily tied and lashed between bulkheads. Apart from the slight scent of diesel and pine tar, another faint but somewhat familiar odor prevailed.

"By the lord Christ, it's good to be out of that weather, but what is that God-awful smell?" Brian was looking around as he asked and did not notice Billie and Peter regarding the three plastic bundles.

"Never mind, Argentina," Billie answered tersely. "Let's get forward and see what's wrong."

With Peter and the lantern light leading the way, the old hull creaked with every roll, rose and fell wave with every wave, and seemed to heel even more as the final steps into the hold disappeared into sloshing green water.

"Holy Mother of God!" Brian's oath was a whisper above the muted storm.

"Christ! It's real!" Peter responded quietly as he held the lantern high. "It really *is* a king's treasure!"

Billie was speechless. Her experienced and critical eye temporarily blinded. She knew that she must act quickly and redistribute the awesome weight that had been shifted when the schooner began to sail, but she was frozen somehow. She simply could not believe what she was seeing. It was as if her mind was in a dream and forced to move too slowly. She had never imagined anything as dramatic. Never in her life, could she ever believe that...*this could be true.*

The entire length of the hold was glowing and reflecting the lantern light. All the way aft, until the hull began to narrow and a bulkhead stopped before the engine compartment, the eerie light reflected upon hundreds if not thousands of flat and shining, rounded gold bars. Some were tumbled and submerged in the green water, but even under the over-flow from the bilge, the golden light shimmered through the diesel-tainted water. Many, many others of the ancient gold bars were dry and strewn along the planking or resting in piles between the ribs of the tilted ship.

"Billie," Peter's voice broke the spell. "The water," he gestured. "Are we sinking?"

"No—at least I don't think so." Billie shook her head. "With the hull heeled over, all of the bilge water has shifted with the..." she stopped, staring at the shinning and tumbled cargo.

"Billie!" Peter spoke harshly as he grabbed her by the shoulders and made her face him.

"We must think clearly," he said with his voice almost a whisper. "We are in great danger."

Brian moved silently past them staring, his hands moving to touch the gold and his feet sloshing in the bilge water. Slowly he began, lifting one after the other, two at a time, moving the bars to the other side of the hold. Without stopping and without looking up he spoke over the groaning hull and the waves pounding through the timbers. His words were in Spanish, but after the first of the lilting phrases, he switched to English and began to recite, *"Her timbers, below decks grown a continuous bedlam, as the howling winds aloft scream to declare a terrible blasphemy."*

"Peter, do you remember the words," he said. "The words from Diego's log. *'Green water is climbing in the hold and makes a mockery of the knowledge that we are heavy with a King's treasure.'* Well, maybe there's something to it," Brian exclaimed. "What if the gold does have a power? A supernatural strength when accumulated in vast amounts. That would explain the ninety-seven shipwrecks, the ninety-seven hard returns of the satellite, the power over the weather, the greed and the ever-opposing odds…and all the bad luck. The *real* explanation of why all the treasure ships have sunk."

Suddenly Brian stopped and looked up, his face strange in the eerie glowing light. "Peter," he said gravely. "If we become like the others we have no hope. Just like Diego and Midas's Captain and all the rest. But don't you see, maybe they gave up. Maybe they were consumed by the greed and therefore the guilt. They could have been defeatist or didn't have the courage to try—the courage to try and fight the greed, and the understanding of how to defy the cargo. We must be stronger, that's our only chance. We can't give in, or give up, we simply can't. We must shift the gold and try to save the ship. But the answer to our success must lie with an inner strength—we must make a promise to send the gold back."

"Well, one thing is for certain," Peter, said darkly. "We can't do this alone. We have to have help. Billie," he looked into her eyes. "We need the three Turks, the two that we captured and the one who bashed me on the head. With Cedric Bowles and his henchmen at the wheel we need the others to move the weight."

Billie nodded, now determined. "Alright," she said. "But there is so much to move, I don't know if we have enough time, or enough help. We really need every—"

Before she could finish, a heavy swell lifted the old hull and the angle below decks tilted even more dramatically. After an eternal moment, the schooner righted herself a little and once again began to plow along.

"Christ!" Brian was looking upward to the overhead timbers. "I thought that was it. I thought that we were rolling over."

"She won't take much more of this," Billie was also regarding the undersides of the deck beams slanting toward the shifted mound of gold.

"Billie," Peter said with a steady voice. "I'm going on deck, and I'm going to get the Turks—all of them, and Cedric Bowles. Do you think you can steer alone? Is there some way you can manage, some way you can tie the wheel? Just as you said, we are going to need a lot of help and we're going to need it fast.

"Brian? Can you cope?" Peter asked, his attention shifted, "What about your claustrophobia?" Peter's mind was racing and very concerned. His best friend had never spoken of the supernatural, of curses, or of anything not anchored in hard scientific fact.

"I'll manage, I'm afraid we will all have to," Brain offered with a weak smile. "There's really no choice is there?"

"That's right, Argentina," Billie said bravely. "But listen, boys, we *are* going to beat this. I don't care if we give the gold back, dump it into the ocean, whatever. All I care about is you *two* and the chance to live and play again. You guys have shown me something more valuable than all of this." Billie gestured to the misplaced bullion glowing in the lantern light. "Before I met you, it was like I wasn't even alive. I was just going through the motions of survival. Doing the things I had to do, just for a glimpse into the past." Billie paused staring, her eyes shifting from Peter to Brian.

"My dad's old sailboat, the *Valkyrie*," she continued. "That was keeping me going. It was a private thing. Caring for that old boat kept my childhood alive—my only strand of hope was to capture the happy times of childhood again. The *Valkyrie* was the only link to my dad, but now I realize that wasn't even important. You two brought me out of that—you gave me my life back." Billie shook her head and pointed to the gold. "And I'm damn sure not going to lose it tonight just because of a spooky old boat filled with bad luck."

Peter nodded. "Brian, you had better keep moving, shifting the gold to the other side of the hold."

"Yes, yes of course," Brian volunteered. He turned, sloshed through the water and bent to the task, two bars at a time, one side to the other.

Peter looked at Billie. "Can you do it? Can you tie the wheel and steer alone?"

"Don't worry about me," she said. "Just follow me up and get those bastards down here to help. And, Pete," Billie added as she reached under her sodden turtleneck. "Take this so you can handle that devil—that cocky bastard who *I know* burned down my marina." In the lantern light, Billie handed Peter the Luger she had retrieved after he had fallen. The Luger she had hidden under her turtleneck in the waistband of her jeans.

Chapter 47

After Billie lashed the wheel against the horrible force that wanted to turn the schooner downwind, she watched as Peter shouted the orders to release the waterfront Turks. He had not threatened to use, or even shown, the German pistol, but relied only on his logical charisma to lead every man below. Even the South African bastard with the combover had followed—he too knowing, as did all the Turks, that without a major and united effort, the ship and all the gold would be lost as well as the lives of everyone onboard.

When Billie was alone, and quite satisfied with the two sturdy lines she had tied to the wheel, she looked at her watch. Unbelievably, it was only midnight. So much had happened in such a short time.

Apart from the wind in the rigging, the only sound was the hissing of the waves and the occasional creak of the wooden deck. After another look aloft to examine the set of the sails, she shook the tangles out of her hair and realized the rain had stopped. The lightning, which had been so persistent in the leading squall line, was now past and the wicked wind that had seemed possessed and all-powerful was beginning to subside. With the single lantern below, the decks of the old schooner were completely dark, the mainmast naked and without sail, still tilted at a most alarming angle.

Forward, in the shadows, the foresail appeared to be a sheet of solid stone, too heavy for the shorter mast to hold up and determined to carry the bows of the old trader under. But as the little ship continued onward, to lift and plow through the lessening waves, there was an imperceptible change in the dangerous incline of the decks.

After only an hour, the eight men below were beginning to shift the weight. Billie had no doubt it was Peter's authority and quiet determination that had led the way. He was perfect, she considered, in every way. He was calm, always centered, and his level of confidence unswayable. He was as solid as a rock and his character as chiseled as his handsome features. Brian was also great, but in a different way. He was such a little boy. A fun-loving, grown-up, little boy with an enthusiasm for life that she had never seen equaled—ever. Peter also carried that youthful hopefulness, but there was a darker side and even that was intriguing.

Yes, Billie thought, as she scanned the rolling waves and searched the darkness for the fantailed launch. I'm alive now, I know I'm going to live, and I know what I want. Suddenly she frowned. *But...I'm not quite sure how to act, or what to do.*

She knew about the wife and daughter killed by the terrorists in London. Brian had told her. She also knew that the terrible incident had left a deep emotional scar. A wound that he thought was incurable, but a hurt that *she could* heal—she hoped.

With another vigilant appraisal, up and down the decking and then over the taff-rail to the following seas, Billie continued to let her mind wander and her mood elevate. With the waterfront Turks far behind in the darkness and unable to keep up in the heavy seas, and with the salty old trading vessel beginning to sail upright, the unbelievable possibilities of what was really happening were beginning to take hold.

With a sigh, Billie settled into the windward railing, tucked her legs in close to her chest, and rested her chin on her knees. She glanced at her watch and was surprised to see another half hour had passed. She yawned.

He also thought he was too old. Maybe he thought that she was too young, too young and damaged goods, damaged forever by an abusive husband. Well, she considered, no one is perfect.

Billie was startled away from her thoughts by a presence in the companionway. She recognized Brian and relaxed once more. He crossed the deck quickly and joined her on the seating that wrapped around the after-bulwarks.

"How's it going down there?" she asked.

"More than half of the bullion is shifted," Brian offered. "And one of the Turks knew how to start the pumps. The water in the hold is gone—at least it's not rising anymore, but Christ am I tired!"

"Me, too," Billie volunteered, and asked, "How are the Turks and that bastard from Texas—the one I'm certain, who burned down my marina?"

Brian shook his head. "Peter is amazing. The greater the pressure, the better he performs. He has asserted some kind of authority and everyone is working like a team. Although, Cedric Bowles still acts as if he is in charge—brandishing that flare gun as he works and stares at the gold."

Billie frowned, her features hard to see in the darkness. "As soon as the cargo is shifted and they know the boat is safe, that's when the trouble will start. The greed will take over."

"I agree," Brian said, as he looked around the afterdeck. "But my God," he exclaimed. "Maybe we are closer to safety than you can realize from the hold."

Billie nodded and yawned. It was true, she thought, the storm line and the squalls were well past and the lessening wind sweeping away the clouds to show a few stars. The schooner was heeling much less with the lighter, but still strong breeze, and it was obvious that even though the old trader was still heavily loaded she was once again sailing as designed. Breaking waves churned alongside, but now the railing was not underwater nor the decks slanted at such a dangerous degree; and the dreadful leaning masts, the masts which had threatened to roll over and embrace the water, were now once again standing tall.

Brian stood and crossed the decks. After taking in the much-improved situation, he breathed deeply and smiled. "Christ it's good to be alive, be on deck, and away from that horrible smell below. It smells like something died."

Before Billie could respond, Brian continued urgently, his eyes searching the waves that were still creaming white. "And speaking of smelly," he asked. "What about those blokes with the machine guns—our bloody *friends* from the waterfront?"

"Maybe I dozed," Billie confessed. "But after I saw the hull coming upright and I knew that we weren't going to have a knock-down, I knew I could relax. I watched them following until my eyes hurt—trying to tell if they were gaining, or if with the rough seas we were still out sailing them." As if to confirm her confidence, Billie turned to examine the wake of the schooner—the speed of the old trader in the lessening wind.

"But that was when it was still raining," she recounted. "Like I said, my eyes were hurting so I closed them. I thought for just a moment, but when I looked up again they were gone," she shook her head and ran her fingers through her drying hair. After a moment, she sighed.

"I guess," she said. "They could have been blinded by one of the bursts of rain and lost us. Or, they could have run out of fuel or been swamped by a wave. Those seas were running pretty big. Maybe their engine was flooded. I don't know."

"Well, no sign is a good sign," Brian ventured as he once again scanned the horizon. "But perhaps, the most important question for the moment is, where are we now?"

Billie shrugged. "One thing is certain," she offered. "We are well out of the harbor and into the Black Sea. Before we went below and found the gold, I checked the compass. We were port tacked and on a northeasterly heading. As far as I know we don't have any charts, but I haven't been in the salon to look. I was afraid to leave the wheel."

"I do remember that the Turkish coast should be running alongside, and that by morning we might be able to see land. If we don't, we can tack and work our way in toward shore."

"Then what?" Brian asked as he reached into his pocket and retrieved a pack of sodden cigarettes, "Christ what I would give for a dry pack of smokes."

"A king's treasure?" Billie suggested.

"Quite possibly it will come to that. What would you trade Billie—to be safely onshore, away from the bad luck, the curses, and the villains?"

"Don't think that I haven't been considering just that." Billie smiled in the darkness and reached out to touch Brian's hand. "You'd better get below and watch out for Peter. The Turks are one thing, but that bastard with the flare gun is another. He's a bad one," she said earnestly. "He's real dangerous—I just know it."

"Don't worry, and don't forget—unbeknownst to Cedric Bowles, Peter has the pistol. He also has the determination and the fortitude to deal with that South African rubbish." Brian offered his own smile and pulled Billie's hand next to his lips. He kissed the back of her fingers and started for the companionway.

Before he reached the steps, Billie asked. "Argentina, how old was Peter's girlfriend from Texas—the one who was murdered?"

"She was thirty-five, but she was not really his girlfriend. Why?"

"I was just wondering about age."

"Whatever for?"

"I'm thirty-three—thirty-four next month."

Brian stopped, and stared open mouthed. "Oh my God! Not you, too!" he exclaimed loudly.

"Shhh! Quiet!" Billie urged. "What do you mean? Don't you dare say anything! You just keep a close eye on him and take care of yourself. And listen, when all the gold is shifted make sure it can't move again. Then, when everything is done and lashed down tight, bring everyone back on deck."

"What for?" Brian was still overwhelmed by Billie's earlier questions and their ultimate implications.

"I don't know yet, but let that bastard from South Africa come up last. He will want to cover everyone as he has the flare gun. Make sure that Pete understands that *the bastard* comes up last."

"Billie, please don't do anything untoward—nothing that you, or *we* will regret later. It's true that Cedric Bowles is a cold hearted bastard but I really don't th—,"

"Oh, for Christ's sake, Brian," Billie exploded quietly. "I don't plan on *killing* him."

"Oh, I was just worried."

"Me, too, but listen," Billie looked at her watch. It was 1:15 AM. "How much longer before the gold is secure and tied down?"

"Three quarters of an hour—maybe a little more."

"Good! Now get below and keep an eye on Pete—*and* yourself," she added.

After Brian disappeared down the companionway, Billie scanned the horizon once more, checked the wheel and the compass, and then settled back into the taff-rail seating. The wind was still very fresh and the clouds were clearing. The waves were sluicing along the hull with a rhythmic pulse, but they were no longer pounding, no longer dangerous. Above the towering rigging, the strongest stars were shining brightly. There were even faint shadows crossing the deck.

Billie tucked up her legs and rested her chin once more. After a few moments, she yawned. There was still plenty of time. She would rest her eyes for just a few seconds.

She was very tired.

Chapter 48

When Billie awoke, The Wolf's hand was over her mouth. She of course, did not know that the large, very strong man was known as "The Wolf," but she did know she was in trouble and that she had failed in her duty to Peter and Brian.

Her mind screamed, *goddamn it*, as she struggled, but then she was pulled from the taff-rail where she had slept and forced to her feet. When she looked about the quarterdeck and saw the two men holding machine guns, she felt a new wave of rising dread. Even in the relative darkness, she could see the greed and desperation molded on the men's features, and the triumph of recovering what had been lost.

Without speaking, the largest of the waterfront Turks signaled his men and an older man in a raincoat moved to stand at the wheel. The two men with machine guns disappeared down the companionway. In less than a minute shouts were heard. After the shouting stopped, Brian appeared on deck followed by Peter and the creepy man who had followed them from Texas. All of the other Turks followed and immediately erupted into several different conversations. It was at once obvious the three waterfront Turks from the schooner had been rescued by the rest of their group and their leader. The two Turks that had boarded with Cedric Bowles now appeared very concerned as they spoke in muted whispers.

Brian was very pale and sweating, as was the bastard from South Africa, but Peter appeared calm enough and even unsurprised. He merely walked across the deck and stood facing the obvious man in charge.

"Do you speak English?" he asked with a steady voice.

224

"Enough to deal with a thief," the big man replied with a crooked smile.

Peter shook his head. "I am not a thief. Nor are my companions. We are scientists and ultimately responsible for what has been found. It is you that has plundered our research and taken what is rightfully ours."

The Wolf laughed softly and took out a pack of cigarettes. After lighting up, he offered one to Peter. Peter shook his head, but nodded toward Brian standing nervously next to Billie.

"I have never been a smoker, but my colleague will accept your offer," he said simply. "And then perhaps we could discuss a compromise."

"Of course." The Wolf smiled again as he gave Brian a cigarette and a light. Brian's hands were shaking as he gratefully inhaled the tobacco.

"I am Tarik Oclay." The Wolf explained as he smoked. "I am the headman of Sinop. These men are my colleagues, but I am afraid they are in no mood for any sort of a compromise. You have taken my ship and my gold, and there can be only one possibility for your future."

Brian's face drained at the latest remark as he looked sharply to Peter and then to Billie. Peter was stoic, but Billie, even in the near dark, regarded the headman with contempt.

"You don't understand our position," Peter began. "What I am about to—"

"Enough!" Oclay interrupted harshly and stepped forward to grind his cigarette onto the deck. "It is *you* who does not understand, Mister British," he spat rudely. "Perhaps you have not examined our entire cargo." After his statement, the big man with the gray hair spoke roughly to his men and when the Turkish words were finished, two of the original waterfront Turks disappeared below decks.

The Wolf turned to the old man in the raincoat who was now steering the schooner. With the wind and seas much calmer, the man at the wheel had untied Billie's restraining lines and was sailing the old trading vessel single-handed.

"Tell me, old man," The Wolf demanded in Turkish. "Where are we? And how far until we reach Toplu?"

"I am not sure, lord," the fisherman began, but added quickly after receiving a withering scowl, "By my reckoning we are near the coast, with Toplu only a few kilometers away. After morning prayers and Allah brings us the light, I believe I can find the way."

Oclay glanced at his watch and then up to the stars shinning above the forward sails and the mainmast rigging. "How much longer?" he demanded. "The wind is lighter now and our travel is slow."

"Yes, lord. That is true—Insha'Allah "

"Is it possible to go faster—if we use more sails."

"Yes, lord."

"Then do it. You are in charge of the ship. The others," Oclay jerked his thumb. "They will obey your instruction, but I will have sighted Toplu before night falls again. Do not fail me or by the prophet you will follow this example."

Tarik Oclay pointed to the companionway as Yarin Dun and Sali Tuz pulled the first of three plastic bundles onto the quarterdeck. Emil waited as two more of the heavy black plastic bags thudded onto the deck, and stared malevolently as he cradled his bandaged hand along with his Ak-47. His impatient attention was equally divided between the three plastic containers and the prisoners of the Wolf.

Cedric Bowles stood by his hired pilot and guide, his eyes darting like a reptile looking for an insect. Peter, Billie, and Brian stood slightly apart from the security director and his men, but the fully automatic weapon easily covered all six captives.

The Wolf now crossed the deck and stood in front of Peter. "You have spoken like a brave man Mister English—like an actor in a Hollywood film. But now I will show you reality."

With a quick burst of Turkish, the Wolf gave his order and Yarin Dun slit open the first of the three bags. As he hurried to step away from the odor, the ruined and bloated body of Benjamin Farouk tumbled onto the decking.

"My God!" Brian exclaimed before he wretched. He hurried to the bulwark and was sick over the rail. Ahmed, the young aviator followed the afflicted example and was also drained white as he heaved over the side.

Billie tucked in close to Peter and buried her face in his chest.

"Now, Mister English, perhaps you can understand your future, and the state of your misfortune. The end result of your proposed compromise." The Wolf's jagged smile was infectious and all the Turks from the waterfront smirked at the calculated response.

"Yarin, Sali," the Wolf's eyes shifted to his captives as he continued in English. "Put them *all* over the side, the living, *and* the dead. I wish to cleanse my little ship. I wish to clean away the odor of rot, and the stink of the English infidel—the infidels and their lackeys!" With a crude gesture, Mustafa and the hired pilot were also included.

"And the woman?" Emil spoke in accented English as he took a step forward. His AK-47 leveled despite his bandaged hand.

"Why would you spare the harlot?" Oclay hissed in Turkish. "Perhaps you covet the American whore. You would wish to enter her loins? No! I am telling you! Put them *all* over the side—do it now!"

"Yes, *Aga*," Emil stepped forward again but winced with pain as he hobbled, his ankle still tender from the episode on the hotel balcony.

Before Billie could do anything but close her mind against the nightmare and clutch Peter tighter, the older Turk at the wheel, the man in the raincoat who suddenly reminded her of Dotson, interrupted the big man who was the waterfront leader. The old sailor's eyes were forward as he rattled off the Turkish words, but he spoke forcefully and made gestures aloft into the rigging and then out to sea.

"*Aga*, have you not trusted me to guide you?" the old fisherman began in the local dialect. "Out over the waves and the power of the Poyraz? We have prevailed by the prophet, but now I must offer the experience of my counsel. This vessel lord, she is old and full of treachery. Why do you believe that she was abandoned?" The older man paused as he looked into the eyes of the Wolf. He continued carefully.

"We are still out to sea and do not know our exact position. I believe we are near Toplu, but I could be mistaken. The Poyraz was very strong and the ship may have suffered. Many things can happen, Insha'Allah. Believe me, lord, *many* things can happen. You have asked that I set more sail so the ship will go faster, but how can I do this alone? The largest sail is not yet set and you and your men are clearly exhausted. How long *Aga*—how long since you have slept?"

As he waited for an answer, the old mariner shook out a cigarette and lit the tobacco with an old-style Zippo lighter.

"I know that you have threatened against it, lord, but forgive me," the mariner exhaled. "Toplu, under sail might be two days away. We could be far off-course and lost. At sea lord, there are always many things to consider. At *sea* all we can do is pray and be prepared."

The fisherman shrugged and gestured ahead and into the darkness. He turned away and fixed his eyes forward.

After a moment of silence, he offered a final suggestion anchored in the comfort of logic. "*Aga*, before I moved to Sinop and began to fish, I worked onboard ships. There are schedules that must be kept. The captain and *some* of his officers must rest while others keep the watch. We could be days away, the weather could go bad again, and we must have help to sail the ship. We must have *their* help." The older man tilted his head toward the six figures gathered at the bulwark. His words had been loud enough so that every man could hear.

Emil still cradled his weapon tightly, his prisoners covered, but now he was looking over his shoulder, waiting hopefully for a positive response. His hand was in need of desperate attention. His ankle still throbbed badly, he was beyond exhaustion, *and* he was starving.

Quickly, Yarin and Sali gathered by the old ship's wheel. With a side-long glance at the seasoned mariner, Sali began quietly, "Perhaps the old man's right, Tarik. We don't know where we are or how long we will be out."

"One thing is certain," the Wolf's voice was dangerous, "the two of you were defeated without a struggle, captured by the two Mister English and a single American woman."

Oclay had already been informed about the events leading up to the boarding and the circumstance involving his own fan-tailed launch.

After his stinging reprimand, Sali and Yarin lowered their eyes. Satisfied with the reaction, Tarik Oclay relented. "Very well," he sighed. "I am not a man of the sea, and neither am I a fool. We will follow our *Captain's* advice until we see the sandy stones of Toplu. We must consider our cargo." The Wolf now raised his voice and spoke in English, "Spare the foreigners and their lackeys but throw the corpses overboard," he boomed. "Have the Mister English do it!"

Emil grinned savagely in the half-light and motioned with his weapon. "You have heard the *Agam*," he spat. "Obey, Mister English, and know that you will soon follow your young little captain."

Brian was clearly appalled, but torn between the order and the repeated signals from his abdomen. The stench from the knifed open body bag was overwhelming. He took two tentative steps as did Peter, but his stomach revolted. With an abrupt rush, he was once again sick over the side.

The waterfront Turks laughed until Emil roughly gestured with his gun, this time in the unmistakable direction of Cedric Bowles. "And what's wrong with you Mister English—you heard the *Agam*! Over the side!"

Even in the near darkness, with only the starlight and the white curl of the waves it was obvious that the sandy-haired South African was revolted to be classified as English. His frustration with the mistake lasted only seconds before repeated gestures with the AK-47 spurred him onward. Onward to help Peter lift the ruined body of Benjamin Farouk overboard. With the Black Sea churning and sluicing alongside, the impact of the splash was hardly audible. Before the two men could turn and begin with the next of the black plastic bundles, a Turkish chant began.

All the Turks from the waterfront had stepped forward and were directing their voices at Brian who was still retching over the rail. Their voices were in a rude chorus and mocking.

"Mister English…Mister English…Mister English," clearly the Turks were taunting the overwhelmed Brian, and their tone and demeanor was both humiliating and dreadful.

"Mister English…Mister English…" the taunt continued. Even the

Wolf had joined in, his jagged smile frightening.

Brian, in between heaves, could only look up in apprehension and disgust. Even in the relative darkness, his color-drained face was pitiful.

"That's enough of that by God!" Billie shouted the words defiantly as she stood with her hands on her hips. Before anyone could react, she was bent at the knees and lifting one of the body bags in the classic fireman's carry. She was then at bulwark railing and the bundle was gone over the side. Without a pause, she was back and bending for the final black plastic bag just as Peter rushed to her side. With his help, the last of the young Turkish divers was returned to the sea.

The childish and mocking chant stopped as soon as Billie shouted her defiance, and in the following silence the erupting laugh of the Wolf reclaimed all attention.

"I have been told that you were a Hell-Cat," the big voice boomed. "And now I know that this is true. But no matter," he continued. "You will serve me well, or I will have Yarin cut the fat one." The Wolf tilted his head toward Brian. "He will bleed like a lamb and you will watch more than his sickness going over the side."

"You bastard!" Billie's response was automatic and so was the Wolf's reoccurring laugh.

Chapter 49

Cedric hated not being in control, but as a realist and a survivor, he knew that he must remain calm and consider his options.

There were eight hostiles, including the old man who was steering the ship and the big man who was the obvious leader. Two of the men from Sinop were no more than teenagers, but clearly enthralled and fanatic. Mustafa and Ahmed the pilot could not be counted on for any kind of support unless a drastic change of command was initiated. Pauliss was useless, but Clopec and the Florida woman did have potential.

The security director's mind was in overdrive despite the task in which he was currently employed. Under orders from the Turks, he was below decks in a corner of the main salon which was designated as the galley. At present, he was reduced to steward and charged with the responsibility of feeding everyone onboard.

Several large baguettes, which were almost as hard as stones had been roughly sliced and huge slab of feta cheese had been pulled out of a bucket of brine. Another bucket was also filled with the same salty liquid, but full to the top with bobbing black olives. A hanging string of garlic mixed with onions was also available along with some dried peppers and olive oil. *Turkish camping*, Cedric thought—with no refrigeration.

As the security director worked under the moving shadows of a hanging lamp, he prepared one meal at a time, crumbling feta stuffed into the bread with garlic, onions, and olive oil, wrapped into wax paper with a single pepper and a hand full of olives. The only drink onboard was gallons of the strong Turkish tea. All totaled, with possible friend and foe alike, the little ship's company numbered fourteen. There was enough of the boring food Cedric imagined, to last about two days.

As he completed another of the primitive sandwiches and folded the waxed paper, his training from the South African Security Force took over—the military theories taught by one of the most thoroughly trained reactionary contingents in the world: assets and liabilities, surprise and distraction, and above all, until it was time to strike, discretion...discretion ...and certainly in this case, *more* discretion.

Currently, Cedric was alone and unguarded. This, he imagined was because the stupid Turks considered him to be British and therefore sympathetic toward Pauliss who was being held as the hostage among hostages. The leading Turk, the big man with the most intelligence had given his orders, ranked his subordinates, and was sleeping on deck immediately after he had eaten the first of the sandwiches. The first of the meals prepared by one of his men before the security director was chosen as galley steward. After eating, most of the hostiles were resting with the exception of the old man who drove the ship and the armed man with the injured hand who always held the AK-47.

With his mind torn between the gold bullion, the Turks, and the English fannies, Cedric roughly considered his own experience with the Russian weapon system. In South Africa, during Mandela's transition period, everyone knew that the whites of the security force used the American M-16, the weapon system originally developed by an American toy maker. Everyone knew that the AK-47 was Soviet and smuggled into South Africa by the communists. If an AK-47 was used it would be clear that no one from the security force was responsible.

This was the reason Cedric utilized exclusively, the Soviet weapon, to throw the blame onto the Kaffir loving communists. He knew *that* weapon like the back of his hand, like an old friend. Although, right now his old friend was in the hands of a stupid and injured Turk—an enemy. Another of the hostile Turks was also armed with Russian automatic, but he appeared overconfident and relaxed as he wore his weapon loosely strapped to his back.

Once again, timing was the critical issue.

Abruptly, one of the Turks descended the companionway and appeared in the light of the hanging lantern. The man was apparently unarmed but for a stiletto-type blade in a sheath on his belt.

"The morning prayers are over and the sun had risen," the man announced. "Prepare fresh tea."

"Yes, of course," Cedric replied, and then asked with a subservient tone,

"And the foul weather? The storm is passing?"

"As God wants," was the automatic reply.

"It seems much better from down here," Cedric continued quickly. "Not so much motion. For a time I was very ill. I do get quite seasick. I was wondering if it might be possible that I go on deck with the others? I was wondering if I might go up into the sunlight and take the fresh air?"

"What? Do not speak so fast! The sound of the British hurts my ears."

"Will you have some tea?" Cedric moved forward with a large pitcher. "I'm sorry if I speak too fast." The security director continued even faster. "It's just that I feel sick down here. The smell of the dead still lingers and the feta and the brine. I'm afraid I'm quite miserable. He made a staggering motion and spilled over half of the tea onto the galley table and onto the Turk.

"By the prophet, I should cut you like the others!" Yarin spat out the English words as if they left a bad taste.

Even in the lamplight, it was clear that the local from the waterfront was disgusted. The infidel British had spilled the tea and soiled his clothing, and he had just dried himself from the final passage of the Poyraz.

"Look what you have done," he ranted, his right hand moving toward his knife. He reconsidered as he remembered the Wolf's earlier reprimand.

"I am so truly sorry," Cedric lied, and continued in a made-up cockney accent. "I'm very clumsy indeed. Can you please forgive me and allow me on deck?"

Yarin's eyes burned with disgust before he stated, "If I see you on deck in the sunshine and fresh air, you will see *this* blade buried in your flesh." He was gripping the handle of his knife.

"You will stay below until we reach the land, and then you will break your back moving our cargo. I will send someone for the tea!"

After the Turk stormed out and disappeared up the companionway, the early morning sunlight began to filter down. After he reached into a pocket and retrieved his sunglasses, Cedric Bowles placed the eyewear on his head and began to giggle.

232

Chapter 50

Billie stood by the spokes of the old wheel and looked forward. The Black Sea was as calm as a lake with the hot Turkish sun burning high overhead. All of the schooner's sails were down and tightly furled and the fan-tailed launch rigged forward as a towing vessel.

The old mariner who had intervened and saved their lives was piloting the thirty-foot launch beneath the shade cover of the luxurious harbor craft. The leader of the waterfront Turks was also aboard the tow vessel and just visible as he rested under the shade and chain-smoked.

All the weather from the powerful squall was gone as was the wind driven waves from the Russian storm system. The aftermath was a mirror-like sea that allowed the exhaust of the towing vessel to hang in the air until the forepeak of the schooner parted the diesel haze like a persistent hound in search of a scent.

As the day dawned, the wind failed and the sails became useless. It was as if the kneeling and chanting Muslims had focused their morning prayers to take away the breath of the oceans. With every degree that the sun rose higher and dried the steaming decks, the horizon seemed to vanish as the glassy water reflected the sky. After the wind dropped to a breeze and the zephyr that followed failed into a wallowing calm, the mood on deck rose and fell as the old trader followed obediently in the modern wake of the fan-tailed launch.

"Hey, you," Billie called over her shoulder to the skinny Turk with the machine gun. "I need someone to go forward and keep an eye on the towing line. It could be chaffing and it could break," she explained. She wiped the sweat from her eyes with the sleeve of her turtleneck. Her jeans and black sweater had dried with the morning sun, but soon became soaked again with her own perspiration.

From the aftermost taff-rail seating, under a rigged shade awning, the waterfront Turk with the bandaged hand spoke harshly to one of the men who had boarded with Cedric Bowles. After a brief Turkish exchange the man Billie had named "Mustache" moved forward along the decking, his pace sullen and defeated.

"I also need someone to go down below and check the bilge. After the storm and all the weight we are carrying, we could be taking on water. The steering is beginning to feel heavy."

After receiving only a baleful stare Billie insisted. "OK, it's up to you, but don't say that I didn't give fair warning. I don't think your boss would like it if we start to sink. I know that you understand me, I know that you speak English. I know that you were the *one* on the balcony."

"Enough!" Emil shouted. "Hold your tongue, woman, or I will put you in the water. I will see how long it takes *you* to sink!"

Billie's chin jutted as she turned back to the wheel and faced forward. "Whatever," she muttered, just loud enough to be heard.

"Ayeeyah, woman! You mock me? You mock me when I tell you to hold your tongue?" Emil was now off the after-rail seating and hobbling forward dangerously. "You are truly a harlot from the great Satan!" he shouted. "But *now* I will show you your place!"

Before Emil could gain Billie's position she spun the spokes on the wheel and the deck of the schooner lifted as it rolled. The movement was not drastic, but enough to make the advancing Turk stumble.

The enraged local was now beyond livid and his face glowed with anger and then embarrassment. He regained his footing and raised his rifle to use the stock of the weapon as a club.

"Don't touch her," Peter and Brian said together as they stood, neither surprised that they had spoken the same words at the same moment. They were also under the shade of the rigged awning with the Turkish aviator hired by Cedric Bowles. Everyone had been under guard by the man with the automatic rifle since the wind had failed and the old mariner had suggested the tow. The old man had also recognized Billie's marine aptitude by the knots she used to tie the little ship's wheel. He insisted that she steer the schooner as he piloted the towing vessel.

"Please don't hurt her," Brian added after the Turk turned to stare malevolently—as if his eyes and ears could not believe that anyone would question an angry man with an AK-47.

Suddenly the rage of the skinny little man seemed to boil over, he was appalled. His bandaged hand redirected the barrel as he leveled the weapon toward Peter and Brian at the taff-rail. While his back was turned, and he was dealing with Billie, Peter and Brian had stood and taken silent steps forward in Billie's defense.

While the undamaged hand tightened around the trigger mechanism and the man dressed in dirty coveralls readied his stance against the fully automatic recoil, another older Turk emerged from the companionway.

"Emil, what are you doing?" the Turkish voice demanded. "Can I not leave you alone long enough to go to the toilet? Do you have wax in your ears and pus in your eyes? What do you think Tarik will do if you kill the foreigners before he says to do it?" The man that just gained the quarter-deck shook his head. "Believe me," he warned. "You would live only minutes longer than they do."

"Ayeeyah," Emil complained. "But she makes a mockery and they rise behind me to help her."

"Forget it!" Sali Tuz switched to English. "Both of you sit down—do it now."

Peter nodded and he and Brian were once again seated.

"He was going to hit her. He was going to hit Billie with the rifle butt," Brian was pointing.

"He will do nothing, and you will do everything—" the older Turk motioned ahead to the towboat. "Everything and anything the *Agam* might order."

"Ayeeyah," Emil began a Turkish curse and hobbled to the far side of the quarterdeck. He sat and began to unwrap the bandages on his injured hand.

"I will give you a warning," the Turkish mechanic lowered his voice and tilted his head toward the man with the rifle.

"Emil has the brain of an animal. He will react when provoked and will not consider the consequences until it is too late—too late for him but especially too late for you."

Chapter 51

After the sun began reaching for the west and casting the slanting shadows of the schooner's masts forward, the leader of the waterfront Turks rose from his position in the towboat and began shouting as he pointed to the southeast.

With the sun well astern and the copper light pouring forward, a land mass began rising from the hammered surface of the sea. With the distant coastline sighted and the day falling short, the Wolf directed the old mariner to increase power and abandon the low-speed throttle setting, intended for saving fuel.

Within minutes, the towline stretched taught as the aged schooner pitched forward and aft, then rolled from side to side with an unnatural movement for which she was never designed. Diesel smoke poured from the fantail launch as the 30-foot pleasure craft worked as never before to pull the overloaded tonnage through the still and becalmed water. The long black hull labored through wake of the towboat like an elderly grandparent being dragged forward by an impatient and spoiled child.

Throughout the long, hot day, the mood on the treasure-laden schooner had been drifting into depression. Especially after Sali's warning to Emil and the ultimate implications of everyone's fate after they were no longer useful. The Turks appeared to be absorbed, distracted, and overwhelmed with the task at hand, and the tension onboard was mounting with each hour that land was not sighted. The considerations of running out of fuel and being boarded by the Turkish authorities were clearly weighing heavily until the rising headland became a solid reality and not a hopeful mirage.

236

"My God is it safe to travel this fast?" Brian asked softly. He, like Peter, had stood from the taff-rail seating and joined Billie by the wheel. The old schooner was clearly traveling at maximum hull speed.

Immediately, after their leader had sighted land, the waterfront Turks ran forward along the decking and were now a gathered knot at the fore-peak of the schooner. They were cheering and obviously jubilant that the familiar coastline had been confirmed.

"Argentina, if this old boat can weather that storm she can certainly handle a full speed tow. Besides, now that they have found what they're looking for, we'll be safe enough until we help with the offloading and the gold is safely onshore. After that...?" Billie shrugged.

"She's right, Brian," Peter offered. "If they had run out of fuel, and with the wind remaining calm, our presence onboard could only be a liability. Now, once again, we are needed."

"What are our chances? What can we do?" Brian's voice was the whisper of a conspirator.

"Well, they are surprisingly lax as they watch over us," Peter began, his tone muted. "Even with all their passion and anxiety, I would have thought that as prisoners, we would be confined below decks or at least our hands and feet tied."

"They're lazy," Billie remarked with contempt. "And they feel overconfident because of those automatic rifles. There's no place for us to go except overboard and they know it."

Peter nodded. "Billie your right, I never expected to be allowed to go below for the toilet, but the skinny one with the bandaged hand just pointed his rifle at the companionway and grunted. And when I went below, I could have done anything—no one watched and no one followed."

"What about the Luger? What happened to the German pistol after I fell asleep? After I fell asleep and screwed everything up?" Billie's voice dropped to the conspirator level as she looked over her shoulder to the two Turks that were still seated on the taff-rail, the men that had boarded with Cedric Bowles.

Peter shook his head. "None of that," he said softly. "Billie you were exhausted as we all were. There can be no blame except for Brian and me pulling you into this. Everything here is totally our fault. We were ill prepared."

"Peter, for Christ's sake," Brian erupted quietly. "What happened to the pistol? I didn't see anything but that bloody Cedric Bowles trying to hide—after the Turks caught us unaware. I know they searched you—they searched everyone. What happened to the pistol?"

Before speaking, Peter tilted his head to the forepeak where the hostile

Turks were still gathered and distracted. "Think, Brian. When this lot showed up we were just finished with restacking the gold. I heard the shouts and then saw their faces in the lantern light."

As he stopped to reflect, an expression of anger, anguish, and regret crossed the chiseled Hungarian features. He continued as if with a confession.

"I thought for a split-second about having it out right then, an old fashioned shoot-out just like in a film. I thought that I just might manage to stop them before they stopped me. But somehow, Billie," he paused as he held her gaze. "Life just seems a little more valuable with you around."

"Oh my God!" Brian spat out the words quietly as he scanned the eyes and faces that were locked onto each other. "You *two* have absolutely gone over the top." He continued in a low hiss, "Here we are, about to be bloody well buggered to death, and you two are acting like school children! Well snap out of it, and tell what happened to that sodding pistol! And what are we going to do to get out this bollocking situation?"

Peter responded quietly, but he was captured by Billie's smile. "During the excitement, when Cedric Bowles tried to hide and they took the flare gun, I covered the Luger with some shifted bars of gold. No one saw me. This lot," Peter shifted his glance to the taff-rail. "They blocked the others from seeing, and they were too busy with their arms in the air to notice me behind them. Besides, I know that no one found it because it's still there—I checked when I went to the toilet."

"Then you could go down and get it right now?" Brian looked nervously to the shadowed entrance of the companionway.

"Now you can understand my earlier thoughts—at least some of them." Peter confessed. "What are you going to do? Come up with an old pistol against two fully automatic machine guns?"

"What about Cedric Bowles?" Brian asked in a whisper. "We could tell him and he could do the shooting."

Peter shook his head. "No way, not him. I think that he is ultimately more dangerous than the Turks."

"You got that right, Pete!" Billie confirmed, "That bastard is as cold as a fish—make that a shark."

"Then we are agreed. We keep the Luger secret until the time is right."

"But how in the bloody hell do we know what to do and when to do it?" Brian shook his head as his attention was drawn forward.

The Turks from Sinop were filing aft, their mood obviously delighted and triumphant. Land had been sighted, and their leader was happy. They were all *hopefully* about to become the richest men any of them could ever imagine, and did not seem concerned that the two Englishmen had gathered next to the American woman steering the ship or that they were in obvious discussion.

"Well, boys, it looks like the party's over." Billie sighed. "What are we going to do?"

"I don't want to sound brutal," Peter offered. "But I think we might have to get our hands dirty—very dirty. There can be no doubt about what will happen if we don't. At the end of the day, it all boils down to survival, and self defense."

"I agree, full stop—but what are we to do, and when?" Brian's voice was urgent and filled with desperation. The Turks were past the mid-ship mark and coming astern.

"Argentina, Pete's right. If we are going to make it through this, we're going to have to get down and dirty." Billie lifted her chin. "Hey listen—I just thought of something, something that's been going around in my head. A children's song from a long time ago. 'One little, two little, three little Indians', and then there were none."

They both gave her an odd look.

"One by one," she whispered.

Chapter 52

After sighting the Black Sea coast, the fan-tailed towboat turned toward shore until the sandy stones and the dunes of a beach were
easily visible. With the heavily loaded schooner wallowing behind,
a rich green tumble of rising hills rose above the swaying masts as the
modern and antiquated vessels traveled along the deserted shoreline. Excitement levels rose among the Turks, peaked, and finally dropped
dramatically when the white sugar cubes of a small coastal town appeared
on the headland. This was when the Wolf ordered another course change
and the fan-tailed tugboat slowed once more and chugged again further
offshore. The heat of the day passed with Toplu, and now the settling sun
was much lower over the still calm and glass-like sea.

"I don't like it," Yarin complained as the Wolf's towing boat turned in
again toward a cliff-lined shore. He was standing next to Sali on the quarterdeck as both men strained to see the approaching coastline.

"Well, little brother," Sali began. "One thing is certain. Tarik doesn't
care. He doesn't care about anything except what we carry below decks. I'm
worried," the mechanic confessed. "What if we are no longer useful? What
if we are only needed until we rendezvous with the *special* men who come in
the *special* trucks?"

Yarin shook his head as if to shake away a distressful image. "We
should have gone into Toplu," he stated grimly. "We should have gone in
and docked, with all the British below decks. Then after dark, we could
have made arrangements. Even now we could be safely moored in Toplu."

"I'm afraid you might be right," Sali glanced around and lowered his
voice to a whisper. "What if Tarik has called his old companions in Italy?

Everyone knows he was connected with their Mafia. What better way to ensure his safety and what better way to drop us as if we are tools that are no longer necessary."

"That's right, elder brother. And don't forget Tarik is a Christian. He pretends to pray as we do, but I'm certain he was converted when he spent time in Italy."

"That would explain a lot. Has he not always criticized the fundamentalist Mullahs? Perhaps he has no feeling of loyalty—for our last five years of service."

"Yes, what you say is true," Yarin agreed. His hand went involuntarily to the handle of his stiletto. "Perhaps we should make our *own* special arrangements."

"Little brother," Sali nodded. "You can see the thoughts in my head. But who can we count on—other than each other?"

"Emil is a fool and a coward before the Wolf, but if Tarik were gone, or he had an accident, you and I would be in control. Emil and the others would do whatever we say. And the special men with the special trucks could be avoided." Even as he spoke, Yarin's right hand was tightening around his weapon.

"But Tarik has the other rifle and he has wisely gone in the other boat." Sali looked ahead and stared at the towing vessel with contempt.

"Yes and we are getting closer to the coast, and running out of time." Even as he spoke, and even with the fading light, Yarin could see the details of the sandy cliffs capped with vegetation.

"We could act now, go below, and eliminate Emil. We could take his rifle, and then cut the towrope. Then, when Tarik orders the old man to turn around and see what has happened, we rise up over the side and take him unaware. We use a magazine on him and the old man, and then we can force the American woman into operating the boat and towing us back to Toplu."

"Ayeeyah, elder brother, that is a bold plan, you truly do have a gifted mind."

"Yes, but is it only a simple logic, grounded in common sense. We must act while we still have time, and before we are useless."

"But the sun is all but gone. After we finish Tarik, we will be left with the darkness."

"Better the darkness of night than what waits for us on the shore." Sali jerked a thumb away from the setting sun and toward the approaching coastline.

"Elder brother, you have spoken like a prophet. Only fools like Emil would follow lambs led to the slaughter."

"Then we are agreed. It's time to act," Sali looked over to the woman at the wheel and then to the others seated on the taff rail, the two English and the two strangers from Istanbul.

After an appraising moment, the mechanic nodded. "Go below and deal with Emil. Surprise him, finish him, and make his departure quick and painless. He is low-brained and will suspect nothing. Tarik's nephew and his friend are another problem, but only small ones. You will know what to do with them when they see what happens to Emil. They will fight, or succumb, but either way, they are only boys and nothing before your knife." The older man paused as he regarded the sheathed stiletto in the fading light.

After a silent moment, the life force strengthened, and the power of the bullion prevailed.

Sali nodded abruptly, his decision inevitable. "I will give you five minutes, and then I will go forward and cut the towing rope. When Tarik comes back to investigate we will use the Russian weapon. With the setting sun, it will be easy."

"And the others?" Yarin glanced over his shoulder.

"We will need the woman to steer the ship, but the others…" Sali shook his head.

Chapter 53

"Hello?"

"Miss Taggart, this is Angela Barnes calling. We met when you came to my office."

"Oh, Hi,"

"Miss Taggart, may I call you Pauline?"

"Oh sure, why not? I'm not in trouble or anything…am I?"

"No, not at all. It's just that I have been considering our conversation about what you told me in the office. About what you said about the OPC security director and about how you have been worried about Doctors Pauliss and Clopec—about their whereabouts."

"Well yes. I'm very worried. It's been over three weeks since I heard from Brian, and now Mister Haggly-Ford is dead. He's dead and everyone is saying that OPC will soon be closed. Closed because they're bankrupt. They're also saying that maybe he really didn't have a heart attack, and maybe he was murdered, just like Becca."

Pauline now paused, gripped her telephone tighter, and was glad she could say what she really wanted without having to look into the elegant lawyer's piercing blue gaze.

"I also heard that you were there…when Mister Haggly-Ford had the heart attack. I heard that he was screaming at you. I heard that you are the one who called 911."

"Miss Taggart, let me assure you that the rumors about Alex Haggly-Ford being murdered are completely erroneous. He died of natural causes, and that has been proven, *and authenticated,* by the county coroner."

"I thought you wanted to call me Pauline?"

"Oh yes, of course... I did, I mean...I *do*..."

"Ms. Barnes, I didn't mean to make you mad."

"No, please understand. I'm not angry. It's just that with my lifestyle, I can sometimes get a little intense. This business with OPC, there's a lot at stake, a lot of money involved."

"So you were there? You were there when Mister Haggly-Ford died?" Pauline gripped the phone even tighter as she waited for the response.

Angela smoothed a wrinkle in her pants suit and leaned back in her chair. "Yes, "she said carefully, "I was there, and I did call 911."

"OK, thanks for telling me the truth. You see, I know that you were there, because I know Charlene—Mister Haggly-Ford's secretary. She told me you were there and she also told me about his screaming—about his screaming at *you*."

"Yes, but please understand there was no foul play—only a terrible reaction to some bad news, information that upset Mister Haggly-Ford."

"Was the bad news about *you* taking over the company? I heard that *you* started a stock sell off and then bought back in later. Most people are saying that OPC is broke and going to close, but a few are saying that *you* now own the whole company. I would like to know which one is true. So if I need to, I can start looking for another job. I mean, now that I can trust you—now that I *know* you told me the truth."

In her law office, Angela Barnes paused to take a therapeutic deep breath and tried to keep the attorney's edge out of her voice. "Pauline, do you remember that I called you?" she began with an earnest tone. "I called *you*, because I have some questions to ask *you*."

"Oh! I'm sorry. I forgot. It's just that me and my friends are all real worried. Everybody in Midland and Odessa are worried about OPC." Pauline nervously continued, "They're worried about the company and their jobs and the whole town, and I'm worried about Brian. I'm worried about Brian *and* Doctor Clopec, *and* about whether they're being followed or chased by that awful security man Cedric Bowles."

"Miss Taggart. My offices have been overrun with these types of questions and I have no intention of—"

"I thought that you wanted to call me Pauline?"

"Well...yes, I do."

"I thought you had some questions for *me*? You sure do get upset easy, Ms. Barnes. Maybe you need to find a boyfriend? You know—someone who could help you with the stress. I know that I sure do miss Brian—I mean Doctor Pauliss. We were good for each other—like *that*."

Angela Barnes pulled the handset away from her ear and stared at the

244

receiver. For a brief moment, she was furious at the insinuation, but then she remembered her Texas childhood, her life experience before Radcliff, and how she had compared the brave young woman who came to her offices wanting information to a younger version of herself, the young woman who wanted information. Or did she want to *give* information? With only seconds to contemplate her overly busy schedule, and her lengthy celibate lifestyle, Angela Barnes, attorney at law, allowed the crack in her armor to widen and she began to laugh.

"Ms. Barnes?" Pauline questioned when she heard the unusual sounds coming through the telephone.

"I'm sorry, I didn't want to make you cry," was the mistaken statement the Radcliff lawyer heard when she finally replaced the handset next to her ear. Then the irony of the young woman with southern accent struck home. The thought that *she* had made *her* cry became hilarious, and Angela laughed harder.

"Ms. Barnes? Are you OK?"

Angela dropped the receiver as the tears of laughter rolled down her face. She could scarcely catch her breath. As she laughed, she realized what a great floodgate had been opened, an emotional door that had been closed for far too long. After a moment, she pulled herself together.

"Pauline?" she asked attentively. "Are you still there?"

"Yes, but maybe we should talk later—when you're not so upset."

Angela had to bite her lip to gain control, but then she wondered if the tears were really from laughter or if the emotional dam that had broken was actually all of her feelings being released at once. She refocused and gripped the phone.

"Yes Pauline, I'm here and I'm fine, but I still have one or two important questions."

"OK, if you're sure you feel up to it?"

"Yes, I'm all right now," Angela said, but really wondered if she was. Was *that* kind of outbreak normal? Quickly, she continued. "Pauline, do you remember Doctor Pauliss'—I mean *Brian's* cell phone?"

"Oh, yeah, he was really proud of that. It was very expensive. He loved to show it off. He was always telling me how he could use that phone anywhere in the world. It's connected to every cell phone server and even some satellites—all over the world.

"Do you remember the number—I mean, have you been trying to call him, or were you waiting for him to call you?"

"Hell," Pauline said. "I'm not proud—or hard to get. I've called him every day for the last three weeks. That's one of the reasons I'm worried, Brian used to always like to talk on the phone. I think in his own way, he

245

really loves me—at least I hope so."

"Pauline I don't want to sound rude or scare you, but maybe you should give me Doctor Pauliss' cell number. Maybe he's in trouble and needs my help." Angela leaned forward with a pen and notepad at-the-ready.

"I have a friend down in Houston," the lawyer continued smoothly. "She works for NASA. She might be able to use a satellite and track him down—and Doctor Clopec. It might be possible to track the cell phone number and find out where they are."

"Really? I never heard of such a thing." Pauline sounded doubtful but hopeful at the same time.

"Well," Angela continued carefully. "We won't know unless we try. I really would like to speak with them. This could be very important—important for everyone at OPC."

"But Brian is not answering his phone. I know because I've had other people try, just in case he saw that it was me calling and he didn't want to talk."

"Why don't you give me the number and we'll see what happens? Maybe I can help."

"OK, but please keep me posted. Like I said, Brian is very special to me."

"Of course," was the personalized but professional response.

Pauline quickly recited the number with the extra digits needed for a satellite-connected, international cellular phone. It was obvious when she repeated the number for accuracy that she had the vital integers memorized.

"Oh, and Ms. Barnes?" Pauline added hopefully.

"Yes?"

"Is it true that you now own OPC?"

"I do own controlling interest—a majority of the stock."

"Then can I ask a question? I don't want to upset you, but can I ask about our jobs? My job and all my friends at OPC?"

"Pauline," the litigator voice took over. "I am not at liberty to discuss the welfare of *our* company at this time, but I can tell you that if we find Doctors Pauliss and Clopec, and *if* what I have learned is true, there could be wonderful opportunities for everyone involved."

After a moment Pauline answered, "Well, that's good news, I guess."

"Yes, it could be *very* good news. Thank you for talking to me, and thanks for the number."

"Oh, that's alright. I'm glad to help. Will you please call when you find out something?"

"Of course," and then the line was dead.

Chapter 54

"But, *Aga*, the passage between the stones, it doesn't look deep enough. This old ship," the aged mariner tilted his head astern, "she swims very deep and she is over loaded," he insisted.

"It's deep enough for a submarine," The Wolf replied with confidence. "I have been here many times." He was stationed beside the elderly fisherman as the older man steered the towboat.

The fan-tailed launch was very near the coastline, and facing an advancing wall of towering sandstone. A deep crevice split the hanging greenery at the top of the cliffs and dropped with sheer sides into a very narrow channel. With every meter gained toward the tightening waterway, the vertical ramparts of stone dwarfed the masts of the approaching schooner.

The sun had disappeared below the western cliffs and the edge of the sea, and with the last light of the day, the fan-tailed launch chugged slowly forward as the battered hull of the schooner wallowed behind.

The Wolf smiled as he regarded the expression of doubt and concern on the old mariner's features. The passage did appear unyielding and with a narrow channel between the high cliffs, the logic that the water was shallow was easily understandable.

"Is it true, *Aga*, that a submarine traveled this passage? You saw this?" the old man asked nervously. His eyes darted from the closing cliffs and then back along the shortened towline to the huddle of men gathered on the forepeak of the schooner.

"No." The Wolf spoke carefully, "I did not see the submarine pass through, but I saw it on the other side."

"Forgive me, lord, but what is this place? I have fished this coastline for many years, but I have never heard of this blind passage, this channel that hides between the stones."

"You have no knowledge, because this place does not exist—at least not officially." The Wolf's comment was given freely and without his usual scrutiny. He was preoccupied. As the launch motored forward, he was raking the cliff tops with a pair of binoculars. He continued smoothly as if the release of his words relieved an inner tension.

"I should explain myself," Oclay commented. "This watercourse and what lies beyond the cliffs is not like the rest of our country, not ancient, but new. Originally, there was only a narrow waterway that led between the rocks, but this was before the Americans came, the Americans and their CIA. The basin that lies beyond was discovered with aerial photographs. A perfect little harbor was found hiding among the cliffs, and the watercourse enlarged with blasting and excavation."

"But why, *Aga*? Why would the Americans do such a thing?" The old fisherman still looked doubtful as he began to thread the needle of stone, his eyes judging the speed, the towline, and the bow-angle of the little ship that now followed closely. The cliffs were at least a hundred meters high, and the passage in between the sheer walls under twenty.

The Wolf laughed softly, but his eyes were glued to the binoculars as he continued to scrutinize the hanging greenery at the top of the cliffs. "It is a new place, but not that new. Think old man!" Oclay demanded. "When that running pack of Soviet dogs had their time with Russia, the Americans were mad about finding out what was really going on. They built this place to service their spy vessels. I have seen small submarines, fishing trawlers and even millionaire's yachts from Greece. All ran by the CIA and all controlled and dispatched from this hidden harbor."

"Forgive me, lord, but how do you know this?"

Oclay lowered his binoculars, apparently satisfied with the empty cliff tops. "Because," he said, "I worked for them. There was a time when the Americans paid out money like water running out of a tap. It was simple work, interesting, and I learned a great deal. You must understand, during those times it was common knowledge that Moscow would have swallowed Turkey if not for the Americans. I was glad to help, and I was well paid."

The fisherman nodded his understanding as his gnarled hands moved to turn the wheel. Even with the fading light, it was now obvious the passage was manmade. As the two vessels entered the chasm, and the walls began to turn with the channel, drill marks for blasting were easily observed dropping below the water.

After the first turn, the narrow channel began to widen, but as the two

248

vessels coasted ahead, they were enclosed in darkness. A pool began to emerge, growing larger as the echo of the chugging diesel drummed against the confined space. Then, in the distance, across the opening lagoon, the silhouette of a long dock was visible. Behind the dock, and deep in shadows, a depot type structure was erected in front of another sheer rising cliff.

With a thumb on a switch, Tarik Oclay clicked one of the marine spotlights and cast the light beam across the water and onto the abandoned pier. He searched the empty windows of the waterside depot and finally cast the light beam aloft. The light traveled upward and probed the covered cliff tops. After a few moments to complete a thorough survey, the light beam returned to the water's surface.

"We are here!" he shouted. "Our voyage is complete!"

At that moment, the towline went slack.

Chapter 55

P eter gauged the moment and stood up. "Come on," he said quietly, "everyone quickly."

After Peter's muted, but urgent suggestion, Brian rose and motioned to the Turkish men who had climbed aboard with Cedric Bowles. Reluctantly, they stood from their positions on the taff-rail and came forward. Within seconds, they were all gathered around Billie at the wheel.

"What's wrong?" Brian's words were a whisper as he watched the waterfront Turk who was rapidly filing aft—the man who was the obvious mechanic and the older man who had struck Peter with the wrench.

"He's cut the towline," Billie explained. "He's cut the towline and now we are adrift."

"But why would he do that?" Brian's question was incredulous as he strained to look around. After passing between the cliffs and into the hidden basin, the lighting had failed almost completely until a spotlight on the towboat began sweeping over the water.

The low building and the dock system appeared long since abandoned, and when the spotlight climbed the cliffs and searched overhead, the answer for the abrupt darkness was complete. A series of cables crossed high across the cliff tops and supported a torn and tattered, but nonetheless still intact, canvas covering. One hundred meters below the cables and the rigged camouflage, the spotlight on the towboat was the only illumination.

"Something's up, and *something* not good," Billie remarked as the fan-tailed launch turned abruptly and approached the schooner. When the towboat was almost alongside, the spotlight hit the Turkish mechanic who had been striding back from the forepeak and the severed towline.

The man was immediately stopped by the light, and seemingly as frozen as his shadow. His mouth worked, but no sound came out, and his eyes darted for the companionway. Disappointment flooded his features as the growl of the diesel rumbled alongside and fell silent. He was alone on the deck, except for his neglected prisoners who were crowded around the woman at the wheel.

"Sali? What have you done? What are you planning?" The Wolf's Turkish voice boomed out across the two vessels, very loud against the now silent engine.

Quickly, with his words a whisper, Mustafa translated for the group at the wheel.

"Where is Yarin? Where is Emil?" Oclay demanded, but the spotlight never wavered. His voice was the light, and his boat and surroundings, a complete silhouette, a powerful entity, separate from the schooner.

"Sali," the Wolf continued, "I can see your thoughts. Your misgivings are written across your face. You have chosen to betray me! After all our time together and all that we have shared, I am surprised." As the booming Turkish words flowed and echoed across the water, Mustafa continued his running translation in a murmuring undertone.

"Ever since we discovered the old king's treasure, your mind has swollen like a boil about to fester. I must confess, I did imagine it would be you. After all, are you not the most intelligent? However, I am truly disappointed. I had hoped that you could have been stronger. I can't believe that you are such a fool," he added. "Do you think I would leave Emil with a loaded weapon? Do you really believe I would be that stupid?

"Before I crossed to the launch, I switched rifles. I chose to travel in the launch because I *knew this* would happen. I knew what I would have to do." Suddenly, there was venom in the words that surpassed any language barrier. "Have you ever known me not to be prepared?"

Before Mustafa could finish translating, the muzzle flash of the automatic weapon shattered the darkness and the sharp crack of the Ak-47 reverberated loudly against the sheer walls of the stone basin. The mechanic jerked as if the tracer rounds from the Russian automatic were stitching threads of fire. Orange streaks of light somehow gripped and held him upright, terrible glowing strings pulled by the ultimate puppet master.

When the flashes stopped and the echo of gunfire was replaced with a heavy silence, a splash sounded as Sali Tuz made a final plunge and joined Benjamin Farouk.

Billie pulled Peter close, beside her at the wheel, as Mustafa and the Turkish aviator crowded next to Brian.

"Yarin! Emil! Kemal!" The voice of the Wolf echoed as the spotlight searched fore and aft. "Show yourselves," he demanded.

Once again Mustafa translated.

After a few heavily weighted moments, with his hands in the air, the thin and dangerous Turk with the stiletto climbed out of the companionway and stood uneasily on the deck. The man's trademark weapon was in the sheath on his belt, but he seemed instantly deflated as the Wolf captured him with the light.

"Tarik, do not shoot," he began. "There has been a treachery," the new man in the light pleaded.

"Emil is dead!" he screamed. "His throat has been cut. And Kemal your nephew. They have been murdered. Murdered by someone onboard," the voice was pleading.

As the last of his words echoed away and as Mustafa finished the whispered translation, every eye focused on the dark stains on the Turkish man's hands. His palms were facing the light, but even from the side there was the unmistakable evidence of walnut colored smudges.

"Christ, what now?" Brian offered gently.

"Quiet, effendi," Mustafa suggested.

In the following seconds, the powerful searchlight from the towboat claimed all attention—a harsh circle of illumination that focused the surrounding silence. It was as if the statement from the man with the blood stained hands was incomprehensible, incomprehensible because it was an unforeseen development, not predictable, and therefore unexpected.

The light remained fixed and seeming to hold the Turk with his hands in the air, but slowly as the seconds passed, the sounds from the surrounding darkness began to intrude. A creak of the wooden deck after an inevitable but subtle movement of the hull, and beyond the edge of the light, a gurgle of water crossed between the two vessels, moved across the lagoon and climbed the chasm with the trace of an echo. Just as the ears became as focused as the eyes were by the light, the metal-oil-smoke of spent gunpowder drifted beyond the search beam and offered a reminder of what had just happened.

Without warning, the booming laugh of the Wolf carried over the water suddenly sounding very close. Without the slightest indication and with the startling revelation and surprise of a magician, the big man stepped aboard the schooner and into the light. In the darkness, and without a sound, the towboat had pulled alongside the schooner.

"Put your hands down, Yarin, you look ridiculous," he said. "Now tell me all about what you have been doing and all about the Mr. British."

Chapter 56

Silently, Cedric stepped forward with the others and tried to control his breathing. It was difficult. He had just hurriedly made his way forward, past the salon, past the galley, and past the stinking toilet-stall to the forepeak of the schooner. He had climbed into a small access hatch and found his way across and over the barnacle encrusted anchor rope. After scratching himself several times, he wiggled through the deck opening for the ground-tackle-storage and watched carefully from behind the jib boom as the dirtiest and greasiest of the Turks was dispatched with the ultimate weapon, his beloved AK-47. He had smiled in the darkness, cleaned and wiped his hands on the heavy sailcloth, before making his way aft along the deck on the shadowed side of the cabin house. This was when the second man emerged, surprised, shaken, and unhinged.

As he knew, all attention would be centered on the Turk with the stiletto. Especially since even from the forepeak, it was obvious that the man's hands were covered in blood. He would certainly be the logical suspect as he was the one who so blatantly carried a knife, particularly when one considered the circumstances below decks.

The two bodies below would never share in the gold, or for that matter share in anything but the nearness of their deaths, the untidiness of their undoing, and the mess that was the necessity of horror.

The security director now had to bite his lip to keep from giggling. He was standing behind Mustafa and the pilot and to the left of the blond woman and the two English fannies. They had no idea that he was behind them, or on deck, or about the graphic scene that waited below. They were too busy watching the Turkish leader regain the deck and step into the light.

Earlier, Cedric had realized upon seeing the coast that the time for action was at hand. He had taken a quick evaluation as the sun was low in the sky and determined that the need for discretion was over. He had been below decks as instructed and pretending to clean the galley, but with nightfall approaching his impatience took over.

Having been below decks for most of the day had provided the perfect opportunity to prepare his plan and make the most of the materials at hand. It was obvious that a serious doubt had to be cast among the Turks— a doubt and fear so ruthless that the waterfront thugs would begin to fight amongst themselves. Divide and conquer, his training had taught, would be most useful strategy when unavoidable changes drew near, changes like the approaching coastline and the ultimate implications of an end-of-route—harbor-side destination.

When all the Turks were above decks and obviously excited about the first discovery of land, the security director abandoned his pretense at the galley chores and made his way aft. With his senses heightened and his background-training taking over, Cedric prepared himself. He had made a thorough evaluation of the galley, and the salon, and for as long as he could stand the stench, the lavatory. Quietly and slowly, he moved past the gold (which seemed to glow even without light) to the lazarette and the engine compartment.

In an abandoned, rust-choked toolbox, a small coil of copper wire was found. The wire, although green with patina, was about two meters long, braided with strands, and very strong. After a quick giggle and without a second consideration, the wire was tucked away in a pocket along with two rusty screwdrivers. It was only after finding the braided wire cable that the security director knew that he had a plan that would work. There would be, without a doubt, obstacles. However, a good operative could always be inspired with confidence. After all, confidence, planning, and surprise were the ultimate components of any winning stratagem.

After returning to the galley, the security director retrieved two of the large plastic trash bags. Quickly, he found the bottom of the bag and began to make a kaffir raincoat. He used his teeth to tear out a center hole for his head, and on the sides, two holes for his arms. When finished, he stood standing with the black plastic covering most of his body. As he admired his ingenuity, he roughly considered that he probably looked like one of the homeless in an afternoon thunderstorm. This thought produced a giggle as he quickly used torn pieces of another bag to cover his arms.

He took a tentative glance up the companionway and listened. There was no apparent activity and he heard no voices. Satisfied that he had a few minutes alone, he began work on the weapon. The braided copper wire was uncoiled and quickly laid out on the galley counter. After judging the correct distance, the wire was folded in half and carefully twisted into a single strand.

As Cedric ran his fingers along the surface, he considered the wire braids were almost like a saw blade and this perforated edge was made even more severe by the fact the copper cable was doubled. The two screwdrivers were easily attached, one on either end of the newly twisted strand and after the new weapon was complete, the security director tested the screwdriver handles for strength. He placed his feet on one end and tried to pull the handles apart. Even with the full extent of his muscle, both handles remained securely in place.

For a distraction and diversion, another trip to the hold was completed and two of the rounded gold bars were placed strategically on the floor of the galley. The two golden samples of bullion were almost out of sight—almost, but not quite.

Cedric waited.

He waited behind the stairs of the companionway. He was completely hidden and out of view, and even if someone had known he was there, the lack of lighting in the cabin and his black plastic raincoat was hiding him nicely. As the sun set lower and the light in the galley began to fade, the black plastic rustled as the security director moved to light the hanging lantern swaying in the salon. For the plan to work there must be more than enough light to see the distraction and the diversion.

Just after the security director was positioned behind the stairs and starting to giggle, the Turk with the AK-47 started down the companionway. The man was an idiot, overconfident and had clearly forgotten any military training. He immediately saw the distraction of the carefully placed bars, and after he had lowered his weapon and knelt to examine the shining golden lozenges, silent steps were taken and the braided copper wire was slipped over his head. As planned, a kneeling victim was the most easily dispatched.

With a knee on the stupid Turk's spine, the makeshift garrote had been closed with surprising speed and efficiency. The man's struggle had lasted under a minute. He died without making a sound. When the victim's death was certain, Cedric began the sawing motion necessary to imitate a violent knife wound. After two minutes, the image was complete. Even though the man's heart had stopped, his blood flowed from the neck wound as if his throat had been cut.

Before Cedric could admire the procedure and check his blood-proof plastic suit in the lantern light. A second Turk started down the companionway. Surprisingly, the youngest of the Turks descended the wooden stairs completely before he saw the fallen shape that was his compatriot lying in an unbelievable pool of blood. His startled expression lasted only a second before the security director smashed in his nose with the rifle butt of the AK-47.

As the youth fell unconscious from the abrupt head wound, he never felt the bloody garrote close around his neck and the sawing motions begin. After another moment of effort, the blood from both bodies mingled and made a black pool covering the floor. Before he carefully stepped away from the mess, the makeshift garrote with the screwdrivers handles was dropped into an access panel for the bilge.

With more than the first stage of his plan complete, Cedric pulled off his blood-spattered trash-bag-coat, turned the plastic containers inside out, and made his way through the hold just as the Turk with the Stiletto descended the stairs. As the security director now stood on the deck, he considered that his timing could not have been more perfect. He had to bite his lip to keep from giggling.

Chapter 57

"Pauline?"

"Yes?"

"This is Angela Barnes."

"Oh, hello, I'm glad you called. Have you heard anything—or found anything out?"

"Well yes, and that's why I'm calling. But before we get into that I need to ask you a few questions."

"OK, sure. But, Ms. Barnes…I want you to know, if there's anything I can do to help, please tell me."

"Thank you, that's very reassuring. Do you have any idea why Rebecca would have met with Doctors Pauliss and Clopec? Why she would meet them at the Kinko's store at midnight?"

"No, I only know about *that* from the security tape—the videotape that I showed you. Why?"

"Pauline, what I have to say is too important to discuss over the phone, but I think I know where we can find Brian Pauliss and Peter Clopec."

"Wow! That would be great. I really am very worried. Even if Brian doesn't want to see me anymore, I still care about him."

"Yes, I understand, but I have a couple more questions and then perhaps we could meet."

"OK, that sounds all right."

"Did Rebecca ever mention a compact disk—a computer disk that she had copied from OPC?"

"No, she always hated to talk about work. Why?"

"I have reason to believe she copied some data from the satellite before it went offline...some data that Mr. Haggly-Ford tried to keep secret."

"Oh my God! Is that why she was killed? Is that what happened?"

"Miss Taggart...*Pauline*, please," Angela corrected. "As I said, this is not the type of conversation we want to have over the phone. Now if I may continue, I have a couple more questions and then perhaps we can meet."

"Alright, I'm sorry," Pauline sounded defeated. "I forgot," she conceded. "How can I help?"

"At Rebecca's funeral, or afterward, did Doctor Pauliss or Doctor Clopec mention a compact disk, a disk that they were interested in?"

"Well, that night after the funeral, Brian stayed at my place until early in the morning. It was even before the sun came up when he mentioned that he needed to get back to his apartment and check on some data—some data that he hoped would get him and Doctor Clopec out of all their troubles. All of their problems with Mr. Haggly-Ford."

"Is that all?" Angela Barnes tried to keep the edge out of her voice.

"Well, that morning. Brian also said that if everything fell into place I wouldn't have to be sad anymore, wouldn't have to be sad about Becca or about anything—ever."

"What do think that means?"

"I don't know, but now I'm wondering if it has anything to do with that data you're talking about—about that data from the satellite. Do you think—?"

"Pauline, not over the phone," Angela interrupted carefully. After a pause she asked. "I have just one more question."

"Ok, what?"

"Do you have a passport?"

"Well, sure. Me and Becca we used to go to Cancun every chance we got—" Pauline was poised to ask why but stopped herself.

"Pauline, aren't you going to ask me why?"

"No, Ms. Barnes, I'm not," the tiny voice offered. "It seems to make you mad."

"Alright good, now listen, I want you to pack a bag, bring your passport, and meet me at the airport. I want you to meet me in three hours at El Paso International. Do you understand?"

"I understand, at one o'clock." Pauline was looking at her watch. "But—" she began.

"No buts, just follow directions. Remember you're working for me now. After all, I'm the new boss at OPC. And, Pauline?

"Yes?"

"If everything works out you just might see Doctor Pauliss within a few days. Maybe within a few hours. How does that sound?"

Oh, Ms. Barnes, I don't know how to thank you." Suddenly Pauline was crying, her emotional dam breaking and the safety valve of her stress and worries releasing an inner pressure.

On the other end of the phone, Angela Barnes smiled and waited. After a moment she spoke. "Pauline, don't worry about finding me at the airport. Listen to the intercom and I'll have you paged. Oh, and, Pauline?"

"Yes?"

You had better bring jeans, some long sleeved blouses, and something to cover your hair."

After a moment of silence, Angela asked. "Pauline, aren't you curious? Don't you want to know why?"

"No, I'm not going to ask because I guess I'll find out soon enough."

"That's my girl. See you at the airport."

After she hung up with Pauline Taggart, Angela punched in the numbers for Roy Hartock's cell phone.

After five rings and just enough time to identify the caller, "This here's Roy," was the gruff answer.

"Roy, it's Angela, I've got a one-time offer for a once in a lifetime deal. Are you in?"

"Well... Hell fire and save matches little lady. I know if you have your hand on the handle, it's bound to be a good one. What are you up to?"

"Roy, I'm going to ask you to go into this one blind. You're going to have to trust me."

"Now goddamn it, Angela, that last mess with OPC screwed me up. I got hurt real bad on that one." It was obvious even through the cellular static that Hartock was lighting a cigarette.

"Roy," Angela spoke carefully. "Maybe OPC is not as bad off as it seems—you know I *did* buy back in...at the last moment."

"Hell, Angela! Do you honestly think I didn't know that? You bought in at somewhere around six dollar and forty cent a share—and now have controlling interest. Hell, little lady, you can pick who ever who want to sit on the board. It's going to be your whole show. But what I want to know is, why? Alex is dead, them other Englishmen have run off, and as far as I can tell that whole mess was just one big swindle.

"Why in the hell did you buy something that ain't worth nothing? This ain't like you, Angela."

"Roy, have you ever known me *not* to be careful?"

After a significant pause, and enough time for Angela to picture Hartock blowing out a thin stream of cigarette smoke he answered. "No," he said. "I have not—so tell me what's on your mind and how much is it going to cost?"

"No, Roy, like I said, you're going to have to trust me. I need a favor, a big one."

"And what's in it for me, little lady?"

"Once again, like I said, this is a once in a lifetime deal. You help me with this one favor and I'll cut you in for two percent of the new company."

"Aw hell, Angela, two percent of nothing is nothing that I would be interested in. I'm sorry but I just don't have time to—"

"I have proof that the satellite really did find gold."

"What?"

"Yes, Roy, proof. It was probably the only thing Alex Haggly-Ford didn't lie about."

"Now, little lady, you sure are talking big."

"Roy, why do you think I bought back in? OPC is legally the only possible owner of the satellite research. The only possible owner of a compact computer disk that I have had copied several times and a disk that I have researched through an expert at NASA, a disk that shows ninety-seven survey points around the globe with a positive analysis for gold. All of the survey points are over water and I have spoken to a salvage expert from Florida. He was with Pauliss and Clopec when they found an old shipwreck, an Old Spanish Galleon wreck from the 1700's. Roy, it's all fact." Angela embellished and then enticed. "Can I count you in?"

"Goddamn it, Angela, this sounds like insider trading issues."

"No way! I have documentation that I acted only on instinct, and found the satellite disk only after I acquired the company. I have names dates and witnesses and a very helpful administrative assistant in security, a lovely Spanish lady who has been most helpful with all kinds of detailed information. Roy, I also have proof that Haggly-Ford crashed the satellite. Proof that he crashed it, and proof that Clopec and Pauliss reprogrammed it. Proof that they reprogrammed the satellite to look for gold—and that it worked."

"Alright, I'm convinced," Hartock's voice revealed his interest and Angela smiled. The more concentrated he became the less he talked like a hillbilly. "Now what's that big favor, and what have you got on your mind?"

After he listened in detail, Roy Hartock lit a fresh cigarette and pulled his Mercedes 500 SEC onto the next exit ramp of I-40. This was too much information to handle while driving. After he parked safely in a McDonald's parking lot he opened his briefcase and began scribbling notes. The information of Angela's request was highly detailed and he was duly impressed.

"Ok, Angela, I think I got it covered. But a favor like this is going to cost more than two percent."

"Roy, like I said from the beginning. This is a once in a lifetime offer and good only for today. I have to be at the airport in two hours and forty-five minutes, and before I go, I need that connection of yours. Roy...I need this real bad. I'll go to four percent..." Angela left the last words hanging.

After a quiet moment the gruff voice continued, "Alright, done. But I have one condition."

"And what might that be?" Angela tried to control her elation but she knew her voice was smiling.

"I want to go."

"Roy, don't be silly."

"Angela, it's not a request. It's part of the deal. Either I go, or no favor. Besides who's going to look after you and that pretty little girl? No, I'm serious. I'm going or no deal. What do you say?"

"Roy, you old softy, I must say that I'm touched. Now listen up—meet me at El Paso International, one o'clock. Can you make it?"

Before he began to speak, the gas pedal on the 500 SEC was floored and the Mercedes was barreling toward the I-40 access ramp in the opposite direction he had been traveling earlier. "Angela, when I get there, I'll have you paged."

"I know. See you then."

After he pressed "End" on his cell phone, Roy crossed into the left lane, set the cruise control on 100, and punched in a new number on the phone.

"Good morning, this here's Roy Hartock and I'd like to speak with the governor."

Chapter 58

Carefully the old mariner asked, "What now, *Aga?*"

"We wait, old man," Oclay replied. "We wait until help arrives."

"But how long lord?"

The Wolf shook his head. "It doesn't matter," he said. "The men that are coming can be counted on like the rising sun. After the message I have given them, I am surprised that they are not here already."

"Perhaps something has happened," the fisherman commented as he reached for his cigarettes. After offering one to the headman he cracked open his American lighter.

"No, nothing will happen," the Wolf inhaled. "All the men who would give me trouble are now gone."

"But the others that are coming," the fisherman blew out a stream of smoke. "The others when they see what you have found...they will also change."

"Then so-be-it! I will handle that problem when it comes as I will deal with any other obstacle." Oclay drew deeply on his cigarette, his eyes narrowed, and he focused anew on the older man before him. "Any obstacle," he said. "Even you, old man."

After the bodies had been found, a dark mood swept over the schooner, it was now obvious the life force of the gold had manifest into the ultimate betrayal. It had taken only a brief inspection of the Wolf's most loyal underlings to produce an instant decision. With a rage so violent and so brutal it was hard to imagine, Yarin Dun was killed as he tried to defend himself with his cherished weapon.

Tarik Oclay after inspecting the horror that was Emil and his nephew, reacted instantly and blamed the knife wielding man from the waterfront. After a quick but pitiful struggle, Yarin was pistol whipped into submission and then given the coup-de-grace with a single pistol shot to the forehead. His body, along with the others, was weighted with chains and thrown over the side.

"All right, now what?" Peter asked with disgust. "Should we tie each other's hands and also go over the side?"

"No, Mister English, as you can see, my company had been greatly reduced, but I also require your services in the way of your expertise. You are men of science. You told me this before." The Wolf's eyes narrowed.

After he spoke, Tarik Oclay crossed the deck of the schooner and regarded the light coming from the dockside depot. The schooner and the fan-tailed launch were alongside the abandoned dock system and the old mariner had been instructed on where to find the installation's generator.

"Good sweet Christ, Peter," Brian whispered when the waterfront leader was beyond the range of hearing. "I didn't think you had it in you," he added.

"What are you talking about?" Peter rebuffed.

"Killing those blokes, what else? And how did you do it and why didn't you use the gun? Oh I see..." Brian nodded in the near dark. "The pistol would have been too loud, but my God how did you do it?"

"Are you mad?" Peter was staring.

The events after traveling through the chasm walls and into the hidden basin had progressed with such a terrible momentum that even the headman from Sinop was having difficulty processing all that had happened.

After the accused Turk had pulled his stiletto in an act of final and frustrated defiance and the Waterfront leader had reacted, only a few moments had passed until the ruined bodies had been hauled on deck, trussed in chains, and then thrown overboard. There had been no chance to even whisper let alone discuss anything.

Billie stepped forward protectively and placed her arm around Peter's waist, her eyes following the waterfront leader as he walked the dock and entered the abandoned waterside depot with his AK-47 in hand, deadly and held at-the-ready, and the older mariner following behind. The only other hostile Turk remaining was the youngest, no more than a teenager, and clearly terrified by all that had happened. He was nervously standing at the taff-rail smoking and covering his prisoners with the other automatic rifle.

"Pete," Billie asked. "You didn't kill those guys, did you?"

"Of course not," Peter's voice was soft but his tone was adamant.

"But you were the only one below decks," Brian shuddered at the thought. "The one with the knife—the one that was shot—he wasn't down there long enough to create that kind of havoc."

The two men below decks had been almost decapitated and the blood spoil was incredible. Earlier, Peter had gone below with the pretense of using the toilet, but had actually gone forward to retrieve the hidden Luger, the pistol hidden between the gold bars that was now tucked into the waist band of his trousers. He had returned to the deck just after the mechanic had cut the towrope.

"If you didn't, then who did?" Brain asked carefully, his focus on the teenager with the rifle who was smoking.

"There can be only one answer," Peter tilted his head toward Cedric Bowles and his two hired Turks, also waiting by the taff rail.

"But he was on deck when both of the men were shot, and when the headman came back aboard."

"He was up and down a lot, Argentina," Billie shook her head. "But I think that was part of his plan, to make himself visible. If he were visible, he would be no more of a suspect than the rest of us. You have to admit, he was damned clever to do it with a knife—to make the leader think it was done over greed and done by the stiletto."

"Well, one thing is for certain," Brian added quietly. "There are less bad guys, and those three that are gone, they were the worst of the lot."

"No, Brian, that's not quite right," Peter's tone was grave as he turned his head and nodded toward Cedric Bowles. "He's the worst one of the lot, and by far the most dangerous."

Across the pier the Turkish leader's voice rang out, "Hey, Mister British! Mister Hollywood British! I need you here! There's something you need to see!"

"Well," Peter looked first to Brian and then over to Billie. "I guess I don't have much of a choice."

"Pete," Billie took his hand. "I'm going with you—at least down to the pier," she gestured over the side. "This hull and the launch—they're not even tied up."

Chapter 59

When the earthquake began, it started as only a tremor. A slight rumbling as if from a far away freight train, but a train that was moving too fast and a locomotive that was arriving without a whistle, an unscheduled engine rattling up from hell.

Billie had just crossed over a makeshift gangway from the afterdeck of the schooner to the concrete pier facing the depot. She was making fast a spring line when the first sensation of vibration moved through the air.

At first, she thought it might have been the diesel generator started beside the dock-house and tried to connect the growing buzzing effect with the electric lights that had so recently been illuminated. As she stopped and stood from beside the dock-cleat, she saw that everyone was frozen in place and looking around as she was.

Then it happened: a great hammer strike from under the ground, a lifting, shattering, splintering motion that was so intense Billie felt as if her ankles had suddenly been broken. She was falling, as was everyone.

Even though she knew that only seconds had passed since the world began to come apart, the drifting dust coming down from the cliff sides blurred the shuddering scene into a hazy, slow-motion nightmare. Her first thought, even before she had time to consider that she had fallen, and what was happening, was: *How do we get out of here?*

The little-harbor basin within the chasm of stone was certainly a perfect anchorage, but not with the precarious cliffs trembling high overhead. After the carved-out channel leading to the sea, there was only one other apparent exit—a railway sized tunnel excavated into a sheer wall of stone, a tunnel leading presumably out of the walled-in basin and onto some type of coastal road. The entire setting was the perfect smuggler's cove—except when the tops of the cliff sides began to rumble apart.

Down on her knees but beginning to rise, Billie immediately scanned her surroundings, but neither Peter nor Brian was visible. Only seconds ago, the big man that was the waterfront leader had disappeared into the dock-house with Peter. Brian however was still on the schooner under guard, as were the others, by the Turk with the machine gun. As she looked, everyone remaining onboard rushed to the side and was staring as if they were reluctant to accept the severity of the earth gone mad.

After another glance to the dock-house, Peter was visible in the entrance to the waterside depot, the Turkish leader beside him. Both men's faces registering shock at the sight and sounds of such an unbelievable seismic event. Beside the pier-side depot, the exit tunnel glowed with a string of electrical lights but also began to exhale a cloud of dust from deep within the passageway of stone.

When the hammer blow struck, the old sailor who was the maritime expert fell to his knees and locked his disbelieving eyes onto Billie as she also struggled with the staggering reality of what was happening. As the quake continued, and a terrible rolling-rumble began to build, rocks from the cliff tops started to tumble down.

For a split second, Billie recalled the old children's nursery rhyme of Chicken Little and the sky falling. This brief thought was reinforced forever as a tremendous boulder broke from the height of the cliffs and crashed onto the roof of the dockside depot. Before she had time to consider that Peter was on the threshold of the damaged building, an avalanche of more stones began to tumble down.

Most of the rubble was bowling ball size, but as the loosened cliff tops began to crumble, entire sections of the old Turkish coast began to slide and plummet into the water. With the collapse of the cliff walls starting to resemble a landslide, a descending veil of dust began to fog the scene with a surreal quality that made the elapsing time sluggish.

High overhead, a new effect of the earthquake demanded attention as at least some of the wire cables stretched across the chasm began to part, a high pitched whip-snapping reverberation that told the tale of a tremendous displacement at the top of the cliffs. As the cables stretched beyond their limits, or the anchors in the stone gave way, the heavy camouflage canvas dropped from the heights and reinforced the image of a dreadful falling sky. All around the circular basin the little harbor was erupting with geyser spouts where the falling wedges of stone displaced the unsettled and trembling water.

As the surface of the basin began to churn as if ready to boil, the tee-naged Turk gripping the automatic rifle staggered for the gangway and the imagined safety of solid land. He made it only half way when the schooner began to roll away from the dock.

As fast as the little ship moved away and spilled the gangplank, the inevitable roll of the hull returned, and seemingly with a vengeance, crushing everything between the concrete pier and the wooden wall of timbers. The Turkish youth's final cry was ground out before it could be finished, and without delay another episode of hydraulic chaos was on the rise.

As suddenly as the quake began, and as suddenly as the water in the little harbor began to tremble, the first of the crashing waves was followed by a dramatic drop in the seawater level. It was as if some unbelievable drain had opened and the entire manmade lagoon began to empty. Before Billie realized that the rumbling tremor was still growing, and the carved out entrance to the sea was collapsing, another tremendous crash sounded and the electrical lights flickered and then went out. With the dry dust mixing heavily in the air, the seaward entrance darkened, and nightfall complete, all of the normal senses were wiped away and replaced with the bedlam-filled horror of the still growing quake.

In the shadows, the masts of the schooner tilted and then dropped, then rose again, as did the battered black hull. Even in the near dark, and even with the air thick and choked with the red powder from the cliffs, Billie knew what was happening. The narrow entrance to the sea was darkened with a rising wall of water—a tidal wave surge created by the earthquake.

With a rushing force of staggering proportions, the Black Sea water re-filled the chasm lagoon, flooded over the pier, and rushed into the entrance of the dockside depot. As the misplaced sea continued to rise, the fan-tailed launch lifted beside the schooner and rushed into an inevitable collision with the depot-house and the sheer wall of the cliff face.

Once again, before there was time to react, Billie was rising with the wall of water, struggling to breathe and stay afloat while her mind raced to deny what was happening.

"No!" her innermost fears screamed. "Not Peter and not Brian! Not when I'm just starting to live!"

The Black Sea did not hear and would not stop. Her ancient waters rushed in and climbed the cliff sides. Relentless in her pursuit of the dry reddish stone the rising waves churned, boiled, and pushed until reaching heights untouched since the great flood. She then crested and withdrew into herself, and finally collapsed back into the depths of her existence. As the waters receded, and the final waves settled with the trembling earth, a beautiful spangle of stars glistened above a newly formed mountain.

Chapter 60

R oy Hartock shook his head in disgust. "Now goddamn it," he said. "What in the hell is that supposed to mean?"

"It simply means, Mr. Hartock, that Brian Pauliss and Peter Clopec are British subjects. Any investigation into their activities, or their whereabouts, is certainly of interest to Her Majesty's government."

"That sounds like a load of horse shit to me. Angela, what do you think?"

"Gentlemen, may we have a few minutes—a few minutes in private?"

"Certainly," the taller of the two Englishmen courteously replied, his accent patrician.

With a polite nod, Angela Barnes led Hartock over to a large bay window overlooking the Attaturk Boulevard. They were in the second story offices of the American Embassy in Istanbul. The day outside was pleasant and bright with the afternoon sun just starting to cast shadows. The traffic was heavy and pedestrians were everywhere.

Angela looked over her shoulder to the two English diplomats waiting by the desk. The Englishmen had arrived just before the scheduled meeting with the American Ambassador. She glanced across the office and smiled at Pauline. After a tentative, but positive response from her novice travel partner, the Texas lawyer returned her attention to Hartock.

"Roy, I think that maybe this is best. Maybe these people can help. They obviously speak Turkish and seem to know their way around. Finding Clopec and Pauliss might be harder than tracing the latest signal from a cell phone."

"Well, Angela, this is your little ballgame, but I always liked things a little more private. I got a feeling that *they* know something that we don't." Hartock paused to light a cigarette and stare at the two intruding Englishmen.

After his phone call to the governor in Texas, and the subsequent calls to the state department in Washington, and then onto Ankara and Istanbul, the Effendi Hartock and his two American women had been received at the airport with all the courtesy afforded to the highest level diplomats. Without delay, the Americans had been rushed across the afternoon traffic, ushered into the embassy, and awaited to speak to the ambassador when the men from the British envoy arrived and forced their introductions.

The British were well informed. They knew the precise moment when Peter and Brian entered Turkey. They knew about the American woman with the German name, Irmgard Finkelmeyer, and they knew about the hired car taking them along the Black Sea coast to arrive in Sinop. They even knew about an empty set of hotel rooms to which no one had returned.

All thoughts and concentration was broken as a large set of double doors opened and a military attaché stepped forward. The man was a strikingly handsome Sergeant Major in the American Army. He was Afro-American, very tall, and his head completely shaved. Angela smiled, glancing at the ironed creases on his uniform, sharp enough to cut. Roy Hartock smiled when the diplomatic soldier spoke.

"Ladies and gentlemen, the Ambassador will see you now," the Sergeant Major said with a southern accent.

After standing to receive his guests, the American Ambassador, Phillip Enwright, shook hands with the women, then Hartock, and finally like old friends with the two British diplomats, Stanley Grey and Samuel Marsh. When the introductions were finished everyone but the Sergeant Major sat down.

"Stanley," the Ambassador began, "why don't you do the kick-off so we can get this thing rolling. As you know, we have had a very serious earthquake in this area of interest and I would like to expedite any action from our end as soon as possible."

"Of course, Mister Ambassador. I understand perfectly." After a moment to make eye contact with each of the visiting Americans, the Englishman began. "What I believe his emissary is suggesting is that you should be informed of some rather closely guarded secrets."

After a nod from Enwright, the upper-class accent continued.

"Very shortly after Doctors Pauliss and Clopec cleared Turkish customs along with the American woman, another man who was apparently on the same flight was also allowed to enter the country." After a pause to examine reactions, the Englishman continued. "This man however, was recognized and flagged as an undesirable by the Turkish Government. Apparently, he is wanted in South Africa, but currently Turkey has no extradition treaty with Cape Town. He was nonetheless flagged as a criminal element and an undercover operative was assigned to him before leaving the airport."

Another pause. "A second man was assigned after it became apparent that the South African was following Pauliss and Clopec." Stanley Grey now stopped to consider the ashen expression on the youngest of the three Americans. The young woman who appeared drained of color and ready to faint. Carefully he continued, "There have been no recent or up-to-date reports regarding the whereabouts of the undercover team, their subject from South Africa, or Doctors Clopec and Pauliss. Or of course," the Englishmen added dryly, "the only valid American interest in this case, is the woman from Florida."

Ambassador Enwright was sitting quietly with his fingers in a steeple of thought. After it was clear the well-polished Englishman had finished, the American envoy leaned back in his chair and shook his head.

All United States ambassadors were well chosen, and Enwright was no exception. He was a tall, handsome man with iron gray hair dressed in an elegant suit. His air was firm, his manners impeccable, and his experience in the diplomatic corps extensive. When he began his dialogue with a shake of his head, his demeanor seemed regretful.

"Mr. Hartock, you and Ms. Barnes have been placed very high on the state department list of VIPs, but quite frankly, I don't know what I'm expected to do to help you. After all, I'm only an American envoy on foreign soil and not the commander and chief. I cannot send out the army because of one American woman and two British nationals. This is a Muslim country and any American show of strength could be regarded as an international incident." After a pause and another shake of his head he added. "You must understand, our position here is most delicate."

"Mister Ambassador," Hartock broke the following silence. "Did you have any luck with those cell phone coordinates we provided—the latest ones from Doctor Pauliss's satellite phone?"

Enwright nodded again, this time to the other Englishman. "Sam," he said. "I believe this is your area of expertise.'

With a curt nod of acceptance, Samuel Marsh reached beside his chair and opened his briefcase. A large glossy photograph appeared, and as the satellite map was passed around, another upper-class English accent explained. "As you can see, the red circle indicates the latest viable signal from Doctor Pauliss' cell phone. The latest signal I might add is over forty-eight hours old, weak and uncertain, and was observed from an offshore position in the Black Sea. Every indication would point to equipment with a flat battery, or cellular equipment that has failed because of inherent moisture."

"Moisture?" Suddenly Pauline was standing as she looked at the map. "Inherent moisture?" she repeated.

"Ms. Barnes," Pauline spoke as she shifted her gaze as her tears began streaming. "Does he think that they were in a boat—a boat that sank? Is that what he is saying? Is he saying that he thinks Brian's dead and there no use trying to find him?"

"Now hold on there!" Hartock interrupted loudly, leveling his best corporate gaze directly at the two Englishmen.

"Nobody's saying nothing like that. Are you, son?" he added forcefully after he had stood to embrace Pauline. His glare was withering.

"Certainly not!" Enwright's voice intervened and left no doubt as to why he was the ambassador. He continued smoothly although his focus had also shifted and his eyes narrowed. "What we have to understand is that Stanley and Samuel are professionals and deal only in facts—facts that are sometimes worded rather badly." As Enwright finished there was no room for argument.

"Quite right, Mister Ambassador," Stanley Grey conceded. "But I do feel the need to point out there was a severe storm that swept along the Black Sea coast. Perhaps Doctor Pauliss' phone was disabled by the rain. There could be any number of factors contributing to a satellite phone's failure."

If Angela Barnes knew anything, it was timing. Everyone was off guard and concerned about offending Pauline, her near breakdown alarming for the British as well as the ambassador, who was all-too-well-aware of failing to rally to state department requests and VIPs with connections all the way to the Whitehouse.

"Mister Ambassador," the Texas lawyer began sweetly. "Did you mention that there had been an earthquake—an earthquake in the vicinity of the latest transmission from Doctor Pauliss' cellular-satellite phone?"

"Well, yes I did," Enwright confessed, "A terrible tragedy. As you must know, Turkey sits on a very unstable fault line. Turkish earthquakes are always listed as some of the most severe in the world. This latest coastal quake has caused major damage in some remote areas."

"The type of remote areas that would need assistance?" Angela's question was probing, "The type of assistance that could be brought in by helicopter—military helicopters on a mercy mission?"

After a moment of silence, and with a glance toward the two Englishmen, she added. "Perhaps a joint effort," she said. "British and Americans helping their Turkish hosts with a much needed mission of mercy, a mission to try and help stranded mariners or shipwrecked sailors. I feel certain there would be coastal townships that will certainly require additional medical assistance." Angela crossed her arms and smiled. "The type of assistance that always breeds goodwill in diplomatic circles."

With the two British diplomats now openly staring, and Phillip Enwright beginning to nod his agreement, Angela knew it was time to press home the attack.

"Mister Ambassador, "she continued. "I know when we find Doctors Clopec and Pauliss we will most certainly find the man from South Africa—the man the Turkish authorities are looking for. Wouldn't that also be another feather in your diplomatic cap?"

After noticing Enwright's eyes narrow, and thinking that she might have gone too far, Angela quickly back-paddled. "What an achievement," she added. "Helping the Turks with a national disaster, finding a criminal on the loose and also helping a poor lost American woman and two British nationals. It certainly would be an incredible opportunity."

After her proposal, Angela watched as the ambassador once again sat back in his chair and raised his fingers into a steeple. Stanley Grey and Samuel Marsh also sat back in thought and after a few moments, the Ambassador said what was on all of their minds.

"Ms. Barnes," he asked quietly. "What's the real reason you want to find these people?"

Angela didn't miss a beat, she looked the ambassador in the eye and improvised with what she hoped was the truth.

"Because," she said. "That bastard from South Africa—the one that is following Doctors Pauliss and Clopec, his name is Cedric Bowles. I want him found so he can be charged with murder. I believe he brutally raped and killed a young woman that was working for me and I want him brought to justice!"

Across the room Pauline looked up, her eyes still puffy from crying. "I knew it," she began, as did a new episode of tears. "I knew he killed Becca. I *knew* it all along!"

As Roy Hartock once again offered his shoulder and placed his arm around Pauline, the American Ambassador to Turkey shook his head with disbelief. He excused himself, dismissed the British envoy, and turned to the Sergeant Major and asked him to make transportation arrangements as well as hotel accommodations for all of the American guests.

After Hartock, the British agents, and Pauline had left with the Sergeant Major, Phillip Enwright lowered his practiced gaze and stared hard into to piercing blue eyes of Angela Barnes. He hesitated for a very quiet moment then spoke. "Ms. Barnes, have you ever been in the diplomatic corps?"

"No, sir," Angela replied evenly.

"Well, you should have been. Your timing and manipulation with that young woman, and the way you skirted Grey and Marsh...I really do believe you missed your calling."

"Mister Ambassador, my intention was not to—"

Enwright interrupted by raising his hand and shaking his head.

"I'll give you two helicopters and make sure the English do the same. We'll slap red crosses all over the aircraft, but I need to know the truth. What are you *really* up to?"

"Mister Ambassador if I told you, you wouldn't believe it. But I *can* make a promise."

"And, what might that be?"

Angela smiled sweetly and winked. "I'll tell you when I find out."

Chapter 61

When Billie came to and knew she was not dreaming, she sat up, opened her eyes, and suddenly realized that she *truly* was in a nightmare. There was no light. When she held her hands in front of her face, the darkness was as complete as if she were blind.

After a moment of trying to see any sign of light, and trying to calm her breathing, she heard the voice of her father with one of his unforgettable lessons for life: *Don't panic. Panic is the killer, and fear is panic's predecessor. Whenever in danger, take your time, control your thoughts, and systematically take an inventory. Taking an inventory will keep your mind in order and no matter what you find, focus on the positive. The negative will turn your thoughts to fear, terror will follow, and that path leads to disaster.*

After remembering his words, Billie tried a deep breath, but the air was too thick and filled with dust. She coughed and was surprised by the sound. At least her ears worked, she thought, and somewhere in the darkness, a trickle of water claimed her attention. As she turned her head to determine the direction, she realized that she was sitting upright, her legs were out in front of her, and her hands were at her sides touching the ground.

Am I on the concrete pier?

She didn't know.

How long ago had that been?

How long since the earthquake—and what had really happened?

Reacting quickly, even before she finished her next thought, Billie lifted her left hand and peered at her wrist. It was there, thank God, and with a rush of emotion, she knew that she was not blind. Her dive watch, the Luminox with the beautiful tritium lights was glowing brightly. The green, radiant dots and the sweeping hands that never needed external light to recharge. The time was 2:10, but she had no idea if it was AM or PM or even what day it was. The date indicator on the watch was not illuminated.

But how did she become unconscious? And what about Peter—and Brian? She started to call out, but a sharp pain stabbed as she tried to open her mouth. With a gritty hand to the side of her face, she jutted her chin and then worked her jaw. It moved, it worked, but she was stiff and there was some pain.

Then she felt the wet. The sticky thick wet from the front of her ear up into her hairline.

After a quick check, she felt the abrasion and then the tear, but the wound was small. She had been bleeding, but the blood had clotted and partially dried. Again, the question popped into her mind: How long and what had happened? Did she fall, and what of the others?

Just as she tried to call out again, another tremor began. Even in the darkness Billie felt the air diminishing as the tiny expanse of her existence filled with dust. Suddenly, she imagined herself in a tomb—a tomb under a great mound like King Midas, an ancient crypt where her cries for help were always to be muffled and any chance for companionship ultimately denied. Thankfully, the rumbling tremor began to subside, and finally stopped.

When all was quiet again, she directed her fearful thoughts back to her father's admonition of taking a basic inventory. *Just an aftershock*, she considered. This was the term the experts used. An aftershock was the aftereffects of the major quake—a series of lesser quakes and a resettling of the tremendous weight that had been so violently shifted.

As she sat alone in the darkness, the sound of trickling water resumed, as did the occasional resonance of falling stones. The dripping rocks sounded more like pebbles, and as she thought about the sound, she realized there was a tiny bit of an echo.

With the echo came hope, and for the first time the idea materialized that she was not trapped and buried alive. Her immediate reaction was to shiver with relief, but as hope glimmered, and she remembered her inventory, she tried to stand. With one hand raised to protect her head, and the other pushing off from the gravel on the ground, she found that although stiff, she was able to slowly rise. In the darkness she reached high overhead and felt another rush of hope when she realized she was not trapped in a tight cavity. She was alive, unhurt, and able to move freely.

The trickling water continued. As she stood, Billie tried to focus on the source of the sound. She turned her head first to the left, and then with some pain to the right, but the ever-present gurgle continued. She concentrated on the echo of stones still dropping from the aftershock, augmenting the sparkling water sound. Unfortunately, with the sporadic echoes, the trickling water could be coming from anywhere.

Slowly, and with her hands outstretched and searching before her, Billie moved gradually forward, one step at a time, over the flat but rubble-covered surface. She recalled that the large concrete pier where the schooner had been tied was in the shape of a rectangle, and that the old coastal vessel took up most of the mooring capacity. What she did not know, however, was which way she was positioned, where the water was, or if she was the only one left alive. With considerable effort she refocused her thoughts toward the positive, away from the fear that welled up inside her, and she tentatively continued her exploration one step at a time.

Billie knew the quake-driven wave had washed over the pier and flooded the depot and the tunnel leading presumably to the outside, but the elapsed time between the quake, the wave, and the ultimate collapse of the high-walled basin was confusing. Dust in the air was obviously still very thick, but the ground on which she found herself was apparently dry. As she moved blindly and carefully forward, the ever-present question returned: How long had she been out, and where was everyone else?

After every few steps, Billie would stop and evaluate the sounds that she heard. The water trickle, she thought, sounded louder and *hopefully,* this meant she would find some kind of boundary, an edge or a side to her newest existence. From one boundary, she could count her steps, find other sides to the puzzle, and possibly find some light to lead her out.

After another glance at the glowing face of her watch, and an upward look into the darkness, the ever-returning question rushed to the forefront of her mind: Was it daylight or dark?

If it was day, then the entire harbor-basin was covered in rubble and she was in an air pocket enclosed in stone. She shuddered and suddenly felt an overwhelming flood of claustrophobia. All around the inky-black darkness rushed in, closing like a smothering blanket, and pressing down with a terrible suggestion of time without end—and life without light. Her only perception of survival was to look again at her watch and its beautiful green lights. Suddenly, everything seemed hopeless.

"Stop it!" she said, and was surprised and utterly horrified by the sound of her voice. Her words had bounced back almost immediately.

She was definitely in a smaller place than she first imagined and not on the concrete pier where she blacked out. She was not out in the open, and in the center of what she hoped was the middle of the dock, but trapped in an enclosed pocket. Trapped like a miner in an underground cave-in.

"Help! Is anyone there? Help! Can anyone hear me?" she shouted.

After her voice mocked her effort in a quick bounce-back return, she stilled herself and began moving forward, determined to find the boundaries of her confinement. With her arms once again outstretched and searching, Billie was surprised when her feet moving too fast tripped over an unseen obstacle and she went down hard. Her hands scraped against the gravely ground, but this time the surface was not dry. She had fallen over something and even before her fingers began to explore, she gasped with the realization that she was laying over a body—a body that was still damp from the rushing wave, but also cold and stiff.

After she felt the tears begin to stream, and a sob rise from her chest, Billie shook her head and pulled herself together. She sat in total darkness and began to pray.

"Please God, Don't let it be Peter or Brian, Please!" When the snap-back of her words died out in the stone, she slowly and methodically began to search the body. Almost at once, she sighed with relief when she realized the deceased was wearing a foul-weather jacket.

Her thoughts quickly turned to sorrow when she thought of the old mariner who reminded her of Dotson, the older Turkish fisherman who had intervened and saved their lives. This was the man who without a doubt had convinced the waterfront leader not to throw everyone over the side, the old man who was obviously no part of the waterfront thugs, but captured somehow by the series of events that ended up to be his destiny. This was the old fisherman who knew his waters, knew his weather, and knew a fellow mariner when he saw one.

With an abrupt flash of thought, Billie's mind erupted in the darkness—the old man who was constantly smoking, the man who lit his cigarettes with the old-style Zippo lighter. Before she realized what she was doing, and as part of her mind screamed "don't get your hopes up," Billie's fingers were exploring for pockets, searching for the lighter that she knew the older man carried.

The first big pocket in the foul-weather gear was empty, but as she continued with her blind and desperate search, her hopes and fears doubled, tripled, and battled into a menagerie of fireworks that only she could see inside her head. In the third pocket, an upper breast pocket of the weatherproof gear, she felt a crumpled pack of cigarettes. Beside the cigarettes was the cool steel of the unmistakable—the cool, sweet, metal square of that old Zippo lighter.

With trembling hands, Billie pulled back the cover and heard the metal click of reality. She held the opened lighter close and drew in the sweet-home smell of pungent lighter fluid, the smell of Dotson lighting his pipe

277

and the scent of her dad cleaning his tools, the smell of her childhood and South Florida baking in the sun.

With a trembling effort, and a reminder to keep her thoughts focused, and not to get her hopes up, Billie found the rounded wheel of the striker and rubbed it with her thumb, uttering the words. "Oh, please God, let it work!"

The first attempt failed, but before she could consider the unthinkable, she once again thumbed the wheel and watched the sparks. After the sixth or seventh try the wick caught, the flame began to grow, and Billie began to breathe.

When the light came, it was the most wonderful sight ever—a rich yellow and gold more valuable than any treasure, a growing beacon shinning with hope and a promise of new horizons. The flame was a signal of new life, and for the first time since the quake, a chance for the future.

All of these thoughts occurred in as many seconds, but were dashed by the pitiful figure resting by her side, and the illumination of her predicament. Billie was down on her knees, her pant legs torn and filthy, as was her turtleneck top. Her hands were streaked where water had splashed the dust-caked grit and bloodstains soiled her fingers.

Nevertheless, lying at her side, at the base of her knees, was the only possible focus of her attention. Beside her on the rubble-strewn ground was the old Turkish mariner with his lifeblood spilled from a devastating head wound. The old sailor must have been caught in the wave, as was Billie, but not as lucky when he was washed away and forced into the tunnel.

As she began to rise and hold the flickering lighter high, she knew now was not the time to pay the old man homage, and more importantly, that the fluid in the Zippo would not last long. She also sensed, somehow, that the old mariner would have wanted her to press on. With the golden light revealing a corridor, her decision on which way to go was easy. Ahead was an open tunnel, and behind her was a caved-in passageway that had once led to somewhere, presumably through the mountain and onward to the outside.

After another look down, Billie whispered, "God help him."

She slowly retraced the path in which the surging wave had pushed her, and after only fifty or sixty feet, she was out of the excavated tunnel and standing in the open. With the old seafaring Zippo held high overhead, Billie stood in awe-struck silence and tried to comprehend what she saw.

First and foremost was the battered hull of the old trading schooner. All of the hundred-foot vessel lifted by the wave surge, had smashed down on the concrete pier, pierced by the concrete pilings. Her black hull was holed and her planks broken, but now she was high and dry and resting on

the pier. Billie realized that the trickling sound she heard was water drain-
ing from the old trader's bilges, the remainder of the rising green water
ebbing back into the lagoon, and the last of the little ship's blood flowing
back into the sea.

As her eyes lifted and followed the two rising masts upward, she was
dismayed that where once there had been an overhead opening, there was
now only slab after slab of the torn-away cliff sides. The cliffs that had collapsed to form a pyramid shaped roof structure. With the dim lighting, it
was hard to see, but as Billie stood staring, she was not sure if the broken
tops of the old schooner's masts were not responsible for holding up what
looked like most of a mountainside. As for the entrance into the basin,
there stood only more sheered cliff sides. The slabs of stone seemed to deny
there was ever any opening leading out to the sea.

When Billie stepped forward to the edge of the pier and listened to her
footfalls, she observed that the water level was back to normal. She also
could not fail to notice the bottom of the schooner was opened by the pier,
and all of the golden cargo was once again buried underwater, reclaimed by
the violence of the quake.

Billie shuddered at the thought of Brian's earlier supernatural suggestion of a curse. She then turned her gaze to what was left of the dockside
depot. Her earlier triumph of finding light in a terrible world of darkness
was rapidly fading as she could not help but consider that she was indeed
the only one left alive—indeed, cursed and trapped with a fortune of King
Midas's Gold.

After a deep breath and a stifled sob, Billie turned away from the
wrecked underside of the schooner and started for what was left of the waterside depot.

More water ran in rivulets along cracks in the pier. As she made her
way over scattered debris, she noticed that resting alongside the only standing corner of the dock-house was the upturned shell of the fan-tailed
launch. The once luxurious harbor craft was now resting against a stone
cliff with a torn and bent propeller flagging the highest part of the latest
wreckage. Strewn all around the upside down vessel were the unmistakable
flotsam and jetsam of a tragedy from the sea.

Even with the flickering and dim lighting from the Zippo, the univer-
sal color of life-jacket-orange was brighter than the surrounding debris. As
she was starting to turn away and begin her search for Peter, a tiny nagging
thought began pecking away. But the search for Peter reclaimed her focus.
The search that was now weighing very heavily on her heart—the search
that she was afraid to begin. She could not even think about Brian not being here, or of being hurt, or worse. Just the thought of Peter's special

smile ripped her apart, and then there was the thought that she might not have enough lighter fluid to find them even if they were alive.

As the all too familiar fears started to lead to panic, her defenses dropped even more with the knowledge that the precious lighter already felt *very* warm, and would have only at best a few more moments of fuel, only a few more moments before she was back in her earlier world of darkness, only a few more minutes...

Then she saw it.

Or perhaps the tiny nagging thought had finally pecked its way through, or during the rising panic, her father's ingrained logic regained control. But it was there! Yes, there, on the nearest *lifejacket,* was an emergency, waterproof, beacon. Just like the ones so familiar from Florida—a little waterproof, very bright, flashlight!

Once again, before she realized she was moving, Billie was down on her knees with the Zippo placed carefully at her side, the light still strong and steady. She ripped at the lifejacket and unpinned the safety-pin-style lamp attachment. With another little prayer, she thumbed the switch and the light that erupted was so bright it hurt her eyes.

"Oh! Thank you, God!"

As fast as she could, she set down the light and closed the Zippo. She unpinned the next lifejacket lamp and then the next. When she was finished, she had seven functioning lights and one dud. After another round of almost tearful thanks to God, Billie turned off all but one of her lights and pinned the others to the bottom of her tattered and torn turtleneck.

Fortified with a new strength, she started for the ruins of the dock-house depot. The last place she had seen Peter standing. With every step forward and as she worked her way around endless pieces of debris, she was awe-struck again at the power of what had happened. It was if the world had had enough. Enough of the greed that turned to murder, the selfishness that led to doubt, and the general misplaced logic of what was really important. Again, she was overwhelmed with the thought that Brian was right and the gold did have a supernatural strength. Maybe this was all punishment for the greed of man.

"Oh please, God," she muttered as she began to search the ruined building. "Please let Peter and Brian be OK. They're all that's important. I know that now. I knew it before."

After she climbed over and ducked through what she imagined was once a depot window, her waterproof lamp cast more shadows than light. The roof trusses slanted downward in an impossible effort to hold up what must have been a collapsing cliff side. What remained of the outer walls and inner framework was now no more than twisted timbers and soggy plasterboard crushed by the rushing wall of water.

Deep in her mind Billie's father quoted another powerful point of training: *Rushing water is the most powerful force on earth. When the volume is great enough, nothing can withstand it. Battering waves always happen when you least expect them.*

It was true she thought, one minute everyone had a plan, be it for good or bad, and the next the earth falls apart and a wall of water rushes in to cancel everything. As she continued through the rubble, the splintered wood, and the broken rocks from the fallen mountain, Billie's newfound hopes began to fade.

The wreckage seemed impossible and too much for one person to search. The more she looked, the more desperate she felt. She was only one person with a little life jacket light, and as she continued to peer into the shadows, she recalled television news clips of similar situations, of earthquake or mudslide scenes teeming with trained rescue workers and dogs that could find victims by using their sense of scent, amid hundreds of volunteers equipped with unlimited resources and contingency plans for every situation. As she moved over some heavy trusses, her fear once again began to rise, and with the growing terror, a new sense of hopelessness.

"Oh God," she began to shake her head as she spoke, "Oh God, how can I help? What should I do?" The only answer was from another trickle of water and the echo of a falling stone.

Just as her frustration was mounting and another emotional damn was threatening to burst, Billie caught sight of a shadowy image that made her heart stop. When she held her little lamp closer, she saw at first a twisted foot without a shoe and a leg that disappeared under a section of plasterboard. The flesh was very white in death, perhaps more so in the light of the bright rescue torch and not the warm glow from the Zippo. Even before she began ripping away at the water-soaked plaster, her voice was once again sounding away from the light and bouncing off into the darkness.

"Please, God, no!" she shouted. "Don't let it be Peter! Don't let it be Peter! Not Peter! Noooo..."

Nevertheless, as she tore at the plaster and the wooden frames, the foot turned to a leg, and on the leg, the torn fabric was dark—dark like the black turtleneck and trousers that they *all* wore when they bordered the schooner.

"No!" she began again louder, this time in defiance. She knew it was true, but she would not believe it until she saw his face. She dug harder, and faster, and suddenly she felt betrayed.

She winced when a nail or screw scratched her hand, but with the newfound pain she became even more frantic to uncover the body. Blood was covering her hand and running down her fingers, but she would not stop until she saw *his* face.

After many moments of frenzied digging, and when the last large piece came away she stopped and began to cry. The face in the light was all too familiar yet restful, the features untroubled and calm. It was as if the rush of the water had washed away his every problem and concern. His eyes were closed, just as if he were sleeping.

Billie continued to cry as she looked down at the body. "What now?" She sobbed. "What am I supposed to do *now*?"

"Well, if you could dig me out, maybe we could plan something together."

Billie at first did not believe the voice. For a spilt-second, she thought she might have lost her mind, but then it began again, the voice that she had fallen in love with, that silly accent and *his* funny way of phrasing.

"Billie, I'm a bit confused. I must have bumped my head again. I was unconscious, but then I heard your voice. I believe you were calling my name."

"Peter?" Billie said the name tenderly, and turned with her light.

"Christ!" he exclaimed. "Not in my bloody eyes!"

When she looked, he was shielding his eyes with his hands and sitting up, surrounded by debris and pushing his way out.

Before she could think, she was moving and tearing away the plasterboard covering his legs. He rose unhurt and holding her in his arms. She cried very hard for a few moments, and when she finally caught her breath, she pulled away and looked into his eyes. She was holding him very tightly and had dropped her waterproof safety lamp. The flashlight was down amongst the rubble but casting little light beams up in between them. His glasses were gone, his hair was still wet and too long, and his salt and pepper stubble was showing the beginnings of a beard. She rubbed her cheeks against his whiskers and then she found his mouth. Their kiss was deep and passionate as the moment that brought them together.

She said the words simply, "I love you, Peter," and when she did she realized it was the most truthful statement of her life."

"I love you too, my dear, with all my heart, but right now don't you think we should find Argentina?"

Billie grinned in the half-light, and wiped the tears from her eyes. She then knew with complete certainty that even if they never got out, or they never found Brian, this was the happiest moment she would ever have.

Without another word, she bent to pick up her light and cast the circular beam of the little safety lamp over toward the body of the waterfront Turk, the leader of the men that had caused so much death.

As they both studied the features so peaceful in the light, Billie confessed. "At first I thought he was you, and I just couldn't bear it. Then when I realized it wasn't, I wondered how anyone could have survived, and I guess I lost the strength to keep going. I was suddenly convinced that I was all alone."

Slowly, Peter reached for her and held her once again. "With you by my side," he said, "I will never lose the courage to carry on, and I will never— ever—leave you alone." After another moment of quiet, a distant cry broke the silence, the voice tone and the accent wonderfully pleasing.

"Peter? Billie? Is anyone out there? Peter?"

Peter hugged Billie tight, "Come now," he grinned. "It's time to find Argentina."

Chapter 62

When Cedric saw the light, he giggled. There had never been a more beautiful sight. After the earthquake and the cave-in, the dust made it difficult to breathe, but the security director remembered his sandstorm experience in Namibia. He immediately tore off the bottom of his shirttail and tied it around his head to cover his nose and mouth. This happened after the earthquake and after the decrepit old boat rose with the wave and crashed on top of the pier. As usual for a man of training, the security director braced himself during the seismic event and was completely unharmed.

Upon the first hint of unnatural movement, and after the pier and the sandy walls began to blur with vibration, he had sheltered himself in the reinforced passage leading from the main deck to the salon and the galley. He watched as the cliffs began to crumble, and as the harbor emptied and refilled with the wave that seemed unstoppable. He remembered the feeling of the deathblow to the sailing ship when the old hull rose and fell, and it was very easy to imagine the concrete pilings breaking into the planking. Even over the roaring rumble of the quake, he knew the precise instant when the bottom of the ship tore away and the golden cargo poured out of the hold and tumbled into the water beside the concrete pier.

For many hours, the darkness was complete, but as his eyes began to adjust, images began to form, and the outlines of objects began to appear. Years of dark glasses and his practice of avoiding the sunlight and daylight hours had conditioned his optical senses to virtually see in the dark. The pupils of his eyes, Cedric imagined, must be conditioned to open wider and therefore admit any ambient light. His eyes in the darkness, he envisioned, must be two dark orbs vacuuming in the blackness.

Cedric giggled again when he realized he was panting. The dust was lighter now and with a quick clawing swipe, the shirttail mask was gone and abandoned in the dark. With his eyes opened like dark holes, and his mouth uncovered and his jagged teeth exposed, he realized suddenly, that he was the perfect predator of the cave. As he carefully moved beside the wrecked sailing hull resting on the pier, he once again looked down into the water and studied the light.

It was brighter now and as the security director continued to watch, he imagined an underwater passage open to the sea, a passage that had remained open, even though the cave-in and collapse of the cliffs sides covered everything above the level of the water. The very delicate, shimmering, golden light could only be daylight traveling underwater and reflecting off the gold bullion at the base of the pier.

After a moment, Cedric looked up. The light was certainly getting brighter with the outside light of the day. He could even see how the cliff sides had fallen onto each other to form an apex vault. The masts of the old sailboat were broken off at the tops, but their studier lower portions seemed to be the pillars that held up the mountain. As he watched, a slab of the stone roof gave way and crashed onto the foredeck of the schooner.

When the echo died out Cedric wiped his mouth and realized he was drooling. For some reason he could not stop panting. He tried to understand this new phenomenon, but everything about his life had immediately changed after he saw: *row after row, stack after stack, of the rounded gold bars, the color and the shine, and the overall effect of the massive quantity.* He had never imagined anything so beautiful or anything so all consuming.

The bullion seemed to have some kind of magical grip. He was filthy from the dust, and from not showering for days, but even when he rubbed his chin and felt stubble of his beard, he didn't seem to mind. Normally just the thought of not being hygienically clean, shaved, and correct, was enough to create an image of complete disgust, but all of that, even the fact that he hadn't brushed his teeth, didn't seem to matter anymore. All that mattered *now* was the beautiful golden light below, and what *that* light represented.

As he continued to stare, Cedric mentally confirmed the golden shimmer could only be an underwater passageway leading to the outside. All that was necessary was to rig up a set of the scuba gear he had seen near the galley and make his way into the water and through the streaming daylight that surely led under the caved-in opening. Then he would make his way along the Turkish coast until he found a road and then transportation. All that really mattered was that he knew the location of the gold and that the precious treasure was not going anywhere. All the details of retrieving the bullion could easily be considered later.

The fact the security director had never actually used the underwater breathing gear did not seem to be a problem, what really mattered was getting out so he could come back and be near the gold. Everything else was just trivial details.

Before he realized he was moving, the security director was beside the upturned fan-tailed launch and going through the wreckage. After commandeering the vessel and forcing the storage compartments, Cedric remembered the marine spotlights he had used during the boarding of the schooner.

With very little effort, and with his fingertips searching through the different shapes, one of the very bright lights was ultimately found and then switched on.

The brightness of the halogen bulb was shattering after the twinkling shimmer of the golden beams, but after a startling moment, Cedric removed his shirt and covered the mirrored lens with a makeshift filter of cloth. After allowing a few moments for his eyes to adjust, and his mind to take in the catastrophic surroundings of the collapsed mountain resting above the wrecked schooner, the security director considered the cloth-filtered lighting effect was perfect.

He made his way through the barnacle encrusted, ripped open wooden hull and found the scuba tanks stored in the main salon. He also found, with very little effort, two black canvas bags that contained the mouthpieces, gauges, and black hoses that connected the breathing apparatus to the air tanks.

After a few minutes of trial and error, the security chief found the correct method for attaching the hoses to the tanks and was rewarded by a sudden hiss of compressed air when the valve on the top of the tank was opened. Disappointment followed when the pressure gauge was examined and the indicator needle only registered a fraction off the peg. The air gauge showed only 200 lbs out of a possible 4000. It was obvious that the air tank was all but empty.

Cedric wiped his mouth and realized that he was still panting and drooling. Never mind, he thought, as he inserted the rubber mouthpiece and breathed. The hiss of compressed air rushing into his lungs felt like victory. He knew now that his escape plan would work.

After all, how much air did he really need to go through the subterranean tunnel and out to the other side? Not much, he considered, just a few breaths as he followed the light and surfaced on the other side. With the scuba tank and hoses tucked under his arm, and with the cloth-wrapped searchlight showing the way, Cedric climbed back though the broken hull and made his way along the concrete pier to the best vantage point where once again he could see the golden light.

With the scuba gear resting on the edge of the pier, a thumb on the spotlight switch reduced the halogen filament to a dying red ember. After a few moments to allow his eyes to readjust, the shimmering illumination of the gold returned. As the moments passed…water continued to trickle… the occasional stones resettled or dropped…and the beautiful light continued to flow. Even the most fleeting thought somehow focused on the gold and what that golden color could ultimately represent.

Beneath the old ship's masts, and within the quietness of the cavern, the passage of time seemed to slow. With his eyes reaching for the golden light, his mind slipped under the water and embraced the fallen treasure.

There were hundreds—perhaps over two-thousand of the ancient golden ingots—an incomprehensible fortune…*all waiting…all his…all alone.*

Suddenly, his tentacles of thought were violently ripped away, his attention brought back to the surface. He was back on the pier and listening.

"Help! Is anyone there?"

Cedric cocked his head to listen and the sound of a human voice echoed in the distance.

"Help! Can anyone hear me?" The voice was an unexpected and somehow obscene intrusion.

It could only be the woman from Florida, the security director reasoned. *But how?* The damage to anything outside of the sailing ship must have been tremendous. How could she have survived? Perhaps there could be others: Clopec, Pauliss, or the leader of the Turks, or even the old man who piloted the vessels. If she were alive, then there could be others—other problems.

As the woman called out again Cedric made a decision. He stripped out of his trousers and made another filter over his spotlight. With only a sliver of the electric lamp showing, the security director began another search, this time for his beloved weapon system—the AK-47.

Once again, it was time for discretion. As he very quietly and carefully began to move through the wreckage, his light shielded except for a tiny sliver moving over the ground, Cedric Bowles realized that he was filthy and naked. He also understood that he could not stop drooling or panting, and that even if he didn't find his choice and favorite weapon he would kill the woman and anyone else with his teeth and his bare hands. When he realized the gold had given him a new power, he very quietly and very carefully began to giggle.

Chapter 63

"Christ does that taste good!" Brian exclaimed as he exhaled. He had just used the old Zippo to light one of the Turkish fisherman's cigarettes.

"And so does this," Billie commented as she ripped at one of the hard pieces of Turkish bread.

"Nothing as good as this tea!" Peter offered as he held a plastic container of the dark-sweet beverage.

After using the life-jacket lamps and finding Brian on the wrecked quarterdeck of the schooner, a quick assessment found the two Turks who had boarded with Cedric Bowles. The men had been surprised by the violence of the wave, thrown to the decks and knocked unconscious, but they were alive and basically as unhurt as Brian. Everyone had apparently rode the little ship when the wave came and had been kept aboard by the quarterdeck railing.

When the wooden hull rose and crashed on the concrete pier, the lower strakes had been cracked open from the weight of the gold. The entire belly of the old trader was torn open, but the topsides were relatively undamaged and the masts were almost vertical. Above the furled sails and the tops of the broken masts, however, was what appeared to be an entire collapsed mountain and the interior of a perfect pyramid.

After hearing Brian's voice and carefully using the lights to climb through the ruined hull and endless debris, a jubilant reunion occurred when Billie and Peter climbed through the companionway and found Brian and the two Turks blinking from the lights. Within minutes the galley was explored, the camping lantern lit with Billie's Zippo, and the meager food supplies and jugs of tea brought out on deck.

"Hey, Argentina, these are for you," Billie grinned as she produced the old mariner's cigarettes. She held Brian tightly, squeezing him as he reached for her embrace.

"Billie, my God!" Brian exclaimed. "The first thing I heard was your voice. You woke me. I was dreaming some crazy dream and then I heard your voice. There was no light, but I knew everything was alright because of your voice—because I heard your voice."

"That's what woke me as well," Peter admitted.

"Excuse me, effendi," Mustafa interrupted. "What do we know of the others? Are we the only survivors?"

Peter tilted his head toward the wreckage of the depot. "Their leader was beside me when the water came. He was crushed in the dock house. After climbing out of the rubble, I can't believe that I'm alive."

"Thank God," said Billie. "Alive and OK. It really is amazing." She lowered her voice. "But the older man who was the pilot of the boats, he was killed." She shook her head with sadness. "And the youngest one with the machine gun, he was caught between the hull and the pier."

"And the man we arrived with?" Mustafa's tone was probing. "The man who identified himself as an agent of the American FBI?"

"I knew it," Billie exclaimed as she stood. "I just knew it!" she said. "I'll bet anything he was the one that claimed to be the FBI in Goodland, the missing man who burned down my marina!"

"Oh my God!" Brian sounded disgusted, "Do you really think it's possible, an arsonist and a murderer?"

"After all that's happened," Peter nodded. "*Definitely.*"

With everyone gathered around the recovered pressure lantern, the tilted quarterdeck was a halo of light surrounded by shadows, a warmth of illumination rising with the masts until the broken spars became one with the slabs of stone resting overhead. All around and beneath the decks of the schooner, darkness waited with a patience that was palatable. As the camping lantern hissed away its finite amount of fuel, a few moments passed before Cedric Bowles stepped into the light.

When he appeared, his image was startling. He was naked except for a brief loincloth. He was very pale, his skin tone resembling white tallow. He wore his sunglasses against the brightness of the lantern and tightly gripped in his hands an AK-47. As he stepped forward into the light, he shivered as if he was cold and leveled the Russian rifle as if for instant use.

"How much air will it take," he demanded of Billie, "to get to the other side?" His voice cracked as if he hadn't used it in weeks and his breath was coming in pants. After no one answered, and everyone just sat and stared dumbfounded, the disturbing figure gripped his rifle more tightly, wiped at his mouth, and rubbed away some spittle. After a few more seconds of silence, he took another step closer to Billie. "Is 200 pounds enough?" he demanded. "Enough to get to the other side?"

"Whatever are you talking about?" Brian's voice was loud, incredulous, and accusing. "Have you gone mad?"

Cedric Bowles giggled and wiped again at his spittle. His breathing was frantic and he did not seem to be able to close his mouth. "I've gone beyond madness, Doctor Pauliss...far beyond," he panted. "Now tell me! Is 200 pounds enough?"

With his startling admission and his latest question redirected at Billie, everyone knew at once that the lunatic they were facing was more dangerous than the earthquake.

"200 pounds?" Billie asked softly, her eyes very worried and focused on the leveled barrel of the Russian rifle. "I guess 200 lbs would be enough, if it's not too heavy."

"No! You don't understand," the bulbous sunglasses shook back and forth and spittle dribbled. "200 pounds in the air tank—in the aqualung! Is 200 pounds enough to go underwater, travel through the passage, and come up on the other side?"

"What passage?" Billie, Peter, and Brian all asked at once.

Without answering Cedric motioned with the rifle until everyone was beside the waterside bulwark of the quarterdeck, with Mustafa standing beside Ahmed the pilot, and Billie in between Peter and Brian.

"Look over the side—down into the water," the security director demanded. He crossed to the camping lantern and turned off the hissing fuel. When the mantled flame went out with a pop the inky-black darkness closed in and compounded the silence. After a moment, all that could be heard was the panting of a madman.

"Can you see it?" the Afrikaans accent demanded. "Can you see the golden light?"

After a moment for everyone's eyes to adjust, everyone *could* see it—the very dim but persistent shimmering of gold, the shimmering that could only be from sunlight streaming in through an underwater opening.

"Well? Is it enough?" the panting voice insisted. "Is 200 pounds of air enough?"

Billie shook her head. "You would never go underwater with only 200 pounds of air," she said. "That's how much you have at the very end of a dive—the safety margin."

"But that's the way out," the panting voice replied in the dark. "The *only* way out!"

"It looks deep," Billie was staring, as was everyone, over the railing, down the side of the ship and into the water, into the glimmering gold.

"Maybe thirty feet," she said, "and then another fifty yards to the outside, maybe more. The opening is probably like a tunnel, a tunnel covered over by the cave-in. You could easily run out of air and be trapped."

"Or, I could make it! It *is* possible that I could make it and surface on the other side."

"You have diving experience?"

"No—none!" the panting continued. "But I must get out, so I can come back!"

"Without basic diving skills you would have no chance," Billie's voice was steeped in concern. She knew this was not the answer the madman wanted to hear. "Maybe if I went," she offered, "I could go for help, I am very good at conserving air."

Cedric Bowles giggled. "No!" he panted. "No one will ever leave this cave-in alive! No one but me!"

"Bugger all," Brian muttered in the near dark and was surprised as anyone when Billie clicked on two of the life-jacket flashlights and thrust the very bright light directly in the madman's face.

He had taken off his sunglasses after he turned off the camping lantern, and before his eyes could adjust, his pupils looked like dark holes above a grimace of sharp jagged teeth. He looked like what he was—a monster that only came out in darkness, a creature of the night. His reaction to the lights was enough to allow Mustafa to reach for the barrel of the Russian rifle, but not enough for the weapon to be forced away from the overpowering and maniacal grip.

Before anyone else could join and lend a hand, the training from the South African Security Force took over. With a violent turning and twisting motion, the one-time security director was away and free from Mustafa's grasp on the rifle, and a hailstorm of automatic fire was ripping into the bulwark where everyone had been standing. Mustafa died instantly as the streaking tracer rounds pierced his chest, and next to fall was Ahmed the private pilot who cried out painfully when several rounds stitched up his leg and into his side.

The madman turned and was trying to hold his weapon down, but as he continued to fire, the barrel began to rise and it was at this moment that Peter grabbed Billie and shouted to Brian. "Over the side!"

Without time to consider the height of the deck from the water in the basin, Brian tumbled over the side and splashed into the water beside Billie and Peter.

Lost and Found

As with any hand held, automatic weapon, after the first few rounds of a fully automatic burst, a virtually unstoppable rising of the barrel occurs and lifts the continuous firing shots higher and higher.

What security director Bowles had not considered was that the Turks had modified the Russian weapon. This AK-47 had a hair trigger that was difficult to disengage. With *this* particular rifle, once the trigger was pulled, the fully automatic sequence continued until the entire magazine was empty.

After the first two victims, the orange line of tracer rounds began to rise and even after director Bowles released the trigger, the recoil spring continued to operate and the firing pin continued to hammer away. The result was a rising arc of orange fire reaching higher and higher, and finally raking up the schooner's masts and pounding into slabs of newly fallen stone. When the final bullet in the magazine fired, but before the light from the tracer round faded, Cedric Bowles saw the falling ton of rock that would end his life.

Chapter 64

After the tremendous crash, silence filled the cavern along with streaming beams of vertical sunlight. The hammering gunfire had loosened the slabs of stone and now an open crack was visible just beside the tilted mainmast of the schooner. With the air full of dust, the sunlight appeared like spotlights pouring down the masts and highlighting the tangled ropes and rigging. All around the broken hull the darkness waited, but it could not deny a single shaft of sunlight reaching down to the water.

"Christ, I can't believe it!" Peter stammered and shielded his eyes

"Well, you Bloody-well better," Brian answered, blinking in the new-found light.

"It's a miracle," Billie exclaimed. "Oh my God! It truly is!" she exclaimed in awe, "It looks like a picture out of the bible."

Billie, Peter, and Brian were all treading water at the edge of the concrete pier. They were clearly in shock by the deaths of Mustafa and the other Turk, but there was unmistakable note of victory in the air. There was a way out. The tilted mainmast of the schooner was a ladder leading to escape and to victory. There was also the knowledge, hopefully, that justice had been done.

As if reading Billie and Peter's thoughts, Brian said, "Well, let's go find out if the bastard is still alive."

The trio climbed back through the torn hull to reach the deck, and it was quickly obvious that the OPC security director had met a most fitting end. His body below the neck, was covered by the huge slab of stone, and he was pinned horribly between the deck of the schooner and the piece of the cavern roof. His head was spared any injury, but the sight of his open mouth with the jagged teeth, and his black eyes staring into the down-pouring sun was oddly unnerving.

"Christ, what a sight!" Brian muttered as all three regarded the remains.

"Well, I've seen enough," Peter said. "But, I can't say that the bugger didn't deserve it."

After a silent moment, Billie tore her eyes away and looked up to the sun streaming down the tilted mast. "Boys," she said. "It's time to get the hell out of here." But before the echo of her words managed to die out, a slight tremor started to rumble.

"Alright, Billie up you go!" Peter's voice sounded above the beginning of an aftershock, "Brian, your next!"

"I'm not a bloody monkey," Brian exclaimed, "I can't climb that!"

"Argentina! *Yes,* you can!" Billie's tone did not leave room for argument.

She tested a halyard that led upward to a tangle of lines trailing from the broken mast top. Dust was thick after the roof collapse, and became all the more dense as the aftershock continued to rumble. As all three looked up into the light, there was little doubt as to the urgency of a hasty escape.

"You *can*, you *will*, and you *are* going to climb," Billie instructed. "Just like this."

She's right," Peter added. "We are both going to climb."

With the aid of the trailing rope, Billie began scaling up through broken rigging until she was just below the new opening in the cavern. After she reached the top, she stood on a broken section of mast and looked outside. "Hey, Argentina, you gotta see this! Come on!"

Bille made her way to where the top of the mainmast was broken and forced into the top of the cave-in, where she tied the end of a long halyard to a secure pulley-block, and then scrambled up through the sun-lit crevice to disappear on the other side.

"After you mate," Peter suggested and then gestured aloft.

"Christ!" Brian commented before he began to climb. But then he was doing it—hand over hand, pulling his weight as he basically walked up the tilted mast. His faith in the line Billie had tied supported his courage, but even before he was halfway to the opening and the crevice, he felt Peter's weight on the rope beneath him.

"Oh my God—I'm doing it! I'm climbing the sodding mast."

"That's right, Argentina!" Billie encouraged, "You're almost here!"

When Brian finally crawled out exhausted and rested beside Billie, he looked around to a sight he knew he could never forget.

Resting high above the sea, and the lightly tumbling waves, Billie and Brian were sitting near the top of what looked like a giant cone or beehive. The sky was clear, and blue, the air fresh and salt-tinged, and a wonderful breeze was pouring up from the water. From the high vantage point, they were on top of the world.

The cliff sides had tumbled together and formed the new little mountain, and now as they sat on the uneven surface, small sandstones began to break away and tumble down the side and roll toward the surf. The sun was high overhead, warm and welcoming, and when Billie saw Brian's expression of relief she was overwhelmed and hugged him tightly.

"Oh, Argentina," she said when she finally let go, "I'm ready to buy you a drink!" Her voice cracked with the last of her words and then she was crying as she hugged him again tightly.

After Brian hastily wiped away his own emotion, he held Billie at arm's length and looked into her eyes. "Billie," he asked with a grin," Why don't you call me Brian?"

Before Billie could respond, another aftershock began and the entire mountain began to rumble.

"Peter!" Billie and Brian's voices tried to override the rumbling quake. They were instantly refocused on the entrance to the cavern below and trying to observe Peter's progress when the quake intensified and they were both suddenly in a landslide and tumbling down the newly formed peak.

"No!" Billie screamed as she slid beside Brian. "No... No... No...!" she repeated as they began to side faster down toward the sea.

A terrible rumbling seemed to erupt from below, the resonance of tremendous weight and shifting of mass that could only be the inner vault of the mountain collapsing—the unmistakable and the undeniable. It was happening before *he* could get out!

Billie knew it was true even as she clawed at the rocks, desperate to stop herself from sliding. Even as she tried to block it from her mind, she knew—*there could be no hope*. The weight shifted and the cavern collapsed. The crevice that opened and allowed their escape was at once a spewing vent of dust and part of the landside that was falling to the sea.

When they finally stopped, when they were standing in the waves and looking upward to the dust and what remained of the mountain, Billie screamed again and again, "No... No... No!"

She fell into Brian's arms, and he held her quietly. When at last, he led her out of the water, they both fell onto the sand. In the distance there was the faint but growing sound of helicopter rotors.

Chapter 65

B rian looked up at the helicopters dumbfounded. He was beyond caring and felt dead inside. He only wanted to turn back the clock so that Peter could have gone up the rope first, or that he hadn't wasted time arguing over climbing the mast and simply done what was obviously necessary for everyone to escape.

Now it was too late.

Again, he felt another overwhelming wave of emotion as he looked to Billie's anguish and examined his own shortcomings. He felt nothing but desolation when the helicopters began to land. He didn't care if they were friend or foe. He looked to Billie's hands covering her face as she cried, and suddenly he did care. He knew just as surely that he would defend her for the rest of his life. He would always care for her, keep her safe and comfortable—*he would do that!*

It was at that moment that he actually scrutinized the lead helicopter and saw beside the crescent moon and the star for Turkey, the red, white, and blue stripes of a Union Jack. His thoughts instantly shifted to Peter. Peter always loved that flag, always so proud to be British.

As the first helicopter landed and stirred up the sand and water at the edge of the beach, Brian stood shielding his eyes with the edge of his hand. Another machine was coming in and beginning to settle, this one with an American flag beside the Turkish, and a Red Cross emblem attached to a side panel. As the third and fourth aircraft touched down, a swarm of figures poured out of open doors, their heads down as they ran under the rotor draft. The first man who reached Brian was wearing coveralls. On his left breast was a Union Jack. The men behind him were clearly Turkish soldiers, well-armed and wearing berets.

The first man's voice pitched over the dying rotor blades and was clearly English. "Doctor Pauliss?" he asked.

"Yes, I'm Brian Pauliss." Brian stood as he spoke. "But how do you know?"

"Doctor Pauliss, I'm with the British envoy, we are here to help."

"Ms. Finkelmeyer?" Stanley Marsh dropped to one knee and looked at Billie. "Are you injured?" he said. "Are you alright?"

"Brian?" Billie asked through her tears. "Maybe they could help. Maybe there is still a chance for Peter."

After Brian and the British agent both turned to examine the collapsed mountain and the rising cloud of dust, the man with the Union jack on his coveralls led the way and the Turkish soldiers followed.

After four hours of exhausting effort, with Billie and Brian helping the American pilots, the British agents, and the Turkish soldiers, another section of the newly formed mountain rumbled and then resettled with a violent aftershock. This was the moment when everyone understood the inevitable, and that any further effort might end with another fatality. When the minor quake subsided, all the soldiers looked around as if they were surprised to be unharmed.

Stanley Marsh once again approached. "We have done our best Doctor Pauliss," he said, "But to continue, I'm afraid...might endanger everyone."

Brian nodded at the logic that was undeniable and held Billie tightly as she once again fell into his arms.

When Billie and Brian lifted off the beach in the final helicopter, the setting sun was a glowing beacon and the Black Sea was a golden path of light. The four aircraft chased the fleeting image, but their westward progress was not fast enough to catch the setting sun.

Chapter 66

"Brian, honey, aren't you glad we came?" Pauline asked gently. "Ms. Barnes went to a lot of trouble to get us here, and Mister Hartock, he even called the Governor."

Brian shook his head, his mind overwhelmed and in denial. "I—of course—Yes," he said. "I'm very pleased."

"Pauline," Angela Barnes interrupted. "Why don't you check on Ms. Finkelmeyer. I would like a few moments alone to speak with Doctor Pauliss, and maybe you could help her pack."

"Oh sure—OK," Pauline said as she stood. She then crossed the presidential suite of the Four Seasons Hotel. After a gentle tap on one of the bedroom doors she asked, "Billie, can I come in?"

After the door opened and Pauline went inside, Angela cleared her throat. "Doctor Pauliss? May I call you Brian?"

Brian nodded, "Certainly, of course."

"Just by looking at you, it's obvious that both you and Ms. Finkelmeyer have been through a lot. Nevertheless, so have we. I mean, finding you wasn't easy. I had to call in all kinds of favors and pull a lot of strings." Angela paused. "I really am sorry about Doctor Clopec. I know that he was a dear friend."

Brian was trying to be courteous and trying to be attentive by holding the inquisitive gaze, but his mind was wandering. He was worried about Billie, and he was worried about himself. He had never, ever, truly been alone—not since the boarding school rescue from the toilet stall. Now he was without his best friend and he was having serious issues coping.

298

"Brian...? Doctor Pauliss are you listening?"

"Yes, by the way, that really is a smashing suit."

Angela leaned back and smiled at the compliment. She crossed her legs and ran a finger down an immaculately pressed seam. After a moment, she looked up.

"Brian," she said. "What did you find? What did you and Doctor Clopec really find?"

"Trouble," Brian replied, thinking of Peter holding the plastic grocery bag at arm's length, the plastic bag with the ultimatum from Haggly-Ford and the Kinko's surveillance videotape.

"What kind of trouble?"

Brian smiled sadly. "Let's just say that we opened a type of Pandora's Box. One that should have been left closed."

Angela leaned forward. "Doctor Pauliss, are you alright? Do you understand why I am here?"

"Yes, I understand everything." Brian smiled again and reached for a cigarette. After he lit up with the old style Zippo, he exhaled and explained. "I understand that you now own OPC, and ultimately all the data from the satellite surveys. What I understand fully, and you do not, is that you must be very careful in what you look for...careful because you just might find it."

"You *did* find gold, didn't you?" Angela's icy-blue stare was gripping

"Oh, yes... Quite a lot actually."

"It's there, under that mountainside?"

"Yes, it's there." He paused. "It's there with Peter."

"Brian, I'm sorry." Angela's icy gaze softened as she leaned forward. "Are there more...many more survey sites, authenticated by the satellite?"

"Oh, yes" he said.

"Do you know what this means?"

Brian stubbed out his cigarette, and shook his head. "Believe me I know exactly what this means."

"You have the data—the satellite imagery on a compact disk?"

Before Brian could answer, an abrupt pounding began on the outer door to the suite. The rapping beyond the foyer was loud, insistent, and bordering on obnoxious. Angela and Brian stared at each other in question as Pauline nervously opened the door to Billie's room. Just as Angela was beginning to consider that the arrogant knocking was from Roy Hartock, he, too, emerged from his bedroom in the four-bedroom suite. As the pounding knocks continued, Billie also appeared in her doorway, but squeezed past Pauline and entered the foyer. Without a pause, she opened the door.

"Christ-all-mighty—girl!" Peter shouted and grinned. "It's lovely to see you!"

"Oh my God!" Brian exclaimed as he rose from his chair and ran across the suite.

But Billie was there before him, and holding Peter tight. Her tears had started again, but this time she was laughing as she cried. Then Brian was also there, his tears mixing as all three hugged.

"Oh my God! Oh my God! Oh my God!" Brian repeated over and over. "I can't believe it—I just can't *believe* it!"

"Oh for God's sake, "Billie said though her tears, and held Peter with disbelieving eyes at arm's length, "Tell us what happened!"

"First some whisky, by God," Peter gestured across the room. "Cocktails for everyone!"

"I can handle that, young feller," Roy Hartock was grinning as he spoke, as his bulk headed for an elaborate sideboard.

"Peter!" Billie pounded his chest. "How did you get out?"

Before she could say another word, he reached for her and pulled her close. Their kiss was long and intimate, and as everyone who was crowded in the foyer could now understand.

Doctor Peter Clopec had arrived.

His clothing was the black sweater and trousers that he wore when boarding the schooner, only now the clothing was torn, ragged, and covered in filth. It was also obvious that the hotel would not have allowed his admittance without Stanley Grey and Samuel Marsh at his side. The two Englishmen were standing behind their recovered victim and the pride in their achievement clearly evident. They did, however, seem to understand that Doctor Clopec carried the odor of the extremely unwashed.

"Doctor Clopec," Roy Hartock began as he stepped forward with a large scotch, "I do believe you should take this drink with you to the bathtub."

"Not yet, Pete!" Billie insisted. "Tell us what happened! How did you get out?"

"Well, my dear," Peter smiled warmly as he sipped the scotch. "It seems that you are quite the scuba instructor."

"Oh my God! Brian interrupted. "You used the diving gear—the diving gear that Cedric Bowles was talking about and went through the underwater tunnel, the path with the sunlight."

"Yes, but after the cave-in and the entrance collapsed, I was forced back inside the ship. I found more diving gear inside the salon and a tank that had almost 900 pounds. The topside of the schooner was hopeless from the cave-in, as well as most of the sides of the ship. I had only one battery light and the camping lantern, and it took most of the night before I could dig my way out of the hull and back onto the pier. When the camping lantern ran out of fuel, and then the battery lamp died, I really did have a few dicey moments—hours actually. When the sun came up I could see the light through the water, just as when we were standing on the decks and looking down."

"And then you swam through?" Brian asked. "You used the scuba gear and you swam through? The exit was big enough?"

"Oh, yes. And Billie, you would have been so proud," Peter grinned again. "I even surfaced in the sunlight with about 200 pounds of air. It was the most amazing moment of my life." He winked at Billie, "So far," he added delicately.

Billie blushed at the innuendo until Brian interrupted, "But Cedric Bowles said there was only 200 pounds in the tank."

Peter shook his head. "Everyone saw the equipment. But there were several tanks. The first one I found after the cave-in showed 900 pounds, the others under 200. The first one I found was lucky, and there was plenty of scuba gear in the main salon. Following my teacher's instruction was the easy part. I just assembled the gear and put it all together."

Once again, Billie smiled and hugged him tight, wriggling her nose. "Pete, maybe Mister Hartock is right. That bath tub might be a good idea."

Angela Barnes moved forward, an outsider to the inner circle. "Please, Doctor Clopec, not just yet," she pleaded. "I now represent the controlling interest of OPC, and have just one question."

After everyone turned to examine OPC's famous boardroom executive, they could not help but notice her eyes fastened to a canvas carryall draped over Peter's shoulder.

"Doctor Clopec?" Her gaze was probing the carryall as her voice questioned. "Would there be anything significant in your shoulder bag?"

The canvas shoulder bag was as dirty and tattered as Peter's appearance. After a silent moment of deliberation, Peter turned to the two British envoys waiting in the foyer.

"May I have your word as gentlemen that what you are about to see may remain private *and* my property?"

"Doctor Clopec," Stanley Grey began. "As you must realize anything you disclose would immediately be privy to Her Majesty's government."

Peter smiled, "Of course."

Before Angela Barnes could protest, Peter unzipped the bag and withdrew the German Luger. He offered the pistol, butt first to the senior British agent.

"Careful, it's still loaded—although it did travel underwater."

With the appearance of the German pistol, every eye focused on the war relic and the previous tension faded into disappointment.

"That's it?" Angela Barnes could not mask her displeasure.

Peter shrugged. "I would like to keep it—as a souvenir of sorts. I realize that hand guns are illegal in Turkey, but I was hoping it could be sent home in a diplomatic pouch."

Stanley Grey nodded as he passed the weapon over to Samuel Marsh. "I believe that could be arranged."

"Thank you," Peter sipped his whiskey and looked over to Billie, his arm snug around her waist. "After all," he said with a wink only for her. "We wouldn't want to become smugglers!"

"Certainly not," Brian chimed in cheerfully. "Well, gentlemen, if you don't mind looking after Doctor Clopec's keepsake, I really must insist we usher my colleague into to the bath."

"I quite agree," Stanley Grey nodded with a smile. He turned to Samuel Marsh who thumbed a lever on the pistol and seemed satisfied when the magazine slipped out.

"No worries, Doctor Clopec, we'll look after your little souvenir."

Brian offered his thanks as he ushered the two British agents into the foyer and out the door. Brian walked back into the sitting room and raised his eyebrows smiling. "That was very clever, Peter."

Peter sipped his whiskey again to hide his grin. "I don't know about clever, but as soon as I crawled out of the water carrying the bag, those *two* ushered away the Turkish soldiers and packed me onto a helicopter. Even with small talk, and during the explanation of my exploits under the cave-in and through the water, I felt their curiosity rising. The whole ride to Istanbul was very polite and helpful, but I felt that any moment I would be handed over to some kind of strip search."

Angela Barnes stepped forward. "I'm afraid that's probably my fault, Doctor Clopec," she confessed.

"Well maybe not just you, Angela," Roy Hartock added. "I did have to tell the Governor and the state department something. The rumors must be running wild."

"No matter," Brian shrugged. "All that matters now is that we are all together. All together, and all part of the new OPC. Especially that Alex Haggly-Ford is out of the picture." Brian continued carefully, still smiling as he motioned for Pauline. "Peter, everyone in this room can be trusted ...everyone!" he assured his friend.

"Too right, Brian, I just wish I had something more than that sodding pistol!"

"Oh Pete!" Billie exclaimed, "That's not fair!" she insisted. She was standing next to Peter, her arm around his waist as his was around hers, but after his wink, she had reached with her fingers to touch the canvas bag. There could be no denying of the solid mass that was hidden inside.

After another sip of whiskey, Peter reached inside and withdrew the first of the golden lozenges. There were only two, the two bars placed on the floor of the main salon by Cedric Bowles.

Silence filled the room after the sound of Angela Barnes' gasp. As the gold bullion was passed around, and all the new comers were shocked and surprised by the density and the weight, Angela Barnes looked up as her fingertips caressed the ancient Phrygian hieroglyphs—the ownership markings of King Midas.

"This bar alone," she said, "must weigh twenty pounds."

"At least," Roy Hartock remarked with a new light in his eyes.

"How many bars are there?" Angela shifted her gaze to Brian, "Under the mountain?"

"Hundreds," he whispered.

"Over two-thousand I should think," Peter remarked after another sip of scotch. "When I followed the sunlight, I could see all of the gold at the bottom of the pier. It would fill this room," he added as he gestured around the suite.

Before anyone could comment, the telephone rang. Without hesitation, Pauline released Brian's hand and crossed the room to reach for the handset. "Hello?"She frowned and looked to Angela Barnes, cupping her hand over the phone. "Ms. Barnes, it's the American Ambassador. He wants to talk to you, and he sounds kind of mad."

Chapter 67

After the ladies were seated, Peter and Brian sat down. The foursome had just been ushered into the Four Seasons restaurant, away from a gaggle of international reporters waiting in the hotel lobby.

"My God," Brian exclaimed, "I can't believe the news has traveled this fast."

"Well," Peter remarked. "I guess we had better get used to it—the press coverage. He reached across the table and took Billie's hand. "Billie, what do you think? Can you handle a little publicity?"

"Forgive me," the headwaiter interjected, as he stepped forward with his two waiter underlings. "I would wager that our heroine of the hour could cope with any situation, public or private." After his smiling statement, he bowed and offered a quick click of his heels.

"Bloody hell, "Brian's comment was agitated, unguarded and enough to make Pauline prod him under the table.

The maître d' ignored the rebuke, and stepped away from the table to allow the wine steward to approach with an ice bucket and a magnum of champagne. Chilled glasses followed, and as the wine was served, the headwaiter clasped his hands together and began his announcement. "Please accept a sample of our finest wine, with the compliments of the staff and a grateful nation."

"*Teşekkur ederim,*" Billie smiled the Turkish words for thank you and reached for her ornately placed napkin and unfolded the linen in her lap.

A brief tug pulled at the headwaiter's smile, but then he was at Pauline's side and unfolding her serviette with a flourish. Before she could react, the Turkish hands were smoothing the fabric above her upper thighs, and after she looked up startled, he and the other two waiters were away with a bustle, their victory complete.

"Cheeky bastard," Brian exclaimed, and everyone laughed.

Pauline nervously lifted her glass, the champagne a pale gold in the candlelight with the tiny bubbles rising like shinning diamonds. "Maybe I have no right to say anything like this," she began with her soft Texas burr. "But I would like to drink to these nice people of Turkey. I'm really glad they are going to get the gold. I mean, it seems to me like it belonged to them in the first place." She looked to Brian and then over to Peter.

"Well done and well said, Pauline," Peter raised his glass. "To the people of Turkey, may their long lost treasure bring prosperity and good luck!"

"I'll drink to that!" Billie lifted her champagne.

"Absolutely!" Brian echoed.

After the toast, Billie giggled. "I know this is real expensive wine, but every time I try and take a sip, it tickles my nose."

"Me, too," Pauline confessed.

Abruptly, Brian raised his hand and motioned for the headwaiter. He insisted that the honor, and the wine, was to be shared with the staff in the kitchen. He ordered a double dark rum for himself and Billie, a Black label—no ice for Peter, and explained how to make a frozen rumrunner for Pauline.

After the wine bucket was taken away and compliments received from the chef and the kitchen, Brian ordered dinner for everyone. Peter sipped his scotch, smiled, and was content to look around the table.

When the waiters were gone, Billie asked. "How did they find out?"

Peter shook his head, but his smile did not waver. "It must have been the Turkish soldiers," he said. "Or someone form the British consulate. After all, it was common knowledge that I swam through an opening—an opening that led to an underground chamber. Someone must have ordered an exploratory dive and found the treasure."

"But why would they do such a thing?" Pauline said. "It must have been very dangerous. What about the aftershocks? Peter, didn't you say that the underwater opening could have closed at any time?"

"Yes, that's true, I was lucky to have escaped." Peter sipped his drink and turned to Brian. "Doctor Pauliss," he said mockingly. "Would *you* have any idea how the Turks found out about their missing treasure?"

"Oh, rubbish!" Brian appeared flustered as he reached for a cigarette. "After you arrived at the hotel and I knew we were all safe. I had an overwhelming feeling of relief," he said as he exhaled. "Then I saw the familiar expression of greed forming on their faces—on Hartock and Barnes—when they saw the gold. I felt as if it were starting all over again."

"So *you* told them!" Billie exclaimed. "*You* told the Turks—the Turkish government?"

"Billie, please don't be upset!"

"Oh. Argentina!" In the next moment she was up and hugging him as he sat. "I am so glad," she said excitedly. "So glad! Trust me! That old ship was filled with nothing but bad luck! Now everything will change. I just know it!"

"Billie, please," Brian said as he nervously looked around the restaurant. "Someone might be watching."

"Well I'll be damned," Pauline whispered as Billie retook her seat.

"Quite possibly, we all would have been," Peter grinned. "Had we taken more than a couple of souvenirs."

"Oh, Pete!" Billie's eyes were only for Peter. "You *knew?*"

"I suspected," he confirmed, "Especially after Doctor Pauliss' theory about the supernatural power of lost gold in huge amounts."

"Then we're free of the curse?"

Peter nodded. "One can only hope."

"But what about Ms. Barnes," Pauline stammered. "And Mister Hartock, they would be awfully mad if they found out."

Brian winked. "Outside of this table, no one will ever find out. Eventually a vague rumor might lead back to the British embassy, that's all anyone should ever need to know. If we are all agreed?"

Brian's suggestion was followed by silent nods from everyone around the table. When dinner came, Peter suggested they all hold hands and give thanks and say grace.

Chapter 6s

After dinner, and Billie's request for the tableside cherries jubilee, the restaurant became deserted once again. Just as before, a single waiter remained in attendance as a few candlelit tables marked the boundaries of the room.

"What now?" asked Pauline. "Do we go back to Texas?"

"We can do whatever we please," Brian remarked. "After all, we are new partners with OPC. There are ninety-five more anomalies waiting to be explored."

"Yes," Peter offered. "But most of those will be handled by local governments in charge of their own domain. Perhaps a few would like the expertise of some experienced treasure hunters, but all in all, I should think that a worldwide holiday is in order."

"That sounds *perfect*," Brian rubbed his hands together. "A trip around the world!"

"Speaking as a new partner for OPC," Peter raised his glass in a toast. "I don't believe financial concerns will be an issue."

Brian grinned. "Not with our new chairperson offering consulting salaries that extend beyond seven digits."

"Brian, honey," Pauline reached for his hand. "Do you really mean it? Would you want me to go?"

"Absolutely." Brian raised his glass and looked around the table. "To the four musketeers!"

Billie sipped her drink with the others, but glanced around the darkened restaurant. After a moment, she leaned forward with a conspiratorial whisper and offered. "But what if there was something *else* to look for—something else that's been lost?"

"Billie, whatever are you talking about?" Brian's voice was a slur. He had been drinking the double dark rums all night.

"Do you remember when Buddy came out to the rig? When he came out drunk and shouted at me?" Billie flushed briefly with embarrassment before she continued. "Do you remember what he said?"

Peter reached across the table and took her hand. "My dear, you don't have to bring that up."

Billie shook her head. "I know that, Pete," she said sweetly. "And thank you, but it's important that you remember. He said that I was just like my Nazi dad, and my Nazi grandpa."

After a squeeze of Peter's hand, Billie began carefully, "Daddy, of course, wasn't a Nazi, but my grandfather was a different story. He was an officer in the *Luftwaffe*. He wasn't in the Nazi party, and he hated everything about Hitler and the holocaust, but he *was* in the German air force."

"But, Billie," Brian interrupted. "What does all of that—"

"Argentina, will you let me tell the story."

"Sorry," Brian apologized and reached for a cigarette.

"My grandfather's name was Erich Boch. He was involved with these top-secret aircraft experiments. An aircraft type that was so secret, they did all of the experiments and test flights at this old castle in Poland. An area that was occupied by Germany, but really remote—a real challenge for anyone to get to. Apparently, before the end of the war they had some very successful test flights."

"But, Billie," Brian began again, and waved his cigarette. "That was almost sixty years ago. What kind of aircraft from the forties could still be a secret or valuable?"

"How about one that doesn't use gasoline—or any kind of fuel for that matter?"

"What?" Peter and Brian responded together.

"I thought that might get your attention," Billie grinned.

"But how is that possible?" Peter was leaning forward, as were Brian and Pauline.

"That's the Texas nightmare," Pauline exclaimed. "Transportation without fuel oil."

"Exactly!" Billie arched her eyebrows, "A concept more valuable than all the gold in the world."

"Christ-all-mighty!" Peter sat up straight. "Now that's something worth looking for. You know about this from your grandfather? He told you?"

Billie nodded, "I met him only once, but I will never forget his eyes. They were green—just like mine. It was like looking in the mirror. He only spoke German, and once when we were alone, he told me about why my dad's sailboat was named the *Valkyrie*. That was the name of the secret aircraft. Apparently it was the brain child of two great scientists—two guys that were killed."

Billie looked around the table. Everyone was mesmerized.

"After the war," she continued, "the prototype aircraft were destroyed, but my grandfather, Erich, he buried some papers in an old cemetery in Poland. He said the papers are in a waterproof box and he gave me the location and the name on a headstone. He said the papers were the plans on how the aircraft worked. He always told me that the *Valkyries* were the greatest flying machines ever. He said that this was the type of technology that could change the world."

"My God," Brian exclaimed. "It certainly would!"

"Well, Pete?" Billie smile was contagious. "What do you think? Does exploring an old castle in Poland sound more exciting than a trip around the world?"

"Definitely," he nodded. "But this time, we bring back up. We *don't* try everything on our own."

"Whatever are you talking about?" Brian asked leaning forward.

"I am simply suggesting that we form a new department in the new OPC," Peter explained. "A department separate from the satellite mining division."

"And what might that be?" Brian's tone sounded incredulous. "What would we call the ultimate research department?"

Peter smiled as he squeezed Billie's hand, "How about lost and found?"

CPSIA information can be obtained at www.ICGtesting.com

224729LV00001B/5/P